THE ATLAS OF US

Tracy Buchanan is a web journalist and producer who lives in Milton Keynes with her husband and daughter and their one-eyed Jack Russell. Tracy travelled extensively while working as a travel magazine editor, sating the wanderlust she developed while listening to her Sri Lankan grandparents' childhood stories – the same wanderlust that now inspires her writing.

To find out more about Tracy, follow her on Twitter @TracyBuchanan or visit her website www.tracybuchanan.co.uk.

TRACY BUCHANAN

The Atlas Of Us

AVON

AVON

A division of HarperCollins*Publishers*
77–85 Fulham Palace Road,
London W6 8JB

www.harpercollins.co.uk

A Paperback Original 2014

1

Copyright © Tracy Buchanan 2014

Tracy Buchanan asserts the moral right to
be identified as the author of this work

A catalogue record for this book is
available from the British Library

ISBN-13: 978-0-00-757935-8

Typeset in Minion by
Palimpsest Book Production Ltd, Falkirk, Stirlingshire

Printed and bound in Great Britain by
Clays Ltd, St Ives plc

MIX
Paper from
responsible sources
FSC **FSC C007454**
www.fsc.org

FSC™ is a non-profit international organisation established to promote
the responsible management of the world's forests. Products carrying the
FSC label are independently certified to assure consumers that they come
from forests that are managed to meet the social, economic and
ecological needs of present and future generations,
and other controlled sources.

Find out more about HarperCollins and the environment at
www.harpercollins.co.uk/green

To the two atlases of my heart: my husband Rob and Scarlett, the daughter I thought I'd never have.

Prologue

Everyone runs except her. Their movements are panicked, eyes wide, arms flailing. But she can't move, legs frozen as she takes in the ferocity of the wave eating up the beach ahead of her. She takes a deep breath and wraps her arms tight around the atlas, her heart beating a strange beat against its cover: slow then fast then slow again.

Just a few moments before, she'd been walking along the shoreline, toes sinking into the warm sand. The soft beach had stretched out vast and gold before her, the walk to the bungalows seeming to take longer than usual.

Now the sea is buffeting against the bungalow three rows in front. It blasts around the sides, its bamboo walls rattling then breaking apart before disappearing into the watery depths.

Someone to her right screams. She turns, sees a long-tail boat thrashing about on top of the oncoming wave. It smashes into a palm tree, its wood splintering as the tree bends back. A man she'd seen swimming in the sea moments before is clinging to it. His eyes catch hers just before he tumbles into the whirlpool of water below, spinning around among deckchairs, beach bags and God knows what else.

Her legs find traction and she stumbles back, breath stuttering as the water surges towards her.

She peers behind her. There's nowhere to run, just more flat ground, more palm trees.

The wave engulfs a small palm tree in front of her, its roar filling her ears. A food stall topples over in its path and careens towards her, fruit churning in the relentless gush of water.

The sharp smell of brine and seaweed fills her nostrils.

It's so close now.

She suddenly feels a strange kind of serenity. She refuses to live what might be her last moments in a state of hopeless panic. This is what she has learned lately, a calm acceptance of what must be. It wasn't always like this. She once fought against her fate, twisted out of its grasp, stumbled on regardless.

Not now.

She tries to face the wave, stand tall and strong, the atlas held against her like it might somehow protect her. But it's no use, fear prevails. She runs into the tiny bathroom, slamming the door shut behind her and sliding down the wall until she feels the cool of the tiles against her thighs.

Maybe she'll survive? She can swim, kick her way to the surface, see the sun and think how lucky she was. She'll go back home, hold tight to the people she let down and never let them go.

Tears flood her eyes as she thinks of all she is leaving behind; of mistakes that may never be remedied.

Thank God she sent the letter.

There's a creaking sound followed by a loud thud. The bathroom door quakes and she realises something has fallen against it.

She's trapped. No chance now.

She quickly scours the room, eyes settling on the plastic bag used to line the bin. She grabs it, wraps the atlas in it then shoves the atlas into the bag slung around her chest, yanking at the adjustments until they're so tight they hurt. She won't let the atlas get destroyed, not after what she went through to get it back. The walls around her vibrate as objects are flung against them. She thinks of the man on the palm tree. That might be her soon, another piece of flotsam on the tide.

Dread overwhelms her.

There's a thunderous rushing noise and someone screams, someone close enough to be heard over the roar.

It's here.

The wall in front of her begins to crack, water tracing a long line down it, finding its path towards her. She pulls her knees up to her chest, pressing the bag against her stomach, taking comfort from the feel of the atlas's bumpy cover against her skin. She closes her eyes and sucks in an urgent breath.

This is it.

As she hears the walls start to tumble, feels specks of water on her cheeks, an unbearable sadness takes over her.

Did she do enough for those she loves?

She closes her eyes as the wall in front of her smashes apart, water ploughing over her. She's lifted with the wave and flung against the sink. The porcelain cracks against her shoulder, pain slicing through her.

The bamboo walls around her crash apart and she's propelled outside with the wave, her body spinning with the force of it as it gallops towards the line of palm trees nearby.

She manages to keep her head above water, gasping for air, and tries desperately to grasp at something, anything, her dark hair blurring her vision as it lashes around her face.

Her fingers graze what she thinks must be the branch of a palm tree and, for a moment, she thinks she might have a chance. But the strength of the wave whips it away from her, thrusting her underwater and spinning her so erratically, she can't tell what is sky and what is ground.

Water gritty with sand and debris rushes into her mouth. She snaps her lips shut, desperately trying to hold her breath as she's pulled deeper and deeper, her chest bursting with the effort.

But the need to breathe is overpowering, every part of her yearning to exhale. Her chest expands, her head ringing. And then she's giving in, mouth opening as she takes one last blissful breath, the faces of all those she loves strong in her mind.

For a brief moment, she thinks she sees red hair, green eyes. She reaches her hand out, but then everything is gone.

Chapter One

Krabi, Thailand
2004

When I close my eyes, the water comes: the violent thud of waves, the tart smell of salty dampness seeping through the cracks of my dreams. But when I look out of the bus window, it's nothing but mangled cars again; boats that have somehow found their way onto the roofs of two-storey buildings; suitcases flung open, their innards spilling out onto the dusty pavements below.

The bus takes a turn and I'm facing the sea again. It looks calm, ebbing and flowing like it's forgotten the devastation it caused a few days ago.

My phone buzzes, a text from Will. I force myself to look at it.

> *Did you get my voicemail? You shouldn't have gone.*
> *Call me.*

'British, love?' There's a woman watching me from across the aisle. Stark white lines dart up from the strapless top she's wearing, disappearing over the fleshy mounds of her shoulders. I feel the urge to tell her about my friend Simone who nearly died of skin cancer.

Instead I nod. 'Yes.'

'Thought so. I saw you at the airport earlier. We're going to see about our son, he's eighteen.'

My heart goes out to her. How would I feel if it were one of my girls missing? 'I'm sorry. I hope he's okay.'

'We hope so too, don't we, Roy?' The woman peers at the man next to her, but he just continues staring bleakly out of the window. 'His friends say he met a girl, spent the night with her. Now he's missing.'

Missing.

That's the word I've been using to describe Mum's status too since getting a call from her friend Jane on Boxing Day. But now that I'm heading to the temple – the endgame – *missing* seems too optimistic.

'What about you?' the woman asks. I can see she's desperate for the comfort blanket of talk her husband obviously can't offer. He's probably like Will, always telling me I talk too much. Even after I'd got the phone call about Mum, he was too engrossed in his new iPod to listen properly as I tried to tell him how desperately worried I felt.

'My mum's been travelling around the islands over Christmas,' I say to the woman now. 'She's not tried to call anyone to let us know she's okay. We're really worried.'

'Oh, poor luv. You've come out here all alone?'

'Yes. I'm all my mum has. We're very close.' I don't know why I lie.

'That's lovely. You're very good to come out here for her.'

Or stupid. That's what Will had called me when I'd woken him in the early hours to tell him I wanted to fly out here to find Mum.

Maybe he was right. Maybe I am bloody stupid to leave

the girls with their dad and come alone to a country more alien than I've ever known. I can smell the foreignness in the scorched spicy air drifting in through the windows; see it in the wires that hang precariously from the pylons; hear it in the strange urgent accents of the Thai people outside.

I feel my chest start to fill with apprehension but quickly swallow it away.

'Have you been putting photos of your mum up on the notice boards?' the woman asks.

I nod. 'Yes.'

'Strange, isn't it? All those smiling faces?'

She doesn't say why. I know what she means though. Strange to think half of them might be dead now, bloated corpses laid out in a temple like the very one we're heading to now.

What if Mum's one of those corpses? Oh God.

'Did you check the patient list at the hospital?' the woman asks.

I clear my throat, trying not to show the fear building inside. 'Yes, I did.' I'd gone *into* the hospital too, waving my mum's photo in the faces of harassed-looking staff whose accents made my head buzz with confusion, the phrase book I'd bought in a hurry at the airport useless.

'You never know, someone might call,' the woman says, looking down at her mobile clutched in her plump hand. 'The embassy photocopied the picture we brought of our son. So nice of them. I'm sure it'll all be fine.' Her hand flutters to the small cross around her neck. 'I'm sure we'll . . .'

Her voice trails off, her eyes losing focus as the bus slows down. A large spiky roof with gold spires comes into view, a mountain shrouded in trees behind it. As the bus draws closer, the whole temple appears before us, curved and ornate with tiered icing-sugar walls and arched windows fringed with gold. Two painted tiger statues adorn its entrance, looking ready to pounce on the frantic relatives and tired-looking officials hurrying around the busy area in front of it. This must be where the foreign embassies are: white canopies, rows and rows of photo boards, lines of desks weighed down with paperwork and flags. I try to find the Union Jack among all the other flags, as if it might blur the strangeness of this place a little. But all I can see is a tiny beige monkey that is weaving in and out of the table legs. I make a mental note to tell the girls about it. They'll want to know things like that when I get back. They don't need to know about the bodies I've seen floating in the sea, nor the turned-over cars. Just this little sprite of a monkey and the bright green lizards I noticed while waiting for the bus.

I think of their faces when I'd told them I'd be leaving them for a couple of days to find their nanna. My youngest, Olivia, had got that look, like she might cry any minute, and it had made my heart ache. They've not spent more than one night away from me and even then it felt like a small kind of torture for them – and me. To make them feel better, I'd told them Daddy was taking them to the show they'd been going on about; the same show he's made every excuse under the sun *not* to go to.

I hope he takes them, I really do. He needs to spend more time with them. He can make their breakfast and ferry them from one friend to another like I do each day, wash their clothes, clean the house, pick up the dog muck in the garden . . . the list goes on. Maybe he'll understand life isn't such a breeze as a stay-at-home mum?

Oh God, what was I thinking? How on earth will he cope? I really was stupid coming here.

We pass under a square blue archway, the red globe lanterns hanging from its ceiling trembling in the breeze.

The woman sitting across from me clutches at her husband's arm. But he ignores her just like Will would ignore me. I want to shake him, tell him his wife needs him. Instead, I reach over and place my hand on the woman's plump arm. The woman nods, her eyes swimming with thanks. But she doesn't speak any more.

The bus comes to a stop beneath a lush green tree, and I try to recognise Jane's son Sam among the crowds from the photo she sent. A man approaches the bus.

It's him.

His tanned face speaks of exhaustion, of sadness and unknown horrors. People stand, blocking my view of him. I rise with them, smoothing my fringe down, checking the collar of my neat blossom-coloured blouse. Despite it being early evening, the heat's a nightmare, sweat making the thin material of my blouse cling to all the wrong curves, curves I usually cover with tailored tops and trousers; strands of my fine hair already escaping from the ponytail I'd crafted so carefully a few hours before. I'm pleased I inherited Dad's height and blond hair, but combine that with my mum's curves and I'm in trouble.

I catch myself mid-moan. How can I worry about my weight when Mum's missing?

The bus driver hauls open the door and I step out, blinking up at the sun and trying not to think about what it must be doing to all those bodies. The other passengers hesitate too, faces white with worry as they take in the temple in the distance. A woman leans her face into her husband's chest and sobs while two young men next to me take frantic gulps of water, the nervous energy throbbing off them.

I feel even more alone now, watching all these people. They're all terrified of what they might find, but at least they're not alone. I look at Sam. Maybe I'm not so alone. I shrug my bag strap over my shoulder, heading towards him.

He turns as I approach, frowns a little like he's trying to figure out if it's the same person in the photo his mum sent. Then he smiles. 'Louise?' he asks, a Northern lilt to his voice.

He's in his late twenties, a few years younger than me, and is wearing a white linen shirt and cut-off blue jeans. This close, I can see the light stubble on his cheeks and chin, the small jewel in his nose, the wheel pattern of the pendant hanging from his neck. He has tanned skin, fair hair, a mole on his cheek. Will would call him a hippy, like the man with long hair who was renting the house a few doors down with his Chinese wife and two children last year. I'd been desperate to invite them over for dinner; they'd seemed so interesting. But Will had always found some excuse or other not to. Six months later, they'd moved away. I wasn't surprised. They didn't look the type to be happy in an estate full of expensive new builds and gas-guzzling family cars.

'Yes, I'm Louise,' I say to Sam. I note a hint of surprise in his eyes. Maybe he was expecting someone like my mum, all bronzed and arty with floaty skirts and flowing scarves, instead of a pale, blouse-wearing, stay-at-home mum from Kent. 'Thanks so much for offering to help,' I say. 'Your mum said you'd been helping out? I'll try not to take up too much of your time.'

'Take up as much time as you want. I promised Mum I'd do everything I can to help you.' He examined my face. 'How are you holding up?'

'The paperwork's a nightmare but—'

'I mean about your mum missing. Must be tough?'

'I – I'm not sure really. It's been a bit of a blur since your mum called. I'm sure everything'll be fine, I'm sure we'll find her . . .' My voice trails off. The truth is, I'm terrified. Terrified I've lost my mum before I've even had the chance to patch things up with her. 'Jane says you live in Bangkok.

Did you travel over here to help out?' I ask, trying to change the subject. Small talk seems out of place here, but it's a type of anchor for us Brits, isn't it?

He shakes his head. 'I came to Ao Nang to visit a friend for Christmas. Luckily, we were staying further inland. As soon as we heard what had happened, we started helping out and I ended up volunteering here,' he says, gesturing around him.

'It must be difficult.'

He swallows, his Adam's apple bobbing up and down. 'Very. But at least I'm doing something to help. Have you done all the form-filling and DNA stuff?'

'Yes, twice. No sign.' I peer towards the temple. 'So, do we go in there then?'

'Not yet. The bodies are back there.' He flinches slightly, like it physically hurts him to say that. 'I'd recommend the boards first, there's photos of each body on there. People find that easier.'

'Yes, that makes sense.' My voice sounds strong, considering.

'Why don't you show me a photo of your mum and I'll go look at the boards for you?'

'You don't have to, really. I can do it.'

This time, my voice breaks as I imagine seeing a photo of Mum up there. Sam gently places his fingers on my bare arm. They feel cool, dry. 'I'm here to help, Louise.'

The woman from the bus approaches from the direction of the photo boards, her face pressed against her husband's chest as he stares ahead, tears streaming down his cheeks.

I look back at Sam. 'If you're sure?'

'Of course. You've probably been asked this already, but are there any distinguishing marks, jewellery, anything that will help me identify your mum?'

'Just a bracelet she always wears. She's wearing it in this photo.' I start digging around in my bag. 'Thing is, I haven't seen her for over two years so I'm not sure if she still looks . . .' My voice trails off. Why did I say that?

'Two years?'

'It's a long story.'

Sam scrutinises my face then nods. 'Understood. So, the photo?'

I pull the photo out and hand it over. Mum looks happy in it, tanned, smiling, her dark hair whipping about her face. Slung over her shoulder is a pink bag with the smiling face of a child embroidered into its front. I can just about make out her precious bracelet, a rusty old charm bracelet with bronze teapots and spoons attached to it. She's wearing the yellow cardigan with red hearts I got her a few years ago too. That did something to me when Jane emailed the photo to me after they'd both gone to some Greek island together last year, made my heart clench to see her wearing the cardigan I got her – like maybe Mum *did* care for me.

Something changes in Sam's face as he looks at the photo. 'That's an unusual bag. I think I saw it last night.'

I try to keep my voice steady. 'With a body?'

He looks pained. 'Yes, I'm sorry. It was wrapped around the woman quite securely. It came in late so if there's any ID with it, it won't have filtered down to any lists yet.'

I sway slightly, vision blurring. Sam takes my elbow, helping me steady myself.

'I'll go out back and check for you,' he says softly. 'Is it okay if I take this photo?'

'Yes.' My voice is barely above a whisper.

'Why don't you sit down?' He steers me to a nearby seat, an oddly shaped bamboo chair that feels rough under my calves. He then runs towards the temple, his flip-flops slapping on the sandy concrete as he weaves between the tables and photo boards, apologising to people as he bumps into them.

I put my head in my shaking hands. Is this what it comes to in the end? I feel a rush of regret and anger. Regret at not working hard enough to rebuild my relationship with my mum again when she stopped talking to me, anger at the fact I'd had to even *try* to rebuild it. It had only been a stupid argument; I'd never dreamt it would have led to her not contacting me for such a long time.

'Oh, Mum,' I mumble into my palms.

I stay like that for a while, trying to grapple with the idea of Mum being gone forever. When Jane had called saying how concerned she was, I knew, quite suddenly, that I had to come out here to find Mum. It wasn't just about finding her, it was about starting over with her, making amends. I'd brewed on it all of Boxing Day as I'd watched the news unfold on TV until I'd had to wake Will to tell him what I'd decided. I could tell he didn't believe I'd go through with it, even when I started packing my suitcase.

I sit up straight when I notice Sam jogging towards me again. He's holding a bag to his chest like it's a newborn baby and there's this look on his face that makes something inside me falter. He places the bag on the dusty ground and crouches down in front of me, placing his hands over mine. I pull my hands away, stifling the growing panic inside.

'There was a passport in the bag,' he says very softly.

He pulls it from the bag and hands it to me. I open it, see Mum's face, her name. I put my hand to my mouth and blink, keep blinking. It feels like there's a wave inside, flattening everything in its path.

'You said the bag was found with a body,' I say. 'Have you seen it?'

Sam nods, face crunched with pain. 'There's a lot of . . .'

13

He sighs. 'A lot of damage to the face. But she has dark hair like your mum's.'

The edges of the world smudge.

I close my eyes and smell Mum's scent: floral perfume, mints and paint oils. With it comes a memory of her smiling down at me, her paintbrush caught mid-sweep, a blot of black ink smudging the eye she'd been painting – her own eye. The ink crawls down the canvas, distorting her painted face. I was eight at the time and had just got back from a disastrous day at school.

'What's with you, grumpy face?' she'd asked me.

I'd hesitated a moment before stepping into the spare room she was using as a studio. Our house was just a small three-bed semi but my father had insisted on turning the largest room into a studio for Mum. It had always felt off-limits to me. But she'd beckoned me in that day, gesturing towards her paint-splattered chair, a bright blue leather one she'd found in the local charity shop.

'Tell me everything,' she'd said, kneeling in front of me and taking my hands, getting green paint all over them.

'I don't want to go into school tomorrow,' I'd said, resisting the urge to pull away from her and clean the paint off my hands. I'd never got on well at the private school Dad had been so keen to scrimp and save to get me into, the teachers always seemed to regard me as inferior to the other, richer kids. Mum had warned him it would happen. 'There's nothing worse for a snooty bourgeois than an aspiring bourgeois,' she'd said. Is that what she'd thought of me when I married a company director – a snooty bourgeois?

'Why not, darling?' she'd asked.

'My teacher told me off today.'

She'd raised an eyebrow, smiling slightly. I remember

14

thinking that mums aren't supposed to smile about things like that and part of me was annoyed. Why couldn't she be like other mums?

'Why'd your teacher tell you off, Lou?' she'd asked.

'I told the truth.' Her smile had widened. 'She read out a poem she'd written to help us with our poems and I said it was rubbish.'

Mum had laughed then, those big white teeth of hers gleaming under the light. 'You told the truth, that's wonderful! "Beauty is truth, truth beauty. That is all ye know on earth and all ye need to know"', she'd added, quoting her favourite Keats poem.

'But she hates me now.' I'd crossed my arms, turning away. 'I can't go into school.'

'Of course you can! You can't let fear rule you, Lou. You have to fight against fear, stare it right in the face.'

'You okay?' Sam asks, pulling me from the memory.

I open my eyes, Mum's words echoing in my mind like she's right there with me.

You can't let fear rule you, Lou.

'Can I see the bag please?' I ask Sam.

'Of course.'

He hands it to me. It's dirtier than in the photo, caked with dried mud, and there's a grotesque tear across the child's face. I imagine Mum shopping in one of Thailand's markets with it, reaching into it for a purse to buy some odd Buddhist ornament, half a smile on her tanned face.

I take a deep breath then unzip it, peering in. There's a hairbrush in there, a bright red lipstick and something wrapped in a plastic bag. I pull the brush out first, examining the hair on it. It looks dark, just like Mum's.

But then lots of people have dark hair, right?

I place the brush gently to one side and look at the lipstick.

15

Mum sometimes wears red lipstick. She's not alone in that though, plenty of women do.

But what about her passport? That can only belong to one woman.

I clench my fists, driving the surge of grief away. It's not over until it's over.

I reach into the bag again for the item wrapped in plastic. It's square-shaped and feels heavy, its surface rough beneath the material of the plastic. I pull it out and lay it on top of Mum's bag. Its front cover is made from strips of thin wood interweaved with each other and an image of the earth is etched in bright turquoise into it with four words painted in gold over it.

The Atlas of Us.

There's a bronzed key lock on the side but it looks broken. I open the heavy front cover, see two lines written on the inside page, the ink only a little blurred – amazing considering how much it must have been thrown about in the water:

To my darling, my life, my world. The atlas of my heart.
Your love, Milo

It feels impossibly romantic. Maybe Mum had met someone? And yet she still hadn't got in touch with me to tell me about them. I can imagine what Will would say if he were here. 'Accept it, move on. Your mother doesn't want to involve you in her life any more.'

I flick through the atlas. On the first page is a hand-drawn illustration of the United Kingdom and Ireland. Opposite is a paper pocket. I run my fingers over it, surprised to feel something inside. I reach in and pull out a dried purple flower encased in cellophane. There are other items too: a yellowed tourist leaflet from a place called Nunney Castle, a ticket to an awards ceremony in London, a photo of a cobweb flooded with light and a business card belonging to a journalist called Nathan Styles. There's a crumpled piece of notepaper too with a pencil sketch of a sheep teetering on a tightrope, its eyes wide with comical fear, a note scrawled in handwriting I don't recognise above it:

Exmoor by Claire Shreve

A watercolour of grey pooling around the edges of moss green valleys, ready to plummet downwards and destroy everything below.

I've never heard of a Claire Shreve. Is she one of Mum's friends? I flick through the rest of the atlas and see more illustrated maps – including one of Thailand – and pockets too, some bulging with items.

'Do you recognise any of it?'

I look up at Sam. 'Just the bag. And the passport of course. I'm not sure about this atlas, I'd have remembered it if I'd seen it. It's quite unusual.'

'Okay. Shall I see if I can find a photo on the boards? Or . . .' he hesitates, '. . . you might prefer to see her?'

My head swims at the thought. Then I remember Mum's words again: *You have to fight against fear, stare it right in the face.*

'I'd like to see her please,' I say.

'I'll take you.'

I follow Sam towards a pair of bright blue gates to the side of the temple, criss-crossed with red stripes, the spikes

17

on top gold. The smell instantly hits me: meaty, horrific. I tuck the note back into the atlas and place my sleeve over my nose as I follow Sam towards the temple. A Thai woman is standing in front of the gates, a clipboard in her hand, a bucket of surgical facemasks next to her. Beyond the gates is a temporary trailer, people milling around it. I'm thankful it's blocking the view of whatever's behind it.

Sam nods at the woman, who hands me a surgical mask. I put it on, gagging at the TCP smell.

'Brace yourself,' Sam says as he leads me through the gate.

I walk around the corner of the trailer towards a large area fringed by spindly green trees, the hill darting up behind them. At first, I think it's dirty clothes spread over the plastic sheets in the middle. But as I draw closer, I see a bloated leg sticking out of one mound, a tangle of black hair fanning out from another and realise it's bodies, scores of them, half covered by different coloured sheets of plastic. People are walking around in blue scrubs and wellies, and then there are the relatives and friends, hands over mouths as they crouch over the bodies, some crying, most looking frantic and exhausted.

I want to turn around and get the hell out of there. But instead, I force myself to follow Sam as he walks towards the bodies and try to control the whirlpool of terror inside.

'She's here,' Sam says softly, coming to a stop in front of a blue sheet. He crouches down, taking the corner of the plastic between his fingers, then peers up at me. 'Ready?'

'Wait.' I look up at the bright blue sky, tears welling in my eyes. Everything will be different after this; even the sky might look different.

I have to do this. I have to know.

'Ready,' I say. I hear the crunch of plastic and look down.

The colour of the face hits me first: dark red, bloated. Then the hair, long, curly and tangled around a swollen neck.

There's nothing there to recognise. It's all distorted, grotesque. How can I find my mum in that?

I quickly look away again, stifling a sob. Could it really be her? It takes a while before I'm certain my voice will sound normal. 'I can't be sure,' I say. 'She has the same colour hair. But I – I can't be sure. Is she wearing a bracelet? She always wore her bracelet.'

There's a pause, more rustling then Sam's voice. 'No. There's a necklace around her neck though, quite distinctive. It's a gold typewriter with blue gems for keypads?'

Hope flutters inside. 'I never saw her wear something like that. Do you think that means it's not her?'

'She could have bought the necklace at a stall here, plus her passport was inside so . . .'

His voice trails off but I understand what he's trying to say. The chances are it *is* Mum. I feel the tears coming, the world tilting, and stumble away, leaning against a nearby tree as I try to control my emotions.

Sam follows me, placing his hand on my back. I don't flinch away from him this time.

'Mum left when I was twelve,' I gasp. 'I've barely seen her since. The last time was over two years ago at a party, it was awful.' I don't really understand why I'm saying all this now, to a virtual stranger. But the words continue to come out in a rush. 'We had a terrible argument and I didn't hear from her after, no matter how many times I called. Your mum keeps me posted with what she's up to. But my mum won't speak to *me*, her own daughter, and – and now I can't even be sure if it's her body back there.'

I start crying again in loud, shuddery hiccups and Sam wraps his arms around me. He smells faintly of sweat and TCP, the plastic of his outfit crinkling against my cheek. I ought to pull away. What would my husband say? But I need this right now, human touch, even if it's a stranger's touch. We stay like that for a few moments, surrounded by death and mourning relatives.

Then there's a strangled sob from nearby. I pull away to see a man with curly blond hair crouching down next to the body we've just been looking at. An Indian man wearing scrubs is standing over him, brow creased.

'This is Claire's necklace,' the blond man says. 'It's hand-crafted, one of a kind. She wears it all the time. Oh God.'

Relief rushes through me as I look down at the atlas in my mum's bag, thinking of the note I found in it. Is it the same Claire?

'What if it's not Mum?' I say to Sam, clutching onto this new possibility. 'There was something in the atlas written by someone called Claire! And if that's Claire's necklace . . .'

'But your mum's passport and bag were with the body, Louise,' Sam says softly.

I refuse to acknowledge what he just said, can't possibly now there's a glimmer of hope it might not be Mum. I look towards the blond man who's now kneeling next to the woman, his head in his hands. Hope surges inside me. 'He seems convinced he knows who she is,' I say.

Sam follows my gaze. 'He does, doesn't he? Maybe it's not your mum.'

I look up at the sky. Still the same. I promise myself that if – no, *when* – I find Mum alive, I'll make her talk to me, really talk to me and we will repair what came apart since she left.

Then something occurs to me. 'Maybe the reason that woman had Mum's bag was because she knew her? If so, that man might know where Mum is.'

I go to walk towards him but Sam stops me. 'Louise . . . give him a minute.'

I look into Sam's eyes. I can tell he thinks I'm grasping at straws. Maybe I am, but what other leads do I have? 'I have to find my mum, I have to bring her back to me, back to her grandchildren. I don't care what it takes, where I have to go, but Mum's going to be on that plane back to the UK with me.'

I shrug off his arm and march towards the man. He looks up when I approach, his eyes red.

I hesitate a moment. Maybe Sam's right. But then I think of Mum out there somewhere, possibly injured in some filthy hospital with doctors who don't speak English.

'I'm so sorry for your loss,' I say softly, kneeling down to his level and putting my hand on his arm. He's wearing a powder-blue suit, more expensive-looking than any of Will's.

He shakes his head in disbelief, tears falling down his tanned cheeks. 'I knew she was in the worst possible place for the wave to hit. But I never dreamed I'd find her body. She's been through so much, gone through so much, and always come out fighting. Oh God.'

His voice cracks and I feel like crying with him. It could have been me kneeling here grieving for my mother. It *was* for a few moments.

'I think my mum knew your wife,' I say gently.

The man flinches. 'Friend, not wife.'

'Friend. Sorry. She had my mum's bag when she was found,' I say, gesturing to the bag slung over my shoulder. 'And there was an atlas with a note written by someone called Claire Shreve in it?'

He frowns. 'Are you sure that's your mother's bag?'

'Her passport was in it. It's quite a distinctive bag too.'

'Did your mother know Nathan Styles?'

I think of the business card in the atlas. 'No. Why?'

He ignores my question. 'What's your mother's name?' he asks instead.

'Nora McKenzie.'

21

His face flickers with recognition. 'The name rings a bell.'

All my nerves stand on edge. 'Really? Did Claire know my mother?'

'No, I don't think so. Sorry, I'm not very good with names, especially now.' He looks down at the body again, face crumpling. Then he takes in a deep breath, composing himself. 'I need to make some calls then I really must sleep. But maybe it'll come to me once I get some rest. Where are you staying?' I tell him the name of my hotel in Ao Nang and he nods. 'I'm not far from there. There's a small café just a few minutes' walk from it.' He pulls out a pen and business card from his pocket and scribbles down the café's address before handing it to me. 'Shall we meet there tomorrow morning, at nine?'

I want to tell him he needs to remember *right now* but then I put myself in his shoes again.

'Perfect.' I look down at the business card: *Jay Hemingford, Journalist.* 'Thank you, Jay.'

He smiles very slightly then looks back down at Claire Shreve. I leave him alone and follow Sam through the gates, the crowds and noise a contrast to the quiet solemnity and hushed sobs of the makeshift morgue behind us.

'Mum mentioned you booked a hotel in Ao Nang,' Sam says. 'There's a bus coming soon that'll get you there. You should go check in and get some rest then start again with a fresh head tomorrow. I can come by the café tomorrow morning after you've met with that man to see if I can help with any information he gives you?'

'That'll be great, thanks.'

'And my mum gave you my number right? So just call if you need me.'

'I will. I really appreciate your help, Sam.'

'No problem. I better get back to it.' He shoots me one last pained look then jogs away.

22

When the bus arrives, I step onto it like I'm sleepwalking, slumping into a chair near the back and staring blankly out of the window as it starts rumbling down the road. There's a young boy crying for his mum in front of me, his dad cuddling him to his chest as he tries to hold back his own tears. I wish I were a child again so I could cry for my mum. I'm relieved that wasn't her body, but that's not to say there won't be other temples, other bodies to see . . . one of which might really be hers.

The bus bumps over a pothole, and something digs into my hip. I look down and realise I still have the atlas. I must remember to give it to Jay Hemingford when I meet him tomorrow so he can return it to Claire Shreve's family.

I hesitate a few moments then lift the atlas to my nose. It smells of salt, of mangoes too, I think. I go to open it, unable to resist. It's clear Claire Shreve wouldn't want random people poking their nose in. Maybe if I just look in the pocket next to the Thailand map? If Mum met Claire Shreve out here and they visited the same places, there might be some breadcrumbs leading me to Mum's whereabouts. And anyway, if they did know each other, surely Claire Shreve would want to help me find my mum?

I find the right page then reach into the pocket. The first item is a photo of three people I don't recognise: a young girl with curly red hair, a petite brunette a few years older than me, then a young blond man. There's a hint of a palm tree in the background and, behind them, a large elephant statue with blue jewels all over it. I turn it over, but there's nothing on the back.

I go to the next item, a creased napkin with a pencil drawing of a rock jutting from the sea, someone standing on it with their arms wide open, like they want to catch the scribbled moon above.

23

And then the final item, a piece of orange tissue paper patterned with flowery swirls. Attached to it with a safety pin is part of a torn note, three words scrawled across it:

The bad things . . .

I shiver slightly, despite the heat, then tuck it back into the pocket before leaning my forehead against the cool window, thinking of that first note I'd found.

A watercolour of grey pooling around the edges of moss green valleys . . .

I'd visited Devon for the weekend with the girls the year before. Will had meant to come with us but something big had gone down at work. He'd suggested cancelling it but I'd thought, what the hell, why can't I do it alone? It wasn't easy. The drive down there was a challenge with two grumpy, tired kids. But once we'd got into the stride of things, it had been a little adventure – just me and the girls enjoying long walks and scones crammed with jam and cream, no frowning husband and Daddy to tell us we'd get fat.

God, how I'd love to be back there right now on safe and familiar ground, away from the fierce heat and the strange smells and sounds. The past few years, I've dreamed of spreading my wings a little. But I'd meant trying a holiday to Greece instead of Portugal; meeting new friends whose lives revolved around more than the school run and bake-offs; romantic dinners somewhere other than the local Italian. I didn't mean *this* – fumbling blind in a country with bamboo houses on stilts. I'd rather see thatched cottage roofs and feel Exmoor's sharp westerly wind fierce against my skin . . .

Chapter Two

Exmoor, UK
1997

In Exmoor, there's a feeling that, at any moment, something might suddenly plummet. Like the sky that September day when Claire drove towards the inn for the first time, a water-colour of grey pooling around the edges of moss green valleys, ready to plunge down and destroy everything below. Or the sheep that stood nonchalantly on steep verges dipped in purple heather, unaffected by the tightrope they walked between the drop below and passing cars.

When Claire arrived at the inn, a white three-storey building that seemed more suited to the plains of America than this windy British valley, she too felt as though she might plummet at any minute. She'd been holding it together so long, but the conversation she'd had with her husband the night before had sent her into freefall, the fragile walls she'd built up around herself the past few years starting to crumble.

She didn't check in as soon as she got there as she normally did on trips for the magazine. Instead, she'd headed straight for the signposted path leading towards the cliffs, praying the fresh air would bring her some peace as it always seemed to on her travels. As she entered the cocoon of trees behind the inn and followed the rippling river towards the sea with her Jack Russell, Archie, she didn't think much, brain muted from the drive there and all that had happened the night before. Instead, she watched as the scenery changed from the lush foliage of the surrounding forest into a valley of grey rocks.

It had rained overnight and now the air was fresh, the sky overhead a light grey mist. Archie clambered over the small rocks, nudging his wet nose under the stones, nibbling at the weeds that lay drying beneath them. She was pleased the inn's owner Henry Johnson had insisted she bring her dog to try out the pet-friendly rooms. She wasn't sure how she'd have coped here completely alone. Sure, she was used to travelling solo with her job, but that was before the floor fell out from beneath her marriage.

Soon the path rose up and away from the river, a steep bank of grey rock either side. In the distance, the river's mouth opened, bubbling over pebbles and out into a frothing sea. As she drew closer, metal barriers appeared with notices warning of sheer drops. She stopped at one of the barriers, looking out over the cliff, tummy wrinkling as she imagined tumbling into the furious waves below. Her publishing director wouldn't be too pleased considering press day was just around the corner.

She allowed herself a small smile before pulling her camera out of her bag and lifting it to her face, taking the usual obligatory photos for the magazine . . . and some for herself too. She had a scrapbook of photos from trips such as these just for herself. They weren't amazing photos; the magazine couldn't afford to send her on a course. But she'd learned on the job how to take a half-decent picture and now she enjoyed it, capturing moments she might have otherwise struggled to remember later as she wrote articles to crazy deadlines.

When she'd taken enough photos of the roaring sea and craggy cliffs, she led Archie down the slope towards the lime kiln she'd read about, a hut-shaped structure that merged into its surroundings. Its entranceway gaped open and Archie ran towards it but she yanked him back, noticing the sign at the front warning people not to enter for their own safety. When she was a teenager, she would've marched right in, regardless of any signs, just like her dad used to. One of her earliest memories was of when she was five and they were visiting the Wailua Falls in Kauai, Hawaii, a stunning double-tiered waterfall that dropped over a hundred feet, surrounded by tropical green flora. Her dad had heard you could get the best photos by scrambling down the steep cliffs towards the base of the waterfall. So, as Claire watched from the safety of the viewing area with her mum and sister, he'd managed to do just that, taking the iconic photo Claire still saw in travel magazines showing two streams of water silver-white as they gushed into the green lagoon below. Looking at that photo, you could almost feel the splash of water on your face, hear the roar of the waterfall.

Ten years later, Claire had visited the Big Falls waterfall in California with her friend Jodie. Inspired by her dad, she'd crossed the river and scaled the jagged hillsides around it to reach the waterfall's base, getting an amazing photo looking directly up the waterfall, the blue sky and bright yellow sun reflected in its sheen.

Put her in the same situation now and she wouldn't dare do that. Life had taught her taking the risky path simply wasn't worth it.

'This way, boy,' Claire said, pulling Archie away from the cliff edge and towards the cluster of boulders leading down to the ocean. They picked their way over the rocks towards the sea, fizz from the waves speckling Claire's jeans. It was strange how still things felt at that moment, so calm and beautiful, despite the frenzied nature of the waves nearby. She was completely alone here, just Archie, the roar of the sea and the squawk of birds for company. Is this the way it would be from now on, just her and Archie? It was unlikely anyone else would take her barren, broken body, after all. Even at thirty-one, it seemed a daunting prospect. What about in twenty, thirty, forty years? Would she end up like her dad, ill and alone in some grotty flat, despite all she'd done to try to avoid a destiny like his? At least she'd been with him at the end. There would be no child holding her hand and mopping her brow now.

She sank down onto a large rock, putting her head on her hands. This was really happening, wasn't it? Ben was leaving her, taking all the dreams they'd shared with him too. What was she going to do now? She felt a scrabbling at her feet and looked down to see Archie peering up at her with his one good brown eye – the other had been removed after a bout of glaucoma. He put his front paws on her knees and nuzzled his wet snout into her jeans. She leaned down, pressing her cheek against the warm fur of his neck.

'At least I've got you, haven't I, boy?'

He wagged his tail in response and she sighed, reaching into her bag and pulling out the book her friend Jodie had managed to get an advance copy of – *Memoirs of a Geisha* by Arthur Golden. That was the advantage of having a friend who was an arts and culture events organiser; she could sate her craving for good books before other people got their hands on them. Claire had met Jodie during her travels with her family when they were both thirteen – Jodie with her bohemian mum and crazy sisters, Claire with her ramshackle family. Jodie had been her one true friend, still was in a way, other friends just ships in the night due to the intense hours Claire worked. Both of them still somehow managed to meet whenever they could, despite their hectic schedules. She wondered what Jodie would say about her and Ben splitting up. Maybe she'd be secretly happy. Jodie had never really warmed to him.

She looked down at the book and let herself get lost in the words. That was all it took sometimes, the feel of flimsy paper between her fingers, the sight of black ink dancing before her eyes and delivering her into another world. Books were often her only companions on lonely nights during press trips. They'd been there for her when she was a kid craving consistency too, curling up in a little nook some-where, the characters she'd read about becoming her friends when she only had her family for company as they travelled from one place to the next.

She reached into her pocket for her other companion – chocolate – and luxuriated in this chance to leave all her troubles behind, occasionally stopping to marvel at the scenery around her, her new fortress of solitude.

But it wasn't long before her fortress of Solitude became a fortress of German tourists as a whole centipede of people appeared on the horizon, trailing one after another on the path above. Among them was a family, a little boy strapped to the mother's chest in a baby holdall. She'd once dreamed of holidays like that with Ben.

She put her book away, reluctantly acknowledging it was time to head back and get on with the job. Her favourite kind of press trip were the ones organised by the tourist offices where she was met at the airport by a media rep then left to get on with it for the rest of the time, with the odd attraction visit and hotel inspection. But on the majority of her trips, most of her time was taken up by her host – usually someone who paid big bucks to advertise in the magazine – escorting Claire here, there and everywhere on a tight schedule, even just a one-nighter turning into a small kind of torture. She had a feeling this might be one of those trips; she'd met the inn's owner before and he was a handful.

'Ready to head back?' she asked Archie.

He wagged his tail as she jumped up. A few minutes later, she was squeezing past the queue of Germans, apologising to them as Archie jumped up at their legs. Once they were behind her, she paused a moment to watch as they marched towards the sea. It already looked different, the blur of their forms blotting the scenery in front of her.

As she walked back along the path the tourists had come down, she thought of the conversation she'd had with Ben the night before. They'd been driving back from a friend's wedding reception and she'd been looking out of the car window as the cat's eyes on the road had blurred into one, creating a jet stream of light down the middle of the windy road. She'd had a bit to drink and had made Ben play Joni Mitchell's 'Both Sides Now' over and over as she'd stared at that light, feeling miserable, thinking of how it was always these nights – these long drives in the dark – that got her thinking about everything they didn't have. After a while, he'd turned to her, the misery on his face mirroring hers.

'Maybe you should use this trip to Exmoor as a chance to think about things,' he'd said.

'What do you mean?'

He'd looked surprised. 'You're not telling me you haven't noticed how strained things are between us, Claire? How miserable you are in particular?'

She'd felt the panic start to rise. Yes, she had noticed, but then they'd only just finished their last round of IVF two months before, then work had been hectic, her boss seeming to punish her for taking two weeks off for her treatment by making her work longer hours, go on even more trips. She'd barely seen Ben, and had kept telling herself they'd go away once things calmed down and get things back on track.

But things had never really calmed down.

'Sorry, I've been so busy,' Claire had said to Ben. 'I'll take some time off, we can go away like we said we would.'

Ben had sighed. 'It's not enough, Claire. Watching Robyn and Richard get married today made me realise just how much we've changed since we got married.' His knuckles had turned white as he'd clung onto the steering wheel. 'We're broken, Claire. We've tried to fix it but it's time we admitted it's over.'

She'd attempted to grab his hand, pleading with him it wasn't over, they just needed to fight for their marriage. But he'd just stared ahead, jaw set. That night, he'd slept in the spare room. The last she'd seen of him was the next morning as he'd watched her drive away, a look of relief on his face.

Relief. Had it really got that bad between them?

As she'd driven away, she'd wondered if he'd realised it was three years exactly from the day of their first embryo transfer. She tried to imagine carrying a toddler in her arms with him strolling beside her. Things would be different then, wouldn't they? She'd have the secure family life she'd yearned for ever since she'd discovered her dad dying and realised a life lived on the edge just left you all alone. But that life was gone and now, instead of that toddler, all Claire saw were six embryos bobbing up and down in the sea, the same six that had failed to implant, leading to a bunch of negative pregnancy tests she still kept in a box in her wardrobe.

Ghosts of lost hope.

'Oh God,' she whispered. She stopped walking and leaned

her hand against the hard grey rock of the cliff next to her to steady herself, gulping in huge breaths as she saw the life she'd dreamed of ebbing away.

Then a bark echoed out in the distance. Archie looked up from the patch of grass he'd been sniffing, back straight as a rod as he tried to detect the source of the sound. Claire followed his gaze to see a feral-looking dog running along a dash of path on the other side of the river. She hadn't even noticed there was another path. Then the dog's owner came into view: tall, dark hair, long stride. He was walking with purpose, eyes scouring all around him, his dark fringe lifting with every step to reveal a hint of long lashes, straight nose, tanned forehead.

Archie let out a woof that echoed around the valley.

The man paused mid-stride and looked up at them. His dog paused too, ears pricking. Then it let out a thin whine that stretched across the river and steep bank between them. The man stepped forward, whole body alert as he reached into his pocket, pulling out a pair of binoculars. He pressed them to his eyes and Claire froze, feeling like he'd actually run across the river and scrambled up the bank towards her. Even Archie stilled, pressing his small black and white body against Claire's shins.

The man lowered his binoculars and pulled his walking stick out from under his arm. That's when Claire realised it wasn't a walking stick he was holding . . . it was a gun.

He cocked it up towards her, pressing his cheek against the flat edge of its top, and all the misery she'd just been battling drained away, replaced by fear.

'Oh Jesus,' she whispered, finally finding her feet and stumbling backwards.

Suddenly, the air was punctured with a sound like a firework going off. She ducked and there was a terrible keening sound from above. She looked up to see a large deer with spindly antlers and fur the colour of conkers staggering around, blood trickling from a small hole in its head. Archie whined and the stag's eyes snagged on Claire's, making her almost choke on the fleeting look of terror and hopelessness in them.

Then it tumbled down the bank, landing with a thump in front of her, one of its antlers cracking in half on impact.

She put her hand to her mouth, unable to drag her gaze away from the deer's eyes, which were now staring into nothingness. Blood was pooling around its head and Archie tried to get to it, yanking Claire out of her shock. She pulled him back and turned towards the man, ready to scream at him – but he was gone.

She jogged back, whole body buzzing with anger. When she reached the inn, a white marquee was being set up on the expanse of green that fanned up from the river. A woman in her fifties watched from the path with a pretty blonde girl, her face lit up with pride. A wedding?

Wonderful.

Claire darted past them then paused as she noticed glimpses of a large farmhouse in between the leaves, dark and imposing, ivy strangling its gutters. Spread out beyond it was a huge hill that sloped into a valley, cows and sheep dotted all over.

She walked into the inn, the soles of her wellies squelching on the pine floorboards. She found Henry, the inn's owner, in the plush-looking bar talking to a girl of about thirteen or fourteen with spirals of vivid red hair. She peered up at Claire, green eyes sparkling with curiosity as Archie's tail wagged against Claire's chest.

'You got here!' Henry said when he saw Claire approach. He bounded up to her, leaving the girl behind and giving

Claire a kiss on both cheeks. He was huge, at least six foot three, with thick blond hair.

They'd met once before during a press trip to the boutique hotel he'd once owned in Oxford. She'd always found him a bit overwhelming and had been dreading spending more time than she needed to with him this weekend. That dread had grown after everything that had happened with Ben; how could she keep up the fake smiles today of all days? That was the thing with editing a travel trade magazine aimed at tour operators: you were forced into situations with people you wouldn't usually want to spend much time with.

'The new hairdo suits you,' Henry said, smiling.

She put her hand to her head. That weekend, she'd impulsively asked her hairdresser to cover the usual brown with bright red and chop it to her shoulders. She hadn't changed her hair in such a long time, her boss preferring her to keep the same style so she didn't confuse the magazine advertisers. But she'd felt like she needed a change. When she'd stared at herself in the mirror afterwards, it seemed to have changed her face somehow, making her brown eyes look even bigger, skin even paler.

'Did you arrive okay?' Henry asked. 'All checked in?'

'Not checked in yet,' Claire said as she tried to catch her breath, hands still trembling half with anger, half with shock at having a gun pointed at her. 'We've just been for a walk. Look, I just saw—'

The girl approached, eyes on Archie, huge smile on her pretty face as she crouched down in front of him. She was wearing muddy jeans and wellies, and a green faded hoodie that matched the colour of her eyes. Archie backed away slightly, wary after the rough treatment of other children.

'Your dog's a bit nervous, isn't he?' the girl asked Claire.

34

Claire smiled. 'He can be. He only has one eye so it makes him quite anxious with strangers.'

'Oh yes, I can see now. You hardly notice with the black patch of hair. Thought it'd be something like that. Dad gets Jack Russells in to kill the rats on the farms sometimes and they're always so confident. Uncle Milo says I'm to get myself to a dog's level if they're scared.'

'That's enough now, Holly, Claire doesn't need to hear your uncle's theories on canine behaviour, thank you very much.' Henry leaned in close to Claire. 'I'm afraid my niece hasn't been taught manners,' he whispered rather too loudly.

Rude git, Claire thought.

Holly frowned slightly at Henry's comment as she slowly reached her hand out to Archie. He hesitated a moment, considering his options, then slunk towards her, head low, tail wagging. She softly stroked his ears and he drew even closer, leaning against her shoulder as she smiled.

'She's a wild one,' Henry continued. 'No surprise considering she's part of my wife's crazy family. I'll tell you all about *that* after a few glasses of wine,' he added, tapping his nose. 'Plus she's not had a proper mother figure all these years and has been brought up surrounded by pigs and tractors in the farm up the road.'

Claire thought of the farmhouse she'd seen just a moment ago. 'Maybe all kids should be brought up on farms then?' she said. 'She's wonderful with Archie.'

Holly looked up at Claire, a hesitant smile on her face. 'Uncle Milo says I should be a vet. But I'd prefer to be a journalist, like you.'

'She's seen the magazine,' Henry said, noticing the confused look on Claire's face. 'Been excited about your visit for days.'

'Oh, it's only a small magazine,' Claire said to Holly. 'How old are you?'

'Fourteen.'

'You have a while to decide what you want to be yet. Why don't you look after Archie while I talk to your uncle?' She handed Archie's lead to Holly. 'Make sure you hold the lead tight though, he likes to chase birds and cars.'

'Just like your uncle Milo,' Henry said, guffawing as he steered Claire away. His face grew serious when they got out of earshot. 'Everything okay, Claire?'

'Not really. I just saw a deer shot right in front of my eyes.'

His jaw twitched but he didn't look surprised. 'Whereabouts?'

'On the path on the way to the cliffs, about twenty minutes from here. It was a man with dark hair, in his thirties I think. He had an old dog with him, it looked like a wolf with grey fur, and—'

'Milo,' Henry said, sighing.

Claire thought of what Holly had said. 'Holly's uncle?'

'Yes, my wife's bloody idiot of a brother. I told you that family is cuckoo.'

She peered towards Holly. 'I don't want to cause a family argument. I just think he needs to be a bit more aware of how terrifying it can be, having a gun pointed at you.'

'Oh, he'll be made aware, all right.' He peered at the clock. 'Do you want to freshen up? Then I have one hell of an afternoon planned for you.'

Claire forced herself to smile. She really didn't want to be here. She wanted to be back home, saving her marriage. 'Great, see you in twenty minutes.'

She turned away but not before she caught sight of her brown eyes reflected back at her in a nearby mirror. She thought of the hopelessness she'd seen in the deer's eyes before it tumbled down the bank.

*

36

Claire picked up the pint of sweet cider she'd just ordered and settled back into the plump sofa, staring out of the window beside her towards the darkening valley and blanket of trees below. Her room overlooked the same scene a floor above. It was all cream carpets, mahogany furniture and plush red chairs, just like the bar she was sitting in. It felt too plush and romantic for just her. She yearned for Ben to be here. She'd told him she wouldn't go when they'd got home from that dreadful drive, but he'd insisted. She'd even suggested to him that he join her. Her company forbade partners from attending trips but this was a special circumstance. But again, he refused. He'd clearly made his mind up and it should have shocked Claire to the core. But the truth was, she wasn't surprised. She'd been in denial and now it was all unravelling.

So instead of Ben being her dinner partner, she'd had to endure Henry all afternoon and over dinner too. Only he could draw what would usually be an hour's tour into four hours. And now she was sat here alone, belly full of Exmoor's finest lamb, head already woozy from the few sips she'd had of her cider. She checked her phone, not that it was much use considering there was no reception here. When Henry had said the place was remote, he'd meant it.

She caught sight of the notepad she'd brought. She needed a distraction. Maybe she could start work on that travel memoir she'd always wanted to write? Except when she opened it, the blank page mocked her. She swirled a pattern in the margins, flowers tangled around the punctured holes like ivy, then wrote the word '*Exmoor*' and her name, then a line – *A watercolour of grey* . . .

A gust of cold air wrapped itself around her, lifting the corners of her notepad. She looked up to see the man who'd shot the deer walk in, dark hair whipping about his head, the ash from the cigarette he was holding dancing towards her. Under the light of the bar, his brown eyes looked almost gold, his lips very red. He appeared younger close up, taller too. He was wearing what he'd had on earlier: black jeans tucked into green wellies, a typical farmer's wax jacket. She had to admit he was very attractive – what her friend Jodie would describe as a 'dasher', all legs, rugged features and windswept hair. That didn't detract from the fact he'd nearly killed her.

A man prowled in behind him. He looked a little like Milo but older, thinner, with hair a shade lighter than his. His brother? He hunched his shoulders and narrowed his eyes as he scanned the pub. Behind him, the feral-looking dog she had seen earlier slinked in. Now she could see it close up, she recognised some Irish wolfhound in it, maybe a touch of German shepherd too. He looked quite a few years older than Archie, his back legs a bit rickety.

Milo stubbed his cigarette out on the wall as he passed her, bringing with him the smell of grass and bonfires. He stared at Claire then looked down at her notepad. She slammed it shut, trying to look suitably indignant. He frowned slightly then strolled to the bar as Claire peeked at him under her eyelashes, taking in how short his hair was at the back, a contrast to his long fringe.

As his dog passed, Archie let out a low threatening growl. The dog paused, surveying Archie with startling blue eyes. Milo tapped two fingers on his thigh and his dog bounced to his side, pressing his face close to his owner's leg.

Henry walked in from the restaurant with a thin, dark-haired woman – his wife, Claire presumed, and Milo and this other guy's sister. She strolled up to her brothers as Henry disappeared behind the bar. Claire could see the similarities between the three of them. Same long, sinewy limbs;

same brown feline eyes; same distinctive bone structure. She thought of what Henry had said earlier about them being 'cuckoo'. She wondered what he meant by that. They certainly gave off a certain energy, the atmosphere in the bar charged in their presence.

The door opened again and Holly bounded in. She was wearing a blue taffeta dress that seemed a little childish for her age, the sleeves too short, the edges frayed. She whirled around the pub before Milo's brother grabbed her arm and reprimanded her, making her pretty eyes fill with tears. Milo frowned and placed his hand on his brother's arm, whispering something to him. His brother relaxed slightly and pinched Holly's cheek playfully as she looked down at her feet, biting her lip. Claire's heart went out to her and she shot her a quick smile. Holly's face lit up and she smiled back at her. But then Milo's brother glanced towards Claire and glared at her. She quickly looked away.

Yes, there was something a bit *off* about that family.

Henry handed a pint over to Milo who held his gaze with a long, cold stare before strolling towards a table in the corner, his brother and niece joining him. Milo sunk into a chair, taking a sip of his beer, his eyes drilling into Claire's over the top of his glass as his brother knocked half his pint back, slamming it on the table and wiping his mouth. Claire turned away again, taking several gulps of cider in quick succession, panicking as she felt the bubbles working their way back up her throat and towards her nose. She coughed into her hand. Milo smiled to himself and she felt a stab of annoyance.

Henry caught her eye and strode towards her, crouching down beside her table. 'Sorry I can't join you, we're short on staff tonight.'

'Oh, it's fine, I'm quite happy sitting here, taking it all in.'

Claire peered towards Milo and his brother. 'Is that your wife's two brothers?'

Henry followed her gaze and rolled his eyes. 'Yes, the infamous James brothers, Milo the Mystery Man and Dale the Deranged.'

'Deranged?'

'Screw loose,' Henry said, making circles with his finger over his temple. 'Came back from fighting in the Falklands one sandwich short of a picnic.'

'He's a soldier?'

'*Was* a soldier, until he spent a few months in a mental institute. I told you that family is nuts, something runs through those veins of theirs, a connection gone wrong in their set up. My wife Jen's the only one who's normal. You know their grandfather shot himself?'

Claire followed his gaze towards Dale who was clenching and unclenching his jaw as he stared into the distance. 'That must have been very hard for Dale, being in the Falklands.'

'We all go through tough times. Don't turn us half-mad, do they?' Henry leaned closer, lowering his voice. 'I talked to Milo about how upset you were. I also told him he won't be paid for that deer he shot.'

Claire thought of the red notices she'd seen on the drive down, the smoke on the horizon, the rotting stench as dozens of herds were culled. She'd even written about BSE, or Mad Cow Disease as it was known, for her magazine after many of the UK's farm attractions had closed to tourists, the disease not only killing cattle but also being linked to vCJD, a brain condition in humans. But tourism was the least of the farm world's problems. The worldwide ban on all British beef exports the year before was crippling them.

'No, Henry, please,' Claire said. 'Farmers need all the money they can get with this BSE crisis.'

'The farm's problems started way before all this BSE nonsense! Thank God I came along and bought this inn off the family, otherwise there'd be no money left.' He raised his voice as he spoke. Milo's brother turned to look at Henry before sliding his gaze to Claire, the anger visible on his face.

She stood up. 'I'm going to call it a night, Henry, it's been a long day.'

'But it's only eight!'

'I'm very tired.' She manoeuvred out from behind the table. 'Don't say anything else to your brother-in-law, all right? And please, don't dock his pay.'

'But—'

Claire looked him in the eye. 'Really, Henry. I'll see you at lunch tomorrow as planned. I want to explore the area a bit in the morning then we can discuss what you have planned for the rest of my stay.'

She found herself taking one last look at Milo, who was now laughing at something Holly had said, then walked out of the bar, Archie trotting after her. As she reached the staircase, she heard footsteps behind her. She turned, thinking it was Henry then froze when she realised it was Milo.

Archie jumped up at his legs, tail wagging erratically.

Traitor, Claire thought.

'I'm sorry about what happened earlier,' he said. His voice was deep with a slight West Country twang. 'Henry said you were upset.'

'I think the deer was more upset,' Claire said.

'It was a red stag actually.'

Claire rolled her eyes. 'Oh, that makes it better then.'

'It does when it's been trampling all over our crops and killing endangered wildlife,' he said with a raised eyebrow.

She felt her face flush. She wasn't qualified to have an argument about this. 'Just be more careful in the future. I didn't expect to have a gun pointed at me on my first day here.'

Archie whined, scrabbling his paws at Milo's jeans. Milo leaned down, running his hand over Archie's back. Then he peered up at Claire from under his fringe, his eyes sinking into hers. 'Sorry, I'm being an idiot. I actually hate hunting.'

'Then maybe you should consider a career change.'

'It's not as easy as that.'

She sighed. She shouldn't have said that. 'I'm sorry, it's none of my business. Goodnight.' She went to walk up the stairs.

'You took the wrong path today, by the way,' he called out after her.

She paused, turning around. 'Sorry?'

'The path you took to Hope's Mouth.'

'I took the official path.'

'The official path isn't always the best path.'

'How so?'

'Secret passages.'

Claire laughed. 'I didn't realise we were in Narnia.'

'Narnia's got nothing on Exmoor.' His face grew serious. 'I'll take you tomorrow morning if you want.'

'Sorry?'

'Via the better path. Unless you have other plans, of course?'

Claire stared at him, not quite sure how to take him. Was he being serious?

His sister came out with a pint of bitter in her hands. 'What are you doing, Milo?' she asked, looking Claire up and down. 'It's Holly's birthday, remember?'

'Thanks, Jen.' He put his arm around his sister's shoulders and led her to the bar, peering over his shoulder at Claire. 'So see you outside at eight tomorrow morning then?'

'I have plans.'

'I won't bring my gun, if that's what you're worried about.'

They disappeared into the bar, laughter ringing out from inside. Claire stood where she was for a few moments, face flushed, heart thumping. Then she whistled for Archie and headed to her room, desperate to disappear into the pages of her novel again and forget all about gun-toting farmers with unbearably handsome faces.

The clouds hovered above like bin bags ready to burst as Claire walked outside the next morning. It was nine; she'd made sure not to show her face before then. If she went for a walk with Milo, how would that look? This was a work trip after all and she wanted to hurry up and get home. Then there was everything that had passed between her and Ben the past two days. It wouldn't be right.

But as she rounded the corner, the first person she saw was Milo, his hands in the pockets of his wax coat as he leaned against a wall, a small smile on his face. Her traitorous lips tried to form a smile in response. She forced them into a grim line instead.

'You're a bit late,' Milo said, looking at his watch.

'I never said I'd meet you.'

'But you're here now.'

'No, I'm heading out for a walk *alone*, with my dog. I need to take more photos for the magazine.'

'Oh, come on. Doesn't the part of you that bought those earrings want to see Narnia?' he said, referring to the striped tribal earrings Claire's dad had got her when they were in Zanzibar.

'Narnia's a million miles away from where I got these earrings,' she said, thinking of the red dusty roads and cracked pavements, tiny children dressed in torn jeans and filthy T-shirts reaching their hands out to her as she passed in the four-by-four her dad had hired. Then there was the other side: the soft golden sands of the affluent coastal resort of Mangapwani; the scent of expensive suntan lotion mixing with exotic spices; couples walking hand in hand as the sky turned orange on the horizon, the same sun that was setting on those children just a few miles away. It was something Claire saw in every place she visited, excruciating poverty in sharp contrast to nauseating wealth. She always tried to touch on it in her writing, her little way of helping in some way, but the lines she wrote were inevitably cut out at subbing stage, her publishing director scolding her as he told her she didn't work for 'bloody Oxfam'.

'Narnia might be far from Zanzibar,' Milo said, snapping her out of her reverie. 'But it's just a thirty-minute walk from here.'

He shot Claire a smile, teeth white and crooked, brown eyes sparking, and her stomach rippled. She wrapped her arms around herself, pressing the handle of Archie's lead into her middle. She wasn't supposed to react like this to another man.

Milo raked his fingers through his dark hair. 'Look, I feel bad about what happened yesterday. I'm doing this to make it up to you. No tourists know about this place, you'll love it. Really. You can write about it in your magazine.'

'I don't know,' she said, peering towards the path she'd taken the day before.

'Fine,' he said, putting his hands up as he backed away. 'I get the message. I'm going up there anyway so feel free to join me. If not, I guess I'll see you across the river on your *official* path in a couple of hours.'

He strode away and Claire stood where she was a few moments. It *would* be good to write about something a little different. She'd got a letter from a reader the other day moaning that all the magazine ever wrote about was information they could get in guide books anyway.

She decided to follow him after all. Maybe that reader would rue their words this time?

Milo slowed down when he heard her footsteps and let her fall into step beside him, shooting her a smile.

'How long have you had him?' he asked as they watched Archie stop at each place Milo's dog did, resolutely covering his scent with his own.

'Five years. No one else would have him at the rescue place – too snappy apparently.'

Milo raised an eyebrow. 'So you're a fan of the underdogs, then?'

Claire thought of the other children she'd try to play with during her travels as a kid: strays and waifs with hidden troubles. 'I suppose so.'

'Holly told me how you stuck up for her in front of Henry.'

'Is Holly an underdog?'

His face clouded over. 'In some ways.' Archie jumped up at his legs and his face softened. 'So how old is he?'

'Seven.'

'He still looks like a pup.'

'Everyone says that. But he sees himself as a *man* dog.'

Milo laughed. 'Man dog. I like that.'

Claire felt a stab of guilt. Ben had come up with that phrase. She wondered how he'd feel about her walking their dog with a man who looked like Milo. Maybe he wouldn't care.

'So how do we get onto this *better* path?' Claire asked, shrugging the thought away.

'Over that.' He pointed towards the river.

'We have to cross the river?'

He put on a mock scared face. 'I know, rivers can be terrifying, all that water trickling over little scary pebbles.'

She smiled. 'Enough of the sarcasm! I just meant there's no bridge and the sign said the river's deep.'

The sign said.

She felt her face flush with embarrassment. Milo probably thought she was a right wuss.

'It'll be fine,' he said. He looked down at her wellies, just shin-high and covered with fat pink flowers. 'They're waterproof, right? And the part of river I'm thinking about isn't as deep as here. I'll show you.'

She followed him down towards the bank, watching as the river gushed over clusters of rocks.

'See, doesn't look so bad up close,' he said, smiling to himself. She noticed he got a small dimple in his right cheek when he smiled. 'Still scared, city girl?'

She rolled her eyes. 'City girl, as if! I've seen plenty of countryside, and not just in the UK either. I'm more worried for you actually. If you fall in, I'd have to jump in and save you, wouldn't I? My hair goes all curly when it gets wet, it'll be a pain to re-style it.'

Milo blew his fringe out of his eyes. 'You think this fringe isn't a nightmare after a dunk in the river?'

Claire laughed.

'And as for the city girl thing,' he said, looking her up and down. 'I was only joking. It's obvious you're not.'

Claire looked down at what she was wearing: the purple leggings she'd discovered in a Californian flea market, the holey jumper Ben had bought her in Belgium and, of course, her flowery wellies, all the way from Scotland.

She smiled. 'I guess not.'

'So you going to put those flower power wellies to use then?'

She felt a funny little thrill in the pit of her stomach, like she was at that waterfall again. But that was ridiculous, it was just a bloody river! 'Why not?' she said.

'Blue!' Milo shouted, pointing to the other side of the river. His dog peered up then bounded across the river, paws splashing into the water, tail wagging. Archie went to chase after him but Claire pulled him back, leaning over to pick him up. He'd be belly-deep in water if she let him walk across.

'Interesting name for a dog,' she said as she looked at Milo's dog.

'Colour of his eyes.'

'Of course.'

'It's a narrow ridge,' Milo said, stepping into the water. 'One step left or right and you're both under.'

She stepped in after him. It wasn't so deep after all.

He peered at her. 'Told you it wouldn't be so scary.'

'I'm disappointed. Nothing like another life or death situation to make a girl's holiday go with a zing.'

Milo stepped onto the river. 'Try milking a herd of premenstrual cows at five am.'

'You were doing that this morning?' Claire asked as she carefully followed him, feeling the squelch of her soles against the water.

'I do it every morning before the sun rises. We have over a hundred cows so it can take a couple of hours. Then I have to feed and clean them. By that time, it's nearly ten. But no stopping there, then it's time to feed the young stock.'

'Lambs and calves?'

Milo smiled. 'Yep. Wriggly little buggers but once they're calm and feeding, it's quite peaceful. The rest of the day I'm mucking stables out, repairing fences, retrieving livestock that have decided to go wandering . . . knackering work really, but worth it.'

Claire breathed in the air, taking in the smell of grass and brine. 'Have you been farming all your life?'

'Yep, the farm's been in our family for generations. My older brother Dale joined the Forces when I was thirteen, so our parents relied on me and my sister Jen to help out. When they passed away, they left the farm to Dale – it always gets passed down to the oldest son.'

Claire thought about what Henry had told her about Milo's grandfather committing suicide. 'When did your parents pass away?' she asked softly.

'When I was seventeen. Dad had a heart attack and Mum died not long after from a stroke. Jen reckons she died of a broken heart.'

'That must have been a tough time.'

'Yep. They had us pretty late so they weren't exactly spring chickens but to lose them within a few months of each other . . .' He sighed. 'To make matters worse, Dale had just recovered from his injuries after getting back from the Falklands.' By injuries, Claire wondered if he meant psychological injuries too, considering what Henry had so indiscreetly told her. 'He was desperate to get back to army life but he had to stay and look after the farm. He did really well at first actually,' Milo continued. 'The farm's turnover nearly doubled, the animals were happier than they'd ever been – fewer visits to the vets, more births. Then this whole BSE thing happened.'

'Were there any cases on the farm?' Claire asked as they reached the middle of the river. It was very dark there, the trees bending right over both sides of the river.

'No, but once a link between BSE and vCJD was made, that was it, milk production and beef sales nosedived. Dale's really struggled to hold things together.'

'But the farm's still here, your brother did well to ride the worst of it. And the profits from the inn must help too?'

His shoulders tensed. 'Hardly. We barely get anything from that.'

'But Henry implied—'

'That he was our saviour?'

'Not in so many words . . .'

'Don't worry, he tells us himself whenever he gets the chance. Yes, the share we get of the profits helps. But if we'd kept the land we sold to him a few years back, we'd have got a much better price for it now. Bloody Henry!'

He quickened his step, striding across the rest of the river so fast Claire had to jog to keep up with him. As they neared the other bank, her foot scooted out from under her and she nearly stumbled. He turned, grabbing the tops of her arms, steadying her. 'Careful now.'

She peered up at him, taking in the fine stubble on his chin, the slight bump in his nose she hadn't noticed before. He swallowed, his Adam's apple rising and falling, and she imagined placing her lips on it.

She turned away in surprise, face flushing. Where on earth had that image come from?

'Come on, we're on the other path now,' he said. 'The better path.'

She followed his gaze towards a small path weaving its way from the bank up into the hills. Blue was already some way up the path, front paws on a tree stump as he looked down at them. Maybe she should turn back? She should have followed her instincts and not come with Milo. She was vulnerable after what had happened between her and Ben, her mind all a fizz. But how would it look if she turned back now?

One walk, she thought, *then that's it, I'll avoid him for the rest of my stay.*

Claire let Archie down and followed Milo up the bank.

Viewed from the path Claire had walked along yesterday, this area had looked like a mass of wild trees and bushes.

'So where'd you grow up?' Milo asked Claire.

'Everywhere. My dad was a travel writer too, freelance though,' she explained. 'We tagged along with him all over the world as he was paid by different newspapers and magazines to write about the places we visited.'

'What about school?'

'Mum's a teacher, she home-schooled me and my sister.'

A memory struck Claire then, from when her family had visited the Japanese city of Osaka when she was ten. They were staying in a hotel overlooking the river so they could watch the famous Tenjin Matsuri boat festival the next day. After coming back from lunch one day, Claire had seen a group of school kids chasing each other down the path below her hotel room. She remembered thinking she'd give up all her travels to be one of those kids, secure at school and surrounded by friends. But the next evening, as she'd watched the beautifully lit boats glide down the river below, she'd thought what a fool she'd been to think that. This was the battle that had always raged inside, her yearning for normality versus her wanderlust.

'Do you have any siblings other than your sister?' Milo asked.

Claire snapped out of her memory. 'No, just Sofia. She has a kid about the same age as Holly actually, Alex. He's great. Holly's your niece, right?'

'Yep.'

'What about her mum?'

His eyes slipped away from Claire's. 'She left a few years back. Dale got sole custody of Holly.' He leaned down to pick up a pebble, cleaning it on his sleeve. 'So did your dad get you into writing?'

'Yeah,' she said eventually, noting the change of subject. 'He even got one of my articles published when I was just thirteen.'

'Impressive. What was it about?'

Claire smiled to herself. 'It was just a short article about the Sichuan giant panda sanctuaries in the south-west of China. But I loved seeing my name in print.'

'Wow, you really have been to some amazing places. What was it like?'

'Wonderful. My dad knows one of the managers so we got a private tour. The sanctuaries are spread across the edge of the Qionglai and Jiajin mountains. I remember being in complete awe of the lush green landscapes and imposing mountains. And that's before we even got to the pandas.' She laughed. 'They're so fluffy, just like they've been plucked from a giant toy box. My dad noticed me scribbling away in my notepad so suggested I write an article. He sent it to the editor of a children's section in one of the national newspapers and he published it.' Claire looked down at the silver globe pendant hanging from her bag. 'My dad got me this to mark the occasion, my first ever published article.'

Milo's eyes widened.

'What's up?' Claire asked.

He smiled, pulling the collar of his jumper down to reveal a bronze globe pendant hanging from a length of black leather twine wrapped around his neck.

'I didn't know you were into travelling,' Claire said, surprised.

'Oh, I haven't travelled much. I'd like to though.' He peered down at the globe. 'This belonged to my grandfather. He was the only James man not to stay and work the farm all his life. He travelled instead after the war, working bars and restaurants, using the experience he got from the inn to hop from one country to the next. Quite a thing to do back then.'

'Would you like to travel like he did?'

He nodded. 'There's a box of letters and photos from his travels that I used to rummage through when I was a kid. It gave me the travel bug.' His face darkened. 'But then my parents died and I had no choice but to stay and help on the farm.'

'You have a choice now, surely? I'm sure Dale could cope on his own.'

He shook his head vehemently. 'No, trust me, he couldn't. It's too much for one person. He needs me.'

'I'm sure he'd rather see you happy than wishing you were on the other side of the world.'

'Nah, I owe him.'

'*Owe* him? Why?'

His face grew stiff. 'Long story.'

Claire didn't push him on the subject. It wasn't her place. 'I'm sorry, I shouldn't pry.' They were quiet for a few moments then she turned back to him. 'Okay, let's pretend you did have the freedom to just travel. Where would you go?'

His face lit up again. 'I'd start in Australia and I'd set up a mango farm.'

Claire laughed. 'A *mango* farm?'

'Hey, it's no joke. My friend Joe has one in Oz.' He looked wistfully into the distance. 'It's perfect. He told me he wakes in the morning as the sun rises and walks out barefoot among the trees, feeling the red sand beneath his feet. He treats those mangoes like his kids, nurtures them until they're ripe for picking. He reckons the satisfaction of picking each mango, then placing them one by one in wooden carts to be taken away for others to taste is the best feeling in the world.'

Claire watched him as he talked, saw the passion in his face, felt the incredible desire he had for a life so completely out of reach for him right now. It made her heart ache.

'So whereabouts in Australia is this mango farm?' she asked, wanting to keep that smile on his face.

'In the Outback, near Ayers Rock.'

She smiled. 'I've been there.'

'You have?'

She nodded. 'I remember the first time I went, it felt like I was on Mars. There's red sand everywhere you look and this feeling in the air like you're the only person on the planet. And Ayers Rock itself – or Uluru, as my dad used to call it – is astounding, rising up tall and proud above you, almost beckoning you to go right up and touch it. It has this power to it that I can't explain.'

His brown eyes lit up with excitement. 'I knew it was as good as Joe said! If I ever go, you'll have to come with me, you clearly love the place.'

She felt her cheeks flush. She could tell he was just joking but still, it made her feel self-conscious. 'I'd make a good business partner,' she said, trying to show she was going along with it. 'I can do all the marketing and stuff.'

'You'll get paid in mangoes, that okay?'

'As long as I get an office,' she teased back.

'Yes, of course. I might even throw in health insurance.'

'We have a deal!'

They did an impromptu high five then burst out laughing. For a moment, she forgot about her marriage troubles and her infertility. It was just her and a stranger laughing in the middle of a West Country valley.

It occurred to Claire then how strange that was: her laughing in the middle of nowhere with a virtual stranger; a stranger who'd pointed a gun at her the day before. But then hadn't she spent the past few years going on guided tours with complete strangers?

She dropped her gaze from his and looked around her. The wild tangle of bushes had petered out into banks of steep grey rock, small green shrubs dotted here and there. It felt like they were in a cave, the sky above grey to match the banks. The pebble path stretched out before them then turned a corner, glimpses of the violent sea flashing between a bank of trees.

'So, we nearly at Narnia then?' Claire asked.

'Nearly. Come on.'

He quickened his step and Claire followed with a smile on her face. Blue ran ahead as Archie trotted after him. 'So what about you?' he said. 'Any plans to live in the Himalayas or something?'

Claire's smile died away. What were her plans now without Ben? Would they sell the house? It had taken them so long to find the Victorian terrace and do it up just as they liked over the years. She felt a wave of nausea as she realised what she was contemplating. Was this really happening?

'Are you okay?' Milo asked, his brow furrowing.

'Yes, sorry, my mind just drifted.' She forced the smile back onto her face. 'Not sure my boss would appreciate me working from my home office in the Himalayas.'

'So is this a job for life then?'

'That was the plan.'

'Was?'

She hadn't realised she'd used the past tense. 'I meant *is*. It's the right path for me.'

'Maybe the right path isn't always the best path?'

Claire thought of her dad. What had not following the right path done for him? 'The right path pays my mortgage,' she said.

Except there'd be no mortgage if her and Ben split up. There was no way she could afford it on her own with her wage. She lifted her fingers to her mouth, nibbling at a loose nail. Milo's eyes flickered over her wedding ring. She pulled her sleeve down to cover it.

'Right, we're seconds away from Narnia,' Milo said, diverting his eyes. 'Sure you're ready? It's just around this bend.' He gestured for her to walk ahead of him so she quickened her step. As she turned the corner, the soft scent of honey drifted towards her and then a truly beautiful sight came into sight: both banks either side of her were completely shrouded in violet flowers, bruised so deep purple it was like she was standing in twilight. Claire stopped, mouth dropping open as Milo appeared next to her.

'You probably saw the flowers on the way here,' he said, reaching for one of them and handing it to her. 'Bell heather. They thrive in full sun,' he said, peering up at the sky. The clouds were gliding away now, rays of yellow sun streaming into the valley. 'They smell lovely too, Holly has them in her room for their scent.'

She lifted the bloom to her nose and breathed in its sweet tones. She then tucked it into her bag for her own room and glided her hands over the others as she closed her eyes. All thoughts of Ben and their future – *her* future – disappeared.

There was just *now*.

She opened her eyes to find Milo watching her, the look on his face making her very aware of the space between them, the thump of her heart, the background sound of violent waves.

She broke his gaze and looked down at her bag, taking her camera out. 'It's beautiful. Really beautiful,' she murmured. 'I must take some photos.' She put her camera to her face, pleased it was covering her flushed cheeks. 'Is that the sound of waves I can hear?' she asked after a while.

'Yep, you can get to Hope's Mouth just through there,' he said, pointing to a small archway in the distance.

'Great, I wanted to take more photos of the sea yesterday but a whole bunch of tourists turned up. Shall we go?'

He tensed. 'You go. I'll stay here with the dogs.'

'I don't have to.'

'No, please do.'

So she did, walking through the archway in the cliff, surprised to find herself at the barrier where she'd been the day before, the waves crashing against the rocks below. It was even more beautiful than it had been yesterday, hints of hazy blue in the sky now, the sun sparkling off the waves. She took out her camera and started taking photos, doing what she always did when a situation unnerved her: slipping into travel journalist mode, hiding behind a camera and notepad.

After a while, she heard footsteps and turned to see Milo approaching with Archie and Blue. He looked nervous, eyes flickering towards the sea then back to Claire.

'Decided to come up?' she asked him.

'Your dog was whining for you.'

She laughed, leaning down to cuddle Archie. When she looked up, Milo's gaze was focused on the sea, face very sombre, eyes glassy. She looked at him in surprise.

'You okay?' she asked.

'Just the wind.'

Was it really just the wind?

They were quiet for a few moments then he nodded towards the cliff edge. 'Shall we walk to the edge? You'll get much better photos from there.'

'Past the barriers?'

He nodded.

'Is it safe?'

He smiled. 'Are we going to have another river episode? Aren't you the girl who travelled off the beaten track when she was a kid?'

'That was then.'

'And now?'

She avoided his gaze. 'I have tour guides telling me where to go.'

'Then consider me your tour guide. You won't fall, I'll make sure you won't.'

He put his hand out to Claire. She glanced at it, heart thumping, then reached her hand out too, raising her gaze to meet his.

Then she heard a cry for help.

'Did you hear that?' she asked, letting her hand drop back to her side.

Milo nodded and shielded his eyes with his hand as he looked in the direction of the sound. Then he whispered a 'Jesus' under his breath. Claire followed his gaze to see two blue ropes tied to a solitary tree nearby, one of them broken off.

'Looks like someone's tried to abseil down the cliff face,' Milo said. 'Both those ropes should be securely tied around the tree.'

He ran beyond the barriers and stared over the right side of the cliff edge. Claire hesitated a moment then followed him, looking down to see the cliff plunge dramatically into the violent sea below, jagged rocks jutting up from the waves like teeth. And there, pressed against the cliff face about a metre above the rocks, was a man, his face twisted up to stare at them.

'The rope got stuck,' he shouted up to them, his voice

carried along by the wind. 'I can't get up. I'm getting bloody married on Friday, Sarah will kill me if I don't get killed by the rocks first!'

'Don't tell me he's the one getting married at the inn,' Claire said.

Milo shook his head. 'What an idiot. He has no idea of the danger he's in. It's not the kind of cliff you want to climb at the best of times, but a few days before your wedding?'

She reached into her bag. 'I'll call—'

'No reception, remember?'

'Then we should go back, call from the inn.'

'The tide's rising, see?' Milo said, pointing to the waves that were lapping at the man's feet now. It was coming fast. 'I'll need your help. Tie Archie's lead around the tree.'

Claire did just that as Milo shrugged his coat and jumper off to reveal a black T-shirt, tanned arms. He slipped his coat carefully under the rope.

'Have you got something on under your jumper?' he asked, his eyes running over her.

She felt her cheeks flush. 'Yes, a T-shirt.'

'Take your jumper off then.'

'Why?'

'To protect your hands. We're going to have to pull him up via the remainder of the rope.'

'Isn't that risky? What if it breaks too?'

'It shouldn't, not with my coat protecting it from the friction caused by the cliff edge. The risk of us doing nothing is greater.'

'Right,' she said, pulling her jumper off to reveal a Bob Dylan 1984 tour T-shirt. She looked down at Milo's hands. 'What about you?'

'I'll be fine.'

'Don't be silly. We can use some of my jumper too.'

'Are you sure? I'll have to tear it.'

She tried not to think about the fact Ben had bought it for her. 'It's fine, really.'

Milo helped her tear off an arm of the jumper and wrapped it around his large hands before running back to the cliff edge.

'What's your name?' he shouted down to the man.

'Matt,' the man shouted back up.

'Right, Matt. You've got yourself into a dangerous situation here. We're going to pull you up via the intact rope. Can you give me some slack please so I can take some of the rope?'

'What if it breaks?' Matt asked, his voice shrill now.

'It won't. My coat's beneath it so it won't get damaged.'

'Hundred per cent sure?'

'No. But I'm a hundred per cent sure the tide's rising enough to drown you soon if we don't try to get you up.'

Matt didn't answer but Claire could imagine his face. She heard movement and saw the rope had slackened. Milo crouched down, taking hold of it.

'Right,' he shouted down to Matt. 'You need to help us by pulling yourself up via any bits of rock you find on the way. But be careful not to swing. I'll shout when we're ready to start.'

He ran back over to Claire, feeding the rope through with his hands.

'What if he's too heavy and one of us stumbles?' she asked him. 'We could go over the edge.'

'I won't let that happen.'

'But—'

'I need you to trust me.'

She wanted to say *How can I, I barely know you!* But instead, one word popped out of her mouth. 'Okay.'

'Good.' He lifted her hands up, tangling what remained of her jumper around them until they were protected by three inches of wool. 'I need you to take hold of the rope there a few metres away and pull when I say – like a tug of war, right?'

He headed to the cliff edge, stopping about half a metre away from it. He then crouched down, taking hold of the rope as he dug his heels into the ground. Claire did the same, heart thumping.

'Ready?' Milo shouted down to Matt.

'Yes,' he shouted back up, voice hoarse with fear.

Milo started pulling, the muscles in the backs of his shoulders flexing as he slowly heaved backwards, feeding the rope back behind him as he pulled the slack. There was the sound of rocks falling in the distance, scrabbling feet, a cry of alarm.

The rope jolted and Claire let out a scream. Milo turned to look at her then started slipping forwards, feet trying to find traction in the ground as he drew closer and closer to the edge. Claire tried to pull him back with the rope but didn't have the strength.

So she made a decision, doing something the old Claire would've done: she took a risk.

She let go of the rope and ran to Milo, crouching down and wrapping her hands around the rope closest to him, her knees against his back.

'What the hell are you doing?' he asked her.

'You need me here. Come on.'

He shot her an exasperated look then turned back to the front, pulling at the rope. Claire did the same, putting all her strength into it and dragging herself back. They staggered backwards and backwards until, finally, a hand slapped onto the cliff's surface and Matt dragged himself up before collapsing onto the ground.

'You okay?' Milo asked him, flinching as he let go of the rope. Claire's jumper was worn completely away and the skin on his palm red raw.

Matt nodded, unable to speak as he tried to catch his breath.

Milo turned to Claire. 'You did great.'

She felt a strange sense of pride. She'd never done something like that, helped save a man's life. It felt good. 'Is this what happens when you take the better path?' she asked Milo.

Milo put his hand on her shoulder. 'Looks like it. Feels good, doesn't it?'

Claire wasn't sure what to make of the thunder of her heartbeat as he touched her.

Then she thought of Ben and moved away from him.

Matt stumbled over to them. 'Thank you so much, both of you.'

'You're very lucky, mate,' Milo said. 'Just a few more moments and you'd have been fish food.'

A few minutes later, as they walked back to the inn, Matt stopped them, pointing into the distance. From there, they could just about make out the cliff face that had been hidden from them before – the part Matt had been climbing away from. On its side was a huge heart messily painted on the stone with pink paint.

'I did it for my fiancée,' he said.

It was the same heart that was shown over and over again on the news in the following weeks.

Chapter Three

Exmoor, UK

When Claire and Milo got back to the inn, they were separated among the back-patting and gasps of horror as Matt regaled a hero's story that made the two of them sound like Greek gods. He even insisted they join the family for dinner that night, and extended an invite to his wedding reception.

As Claire was talking to Matt, Henry came out, face incredulous as he took in all the attention his brother-in-law was getting.

'Ready for our lunch, Claire?' he asked her, frowning slightly. He'd clearly heard she'd gone on a walk with Milo and disapproved.

'I have a bit of a headache actually,' she said. Last thing she needed was to sit across from his judgmental eyes. 'I might just go back to my room. Sorry to be a bore. I got some great pictures though, and I still have two days here. Maybe we can meet for a drink or dinner later?'

He looked over at Milo then turned back to Claire, smiling. 'Yes, of course. You can try our taster menu. Just come down when you feel like it.'

Claire headed back to her room, sinking into a deep sleep with Archie curled at her side. When she woke, the first thing she smelled was the bell heather she'd placed on the table. It instantly brought back memories of Milo's big calloused hands clutched tight around the rope; the smell of him so close, bonfires and musk; the way his eyes had lifted to meet hers.

No, it wasn't right. She needed to drive those thoughts away.

She pulled out her dad's old postcards and flicked through them. Kangaroos and Niagara Falls; golden temples and bone-dry deserts, scenes from all the countries they'd visited as a family: Australia, New Zealand, Canada, Namibia, Iceland, Paraguay, India . . . the list went on, all jigsaw pieces of her childhood that she carried with her wherever she went. Her dad had scrawled on the back of some, messages like 'Littlest Hobo, do you remember the sun rising over that rock? Daddy Bo, xx', every word still scorched into her memory.

But still, she saw Milo.

So she strode across the room and grabbed her phone, flicking through loving texts she'd received in the past from Ben, trying to find an anchor in him too. When that didn't work either, she reached for her book. It took a while but, eventually, her shoulders relaxed, Milo's face disappearing as she sunk into pre-war Japan.

When darkness fell, she put her book aside and walked to the window, peering out across the valley. The skies were clear, stars scattered all over, their bright white orbs lighting the night sky and turning it violet. Claire thought of Ben. What would he be doing right now? Probably watching the news or looking over some documents from work. Would he be wondering what she was doing? When she'd told him there'd be no reception, he'd said that was a good thing; that it would give them proper space from one another. But she yearned to pick up the phone now, hear his voice, have him tell her he'd made a mistake. Her stomach plummeted as she remembered their conversation again and the look on his face that spoke volumes. He was exhausted with the charade, she could see it in the bags under his eyes, the stubble on his cheeks.

She put her fist to her mouth, stifling a sob. Once again, she felt as though she were falling, her body twisting and turning in the westerly wind as she tumbled down that valley into nothingness. What was there for her without Ben and the security he offered?

Thirty minutes later, she was standing in the shadows of one of the cream-painted alcoves in the restaurant, pulling Archie back as he strained to find the source of the delicious smells coming from the kitchen. There was a large table at the back and she could already see Matt sitting at it with the pretty blonde girl she'd seen the day before, presumably his fiancée Sarah.

She felt a hand on her shoulder and turned to see Henry looking down at her, face red and sweaty. 'So sorry, Claire,' he said. 'Two of our staff have called in sick. Hangovers no doubt. They certainly won't be invited back. Means it's all hands on deck. Can we do lunch tomorrow? I've set a table aside for you and have instructed our chef to prepare our famous taster meal. And a sausage for Archie, of course,' he added, leaning down to ruffle Archie's head then snapping his hand back as Archie let out a low growl.

She followed his gaze towards the solitary table overlooking the valley. She was used to dining alone during media trips. But tonight it scared her, made her see more nights like this mapped out before her without Ben by her side.

'Of course,' she said. 'Thank you, Henry, sounds lovely.'

When he rushed off, Claire took a deep breath and looked down at Archie. 'Looks like you're my dinner date tonight, boy.' She headed towards the table then noticed Matt look up.

'Don't tell me you're dining alone?' he called out to her. 'I said you can join us tonight.'

'Oh, I don't want to impose.'

'I insist,' he said.

She looked at her lonely table then took in the large table buzzing with chatter and laughter. She yearned to sit with them all, have her head filled with other people's lives and stories so she didn't have to think of her own. Milo wasn't there, maybe that meant he had to help out in the inn – Henry had said it was all hands on deck?

'Okay, if you're sure?' she asked.

'Of course.' When she walked over to the table, Matt pulled out a seat next to a blond man. 'This is Jay Hemingford, my best man,' he said as Claire sat down. Archie darted under the table as Sarah threw a piece of bread for him. 'And this is my animal-loving fiancée, Sarah,' he said, gesturing towards her.

'Very grateful fiancée too,' Sarah said. 'Thank you for saving my foolish husband-to-be.'

'Yes, I've heard all about your heroics, Clara,' the man sitting next to her said. He was wearing a dark Victorian-style suit, an expensive gold watch around his freckled wrist.

'Jesus, Jay, her name's Claire!' Matt said, shaking his head.

Jay pulled a face. 'Christ, sorry, I'm terrible with names. Claire, Clara, whatever, you're still a hero.'

'Ha, I didn't have a clue what I was doing,' Claire replied as Archie tried to jump up at Jay's trousers. She pulled him away. 'Sorry, he has a thing for ruining expensive-looking trousers.'

'And expensive-looking dresses,' Jay said as Archie turned his attention to scrabbling at Claire's long print dress. 'Is that an Alexander McQueen?'

'Alexander who?'

Jay laughed. 'Maybe not then.'

'I got it from Singapore.'

'Very nice. So, Matt tells me you're a journalist?'

'Yes, I write for a travel magazine.'

'Splendid. Which one?' he asked.

'*Travel Companion*? You won't have heard of it. It's a trade magazine.'

'Ah, no.' He took a sip of the champagne he'd been nursing. 'I'm a journalist myself.'

'Who do you write for?'

'*Daily Telegraph*. I cover the European markets.'

'That's impressive.'

'Honestly, my dear, if you caught sight of my pay cheque, you wouldn't think it impressive at all.'

Claire looked at his expensive suit. She knew exactly how much national newspapers paid. If the *Daily Telegraph* hadn't paid for that, she wondered who had. A gust of cold air drifted in as someone opened the entrance door. She peered towards it – still no sign of Milo. She felt a mixture of relief and disappointment.

But once the starters arrived, he appeared, no wax jacket and wellies this time. Instead, he was wearing a dark grey shirt, sleeves rolled up to reveal his tanned forearms, his hand wrapped in a bandage. His hair looked newly washed, and he'd shaved.

He paused at the entranceway to the restaurant and fixed his eyes on Claire, making her stumble over her sentence.

'Finally,' Matt said, jumping up and placing his hand to his heart. 'My hero.'

Everyone laughed and Milo's gaze broke from Claire's.

'He even looks like one, doesn't he? Tall, dark, handsome,' Matt said, striding over to him and shaking his hand. Milo flinched. 'Jesus, of course, sorry. How's your hand?'

'I'll survive. How's the ego?'

Everyone laughed as Sarah clapped her hands.

'Bruised,' Matt said, leading Milo to the chair across from Claire's.

Claire didn't remember much about the start of that dinner, just the way Milo looked, his lips red from the wine, his dark fringe in his eyes. And how, each time he caught her eye, she felt her skin turn warm. So she avoided his gaze by watching the happy couple instead. Had things been like that with Ben before they married? She thought so, despite how stressful it had been balancing her job with organising caterers and florists and God knows what else. Was it natural, this gradual abrasion of feeling? Or was the infertility just the death knell for a marriage that had been weak from the start? She took a quick sip of wine. Why was she being so bloody negative? She should be fighting for her marriage, riding the good waves and the bad, as her sister Sofia would say.

Milo caught her eye again and she felt the heat rise in her cheeks. Did fighting for her marriage mean blushing every time a handsome farmer looked her way?

Sarah shot Claire a knowing smile as she looked between them. Claire wanted to shake her by the shoulders, tell her she'd got the wrong end of the stick, it was just the emotion of the day, the drama.

When pudding arrived, so did Milo's brother Dale. He pulled a chair up next to Claire. 'I hear my brother nearly shot you yesterday,' he said, pouring himself a glass of red wine, some of it sloshing over the sides. His eyes were like

Milo's: penetrating, intense. But there was something else there too, a detachment that unsettled her.

'Not quite,' Claire said. 'It's all a bit embarrassing now really.'

'It's just the way it is. If an animal needs to die – for food, to put it out of pain, to save a younger animal – you kill it. That's what our father used to say.'

Claire laughed nervously. 'You make it sound like Milo was trying to put me down.'

Dale didn't return her laugh, just stared at her with that dispassionate look in his eyes. Then he turned his gaze to his brother. 'Milo's too soft, you know. When he was sixteen, one of our bitches had a mongrel litter and Dad was about to shoot them all and who turns up but my little brother, the sap. Just goes and stands right in between that gun and those pups, kicks up a stink, saves their lives. Dad told me he beat him black and blue after,' he added, laughing. Claire moved away slightly, feeling uncomfortable. She could see what Henry meant now about Dale. Maybe seeing all he'd seen in the Falklands had made him like this? 'Five of the pups died anyway,' he continued in a bored voice. 'Only Blue survived. Milo reckons it was worth a broken rib to save that mongrel.'

'He does adore Blue,' Claire said, not sure what else to say. Dale gave her a cold smile in response, his gaze holding hers for a beat more than was comfortable.

Claire looked over at Milo. He was talking to Sarah, his face animated as he tried to explain something to her. How different your first impressions can be of someone. When he'd killed that stag, she'd thought him heartless, violent. But it appeared he was very far from that, just a man who cared deeply for his family and the animals in his care. His brother, it appeared, was a different story.

Dale followed Claire's gaze. 'He'll be gone soon enough. He's got the travel bug like our grandfather, always going on about running a farm in another country.' He laughed. 'Wonder if he'll end up putting a gun in his mouth and blowing his brains out like our grandfather did?'

Chills ran down Claire's spine. How could he say things like that so flippantly?

He slugged back more wine, some of it spilling from the side of his mouth, leaving a trail of red down his chin. 'He's definitely got the bug all right. Just needs to save enough money. Then I'll be left alone to deal with all the crap.'

Claire looked towards Jay as a way to escape but he was deep in conversation with the man to his right. She could make her excuses and go to the toilet but what about Archie?

'Ah, the blushing bride,' Dale said, leaning back in his chair and watching Sarah over the rim of his glass. 'They're never as innocent as they look, you know, especially the pretty ones. I told Henry to stop doing the weddings, makes us look like a bloody chain hotel. Makes me sick, every one of them.' He slugged back another mouthful of wine, his face stony, shoulders tense. Milo peered over at his brother, his face clouding over as though he could sense the tension.

'All right there?' he asked, looking between Dale and Claire.

'Just saying how tedious it is,' Dale said in a loud voice, 'seeing one wedding after another here. They all blur into one after a while, one boring sentimental mess.'

The table went quiet and Sarah's blue eyes widened. Milo's face flushed. 'Dale, why don't we—'

Their sister Jen appeared then, exchanging a look with Milo. 'Dale, can you help me get a keg from the cellar? I can't find Henry anywhere.'

'Maybe that's because he's hiding in the waitress's knickers,'

Dale said under his breath, his lip curling. Jay raised an eyebrow and Claire looked at Jen to see if she'd heard but her expression remained unchanged. Dale stood up, nearly knocking over Claire's drink. Milo leaned forward and grabbed the glass before its contents spilled all over Claire's dress, mouthing a 'sorry' to her as Dale stumbled off after his sister.

'What a romantic soul your brother is,' Jay said to Milo.

Milo swallowed, clearly uncomfortable. 'He gets a bit cynical after having a few.' He turned to Sarah. 'Sorry, he didn't mean any of it, not really. He's had a lot of stress recently.'

'Oh, it's fine,' she said, smiling. 'I completely understand, must be very difficult for farmers.'

'What about you, Milo?' Matt asked. 'Are you cynical about love? Or have you managed to find yourself a farmer's wife in between all that muck-clearing and cow-milking?'

Milo dug his spoon into his apple crumble, his expression unreadable. 'No time to look for anyone really.'

'Surely they come searching for you?' Sarah said.

Milo's cheeks flushed.

'You better get a move on,' Matt said. 'Every man needs a good woman to look after him.'

Sarah flicked her napkin at her fiancé. 'Since when did you turn into a chauvinist pig?'

'Damn, I was hoping to keep that bit hidden from you until *after* the wedding.' He glanced back at Milo. 'So?'

'You don't need a wedding ring on your finger to look after someone. A couple can be just as secure without a piece of paper binding them.'

Claire stared at her wedding ring. She'd actually been the one who wanted to get married quickly after Ben proposed. He'd wanted to wait, save more money. But she'd *needed* that piece of paper, that ring on her finger, to prove she wasn't like her dad and to start on her road to security.

Jay turned to Claire. 'Do you agree?'

She glanced up, noticing everyone's eyes on her. 'I don't know what I think really. But my dad's old friend gave his wife a ring made from goat's hair,' she added, hoping to lighten the conversation. 'That sounds fun.'

Everyone around the table laughed but Jay frowned. 'How strange, my friend's father was a bit of a hippy and did the same with his wife too. His name was Josh Pyatt, he worked for the *Independent*. Maybe it's the same guy?'

'I don't recognise the name. But my dad wrote a travel column for the *Indie* so chances are it's the same man.'

'Wait a minute,' Jay said, his blue eyes bright with excitement. 'Don't tell me you're Bo Shreve's daughter?'

Claire looked down at her food, wondering why she'd been stupid enough to bring up her dad. Now she was going to have to keep her emotions in check. Milo's brow puckered as he watched her.

'Yep,' she said.

'He was a wonderful writer, my mother adored his stuff,' Jay said. 'I was sorry to hear he passed away.'

Claire blinked, trying to stop the tears. 'He was a good writer,' was all she could manage. 'It's getting pretty late, thank you so much for inviting me to join you all,' she said, suddenly feeling exhausted with it all. She peered at Archie who was curled up at her feet under the table. 'I better get this little one to bed.' Jay raised an eyebrow and she laughed. 'Yes, he's my little fur baby, what of it?'

He looked at Archie in mock shock. 'That is *one* hairy baby.' His face grew serious. 'It's very dark out there, I can join you, if you wish?'

Milo stood up too. 'I'll go out with you, Claire. I ought

to head back anyway. Yet another early start tomorrow thanks to those pre-menstrual cows.'

She smiled. 'You won't want to keep them waiting.'

When they stepped outside a few minutes later, Claire breathed in the tart air, hoping it would clear her head of the wine and the memories of her father.

'I'm sorry to hear about your dad,' Milo said. 'Did he pass away recently?'

'Nearly thirteen years ago. Cancer.' She saw her dad's thin face again as he stared up at her all those years ago. She peered back towards the hotel. 'Will your brother be okay?'

Milo frowned. 'Yeah, he gets like that when he's had a few drinks. Add that to how tough things are at the farm nowadays, it's not a good mix. Sorry you had to see him like that.' He peered towards the path. 'So, what are your plans for tomorrow?' he asked, quickly changing the subject.

'Just lunch with Henry. Otherwise, I was thinking about driving somewhere, maybe further west towards Cornwall. I'd like to write about some of the places people can visit while here. Saying that, my car struggled enough on the journey down.'

Milo followed Claire's gaze towards her aqua Fiat Uno. 'It's quite a specimen.'

'I swapped Bob Dylan tickets for that old thing years ago with a friend.'

'You missed a Bob Dylan gig for *that*?'

She shrugged. 'She brought me back a T-shirt.'

'Well, if it's just your car stopping you doing a tour, I can drive you tomorrow morning if you want? Can't guarantee you'll get back in time for lunch. But then maybe that's not such a bad thing,' he added, raising a dark eyebrow. 'Lunch with Henry isn't exactly thrilling; he'll just bark on about why he had the restaurant walls painted cream instead of teal.'

'How do *you* know I don't find the interior decoration of West Country hotels fascinating?'

Milo smiled, a swift breeze whipping its way around him and picking up strands of his dark fringe. Claire wanted to reach out, sweep it away from his eyes. She felt guilt burn in her stomach. What was wrong with her?

She turned her attention to Archie so Milo didn't notice her blush. Maybe it wasn't such a good idea for them to spend the morning together? 'I'll manage on my own, I'm sure you've got better things to do with your time.'

'Like terrify tourists with my stag-shooting abilities?'

'I bloody hope not!'

'Never again,' he said, his face very serious. 'Look, I'm due some time off. Dale keeps hassling me to take a break. What do you think?'

Claire held her breath. This press trip wasn't meant to be about *this*. A quickening of the heart, the inability to breathe as some virtual stranger looked her square in the eye. She needed space to figure out a future without Ben – 'see the wood for the trees' as he had said. But she felt like she'd stepped even further into the forest, the wood and the trees blurring even more than ever.

But as the seconds ticked by without her answering, and a frown puckered Milo's forehead, she found herself unable to say no.

So she said yes instead.

Claire was nervous as she approached Milo's Land Rover the next morning. She'd promised herself the night before she wouldn't read anything into every flutter of her heart, every catch in her breath. It was like looking at a beautiful painting when she was around him. Aesthetics and desire, that's all, she reasoned. She needed the company, a distraction from dwelling on her problems with Ben all the time. But that didn't detract from the fact she was anxious.

As she reached the car, she paused. Milo was reading her magazine, his eyes heavy with emotion. She recognised the article, an obituary for the magazine's financial director Victoria who'd passed away a few months ago. She'd always got on with the gentle, kind woman, who was a contrast to the magazine's obnoxious founder. In the article, she'd drawn on a conversation she'd once had with her about how important it was to follow your own path, something Victoria had done by moving from the tiny Italian village where she'd been born to live in the UK, despite her family's protests. Claire had used a quote by Bob Black, the anarchist her dad loved reading: *The reinvention of daily life means marching off the edge of our maps.*

Milo noticed her watching him and smiled, placing the magazine in the back seat and jumping out of the car so he could hold the passenger door open for her. She paused a moment, taking the chance to still her heart as she took in the misty valleys ahead of her, feel the cold on her cheeks. Then she clambered in, placing Archie on her lap as Blue regarded them from the back seat.

'You were reading my magazine?' Claire asked, gesturing to it.

Milo nodded. 'Holly got a copy off Henry after hearing you'd be staying here so I nabbed it off her. You're a great writer, Claire.'

Claire looked down, feeling her cheeks flush. 'Thanks. It took a lot to write that article, I really liked Victoria.'

He was quiet for a few moments. 'It made sense what you said about how losing someone burns a hole in you. But how the love of the people left behind can make new skin grow back.'

'You talk like you've lost someone too.'

'Haven't we all?' He started the engine, the smell of petrol filling the car. 'We better get a move on if we want you back for Henry's thrilling lunch.'

He winked at her and she laughed. 'Your engine sounds a bit dodgy, we may well break down on the way back.'

'Good thinking,' Milo said.

Claire looked around at the car's immaculate interior as it rumbled down the road. 'Nice and tidy. You're a farmer. Shouldn't there be some dead pheasants in the back or something?'

Milo raised an eyebrow. 'Or an African drum like the one in your back seat? Holly noticed it when we walked past your car yesterday. *And* all the books too.'

Claire thought of the back seat of her car, taken over by items she'd picked up from her travels and books taking her back to the distant lands she'd visited as a child: travel memoirs and novels crammed with dusty roads and stunning vistas.

She sighed. 'It's a mess, isn't it? I haven't properly tidied my car since I got it years ago. I like to hoard stuff. My dad used to call me his Littlest Hobo.'

'Like the dog?'

She laughed. 'No! He said I was like a homeless person, collecting all these items during my travels. He even got me a shopping trolley once in Spain which I hauled around a campsite with all my stuff. Plus his name was Bo and everyone said I was a miniature version of him, so it kind of stuck.'

Claire wondered if those people would say the same now. She had a job writing about travel, there was that at least. And a failed marriage on the horizon, just like him too. Claire swallowed, turning to look out of the window at the forest-fringed road to distract herself.

'No wonder your car's playing up if you're treating it like a trolley,' Milo said. 'There are such things as glove compartments, you know. Speaking of which,' he said, leaning across her and opening the glove compartment as she tried to control her heartbeat, 'I can't promise any Bob Dylan but I have some U2 tapes somewhere.'

He pulled a tape out and stuck it on as Claire forced herself to relax. Over the next three hours, Milo drove them around beautiful fishing villages where he seemed to know half the people, waving at them out of his window. When they stopped at a couple of places, Milo led Claire on a wild goose chase to find a 'little tea room with outdoor seating I'm sure's just around the corner' or an 'old open-air book market I swear is just here'. He only seemed comfortable outdoors, hovering outside with Archie and Blue when Claire wanted to pop into a shop or museum.

They drove even further along the coast, stopping to take a twisting coastal walk up a hill thick with grass, sheep grazing in the distance, the growl of waves nearby, the mouth-watering smell of fish and chips from one of the restaurants dancing up the hill towards them. They talked a lot, Milo telling Claire about his childhood on the farm, she telling him about her job and the people she'd met along the way – about everyone but Ben, the person who pulsed between them wherever they went. When lunchtime drew closer and closer, Claire found herself not wanting to leave. As though sensing her thoughts, Milo looked down towards the restaurant where the delicious smells were coming from. 'Hungry?' he asked with a smile.

She thought of Henry who'd be looking at his watch while tapping his fingers on the table. Maybe he'd even called her from the restaurant phone? She didn't dare check. She didn't *want* to check. She wanted to stay here, her troubles a distant memory, just the sea, Exmoor's sloping hills, two dogs and Milo for company.

She matched his smile. 'Very.'

Half an hour later, they were eating fish and chips in a café overlooking sandy, windy beaches.

'You eat very slowly,' Milo said, watching as Claire chewed on a chip.

'It's become a habit, I guess. My dad once said travel writing's about all five senses, so I savour every mouthful to write about it later.' She laughed as she watched Milo wolf down a chunk of cod. 'Maybe you should try the savouring thing too?'

'Have you *seen* the way my brother devours food and drink? I've had to learn to eat quick around him so he doesn't get a chance to steal my stuff.' He took a quick sip of cider. 'So your dad taught you everything you know about writing, right?'

'Yep. Jay was right: he was a really special writer. I have this one article of his I like to read over and over. Funnily enough, it's about a country that's really close to us, Belgium. He visited Ypres with my mum and sister while Mum was pregnant with me and he wrote about how the air was so heavy with loss and torment, he was scared it would infect me as I grew in Mum's belly. But then he saw a solitary poppy, and it reminded him that birth and death are part and parcel of life, with blood spilled both times. It is what it is.'

'I'd like to read that.'

'I'll dig it out and send it to you. It won an award, the Flora Matthews Foundation Prize for Travel Writing. It's pretty prestigious.'

'Sounds it.'

Claire looked down at what remained of her food. 'That's the night Dad left us actually.'

Milo frowned. 'Left you?'

'We woke to find him gone the morning after the ceremony, just a note scribbled on the back of the awards menu I'd kept. *Time to march off the map, my darlings. All my love, Daddy Bo.*'

'I'm sorry. How old were you?'

'Sixteen. Looking back, it shouldn't have been a huge surprise. He'd started taking all that marching off the edge of the map stuff too literally, banging on about needing to leave behind societal pressures – which, in the end, meant his family too.'

'Where did he go?'

Claire shrugged. 'No idea. We didn't hear anything from him over the next few months, not even on my seventeenth birthday or at Christmas. It felt like he'd thrown us away like a piece of rubbish. Mum said we needed to accept we might never see him again. My sister Sofia grew bitter. She'd never been as close to Dad as I was, but that really changed things for her. She pretended like he was dead.' Claire looked down at the tiny globe hanging from her bag. 'But I refused to give up on him. Six months after he left, I used the money he'd left in my savings to go find him.'

'Brave,' Milo said softly.

'I *was* brave back then.'

'Not now?'

Claire shrugged again.

'So did you find him?' Milo asked.

'Not then. I carried on travelling for a year or so, making money from articles. My mum met a new guy, moved to Hong Kong with him – she's still there now. Sofia started training to be a solicitor, the very job my dad despised. It was only me who followed his path, travelling, writing. Then my uncle passed away. Mum couldn't track Dad down to tell him, so I did some investigating and . . .'

She paused, hearing the smash of rain against glass from the day she'd found him. She quickly swallowed down more cider.

'You okay?' Milo asked.

She nodded. 'I – I found him dying in a flat in New York. Turned out he'd been living there the past year, dying of liver cancer, refusing to bend to societal pressures and get medical help. He died in my arms a few days later.'

'Jesus, I'm so sorry, Claire.'

They were quiet for a few moments as Claire remembered how it had felt to see her dad lying there. She remembered thinking, *Is this what marching off the map does – drives people apart, leaves people dying in pain all alone?*

She'd cared for him over the next few days, reading his favourite books to him, sharing memories from her childhood. The third night, he'd gestured towards one of the drawers in his room. Inside, Claire found a sky lantern, just like the ones they used to send skywards each New Year's Eve, all the troubles and negativity of the year before written down on notes attached to them and sent away forever. He scribbled a note with trembling hands: his name, *Bo.* She hadn't understood at first. But when he drew his last breath and her world felt like it was ending, it dawned on her: he wanted her to let him and all the negativity associated with him go.

So that very night, she did what they'd done every New Year before: she sent the lantern skywards, her father's name attached to it.

'I went back to the UK after,' she said, sighing. 'Talked myself into a university course—'

'Talked yourself?'

'I'd been home-schooled, remember? Dad said education was just society's way of brainwashing children so I had no

79

qualifications. So I wrote this long rambling letter to a bunch of admissions directors at various universities and one recognised something, got me in for an interview and that was that. I worked my arse off, came away with a first-class degree in English, got the job at the magazine, got a mortgage, life insurance, the works, everything Dad once despised.' She forced a smile onto her face as she took a sip of cider. 'And now here I am.'

'Why did you do everything your dad despised?'

'Seeing him like that scared me. I realised if I followed the path he had, I might end up dying alone too. I chose a safer path.'

'Are you happy with that decision?'

She swallowed hard. 'I don't know. I can feel it pulling at me sometimes, the desire to just let everything go and fly with the wind.' She paused. She'd not admitted that to herself properly, like the nights she'd feel the urge to just throw open the window and breathe in the wind, Ben protesting it was too cold as she imagined climbing out and leaving.

'What about your husband?' Milo said, his eyes flicking to her wedding ring. 'Is he a writer too?'

She froze. She'd purposefully not mentioned Ben to Milo, aware of her growing attraction to Milo and what a betrayal it might be to her husband to utter his name in front of him. 'No, he's an engineer.' Her voice cracked and she turned away, feeling tears start to well up.

'Are you okay?' Milo asked softly.

'I'm fine.' She smiled to show she was okay but it just made her feel even more upset, her smile turning into a grimace.

'Claire, what's wrong?' Milo asked, leaning towards her and trying to look in her eyes. He hesitated a moment then sighed. 'I saw you crying before I shot the stag.'

She looked up at him. 'You saw that?'

He nodded, his brown eyes full of emotion. 'I know we hardly know each other but sometimes it helps to talk to people who aren't so close to the situation.'

'It's more complicated than you know.'

'Try me.'

She looked into his eyes. They were open, curious, full of feeling. Maybe he was right?

'My husband and I are having problems,' she said. 'He suggested we take a break.'

Milo took in a deep breath. 'I'm sorry to hear that.'

'I don't want you to think my marriage is a shambles,' she said quickly. 'It was good at first, really good. We met at uni, and though we're completely different – I was studying English, my husband was studying engineering – we clicked right away.'

Claire thought about the first time she'd met Ben. It was just a few months into her first year at university and she was starting to regret her choice. It all felt too restricting and regimental, lectures at particular times, meetings with professors, special clubs and different cliques. One night, when it all got too much, she got horribly drunk on snowball cocktails at a party and had to make her way back to her room in the dark. That's when Ben turned up, driving alongside her in his Renault Clio and offering her a lift. Anyone else and she might have steered well clear. But there was something about Ben: an honesty in his soft green eyes, the neat turn of the collar on his shirt, the polite way he talked in his Home Counties voice. When he helped her into his car, she felt instantly safe and on the car journey to her room she unburdened herself, telling him how stifled she felt at university, even confessing she wanted to quit, something she hadn't even admitted to herself. The next day, he talked her out of packing in her course over lunch then asked her out for dinner. And that was that.

'What went wrong?' Milo asked, pulling Claire from the memory.

'We started struggling to conceive.'

She paused, checking Milo's expression. But he looked the same, willing her to continue with his eyes.

'My fault,' she said. 'My insides are a bit of a mess, blocked tubes and dodgy eggs.'

She didn't tell Milo her blocked tubes were caused by swelling from the chlamydia she'd caught from a man she'd met in Paris while searching for her father. She'd been devastated when her GP had told her: yet more proof that travelling off the edge of the map was the wrong thing to do. She'd had an op to unblock her tubes but, when she still hadn't fallen pregnant a year later, more tests revealed she had low quality eggs. IVF was her only chance of ever becoming pregnant.

'We tried IVF,' she said to Milo. 'Three rounds, each one a dud. The last one was two months ago.'

'Claire, I'm so sorry,' he said. 'I've heard IVF can be very difficult.'

'The physical stuff I could deal with,' she said, fiddling with her glass. 'Sure, having your flesh pierced with needles each night isn't exactly a ball. Being poked around by doctors, I guess you grow used to that over the years when you've been through what we've been through. And the effects of the hormones, the headaches and the nausea and the crazy outbursts . . . it was bloody hard, don't get me wrong. But the worst part was how it affected me emotionally.'

She could hear the tremor in her voice but ignored it. She needed to get this off her chest. She'd turned down the counselling that had been offered to her, thinking she could cope. And she'd always put on a brave face with family and friends. As for her and Ben, they couldn't talk about it, not properly, because then they'd need to admit how difficult and painful it all was. This was her chance to vent and she was grabbing it with both hands.

'The idea of never being a mother,' she said, 'never holding a baby in my arms and leaning my nose in to smell its sweet head, never feeling the tickle of its soft hair on my cheek.' She shook her head, eyes filling with tears. 'It's unbearable. I've never been one of those girls whose whole life revolves around the idea of being a mother. But I've always wanted children. And the more you fight for it, the more you want it, you know?'

Milo nodded, his face very sombre. Claire looked out towards the stretch of beach below, the hill they'd walked along earlier spreading out to its right. Two children splashed into the shallow water in their wellies, a little dog jumping up and down, yelping in excitement as their parents watched from nearby.

'Seeing other people's kids grow older,' she said, 'that's been hard too, especially kids who are the same age my child would be if I'd fallen pregnant straight away.'

'I can imagine.'

'And then there are the looks of sympathy you get when you turn up to yet another wedding, still childless. That's all bad enough but then add society's expectations to it all: if you're not a mother, a parent, you're nothing.'

Milo shook his head. 'That's rubbish. It's an important role, yes, but you don't need kids to have a fulfilling life.'

'I guess I know that. But the message you do is in everything I see.' She sighed. 'And now I know all hope's gone—'

'You do?'

She nodded sadly. 'We paid for our first three rounds

83

because the NHS waiting times were ridiculous. Now we're finally at the top of the list and the NHS won't fund us because my hormone levels are too hopeless.' Claire stabbed her fork into her fish. 'It's definitely not going to happen now.'

That consultation had been a month ago. Claire was used to these post-round consultations. With each one, more and more hope drained away, the doctors' once jovial and optimistic demeanours replaced by frowns and serious tones. She'd known something was particularly wrong with this last one because the doctor they saw could hardly look Claire in the eye. When he'd broken the news that her last blood test had shown her hormone levels had climbed, suggesting her egg quality had plummeted, it felt like the swivel chair she was sitting on was spinning her around and around, sending her into freefall. She'd held on tight enough to her emotions to ask all the perfunctory questions, even cracking the odd joke or two. But when she stepped outside, she had broken down, mumbling into Ben's shoulder, 'It's chaos, it's all chaos.' Because how could so many millions of people, some of whom didn't even want to be parents, get pregnant and she couldn't?

Ben had just stared into the distance, trying to control his emotions, jaw tight, the same expression he'd had on his face ever since.

Milo was silent so Claire looked up at him, heart thumping painfully against her chest. 'This is the bit where you're supposed to offer useless advice.'

'What, like relax and it will happen?'

'I prefer "My friend's second cousin couldn't conceive so she gave up and guess what? She got pregnant!"' That's the one my sister Sofia uses all the time.'

She smiled but Milo didn't smile back. He knew what she was trying to do, lighten the tone. Except this was a serious subject, wasn't it?

'If you say it's not going to happen, I believe you,' he said. 'It's not fair to offer false hope.'

'Thank you, I agree,' she said, sighing. 'I did think about getting a loan to pay for another private round but I just can't face it. You hear of people who have loads of rounds and it just takes over their lives. That's one of the worst things too, feeling like you're in limbo. I can't be in limbo any more, I just can't.' Claire watched a woman walk along the shoreline below them, a book in one hand, her sandals in the other, her long blonde hair like candyfloss as it whipped around her head in the wind. 'I think my life can be complete without a child, you know. I think I can carve a place for myself.'

'Definitely. I have no doubt about it.'

She looked into Milo's impassioned eyes and almost believed it herself when he said that.

'And your husband?' he asked. 'Does he feel the same way?'

'No, he thinks we should have another round. He brought it up during our last consultation, but after, I told him I just couldn't face it. Since then, we barely talk, just go through the motions. God, that sounds like such a cliché – married couple runs out of things to say to each other.'

She laughed but Milo didn't. Instead, he placed his hand over hers. She lifted her eyes to meet his, and she saw something in them that made her heart seem to thump a million beats at once. It wasn't just sympathy for what she was going through; there was more to it than that.

'You're trembling,' he said, voice hoarse. Her tummy flipped and half of her wanted to bury herself in his brown eyes and stop talking, just forget all the bad stuff. But the other half needed this, to get it all out, no interruptions from well-meaning friends about different remedies she could try to miraculously become fertile.

'I can't figure out if it's simply the stress of being infertile,' she continued, her gaze dropping from his, 'or because we just don't love each other any more and this would've happened even without the infertility. I think the problem is we married an idea of a *life*. A life with a nice house to do up, visits to DIY stores, life insurance . . . kids. But without the possibility of kids, it feels like that's all gone. And with it, the purpose of our marriage. Does that make sense?'

'Of course,' Milo said.

She put her head in her hands. 'God, I feel guilty talking about all this, he's a wonderful man. I shouldn't be unburdening myself on you either, it's not fair.'

'Unburden all you want! You shouldn't feel guilty. You've been through so much. It can happen at the best of times, but after everything you've been through . . .'

She fiddled with the globe pendant on her bag, trying to control her emotions. 'I don't just feel guilty about how confused I am right now but also because it's me who's got the fertility problems, not him. He's always been the one who's really wanted all that. If it weren't for me, he could have it by now, just like all his friends.'

Milo frowned. 'Is this what this is about? You feeling like you're holding him back? Maybe he doesn't feel that way at all.'

Claire shook her head. 'He does.' It was right at that moment she realised Ben *wanted* it to be over. He was just too kind to do the ending.

And Claire wanted it to be over too.

It all got too much then, the tears starting to come. She didn't want Milo to see her like this so she scraped her chair back and ran to the toilets. When she got there, she stared at herself in the mirror. Her face looked like it was stuck mid-argument; skin stretched, the tops of her cheeks red, eyes angry.

Her face crumpled and she slumped down into the wicker chair next to the sinks, sobbing into her hands. Her marriage was over, and she was terrified. Terrified of what the future held, terrified of the road she'd be forced to take. It wasn't just Ben she was leaving behind, it was kids too. There was the possibility of adoption with Ben. But if she stepped away from her life with him now, that might mean turning her back on ever having a family.

'So be it,' she said, her jaw clenching. 'This is what fate's dealt me. So be it.'

She took a deep breath and got up, patting some water over her face before walking back outside, pausing at the entrance when she noticed Milo leaning over the railings with Archie, pointing something out to him as Blue stood with his paws on the railings.

How could it have taken a farmer from Exmoor to help her see the truth?

She walked towards him.

He turned when he heard her approach. 'I'm so sorry, it's none of my business, I shouldn't have pushed you to talk about it all.'

'No, it's helped. Really . . .' She paused, trying to hold herself together. 'I need to accept my marriage is over. I think Ben has; it's time I did too.'

On the way back, Milo let Claire quietly sob as she digested the acknowledgement she'd just made about her marriage. Her heart ached for Ben and every wonderful moment they'd shared: the footprints they'd made in the sand during their wonderful honeymoon in Sardinia; the way he'd carried her over the threshold the day they'd moved into their house; the long dinners they'd shared with their friends, talking into the early hours. There were sad moments too, the touch of his hand when she woke from being sedated in their IVF clinic, the tears they'd shared at yet another negative pregnancy test.

After a while, they reached a small village crammed with thatched-roof cottages. The sun was starting to set, casting a pink glow over the village. As Milo drove into its centre, a castle appeared. Claire looked up, wiping the tears from her cheeks and smiling slightly.

Milo smiled as he noticed her reaction. 'Nunney Castle,' he said. 'We used to come here as kids – Dale, Jen and me. I thought you might need something to smile about.'

'It's perfect.'

As they drew closer, she could see its exterior walls were discoloured and crumbling, its turrets falling apart, huge weeds curling around their bases. Circling the castle was a moat, grey water glistening in the setting sun, ducks shaking their wings on its banks.

They left the dogs in the car and stepped inside the castle, taking in the disintegrating walls and empty windows which looked out onto the pink sky. Claire pulled out her camera, noticing how perfect the light was.

She started taking pictures as Milo leaned against a nearby wall and watched her. She tried not to get distracted by the sight of him there, his dark hair in his eyes, arms crossed.

'I can imagine you living somewhere with no roof,' she said as she crouched down to take a picture of a cobweb that stretched across a crook in the wall.

'Why's that?'

'You always like to be outdoors. I bet you have the window wide open in your room when you sleep, even in the winter.'

She thought about watching him sleep. She imagined the way his eyelashes would curl over his skin, the way his mouth would open slightly, the way his dark hair would look against a white pillow. She pressed her nails into the skin of her palms to drive the thoughts away.

'I'm not that daft, though I do like to camp out in the summer and sleep under the stars,' he said. 'Funny you say that though. When my grandfather went to Greece, he slept on the beach for a week because he couldn't afford a hotel.'

'He sounds really interesting.'

'He was; it's great reading all his letters. Shame things ended for him the way they did.' Claire thought again of what Henry had told her and Milo rolled his eyes. 'Henry told you, didn't he? I can tell from the look on your face.'

'He did mention something.'

'He probably forgot to mention my grandfather had liver disease and was in terrible pain, according to his final letters. He couldn't take the pain any more.'

Claire thought of the pain her own dad suffered. 'That must've been difficult, making that decision, going through with it,' she said.

Milo sighed. 'I understand why he did it. I'd do the same. But it hasn't exactly helped our family's reputation.'

'What reputation?'

His jaw clenched as he looked down at the dusty ground. 'Mum used to say the James family was cursed – the "James Curse". There's lots of stuff in our family's past going back generations, various scandals. That farmhouse has seen more action than most. If it weren't for our mad family, we'd have a lot more money, that's for sure. I personally think it's more about the James propensity for depression. My dad had problems with drinking, probably the reason he had a heart attack in the end.'

'I'm sorry, Milo.'

'It was hard growing up. Just hope I don't end up the same,' he mumbled.

'You don't strike me as being like that,' Claire said softly.

He smiled. 'Mum said the same. She said I'm different from the other James men. Apart from the sleeping in the open, that is,' he added, raising an eyebrow. He looked up at what remained of the castle walls. 'Reminds me of Venice in this light,' he said. 'Pink crumbling rocks, the strange gaping emptiness of it all.'

'Very poetic. When did you go?'

'School trip ages ago. Haven't you been?'

'No.'

'I found it a tad tacky actually. It was probably nicer before the twentieth century got hold of it.'

Claire smiled. 'I'm pleased you said that. I always thought the same.'

Milo stepped into a large hole in the wall. 'This'll make a good photo,' he said, peering up. 'Come look.'

'Can it fit us both in?'

'Sure.'

It wasn't so dark inside but it was small, just wide enough to fit three, maybe four people. Milo blinked at Claire in the gloom and her heart rebounded against her chest. She wondered if he could hear it in such a small, quiet space.

'Here,' he said, taking her shoulders and twisting her around so she was facing outwards again.

Her arms tingled at the feel of his fingertips through the thin material of her cardigan. She pressed the camera into her chest to try to still her heart.

'See,' he murmured into her ear, his lips close to her neck. 'You get a great angle from here.'

It was true. The sky was framed by the jagged outline of the entrance to this small hideaway, orange light gleaming in through all the different-sized windows. But Claire could hardly focus on it; all she could sense was Milo behind her.

'Look up,' he said, smiling. She lifted her camera but he put his hand on her arm. 'Without hiding behind that camera of yours. Look with your eyes.'

She lowered her camera and did as he asked, taking in the slice of red sky that showed through the gap in the ceiling above. He was so close now, she could feel his breath on the bare skin of her shoulder, almost feel his lips there. She closed her eyes. She had two choices: step away into the safety of the castle, or stay here and see where the moment took them.

Her dad had said something similar a few days before he left.

I want to see where the moment takes me. I want to try a new path.

Where had that led him? Dying of cancer all alone, that's where.

Claire stepped out of the crevice and thought she heard Milo sigh.

'We better head back to the car,' he said after a while. 'It'll be dark soon.'

Claire saw Milo as soon as she stepped into the wedding marquee the next day. He was standing with Holly in a dark grey suit, pulling awkwardly at the collar of his white shirt as he watched Matt and Sarah's wedding guests walk in from the warm autumnal evening. When he caught sight of Claire, he stopped what he was doing and smiled.

She smoothed down her hair then walked up to him and Holly, feeling awkward in her oriental dress, the kitten heels of her shoes digging into the mud.

'I love your dress, Claire,' Holly said. 'Is it from your travels?'

Claire nodded. 'Japan.'

'I'd so love to go there! A Japanese lady came to school to tell us about their culture. It's so different from boring old England,' she said, wrinkling her nose as she looked towards the farmhouse.

Claire smiled. She remembered feeling the same each time her family returned to the UK for a family event. 'Maybe you will go to Japan one day.' She took in Holly's dress, the same blue taffeta one she'd worn for her birthday. 'You look pretty yourself, Holly.'

'I'm not so sure. Dad said he can't afford a new one,' she said. 'It's too childish. They'll all think I'm a little girl.'

'No they won't,' Milo said, putting his hand on his niece's shoulder. 'Claire's right, you look really pretty in it.' Holly looked up at Milo, beaming at him.

Claire pulled the bejewelled clip from her hair. 'Take this,' she said to Holly. 'It goes better with your dress than mine.'

Milo smiled.

'Oh, I can't!' Holly said.

'Please, consider it a belated birthday present. A freedom fighter in India gave it to me when I was about your age so you can wear it and feel very grown up knowing that.'

Holly's eyes lit up as she took it, staring down at it in her open palm as Milo mouthed a 'thank you' to Claire.

'The heroes!' someone shouted out.

They turned to see Matt strolling towards them. He was clearly already drunk but looked happy and very handsome in a black morning suit and pink cravat. He pulled Claire and Milo into a sweaty hug, pressing their faces together as Holly laughed. Then he beckoned some friends over and they spent the next twenty minutes listening to him tell the story of his 'rescue' all over again.

'If I have to hear that story again,' a familiar voice murmured next to Claire, 'I think I'll combust.'

She smiled. 'Hello, Jay.'

He was wearing an usher's suit in a similar style to Matt's but he'd added a dash of his own style with a smart top hat and pink silk handkerchief.

'I'm pleased you're here,' he said, completely ignoring Milo. 'I want you to meet Yasmine. She's an associate editor at *Travel* magazine in the US and was only saying the other day how she needs some fresh blood on her editorial team.'

Travel was big, glossy and had a huge circulation aimed at people who had the money to discover new places without missing out on the luxuries. Her dad would turn in his grave at the thought of her working for a 'sell-out' magazine, as he'd call it. But she'd heard great things about the way they treated their staff, a contrast to her current employers. And if her marriage was really over, she'd need a change. She couldn't face still living in Reading, seeing the same people, bumping into Ben.

Milo took Archie's lead from Claire. 'You go ahead, Claire. Holly and I will take Archie and go find Blue. We'll come back in a few minutes.'

'Good idea,' Jay said. 'Lugging a dog about isn't going to impress Yasmine.'

Milo smiled tightly then strode off with Holly as she twisted around to frown at them.

'Come,' Jay said, steering Claire towards a group of people.

She didn't see Milo 'in a few minutes'. In fact, she spent the next hour talking to the editor Jay had mentioned, as well as a host of 'important people' she couldn't get away from. When she finally did extract herself, she couldn't find Milo, just Holly who was feeding Archie wedding cake under a table at the back.

She stood on her own, imagining what it would be like at future weddings without Ben. She'd cope. She'd always been independent. She glanced at Yasmine. Maybe she wouldn't have time to go to weddings if she was jet-setting around the world with *Travel* magazine? It was a completely different vibe from her magazine, which was run on a shoe-string . . . and from her ramshackle travelling days with her family. She'd be drawn into a different world, a world with money and privilege. Did she want that, no matter how much of a welcome change it offered? She looked over at Jay, who was clearly used to a world like that. One of the bridesmaids he was talking to, a beautiful girl with long black hair, let out an ear-piercing laugh as he whispered something in her ear.

'What *is* he like?' Claire turned to see Sarah smiling down at her. She'd seen her earlier, looking dazzling in her sleek ivory wedding dress, her curly blonde hair piled on top of her head, set off by a silver and pink tiara. 'I thought he was gay the first time I met him. But he's since slept with half my friends. And that fashion sense of his? Turns out he got all his style from his mother, she was a fashion designer. She died when he was young and his dad's a typical rich banker type, hence Jay's job at *Daily Telegraph*. But his heart is in culture and the arts.'

Maybe her and Jay weren't so different.

Sarah peered towards a woman with black hair. 'You must meet my boss later, Audrey Monroe. Have you heard of her?'

Claire shook her head.

'She set up her own foundation, the Audrey Monroe Foundation,' Sarah explained. 'It helps animals affected by war. Our volunteers are in Chechnya right now and I'm due to go to Serbia in a year or so, my first trip for work. We rely on volunteers to pass the message around so please do.'

'I will. Sounds like a wonderful charity.'

Sarah looked around her. 'Where's Milo?'

'I don't know. He just disappeared.'

'I suppose this isn't his kind of thing really, is it? All these people, hemmed in by white plastic?'

Claire laughed. 'No, you're right.'

'You like him, don't you?' Claire's laughter trickled away. Sarah clearly hadn't noticed her wedding ring. 'If I were you, I wouldn't let a hunky farmer like Milo slip from my grasp. In fact, I'd be down at the stream at this very moment.'

'The stream?'

'He's there, I saw him a moment ago when I popped out for some fresh air. Archie's fine.' Claire followed Sarah's gaze towards Archie, who was tentatively lifting his paw towards Holly as she hovered a piece of wedding cake over his nose. 'Go on, go find Milo. Make sure your dog isn't the only one having some fun tonight,' she added with a wink.

Claire looked out into the warm summer evening, the soft tinkle of the nearby stream calling out to her like a siren, the champagne running through her veins making her feel brave and foolish. Maybe Sarah was right, maybe she shouldn't let a man like Milo slip from her grasp? She put her arms around herself and stepped out of the marquee, the grass tickling her toes . . .

Chapter Four

Krabi, Thailand
2004

I look up from the note I'd found in Claire Shreve's atlas, eyes blinking into the sun as I peer out of the window. Huge mountains hover in the distance, large signs and palm trees jostling for position on the dusty roadsides. I think we're in Ao Nang now, I recognise it from the tourist book I got at the airport. But the busy market stalls they showed in the photos are empty, the glimpses of a sweeping yellow beach in the distance clear of crowds. I'd heard it wasn't hit as badly as other resorts I'd seen on the news, hence choosing it as somewhere to stay. Its location meant the power of the waves had dissipated a little by the time they reached its shores. But lives were still claimed here, and I see signs of that now: wood clogging the road's edges, photos hung up on walls, ripped clothes tangled around lampposts. And then there's the eerie silence.

I quickly gather my stuff and stand on shaky legs, moving down the middle of the bus as quickly as I can as it bounces up and down. 'Stop?' I say to the bus driver. 'Can you stop please?'

He seems to be ignoring me. I panic. What if he doesn't stop and takes me to some far-flung town? I shake his shoulder and point out the window. He brings the bus to an abrupt stop and I stumble backwards, my mum's bag dropping from my shoulder, its contents spilling out onto the bus's floor. The Thai couple next to me scramble to pick everything up, even smiling at me as they do so. I'm grateful for their kindness and smile back.

When I get off the bus, I look up and down the street, trying to recognise the orange exterior of my hotel. Then I notice it a few doors down, one of several small two-storey buildings sitting right in the heart of Ao Nang's shopping district. Though the streets are quiet, there are people milling about, including exhausted-looking relatives handing out posters of their loved ones.

I check in, struggling with the heavily accented voice of the receptionist, then head to my room. It looks different from what I expected, more 'Western', with clean white sheets over the small double bed, a dark wooden table fitted to the wall with a leather-topped stool, a small balcony overlooking the quiet streets. A fan whirs above, my shoes making a clicking sound as I walk across the cream-tiled floor. The wardrobe is the only indication of the country I'm in, made from thick pale wood, two square panels with ornate wooden carvings running down each door. As I move past it, I breathe in the faint scent of eucalyptus.

I take everything out of my suitcase, re-folding each item before placing it on the shelves of the wardrobe. I wonder where Mum stayed last. Did she unpack like I'm doing now? Or, more likely, fling her suitcase into the corner, her clothes spilling out of it as she headed straight out onto the streets – to 'breathe in the atmosphere' as she used to say?

After unpacking, I try to call home but it just rings and rings. Maybe Will has taken the girls out. I hope so. I leave a quick message then lie back on the bed, the jetlag catching up on me. But all I can see is Mum painting again, lip caught snugly between her teeth as she swirls pink with white to create her own pale skin on canvas. It's almost like she's there, right in the room with me.

'Don't look so anxious, Lou,' she'd say if she were. 'It'll turn out all right in the end. And look,' she'd add, gesturing towards the window. 'The sun's shining, there's no children yanking you about, no husband insisting on his dinner. Make the most of it!'

I smile to myself. Yes, that's what she'd say. Turn a serious moment into something frivolous.

'I'm going to find you, Mum,' I say to her mirage, my voice trembling with determination. 'I'm going to bloody find you.'

My phone rings and I see it's Will's mobile. The image of Mum drifts away. 'How are the girls?' I ask as soon as I pick it up.

'I told them you'll be back in a couple of days. Jesus, I didn't think you were serious. Do you realise how stupid you're being?'

That word again. *Stupid.*

'She's my mother, Will. Wouldn't you do the same for yours?'

'That's different.'

'Different because Mum doesn't wear pearl necklaces and attend WI meetings?'

He laughs bitterly. 'Funny you say all that now considering you were only telling me last week you'd had enough of your mother not talking to you.'

'That's unfair to bring up.'

'Why? Because she might be dead?'

I open and close my mouth in shock.

'Because let's be frank,' Will continues, 'there's more chance she's passed out in some shoddy hotel somewhere than—'

There's the sound of crying in the background.

Chloe.

He'd said all that in front of her?

'Let me speak to Chloe,' I say, voice firm.

'Why? You're the one who left her to fly to the other side of the world.'

'To find my missing mother, for Christ's sake! Put Chloe on *right* now, Will.'

He's silent for a few moments then sighs. 'Come on, Chloe, your mother wants to talk to you.'

'Mummy!'

I have to use every ounce of strength I have left not to sob out loud. 'Hello, poppet. Have you been having a good time with Daddy?'

'We've been at Grandma's! She helped us make dolls.'

My stomach sinks. So Will drove them all the way to Surrey so he didn't have to spend time alone with his own children?

'That's nice,' I say, keeping my voice cheerful. 'Are you staying tonight?'

'Yes!'

'Daddy too?'

'He needs to *work*, Mummy,' Chloe replies in an exasperated tone, the same tone Will adopts when he's using that excuse.

'Is Olivia there, darling?'

'She's sleeping. She thinks Nanna's in the Nile.'

I press my eyes tight shut.

'But I told her you'll bring her back,' Chloe says, her voice trembling. 'You *are* going to bring Nanna back, aren't you? She can sleep in my room if she wants and draw in my art book again.'

'I hope so, darling.' My voice catches. 'You be a good girl for your grandparents, okay?'

'Okay, Mummy. I love you.'

'Love you too.'

There's the sound of the phone being passed over then Will comes back on. 'I'm sorry for what I said about your mother,' he says, his voice contrite. 'It's just been very difficult with you disappearing like that.'

'I did tell you I'd be going. Chloe said they're staying at your parents. It wouldn't kill you to spend some time alone with your daughters, Will.'

'Says the woman who left them to find her eccentric mother!'

'I can't talk to you when you're like this.' My voice is shaking so hard now, I'm surprised I can get my words out properly. 'Remember Olivia's cough medicine and Chloe needs new shoes so your mum might want to try the sales tomorrow. Goodbye, Will.'

'Don't put your phone down on me or—'

I slam the phone down and the four walls close in around me, making me feel like Alice spiralling down the rabbit hole. I grab my bag, slipping my shoes back on before making my way outside. The heat makes me sweat again, that horrible stench clogging my nostrils.

There's even more sadness in the air now evening is approaching, people sticking posters on lampposts, Thais huddled in groups in café, heads close together, some of them crying. How trivial my argument with Will seems now.

My stomach gurgles, reminding me I haven't eaten a thing all day. A lone street vendor shoots me a toothless smile and gestures to his wok. I lean over it then let out a small gasp when I see huge crickets, cooked legs pulled close to their scorched bellies. I stumble away, putting my hand to my mouth as the vendor laughs. Someone grabs me.

'You want a new bag?' a Thai woman says, gesturing towards one of just three stalls that are now open.

'Sorry, I—'

'I give you good price.'

'No, please, I feel sick.'

I pull away from the woman and lean against a nearby wall, taking in huge gulps of air. Terror starts working its way inside. Will's right, what the hell was I thinking, coming here alone? Before I even realise what I'm doing, I'm scrolling through the contacts on my phone with trembling fingers, finding Sam's number. It rings and rings before eventually he answers.

'Hello?' Northern lilt, voice breathless.

'Sam?'

'Louise? Are you okay?'

'Not really. They're – they're baking insects. It's horrible.' I let out a small sob then cringe with embarrassment. *Get a grip, Louise.* 'I'm just being silly,' I say, pulling myself together. 'I'm exhausted and hungry and—'

'You still haven't eaten?'

'No. Only insects on the menu, I'm afraid.' I peer towards the vendor again. He smiles at me and waves. I force myself to wave back.

'You have to eat,' Sam says. 'What hotel are you staying at?' I give him the name of my hotel. 'I know a place near there,' he says. 'I'll be there in half an hour.'

I pause. He's a virtual stranger. And yet my stomach feels clawed out, my nerves shot to pieces and I'm craving the sight of another English face. 'All right,' I say.

'Wait in reception, I'll come get you.'

I disconnect and notice I've received a text from Will. I place the phone into my bag without reading it.

Thirty minutes later, there's a sound like thunder outside. For a moment, I panic, thinking it might be the sea roaring towards the island as it had a few days ago. But then my eyes snag on something approaching in the distance – a huge chrome motorbike that sticks out like a sore thumb among the tiny mopeds whizzing past it, steered by familiar tanned arms.

I pull my bag close to my chest as I step outside, my forehead already growing slick with sweat. I'd showered then changed into a pair of cut-off white trousers and a pink petal blouse, but now it feels just like I'm wearing my old clothes again.

Sam pulls off his helmet, his gold hair standing on end. He looks even more exhausted, face grimy with specks of sand. He clocks the look on my face and smiles. 'Don't worry, you don't have to get on this. The restaurant's only a five-minute walk.'

Would I have got on the back of Sam's bike if the restaurant weren't so close? What would everyone back home say if I had? What would *Mum* say?

'About time you had some fun,' I imagine, that mischievous twinkle in her brown eyes. 'Look at you, my straight-laced little Lou on the back of a stranger's bike. Good on you, girl!'

Sam jumps off the bike and gestures for me to join him. I hesitate a moment. The heat's making me nauseous and what if he takes me to some far-out place with cockroaches and squat toilets? Then I think of my mum again and fall into step beside him.

'How long have you lived in Thailand?' I ask him.

'Four years.' He looks around him at the debris and exhausted-looking Thais. 'I've grown to love the place so it's difficult seeing it like this.'

We're quiet for the next few minutes, watching as the sea shimmers under the dying light in the distance. I imagine it rising and arching towards us, just as it did a few days before.

Did Mum see it rise?

After a while, we approach a small restaurant with a sign outside in Thai, a yellow flower painted on it. I breathe a sigh of relief: it looks quite normal, not the type of place with squat loos anyway. The entire building is made from light brown wood with exotic-looking trees and flowers entwined around it. It makes me think of Mum's tiny beach-side house in Brighton. It was right in front of the roaring sea and even had its own piano. Mum would play it, and we'd dance and sing and put on shows, the seagulls outside our only audience. We'd buy chunks of cheese and bread and chocolate, lots of chocolate, and watch films I'd never let my girls watch on the banged-up old video player.

Then there are the other memories, darker ones. Like the time I woke in the night to find Mum standing barefoot outside, sobbing. Or the time I accidentally broke the bracelet Mum's best friend had made for her. I still remember the look on her face, the way she'd run from the room then not talked to me all day.

'I gave them a call to check they're open,' Sam says, opening the door for me. 'Not many restaurants are open around here after what happened. No tourists means no business.'

'I guess that's another thing too, the effect it'll have on tourism and the Thai economy.'

'Yep,' he says sadly. Then he plants a smile on his face. 'But at least we'll be contributing something here. You'll be pleased to hear this place does good English food. But seriously, you should try the Thai food, it's delicious.'

'Oh, it's not that I don't like Thai food. But after seeing the stuff the street vendors were serving, I wasn't sure if my version of Thai food is different from the real thing.'

Sam raises an eyebrow. 'They don't serve insects here, I promise.'

When we get inside, a pretty Thai woman greets us, placing

her hands together and bowing her head. Sam does the same but I don't, embarrassed. The place is deserted, no surprise considering. We follow the woman through to a table at the back. It's a small restaurant but the chunky mahogany tables are set out in a way that makes it look spacious. Paintings of the local area line the walls and I wonder if any of the scenes depicted have changed because of what's happened.

The waitress comes over and Sam orders his food. I cast my eye down the menu and am relieved to see there are items I recognise on there alongside the more strange-looking stuff. I think about ordering steak and chips then remember the way Will had looked at me as I'd tried to squeeze myself into that black slinky dress on Christmas Eve. 'Caesar salad, please,' I say.

The waitress scribbles the order down then walks away.

'So all set for meeting Jay Hemingford tomorrow?' Sam asks, stifling a yawn. He can't have had much sleep lately and I feel bad for dragging him out.

'I think so.' I unfold my napkin and spread it out on the table. 'I need to return Claire Shreve's atlas to him too, I took it by accident. It's just so strange Mum had it in her bag . . . and that Claire Shreve had Mum's bag.'

'Maybe they became friends out here? Or maybe Claire Shreve just found your mum's bag and was meaning to hand it in?' He pauses. 'Or she stole it.'

I shake my head. 'Judging by the way Jay Hemingford was dressed, I doubt she's the type to steal something.'

'Don't judge a book by its cover.'

'True.' I sigh, raking my fingers through my hair, which is already sticky with sweat. How can people live in countries like this? 'I don't know, I guess I'll get some answers when I speak to Jay tomorrow.'

Sam leans back in his chair, contemplating me. 'So what do you do back in the UK?'

'Full-time mum.' I brace myself for the 'is that all?' look I always get, usually from Will's work colleagues. If only they knew how many miles I put in running after those kids of mine.

But instead, Sam smiles. 'That must be hard work! I nearly had a heart attack looking after my niece when I was back in the UK and that was just one child for one afternoon. It's important for spiritual growth that children spend time with their parents.'

I stifle a smile. Maybe he was a bit of a hippy? 'Oh, I don't know,' I say. 'I have friends who are working mums and their kids are fab. As long as you love them and feed them and let them watch *Dr. Zitbag's Transylvania Pet Shop* they're happy.' Sam raises an eyebrow. 'Don't even ask,' I say.

He laughs. 'I won't. How many kids do you have?'

'Two. Chloe's seven and Olivia's four.'

I hand him a photo and he smiles. 'They look like you.'

'Everyone says that. They have their dad's brains though, thank God.'

'What does he do?'

'He's a recruitment director. That's how I met him; I was the office manager at the headhunting firm he works for.'

Will had been so charming then, the handsome clever graduate taking me under his wing. That all changed, of course.

'Do you miss office life?' Sam asks.

'No, I was only there while I tried to figure out what to do with my life. By the time I realised, I was pregnant with Chloe and Will wanted me to be at home with her.'

'What did you realise you wanted to do?'

'It's silly really but I wanted to make wedding invitations. I did my own when Will and I got married, and I loved it. But Will was quite right when he said I'd get little financial reward for all the hard work.'

'You'd have been rewarded in other ways though, like seeing your invites used by happy couples.'

'Too late for all that now. What do you do?' I ask.

'I sing. I figured that out halfway through a theology degree.' He nods towards a small stage at the back of the restaurant. 'That's how I know about this place. I do gigs here sometimes.'

'Wow, I had no idea,' I say as the waitress brings over our drinks.

'Your mum came to one of my gigs in London with my mum actually. But I never got a chance to meet her, she had to rush off to get a train. She was a godsend, dragging my mum out, making sure she wasn't stuck indoors all the time.'

I smile to myself. 'Sounds like my mum.'

'What about your dad, is he an artist too?'

'He's an accountant.' Sam looks surprised. 'He met Mum while doing the accounts for a local art gallery she exhibited at.'

Our food is brought over then. My salad looks lame compared to Sam's curry, the fragrant smell of its spices drifting towards me and making my mouth water.

'Do you like your mum's paintings?' Sam asks in between mouthfuls.

'They're not really my kind of thing. But then what do I know? I'm not creative like her.'

'You made your own wedding invites. And you're not half bad at origami.'

He stares at the little swan I've finished creating with my napkin. I quickly unfold it, smoothing the creases out with my hand.

'What sort of stuff does she paint?' Sam asks.

'She used to paint scenic stuff,' I say. 'But then she had a massive argument with her best friend Erin when she came to stay with us once and all she painted after were images of them both together. It's become her trademark.'

'Why did they argue?'

I sigh. 'I think it was about some man Erin was obsessed with – *not* her husband. Mum never heard from her again. Mum tried to find her, even went to the police to report her missing. It really got to her, losing her friend like that.'

The memories come in a rush then. The sound of her angry brush strokes in the weeks and months that followed, the sight of her bloodied fingers the mornings after. Then the spectacle of her night's work: her mouth, grotesque and mid-scream on canvas after canvas, with the image of Erin watching in the background.

The pain Mum felt at losing her friendship had been so palpable, it had seared every minute after, every hour, ever day. And yet any pain Mum might feel at not talking to me and her own grandchildren for two years seems non-existent. How could she not pick up the phone, send an email, even a bloody postcard?

'They must have been very close,' Sam says.

'Yes, Erin was like a sister to Mum. After my grandparents died, Mum was sent to live with her aunt in a tiny seaside village in Ireland when she was just seven. The first week there, Mum found Erin playing with a dirty old doll in a cave near the sea. Mum's aunt had told her an unusually high tide would be coming in so Mum persuaded Erin to come out from the cave. They became firm friends after, creating their own lives in that little cave.'

'Shame their friendship ended.'

I nod. 'In a way, that argument broke up my family.'

'How so?' Sam asks.

'Mum didn't pick me up from a party when I was twelve because she'd driven to Oxford after hearing Erin had been spotted there. I got moderate hypothermia trying to walk home alone. Dad went mental.'

I think about when Mum had come up to my room just before she'd left, eyes glassy with tears. I remember getting that feeling like I was on top of a faulty rollercoaster, ready to smash down into the concrete below. I knew what was coming, had heard about this kind of conversation from the other kids at school. It didn't make it any easier.

She'd knelt down in front of me, taking my hand in hers. 'Your dad and I aren't very happy, Lou. So we've agreed it'll be better if I go stay with some friends in Brighton. You can come and stay any time, and I'll come visit you too. I just haven't got enough money right now for you to live with me. But when I do—'

'Don't lie,' I'd said, interrupting her. 'Daddy's not unhappy with you. He loves you and I *know* he'll be sad if you leave. You're leaving because *you're* unhappy. Not just with Daddy but me too.'

'Oh no, Lou, it's not that. I—'

I'd jumped off the bed then, going to the door and holding it open. 'It's true. Beauty is truth, truth beauty, remember, Mum?'

She'd peered up at me then, still on her knees, and I'd felt strangely powerful, quoting the poem she so loved, twisting it around and using it for my own purposes.

I still remember watching Mum walk down the path with her suitcase a few minutes after that, the feel of Dad's hand, sweaty and desperate as he clutched at mine. She'd turned once before stepping into the taxi, her eyes seeking out mine. But I'd turned away.

Now I have my girls, I understand how she must've felt. There must have been very good reasons why she left. It makes me even more determined to find her and hear her side of the story.

Sam and I eat the rest of our meal in silence, both exhausted from the day's events. As Sam walks me back, I stare out at the blur of black against black.

'Thanks for everything today,' I say as we stop outside my hotel. 'I really appreciate it.'

'No problem. I hope your chat with Jay goes all right tomorrow morning. I'll meet you at the café at ten, okay? Then we'll get on with the search.'

'Thanks. 'Night, Sam.'

When I get to my room, I get everything ready for the next day, just like I'm used to doing at home. But instead of laying out the girls' clothes and getting out their bowls for breakfast, I'm laying my own clothes out. As I place Claire Shreve's atlas in a spare plastic bag to give to Jay, something falls from it. I lean down then hesitate a moment. I mustn't look at whatever it is, it's private ... and belongs to a dead woman whose family should now have it. But this will be my last night with it before I meet with Claire Shreve's friend Jay and what if this item holds a clue to Mum's whereabouts? I quickly turn it over before I change my mind and see it's a photo from a newspaper article of a man with dark hair, signs of a faint scar on his right cheek. There's a caption beneath it: *Milo James will be taking to the stand tomorrow to defend himself.*

Milo. The person who'd written in the front of the atlas?

I stare into his dark, wretched eyes and feel my heart thump against my chest. Defend himself against what? What if he was out here with Claire Shreve, and Mum had met him too? Would she have been in danger from him?

I think about how he'd feel if he knew I'd been poking about in his dead girlfriend's belongings. I quickly shove the article back into the atlas's pages and place it in my bag ready to give Jay Hemingford tomorrow.

Chapter Five

Exmoor, UK
1997

It was a beautiful night, unusually warm for the time of year. Pink fairy lights shimmered all over the wedding marquee and tables had been set up outside with bright lanterns all over them. Claire pulled her cream pashmina from her bag and wrapped it around her arms as she headed towards the stream where Sarah had said Milo was, her small heels digging into the mud. There was a roar in her ears, like she was on the verge of something and it both exhilarated and terrified her.

She couldn't see Milo at first. But as she reached the end of the small meadow that led down to the stream, the music growing fainter and fainter the further away she got, she saw him standing in front of a large oak tree, throwing pebbles into the stream.

She stood on something – a branch maybe – and he turned.

He didn't say anything as she walked towards him, just watched her, his eyes blinking in the darkness.

'Sarah mentioned you were out here,' Claire said when she got to him.

He raised an eyebrow. 'There's only so much seventies music a man can take.'

Claire laughed. 'I tried to find you.'

'And now you have.'

'Yes.'

She peered down at her pretty silk shoes and suddenly felt ridiculous, standing here under the stars across from a man who wasn't her husband. Her life was taking a turn she'd never anticipated, like a current that suddenly changes direction. And yet she didn't *want* to resist it as it urged her along. It felt too good, too right.

'I didn't get the chance earlier to say how beautiful you look,' Milo said softly.

Claire's breath caught in her throat. The night seemed to open up to her then, the sound of the stream throbbing at her temples, the stars above closing in on her. She felt as though she was on the edge of something and was about to step off.

'And I didn't get a chance to say how handsome you look,' she said, taking that step.

'Not bad for a stag-killer.'

'A reluctant stag-killer.'

They were quiet for a few moments then Milo stepped towards Claire. 'That quote your dad liked, the one about marching off the edge of our map?'

'Yes?'

'I understand why it scares you, going on the path less travelled, especially after what happened to your dad. But he went off on his own, didn't he? If you have someone beside you, then it doesn't have to be so daunting.'

He gently took Claire's hand. Her heart fumbled, floundered, trying to find its beat.

'I know you still yearn for it,' he said, 'the adventure of

following the path less travelled. I do too. I've wanted it for so long, this idea of just leaving everything behind and travelling. But I've kept it at a distance, always thinking deep down inside it'll never happen.' His handsome face lit up. 'Until I met you, that is. You make me feel like I can really do it. I think you can do it too.'

As she looked at him, she felt all the dreams she'd once had of living in one country to the next spread out before her. She'd kicked them all away that day she'd found her dad dying in his flat, terrified she'd end up like him. But the travel bug that fought against her desire for normality was always inside, like it was inside Milo, flapping its wings, urging her to return to being the free spirit she once was. Meeting Milo had sent it flying and she wanted to chase it with him.

So she nodded. 'Yes, I do want that.'

His brow creased slightly, like he was considering very carefully what to say next. 'I'm taking a leap of faith here and I know we've only known each other a couple of days. But I think things would be a lot less scary if we marched off the edge of the map together.'

The space between them contracted, shimmered. Maybe she didn't have to be alone, after all? In the distance, people laughed and the music turned up a few levels, birds flinging themselves from the trees above in alarm. But they barely noticed and suddenly they were in each other's arms, Milo's lips finding hers, Claire's fingers tangling in his hair as his hands glided over the bare skin of her arms. The blend of his soft lips on hers and the look in his eyes made her skin dance with feeling.

As his lips moved against hers, his fingers trailing over her cheek, sensations bubbled inside. She hadn't felt this in such a long time, the searing urgency; body selfish and hungry for more. He glided his hand down her neck, grazing his fingers over her nipple, the calluses on his hand rubbing against it through the thin material of her dress as she let out a muffled cry.

She reached down, pulling his shirt from his trousers, gliding her palm over the warm flesh of his taut stomach as her eyes stayed on his. He slipped his hand under the neckline of her dress, dragging the lace of her bra away as she reached for his belt.

They stumbled back towards some nearby hedges, the river shimmering beside them, and Milo pulled Claire to the ground, the mud and grass cold on her skin. He stopped a moment and smiled, his eyes playful, and she smiled back. Then he slowly pushed up her skirt, her fingers clumsily unbuckling his belt. He pushed her knickers to the side as she unzipped his trousers, yanking them down urgently.

He paused a moment, the tops of his cheeks pink, his dark fringe hanging in his eyes. 'This okay?'

Claire didn't need long to consider what they were about to do really; she just knew with all her heart it was right. 'Yes.'

His smile deepened, his dark eyes deep in hers. He manoeuvred himself so he was in between her legs, the coldness of his zip gliding over the folds of her skin.

Then there was the sound of movement nearby.

Someone was limping towards them in the darkness, hands out.

They pulled away from each other and Milo jumped up, quickly doing his trousers back up, belt still hanging open. Claire straightened her dress and slowly stood with him.

'Jen?' Milo said, stepping towards the figure.

His sister leaned down, taking in gulps of air. 'Dale . . . he's got Dad's gun. He's lost it, Milo. I tried to stop him but he pushed me out of the way. He was so angry, screaming . . .' Her voice trailed off as she looked at Claire.

Claire put her hand over her mouth. What was Dale going to do?

'We did it all wrong,' Jen said, shaking her head. 'We – we should've—'

Milo grabbed her hand, face anguished. 'No, Jen. You did nothing wrong, it was me!'

Claire couldn't comprehend what they were both saying, her mind focused on the strange hitch of Jen's breath, the wretched look on Milo's face.

'Do you know where he went?' Milo asked Jen.

Jen peered towards the marquee, and Claire and Milo exchanged horrified looks.

'Where's Holly?' Milo asked.

'She was in there with Archie a few moments ago,' Claire said. 'Dale won't really hurt anyone, will he?' But as she said that, she knew he would; she had seen the darkness in his eyes the night before.

'I – I don't know,' Jen said through chattering teeth.

'Jesus Christ, you don't *know*? We – we need to call the police,' Claire said. She pulled her phone out with shaking hands then remembered there was no reception. 'I'll go to the hotel and call, you—'

'No.' Milo's voice sounded cold, hard. Something had changed in him, and so quickly too. 'It's not safe. I'll go. Both of you stay here.'

That's when the music stopped. Abruptly. And the screams started. Lots of them. A chorus of horror punctured by gunshots.

'Oh Christ,' Milo said, backing away, face distraught. 'Stay here, please stay here.'

He darted away into the darkness as people flooded out of

114

the marquee. Claire couldn't see the expressions on their faces from where she was, but she could sense their horror. Her brain whirred and trembled as it tried to comprehend what might be going on in there . . . and what Milo was running into.

'I need to go help Milo,' Jen said, taking a step forwards then wincing.

Claire put her arm around her shoulder. 'No, you're hurt.'

'But what if Milo needs our help? He can't deal with Dale alone when he's like this. And Holly's in there, what if—'

Claire closed her eyes and imagined Holly's sweet face slick with blood. Then Archie, the terrible sound of his whimpers. Both helpless and innocent with no one to help them.

She opened her eyes, her whole body suddenly buzzing with adrenaline. 'I'll go,' she said to Jen, not quite believing the words when they came out of her mouth. But for so long, she hadn't had control over her life. Right at that moment, she had control. If she went into the marquee, she could save a life, protect a child, ensure Archie felt no pain . . . she might be able to save them even if she couldn't save the embryos that had once grown inside her.

She started heading towards the marquee, the adrenaline still surging through her, tears drenching her cheeks before she even knew what she would see.

In the distance, Jay stumbled out, face stricken as he peered back towards the marquee. He grabbed her arm. 'Don't go in there,' he said, his usually jolly voice quivering. 'Milo's brother has a gun.'

'What happened in there?'

'He was shooting at people. Please Claire, come with me, you can't go in there.'

He tried to pull her away but she continued walking, breath coming in spurts as her mind tried to grapple with what she might see in there. When she got inside, it was worse than

115

she could even have imagined, the fairy lights dotted around the marquee illuminating patches of blood on the white walls and dance floor, the beautiful pink roses on the tables splattered with blood too.

She heard a man sobbing to her right so ran in the direction of the sound to find Matt sitting under a table with Sarah in his arms, her wedding dress turned scarlet, her eyes wide open. Matt was rocking her back and forth, tears streaming down his face as he looked down at her.

'She's dead,' he whispered. 'My God, she's dead.'

Claire pressed her fist to her mouth to stop the sob coming out then knelt down, checking Sarah's delicate wrist for a pulse. *Nothing.*

'Where's Dale James?' she asked.

'Over there,' Matt said, pointing towards the back of the marquee, Claire's view blocked by a toppled chair. He looked back down at Sarah and started sobbing.

Claire put her hand on his arm. 'We need to get you out of here, I—'

A shot rang out from the back of the marquee, making her ears ring. Someone started sobbing then a dog barked – Archie. She jumped up and started heading towards the back of the marquee, resisting every urge inside to run away.

Milo came into view then. He was sitting on the floor at the back of the marquee, legs flat out in front of him with a figure crumpled in his arms. There was a bad cut over his right cheekbone and blood was seeping out of it. A rifle was leaning against the wall near his shoulder and he was staring blankly into the distance.

As Claire drew closer, she realised it was his brother he was holding. Dale's eyes were closed, a blunt, red hole in his forehead.

Claire stifled a cry of shock.

116

Milo peered up, his eyes locking onto Claire's. He looked utterly broken.

'Are you hurt?' she asked, crouching down in front of him and placing her hand on his leg as she tried not to look at Dale.

'No,' he said in a monotone.

'Where's Holly?'

His eyes slid to his right, towards a table. Claire saw two blue shoes there. She shuffled over to find Holly huddled under the table, her beautiful eyes wide with shock. But she was unharmed, thank God. Blue was lying across her legs, Archie curled up in her arms. He let out a whine and struggled free, hurtling towards Claire. She picked him up, checking him all over. He was fine, completely unharmed. She placed him down and crawled under the table, reaching her hand out towards Holly.

'Come on,' Claire said to her. 'It's safe now, sweetheart.'

Holly's face was very white, her teeth chattering. Blue stood up, slinking out from under the table and making his way to Milo. Holly put her hand out and Claire took it, helping her slide out.

'Close your eyes,' Claire whispered, pressing Holly's face against her shoulder as she led her away from the table. 'Don't look until I say. Okay?'

Holly nodded against her arm as the sound of sirens rang out in the distance. Milo looked up at them both, his eyes passing over Holly then sinking into Claire's. There was nothing in them and Claire realised in that moment the Milo she'd spent the day with was gone.

His eyes slipped away from Claire's. Then he looked back down at his brother's bloody face and let out a small tortured moan.

Chapter Six

Krabi, Thailand
2004

I check my watch. Already ten past nine. Jay Hemingford's ten minutes late. Something tells me he's going to be a no-show. Can I blame him? He's lost his friend, after all. I'm not sure I could even drag myself out of bed if I'd found Mum's body at that temple.

There's a cough. I peer up to see two middle-aged women standing over me. One of them hands me a missing poster with two girls on the front waving from the top of a mountain, rucksacks on their backs.

'Our daughters,' one of the women says in an exhausted voice. 'They're cousins. Have you seen them, they were staying nearby?'

I think of my girls and imagine how awful this must be for them. 'I haven't, I'm sorry. But I'll keep an eye out.' I show them Mum's photo. 'Have you seen this woman while you've been here?'

They shake their heads. Then one of them peers towards the line of computers at the back, a misspelled sign saying 'Free for relatevs' hanging above.

'There's a computer free,' she says. 'Better check email, just in case.'

They wish me luck, then both head towards the computers. A man sitting at the end computer stands, stretches, then walks away, leaving that one free too. I take another look at the entranceway – still no Jay – then head to the free computer, thinking of the photo that had slipped from Claire's atlas the night before, Milo James's haunted eyes staring out at me. If it turns out Mum and Claire Shreve met each other out here, maybe he knows where Mum is?

When I type Milo's name into a search engine, a bunch of articles come up. I click on one, my fingers freezing on the mouse when I read the headline.

Bride shot dead at Exmoor wedding

New bride Sarah Levine was tragically shot dead at her wedding last night in an unprovoked attack. She is believed to have died at the scene from a gunshot wound to her stomach. The shooter, local farmer and Falklands veteran Dale James, opened fire at the evening reception before being shot dead by his own brother, Milo James. There is believed to be no connection between Sarah Levine and Dale James other than the fact his brother-in-law owns the inn where her wedding was held. Dale James's daughter, fourteen-year-old Holly James, is now being looked after by relatives.

I'd been silly to think Milo James was a danger after finding that photo the night before. He was just protecting people. The shooting had been all over the news a few years back, but I'd barely paid attention, too busy preparing for Chloe's birth. Surely Mum would've mentioned the shooting if she was connected to any of the people involved? Or maybe not. Once she'd casually mentioned she'd gone to Downing Street for a reception on arts and culture. Why hadn't she told me *before* the event?

I notice the article was written by a Nathan Styles. The name rings a bell. He was the journalist whose business card Claire Shreve had in her atlas, the one Jay Hemingford thought my mum might know. There's a photo next to it of the journalist, a thin man with a squint. I scroll down. With the article is a photo of a pretty redhead, the caption underneath saying it's Holly James. I've seen this face before. I pull the atlas out of my bag, flicking through it until I find the photo of the redhead in front of the blue elephant. I then look at the photo in the article again. She's older than in the article photo but it's definitely the same girl.

Another photo of Holly catches my eye in the 'related articles' sidebar. I click on it to see it's a recent photo of Holly James stumbling out of a nightclub in Bangkok. It's from just a few weeks ago. I shouldn't be shocked. No wonder she acted out like that considering her own father shot a young woman. I can't even begin to imagine what that experience would do to Chloe and Olivia.

I'm about to return to the search results for Milo James but catch sight of the atlas poking out of my bag. Who *was* Claire Shreve? I do a search for her, finding dozens of travel articles from different publications. There are photos with some of them, confirming Claire Shreve is the dark-haired woman pictured with Holly in the blue elephant photo . . . and, it turns out, the woman whose body I'd thought was Mum's. They do look alike in some ways: same dark hair and olive skin; same big brown eyes and slight Roman noses. I know they're not related; I'd done our family tree and knew of every member of my mum's side of the family going back decades. Plus Claire Shreve seems a bit younger than Mum, so that rules her out of being a secret addition to the family: both Mum's parents died when she was little. I once read a review of her work in an arts magazine where the writer said the reason Mum painted herself so much was because she was trying to find her identity. Becoming an orphan so young had made it difficult for her to get a sense of who she really was. Maybe that journalist was right?

One of Claire Shreve's listed articles catches my eye: 'A life without children'. I click on it and read the bit at the top in italics: *Claire Shreve writes about finding her place in the world as an infertile woman.*

Poor Claire. My girls are everything to me. I fell pregnant with both of them straight away. What if I hadn't though? What if I'd watched the months go by, one negative pregnancy test after another?

The thought's unbearable.

I look at Claire's other articles, see they're mainly about all the different countries she'd visited: New Zealand, India, Vietnam, Russia, South Africa . . . the list goes on. That must be fun, travelling and writing for a living. She certainly seemed happy in the photos I catch of her in various magazines. I suppose that's the upside to not having children: the freedom to travel, to follow your dreams. It's tough with the girls, they rely on me so much. Maybe if I hadn't had them, I'd be doing something exciting too, making wedding invites for some celebrity or another and being flown out to their beachside mansion in LA.

I almost laugh out loud. How ridiculous! And anyway, which would I prefer: a jet-set lifestyle or my girls? The girls, of course. But still, what a life this woman led.

An image suddenly flies through my mind of Claire

Shreve's swollen face and long dark hair clogged with debris. I put my hand to my mouth. That life's gone now, all that time ahead of her just wasted.

I go to carry out another search for Milo James then hear a shuffling sound behind me. A queue's formed for the computers now, a distressed-looking couple at the front. It's not fair of me to hog the computer so I log out then stand up, walking past the long queue that's formed. So many people searching for their relatives, desperate for news, hope battling with fear . . . and I'm one of them. I take the chance to show them Mum's photo, but none of them recognise her. Then I realise I never showed the picture to the Thai boy who'd brought me coffee earlier. I show him the photo now. Instead of shaking his head with a sad look on his face like everyone else has been doing, he nods. My heart starts pounding.

'Your lady come in every day for breakfast. She ask about this girl,' he says, jutting his chin towards the wall of photos behind him of various café guests. The one he's pointing at is of a pretty red-haired girl in her early twenties – Holly James!

'Did she say how she knew the girl?' I ask, trying to wrap my head around why Mum was looking for Holly James.

The boy shakes his head then points towards a hotel across the road with a bright pink exterior. 'I think your lady stay at that hotel. I see her go in there after.'

I reach into my bag and scribble down my mobile number, heart thumping so loud I think he might hear. This is the furthest I've got so far in finding Mum! I've found the connection between Mum and the woman who had her bag, *and* I've found out where she was staying when she was here.

I stare at the hotel. What if she's still there? I imagine seeing her silhouette in the window, twirling about as she listens to some local Thai radio, leaning forward to apply lipstick in a mirror, fluffing her hair.

I take a deep breath then head to the hotel. A fan whooshes in the centre of the ceiling when I step inside, lifting the corners of a newspaper nearby. There's a Thai woman around Mum's age on reception, her name badge reading 'Sumalee'.

'Hello. The boy at the café thinks my mother stayed here, Nora McKenzie?' I ask her, showing her Mum's photo and hoping with all my heart that she says Mum's still here.

'Yes, she stay here.'

'Is she still here?'

The woman shakes her head and my heart sinks. She flicks through a beautiful aqua-coloured book with a bejewelled elephant on its front, finds a page and traces her finger down it. 'She check out twenty-second of December.' Her brow puckers.

'What's wrong?' I ask.

'I think she say she go to Ko Phi Phi Don next.'

Oh God, I think I'm going to be sick.

I sink into the leather seat behind me and put my head in my hands. The images I've seen of Ko Phi Phi Don on the news are horrendous. Hotels torn apart, people screaming and crying, twisted metal and bodies floating in filthy water. It was one of the worst-hit islands.

There's the *click click click* of Sumalee's heels on the marble floor then I feel her cold hand on my back.

'Maybe she okay,' Sumalee says. 'Maybe she go back home.'

'I haven't heard from her. None of us have.' I peer up at Sumalee. 'Did she say where she'd be staying in Ko Phi Phi Don?'

She shakes her head, her brown eyes heavy with sadness.

'It's very bad in Ko Phi Phi Don, isn't it?' I ask.

She sighs. 'Yes, very bad.'

'Is it easy to get to from here?'

'Not so easy now, no boats.'

'Then what are people with relatives there supposed to do?'

'Phi Phi very small and not too far, so they bring bodies from there to here. Some even float here too, you understand? But you must think happy thoughts. You must believe your mother okay.'

That's what Mum would say. *Be positive, Lou. Believe good things will happen and they will.*

'You're right.' I pull myself together, quickly scribbling my number down. 'In case you hear anything. Thanks for your help.'

'No problem. Remember, think happy thoughts.'

I smile weakly and walk outside, forcing one leg in front of the other when all I want to do is duck into a nearby alleyway and curl up in the shade. But I don't, I continue walking until I'm back at the café, sinking into one of the chairs to wait for Sam. I look at the queue of people waiting to use the computers and imagine seeing Mum's face among them. But she's not here, is she? Worse than that, she might be on an island that took the full force of the wave.

After she left Dad and me, I'd imagine seeing her everywhere: outside school with the other mums, in the shops, even on TV. I alternated between being desperate for it to be her, to never wanting to lay my eyes on her again. When she'd picked me up in her old Mini two weeks after she'd left so we could spend the day together, I was even more conflicted, my heart bursting with love at seeing her again, my mind twisted with anger at her leaving.

'I've missed you, Lou,' she'd said when I got into her car. I didn't say anything and she'd flinched. I remember thinking, *What does she expect, a welcoming orchestra?*

'I got you some presents,' she'd said. 'New clothes, some jeans – remember the ones you liked when we went to the shops at Easter?'

'You can't buy my love,' I'd snapped back, heart thumping with the guts it had taken to say that. I'd heard a friend's older sister say it to her boyfriend on the phone and had thought it very grown-up.

She'd slammed on the brakes then and I'd darted forward, pressing the heels of my hands onto the dashboard to steady myself. 'Mum!'

She was shaking, the tops of her cheeks red. Someone beeped her so she indicated left, pulling up under a huge oak tree. Then she'd turned to me, tucking her finger under my chin and making me look at her.

'I understand why you're angry at me,' she'd said. 'But I love you, very very much. And I'm here because I want to spend the day with you, do you understand? Let's not ruin things.'

'But you left!' I'd screamed, shocking myself.

She'd closed her eyes briefly then opened them. 'I love you and respect you so I'm going to be honest with you, all right?'

I didn't say anything, too scared to open my mouth, too curious too. Was she going to reveal some big dirty secret?

'When I met your dad,' she'd continued, 'I was young and very bored. And when I say bored, I mean bored with all the bohemian arty boys that kept asking me out after I moved to London. Your dad was different, *completely* different in his Marks & Spencer suit and slicked-back hair. And a car, he had a proper car! I ran into his arms just to show everyone I was *different*.' She'd sighed then, hands squeezing the steering wheel as she'd stared ahead of her. 'But that's never a good reason to be with someone. There needs to be some depth of feeling. Do you understand?'

I'd opened my mouth and closed it, unsure what to say, feeling out of my depth with such a grown-up conversation.

'Your dad's a wonderful man,' she'd said, her face soft. 'But because we never started with strong foundations, with good pure reasons for being together . . . it was bound to crumble when the going got tough. And the going's been getting particularly tough lately.'

'Just because you argued with Erin?' I'd spat, still angry.

She'd got that pained expression on her face that she always got when her old best friend was mentioned. 'Not just that. Look, whatever happened between your dad and me doesn't mean what you and I have isn't strong. You're the one strong piece of foundation we have and our bond is very very special because we're mother and daughter. So don't go pulling faces and getting into a strop. You're very special, you see, and special girls are grown up enough to know the way the world is. And the way it is is simple: I love you and your dad loves you and there's a picnic in the back of this car that's waiting to be eaten. All right?'

Then she'd smiled at me, that huge beaming smile, and I couldn't help but smile back. We spent the rest of the day outdoors, eating food and running around with promises at the end to see each other again in two weeks' time.

But those two weeks went by with not a word from Mum. Then another two weeks, then a month, and my resentment began to build again so that by the next time I saw her two months later, we had to go through the same routine. I'd taken it so personally then, the way she just disappeared, even when Dad said that was the way she coped with her guilt. By not seeing me, she didn't need to face that guilt. If it were me, I'd have dealt with the guilt by seeing my girls as much as possible. But Mum wasn't like that. She crumbled under pressure, just as she had when she and Erin argued.

Maybe that's why she hasn't talked to me for two years: perhaps the guilt is particularly unbearable with Olivia and

Chloe there to remind her of the way I was back then and what she did by walking out on me when I was a kid?

'Louise?' I look up to see Sam standing over me wearing the same T-shirt he was wearing the night before. I wonder if he's been volunteering all night. 'How'd it go with Jay?' he asks, sinking down into the seat across from me.

'He didn't turn up.'

'Shit. Sorry.'

'Not just that.' I try to control the tremble in my voice. 'I discovered where Mum was staying so spoke to the hotel manager. She thinks she went to Ko Phi Phi Don.'

His face drops.

'It's terrible out there,' I continue, desperate to continue talking, anything but stop and break down. 'I've seen the news, I . . .' But it's too late. My voice breaks and I put my head in my hands as the tears come, feeling Sam's hand on my shoulder. After a while, I look up at him. 'I need to go to Ko Phi Phi Don. But I don't think there are any tourist boats going there. Can you help?'

He considers it a moment then nods. 'I know someone with a boat, he owes me. I can make some calls.'

He pulls his phone out and starts talking in Thai. When he puts it down, he looks at me. 'My friend said he'll help get us over there. The authorities aren't letting many people go to the island but he can pull a few strings. He won't be free for an hour or so though, that okay? Maybe we can hang out here, get something to eat?'

After we order some food, I tell Sam about what I've learned from my internet investigations.

'God, yeah, I remember that shooting in Exmoor,' he says. 'How do you think your mum knew Holly James?'

'No idea.'

'Maybe the whole reason your mum came out here was

127

to find Holly James? In fact, she may have come out with Claire Shreve to find her. You said there were articles suggesting Holly was out of control? They could have been coming out to do an intervention or something.'

'But it doesn't make sense. Mum would need to be really close to Holly or Claire to do that and she never mentioned either to me. Unless she met them in the past two years. Can you ask your mum? Maybe my mum mentioned something to her?'

'Yeah, of course. It's the middle of the night there now but I can call her later.' He peers towards Claire's atlas, which is sticking out of my bag. 'In the meantime, why don't you have a look through the atlas properly, see if you can find a connection between your mum and Holly James? And maybe a clue to where she is now?'

I think of Claire again, lying dead in that temple. And here we are talking about pawing through her special atlas. 'I don't know, it's not mine to look through.'

'It's not like you know where Claire's family live to return it to them right now, surely it wouldn't be so wrong if we searched the other pockets to see if there's any mention of your mum? Desperate measures and all that? And anyway, I'm sure Claire wouldn't mind if it meant helping you. I know I wouldn't.'

Maybe she wouldn't mind? She seemed nice in her photos, and the brief glimpses I'd seen of the articles she'd written suggested she was the sort of person who wanted to help people. 'Maybe you're right,' I say.

He pulls the atlas from my bag and lays it on the table between us. 'Ready?'

I straighten my shoulders, ignoring the guilt. 'Okay. Let's do this.'

We fan through the pages until we find another stuffed

pocket, this one next to the map of Serbia. I look inside, finding a pamphlet with a clenched fist printed on the front, then another photo of Milo James. This time he's with Claire and they're staring into each other's eyes like there's no one else on earth.

Will and I never look at each other like that. Is it because we have two little girls jumping on our bed most mornings? Judging from that article Claire had written, she and Milo never had children. Surely two beautiful daughters trump intense looks of love?

Sam pulls out another item, a small article about a Serbian dog sanctuary with a note clipped to it.

Claire,

I thought you'd enjoy this. You must visit again. But no Milo, understand?

Nikola x

'He clearly doesn't like Milo,' I say.

'I guess it takes a certain kind of person to shoot your own brother.'

'But he did it to stop his brother killing others. I think that's quite brave.'

The waitress brings over our toasties. 'I couldn't do it.'

'I could do it for my girls.' I put my sandwich to the side, I really can't face food at that moment. Then I continue looking through the atlas, finding another full pocket next to the map of Finland.

'A Christmas card,' Sam says, pulling out part of a festive card, its pieces taped back together, a sentence or two just about legible on what remains of the inside:

129

. . . can't continue. Please come back for Christmas, we're all worried. Lots of love. M
x

'M as in Milo?' Sam says as he examines the card.

'Maybe.'

In the same pocket is another photo of Claire and Milo, this time with Holly and the blond boy from the Thai photo. They're all smiling and bundled up in layers, hints of a snowy landscape behind them. They look like a family. There's another photo too, of Milo holding a rope above his head with a reindeer in the background, the sky a dewy pink overhead.

I quickly shove the photo back into the pocket and flick through the rest of the atlas, finding postcards with short messages scrawled on the back from someone called 'Daddy Bo'. There are more tourism leaflets too, ticket stubs from concerts around the world, old photos of what looks like Claire as she was growing up against different backdrops: a tiny cherub-faced girl of about six who I presume is Claire with another blonde girl – her sister? – jumping in the air under a bushy olive tree. Then there's another showing Claire as a pretty teenager, one slim brown leg slung over a wild-looking horse while the other leg balances on a plastic box, hands clutched tight onto the horse's speckled mane. She's high up on some mountain overlooking hundreds of dark green pine trees and a huge sparkling lake, and next to her is a man who has her brown eyes, shaggy blond hair and a deeply tanned, lined face.

They look like a happy bohemian family on their travels. How different Claire's childhood was from mine. Our holidays consisted of trips to the UK's miserable seaside towns, invariably always choosing the one rainy week of the summer. We'd hire a freezing cottage with hot water that never worked, and Mum would set her easel up in whichever room had the best view of the windy, rainswept sea. It would have been wonderful to enjoy horse rides on stunning mountaintops and visits to olive groves. My life feels very small in comparison.

But then I've *made* two lives, haven't I? Our three small lives shine bright enough together.

Sam turns to the last map – a map of Australia – and pulls out a small painting of a snake curled around itself, its skin covered with red and yellow dots against a fiery orange background.

'Here's another photo of Holly James,' Sam says, pulling out a photo from behind the painting. Holly's leaning against a large tree, a hazy red landscape behind her. 'That's the Red Centre in Oz,' he says. 'I went there a few years back.'

'What's it like?' I ask, leaning forward. I remember watching a documentary about the Red Centre in the middle of the night once while feeding Chloe the week she was born. I'd yearned to be there, anywhere but in the UK's freezing cold with a husband who barely lifted a finger to help and a baby who didn't seem to stop screaming. I felt guilty when daylight came, cuddling Chloe close and whispering there was nowhere I'd rather be right then.

'It's one of the most fascinating places I've been,' Sam says now. 'I remember the long sparse dusty-red roads the most. Kangaroos would bounce along beside us as we travelled from place to place and then, suddenly, a huge mountain range would appear.' He smiles. 'It was so hot when I went, I needed to take a swig of water every five minutes. It felt like I could smell the heat sometimes, you know? A dusty, scorched kind of smell.'

That's just how I imagined it as I'd watched the documentary that winter night. Scorched and dusty. Somewhere I could only dream of visiting.

'That's it,' Sam says, gently placing each item back in the pockets, scraps of Claire's exciting life.

I sigh. 'Nothing much to help us.' I lean back in my chair, feeling frustrated. 'I think Mum would be mortified if she knew I was the sole person in charge of finding her.'

'Why'd you say that?'

'I spend my days cleaning jam off the walls and explaining why it isn't a good idea to put orange juice into the CD player, that's why. She'd have been better off with someone like Claire Shreve as a daughter; she'd know where to look.'

Sam smiles. 'You're doing a great job, Louise. I'm sure your mum'd be delighted to know you're on the case.'

'I doubt it. I always get the impression she doesn't think much of me, to be honest.'

'Don't say that.'

'Why not? Isn't it healthy to face the truth? Won't it just infect me, keeping it all inside? A hippy like you would think that anyway.'

He raises an eyebrow. 'Hippy?'

'I meant it in a nice way!' I say, feeling mortified. I hadn't meant to say that out loud. Anyway, I did mean it in a nice way. Sam seems so caring, so thoughtful.

'It's fine, it's true,' he says. 'I *would* say something like that. But in your case, I'd actually say dwelling on those negative thoughts is infecting you. Buddhists see forgiveness as a way to keep yourself good and pure, resentment as a way of infecting yourself.'

'I don't resent Mum.'

'I mean yourself,' he says softly. 'By suggesting she wouldn't want you to look for her, that she didn't think much of you. I think you'll find it's not true.'

I look down at my untouched sandwich. Maybe he's right?

'I guess there's only one way to find out,' I say, pulling stuff out of my bag to get to my purse.

'Who's that pictured with your mum?' Sam asks as he picks up one of the photos I'd grabbed of Mum before going to the airport.

'Mum's best friend, Erin.' They're just teenagers in it, arms slung around each other, a harbour in the background, hair swishing about in the wind. Mum looks so young in it, so beautiful, just like I remember. 'Why?' I ask Sam.

'She looks an awful lot like Holly James.'

I stare at Erin and realise he's right: she has the same oval green eyes and vibrant red hair as Holly. I pull out the photo of Holly James from Claire's atlas. Now I see them side by side, I can see just how similar they look.

'Erin did have a daughter, but I never knew much about her. Surely Mum would have told me if her best friend was married to someone like Dale James though?' I say. 'Or maybe not. It's not like we talked all the time, even before her silent treatment.'

'It would explain the connection between your mother and Claire Shreve . . . and why your mother was so keen to come here.'

'To find Erin through Holly?'

Sam shrugs. 'Maybe. If she'd seen the photos of Holly in the press, she'd know exactly where she was. She might have come out here to find her, maybe even thinking Erin was here too.'

I look at the photo of Mum and Erin. So this all comes back to Erin again.

I sigh. Didn't it always?

Chapter Seven

Venice, Italy
1998

Venice reeks of secrets. Its air is heavy with them; its narrow alleyways and shadowed canals tailored for them. As Claire strolled around Venice the May following that terrible evening in Exmoor, her heart was heavy with secrets: the feel of Milo's fingertips pressed against her thighs, the way his skin felt against hers.

And as she looked at Ben across the table from her, all she could do was wrap a fist around her traitorous heart and squeeze the images away, images brought back with a vengeance as Milo's court case for shooting his brother unrolled back in the UK.

'Hello? Earth to Claire,' Ben said, waving his hand in front of her face.

She looked up from the pasta she couldn't eat. 'Sorry. What were you saying?'

'I think we should buy some masks. We can try that night market we passed yesterday?'

God, he was trying so hard. She mentally picked herself up and forced some of the thick creamy Bigoli pasta into her mouth. This was the path fate had steered her down;

the one she'd started years ago with her husband, not Milo. Things were good. Things were safe.

'Sounds great,' she said, smiling.

They ate in silence before Ben looked up again. 'You had another nightmare last night.'

Claire paused mid-chew. 'What did I say?'

'Same. *Milo.*' His voice grew tight, strangling Milo's name.

Claire tried to control her face. She'd said Milo's *name* in her sleep?

'Might be worth mentioning it to your therapist?' Ben suggested.

'Good idea,' she said, trying to keep her voice steady.

Ben smiled. 'Good. I'm sure it's very normal, the sleep-talking. But just in case.'

'Of course.'

She looked out at the shiny black canal that stretched below their window beneath solemn night skies, the buildings across from them turned gaudy gold by yellow lanterns. In the distance, a gondola passed, a young couple giggling as they cuddled up to each other.

Claire hadn't told Ben about what happened that night, nor the therapist he'd insisted she see. As far as he was concerned she'd been in the hotel's toilets when Dale marched into the marquee and started shooting at the wedding guests before Milo accosted him, only coming out of the toilets when the police turned up. That was the way Milo wanted it told, after all.

'You can't tell anyone you were here,' Milo had pleaded just after Claire had pulled Holly out from under the table and Milo's sister Jen had appeared, trembling with grief and shock. 'Do you understand, Claire?' Milo had continued. 'I don't want you tangled up in this.'

'But—'

He'd grabbed her shoulders and looked into her eyes, his own dark gaze desperate. 'Claire, I'm begging you, please don't say anything. You went to the toilet, heard the noise, locked yourself in. Please promise me that's what you'll tell the police? Please?'

She'd looked into his eyes for a few moments, trying to wrap her head around what he was asking of her. Was he doing it for her, a married woman, so the kiss they'd shared didn't somehow get out? It felt like more than that, like he didn't want her tainted with what his brother had done.

A tear escaped one of his eyes and she nodded, mute, watching as it slid into the cut on his cheek, mingling with the blood there and turning it pink. It was all she could do right in that moment, agree with a man cradling his dead brother.

'Go,' he'd said, shoving her away when she'd tried to touch him.

When the police arrived, she'd watched them take Milo from the marquee, his face blank and smeared with his brother's blood. Afterwards, she'd been shuffled into the inn's dining room with all the other wedding guests, her mind a mush of Milo, of the blood, of the terrible screams. In the confusion of the night, she wasn't even questioned by the police: an inexperienced officer who'd since been the subject of a bashing from the media had told her and a few others they could go home. She'd wanted to tell the police the truth, of course. But Milo had been so vehement and she really wasn't thinking straight. So she just kept quiet.

Stupid, stupid girl.

She'd regretted it ever since. It had been difficult avoiding the story for the past few months. At first, she'd been desperate to fill in the gaps of what had happened that night by watching the news reports and scouring the papers; how Dale had strode into the marquee and started randomly shooting at the wedding guests before finally finding what some of the media were saying was his target: Sarah, the beautiful bride. If it hadn't been for the fact that most of the guests were gathered at the back of the marquee at that moment for the buffet, there would have been more injuries; deaths too. He'd injured a further six people. He'd then gone to find his own daughter, Holly. It was at that point that Milo appeared, according to the papers, and wrestled the gun off his brother, shooting him by accident in the process. Holly had witnessed everything.

Ben lifted his fork towards her, a bloody piece of boar's meat on the end. 'You're right, it's delicious. I need to try more of this exotic food! Want to try some?'

'No, it's okay, I'm actually not that—'

'I insist,' he said, the fork coming towards her. 'You won't regret it.'

She forced herself to lean over to take a bite, her stomach churning as she tasted the blood on her tongue. She usually loved boar's meat, first tasting it when she was just six during a visit to an olive tree orchard in the heart of Umbria. As she chewed it now, she realised it was nothing in comparison here in Venice and double the price.

She swallowed it down anyway, quickly taking a sip of overpriced red wine, then forcing a smile. 'Yes, it's nice.'

She'd promised herself she'd make the effort but as each day went past since she and Ben had agreed to make it work, it was getting harder and harder not to regret her decision to stay with him. The horror of what she'd seen that day in Exmoor had made her vulnerable and desperate for safety and stability – something she knew Ben could offer. She'd known it had been selfish, thinking like that, and had resisted his attempts to get back together at first. But he'd persisted and it had felt so easy.

Not now. Now it was even harder than before Exmoor.

That night, she couldn't sleep. She tried to read but the words blurred before her eyes, the red wine she'd had earlier making her head woozy. So she turned the TV on with the volume down, flicking through the channels. Suddenly, Milo appeared on screen. Claire clutched the remote control tight to her chest. It was the same footage that had appeared on TV from a few hours after the shooting: Milo walking down the path from the farm, head down, hair matted with blood; stitches now binding the jagged cut that tore across the top of his cheek. Cameras flashing, the journalists who'd managed to get there jostling for position. Emblazoned at the bottom of the screen was *Exmoor Wedding Shooting*. Then beneath it: *Milo James in court for brother's manslaughter*.

He'd been arrested that night, sources telling journalists that the detective in charge hadn't 'felt right' about Milo's version of events, something backed up by the fact locals told the media the two brothers had a fractious relationship when Dale had returned from the Falklands. But policeman's intuition and idle gossip weren't enough for the Crown Prosecution Service to charge him for murder so manslaughter was the charge in the end. Milo was granted bail, not deemed to be a threat to the public.

Claire had done so well to avoid news of the shooting after her initial desperate need to learn more had worn off. But the past few days it had been everywhere and right now, it was like Milo was right there in the hotel room with her as he stared out of the TV screen. She'd seen the very same footage on the early morning news the day after the shooting. She'd been staying at her sister's. It was on the way back from Exmoor and that was the excuse she'd used at the time. But the truth was, she couldn't possibly return to the home she shared with Ben, despite his desperate phone calls to her after he'd heard the news. Apparently the idea of losing her had made him regret his request for them to have a break from each other. Her mind had been too rammed full of what had happened in Exmoor to face him . . . and of the moments she'd shared with Milo. He'd made her feel like she had before her father died, buzzing with the promise of future adventures. She'd sent him a letter a couple of weeks after that, telling him she was there for him if he needed to talk. It hadn't seemed right to just cut off contact. She got a note back very quickly on a grubby bit of paper, just one line: *It's best we forget what happened between us. Sorry. M*

Her whole body had burned with humiliation after reading that. She realised she had no choice but to treasure those few days as a special memory, nothing more. So she gave up on him, even when she got a couple of phone calls from anonymous numbers and all she'd hear was soft breathing on the other side. She refused to allow herself to believe it was Milo, the memories of the way he'd touched her that night, the catch in his breath as he'd held her turning into figments of her imagination, wisps of smoke swept away on a wind of tragedy.

And it had worked for a while as she focused on her job, agreeing to more press trips than ever. But when she'd got back with Ben, she couldn't help but compare the two men: where Ben dreamed of a bigger house and a new car, Milo dreamed of mango farms in distant lands; where Ben tuned out when she talked to him about the countries she'd visited, Milo had listened, eyes intense; where Ben thought life couldn't be whole without children, Milo thought it might just open up more possibilities.

She peered up at the TV screen again just in time to see Milo lash out at the cameraman in front of him, swiping at his face like a wolf might. Next to her, Ben stirred but didn't wake. She pressed her finger on the off button and ran into the bathroom, closing the door and sitting on the edge of the bath, taking in deep gulps as her nails pressed into the enamel. This couldn't keep happening. She had to get on with her life; a life on the *right* path with her husband and the future they could create together.

The mask Ben handed her the next evening was a sad white one with black feathers dipping over its right eye.

'Like it?' he asked. 'We can hang it in our downstairs bathroom, would look nice with that Eiffel Tower statue we got a few years back.'

She thought of their bathroom – or, as Ben proudly told friends who visited, their 'shrine to travel' – rammed full of all the souvenirs Ben insisted Claire brought back from her trips, as well as items he bought during their holidays. It made her cringe whenever she was in there.

'If you want it,' she said absent-mindedly, trailing her hand over another mask, a red one with a long nose and silver sequins around its eyes. She picked it up and pressed it against her face, turning to Ben. He laughed, and pulled her into a hug, the nose of the mask poking into his cheek. She made herself laugh too, focusing on how handsome he looked when he laughed like that, his smile deep and wide, his green eyes sparkling. She reached up, sweeping his strawberry-blond hair away from his forehead. His grip tightened, his face growing serious.

'Shall we go back to the hotel?' he murmured into her ear.

An older couple watched them, smiling at the happy young couple. But when she looked into Ben's eyes, she felt nothing. Why couldn't she find the roar of emotions she used to feel for him?

'Masks first, young man,' she said, swallowing down the doubts. 'Then I have to take some scenic night-time shots for the magazine.'

'I'm very lucky,' Ben said, wrapping his arm around her shoulders and winking at her. 'Not many people can say they get free holidays as part of the marriage package.'

'Not really free,' Claire said. 'I'm officially working, remember? We could've booked that remote cottage in the Isle of Skye I found instead.'

He wrinkled his nose. 'Bit in the middle of nowhere.' He looked around the shop at all the overpriced masks and fake gold gondolas. 'This is much better, even if you do have to work.' He leaned in close, his lips brushing against her cheek. 'But tonight you have a break, I have other plans for you.'

She laughed. 'All right, all right. Now what mask do you want?'

'The red mask!'

'You sure?'

'Anything to get us back to the hotel as soon as possible.'

When they got to their hotel – a small but ornate building directly overlooking a canal – they stumbled into their room, Ben's lips pressing against Claire's neck, her hand reaching for his belt. Then she suddenly saw Milo's face as he'd looked during the moments they'd shared on the riverbank. She closed her eyes, pleased it was too dark for Ben to see the look on her face.

Ben paused. 'You okay?'

'Fine, just woozy from the wine.' She trailed her fingers down his back, trying to lose herself in the moment. As he touched her and made love to her, she arched her back and made all the right noises.

She needed this to work.

After, he pulled her against his chest and they stared up at the ceiling until their heartbeats slowed.

'I've been thinking,' he said after a while. 'Maybe we should give IVF another go?'

He peered down at Claire, eyes hopeful.

'Remember what the consultant said to us last time we saw him?' she said softly.

'That's just one consultant, Claire. I really think we should give it one more shot.'

The road he had planned seemed to crash through the hotel room, their future spreading out before her. A year, maybe two, of countless injections and sore, bruised thighs; lonely train journeys for yet more scans; headaches and nausea and debilitating mood swings; then the pregnancy tests, all negative, because what else would they be with her problems? There'd need to come a point where they'd admit defeat, maybe during the tense 'weekend away to regroup' that always followed a failed round at some characterless luxury chain hotel. As for the years that would follow, all she saw were silent dinners in their large kitchen; more work trips for her just so she could get away from the tension; then maybe Ben would turn to drink like his father did.

It was better they didn't waste their time filled with false hope.

'Oh Ben, we can't wish our lives away on something that will never happen,' she said as carefully as she could. 'I'd so love it if we could focus on doing all the things we wouldn't be able to do if we had children, like I suggested the other week: taking time off to travel. Make all our friends with kids green with envy?'

'But you travel for work!' Desperation flickered over his face. 'Lauren and Aiden got pregnant on their fifth attempt, Lauren herself said she thinks it's because she did all that

142

positive thinking stuff.' He folded his arms and turned away. 'You're always so bloody negative about it.'

'Lauren hasn't got my problems, Ben! She produced three times the amount of eggs I did each round. We need to be realistic, darling, we need to move on.'

She put her hand on his shoulder but he moved away from her, jaw flexing.

'Fine, I shouldn't have mentioned it.' He jumped out of bed. 'I'm having a shower.'

He stormed into the bathroom and slammed the door. Claire slumped against her pillow, biting her nails. He was so desperate for a family and so intent on glossing over the reality of their situation. But she couldn't give him what he wanted and she felt terrible about that.

She looked around the hotel room; at the bottle of cheap Prosecco glistening under the light of the bedside lamp; the sheen of the silk covers tangled around her feet. Then she stared at the house across from their room. It was falling apart, its walls pink with mildew, bits of it crumbling away. She'd rather be there than here, at least it was *real*.

Pink crumbling rocks, the strange gaping emptiness of it all.

Isn't that what Milo had said about Venice? She squeezed her face into her pillow, driving the memories away of him.

Claire watched Ben approach her table the next morning, his expression solemn, a newspaper tucked tight under his arm. She understood how hard this was for him, but she was the one who'd have to go through all the physical turmoil of yet another round of IVF.

When Ben got to their table, he didn't sit down, instead placing the newspaper on the table and peering over to the buffet area.

'Want some more juice?' he asked in a stiff voice.

'No, I'm fine thanks.'

He strode over to a buffet table, passing the *fette biscottate* she'd opted for, a delicious hard sweet bread, and headed towards the English fried breakfast area just as he had each morning they'd been here.

A waitress approached Claire's table. 'Anything else?' she asked in a bored voice.

She wondered what Milo would go for. Probably a *caffè corretto*. It was the drink her dad always enjoyed during their visits to Italy, a shot of espresso mixed with grappa, an Italian brandy. He used to say it gave him the perfect kick in the backside each morning. She needed that right now.

She ordered it and a few minutes later her waitress brought it over. Claire lifted it to her nose, breathing in its subtle grapey aroma, then took a sip, the alcohol and coffee mixture going straight to her tired brain. As she reached for Ben's paper, she spluttered on her drink. On the front page was a photo of the groom from the Exmoor wedding, Matt Levine. Claire knew she ought to put it aside but she couldn't resist reading the article.

Dale James 'laid down gun before being shot'

Nathan Styles reports

Exmoor groom Matthew Levine told Exeter Crown Court yesterday that he heard Dale James shout out 'Okay, I've put the gun down!' a few moments before his brother shot him, adding to the prosecution's case against Milo James's self-defence plea. Investment banker Levine was recounting the moments just after his new wife, Sarah Levine, was tragically shot dead. As the only witness outside the James family to observe the confrontation between the two brothers,

> his testimony is crucial, especially because it contradicts Milo James's statement that the gun went off by accident while he tried to wrestle it off his brother.

She looked at the photo of the journalist, a man with a squint and receding hair. He must have been referring to the moments before Claire entered the marquee. Was he really implying Milo hadn't acted in self-defence? She'd presumed Milo would easily get let off. Even her sister Sofia, who was a solicitor, had said it was a formality. The police had to charge Milo, but there was no way he'd go down for it. It suddenly all seemed so different now.

Ben approached the table so she quickly shoved the paper back to his side of the table and took a big gulp of her drink.

'They didn't have any bacon left,' Ben said as he sat down.

'Hmmm,' was all Claire could muster, the article still strong in her mind.

'You okay?'

She looked up at Ben. 'Yes, fine.'

He sighed. 'Look, about last night. I shouldn't be pushing you, it's too soon.'

She put her hand over his and smiled with relief. 'It's fine, but I just need some time to get my head around the future. We both do.'

Her eyes strayed back to the paper. Could Milo really be sent to prison for murdering his brother? It wasn't right! Claire had been with him right before he ran into the marquee, she knew his state of mind. He loved his brother and would never have hurt him unless in self-defence.

'So, with time, are you saying there's a chance we might try IVF again?' Ben asked, his voice hopeful.

She looked back at him, the article whirling around in her mind with the grappa and coffee. 'Ben, we—'

'Let's just leave it at that. Keep an open mind.'

'Right,' she said, thinking of Milo locked up in prison. 'Open mind.'

'To us,' Ben said, raising his glass of champagne the next evening. 'Happy anniversary, babe.'

Claire clinked her glass against his just as a cheer went up from the crowds around them. Their hotel was ideally placed to watch the Vogalonga, the rowing regatta that took place in May each year. The building had a magnificent balcony, gilded gold with tiny caricatures of birds all over it. Claire and Ben were two of the lucky few who were being treated to a champagne lunch as they watched the dozens of boats float by. The canal danced with colour, reds, greens and blues, flags fluttering in the wind, oars battling each other as the boats crowded into the water. Claire smiled, feeling more optimistic. Ben hadn't mentioned the IVF thing all day. In fact, he'd talked about looking for a new house that morning, 'somewhere in the middle of nowhere, just us two'. It wasn't quite taking time off to travel, but it was a hint he might be willing to carve out a different kind of life that didn't include having a family.

'So,' Ben said, turning back to Claire, 'we're not just celebrating the fact we've been married for five years today but also how we've overcome everything we've been through the past few months. I really didn't think we'd get here, Claire.'

'But we have, haven't we?' The champagne and the atmosphere were making her feel optimistic again. Maybe things could really work out between them.

'We certainly have.' He took a deep breath, placing his free hand over hers. 'I don't want to dwell too much on the bad stuff. But all those months ago, when I saw the name of your hotel flash up alongside the word "shooting" that day . . .' He sighed, shaking his head. 'All I could think about was that terrible conversation we'd had before you left and how little I'd done to save our marriage.' He leaned forward, looking into her eyes. 'I'd given up on our dream, Claire, we'd *both* given up. Not only on us, but a family too.'

Claire paused mid-sip, disappointment flooding through her. Why couldn't he accept that wouldn't happen?

'I know you need time,' he said, noticing the look on her face. 'But, like we agreed yesterday morning, that doesn't mean we can't try again in the future. We need to keep an open mind.'

Had they agreed that?

A boat passed directly beneath them, carrying five men dressed in striped red and white T-shirts, a length of ruby chiffon draped all around the boat, plump red roses dangling from its sides. One of the men peered up at her and bowed before blowing her a kiss. Claire waved back, trying to force herself to get into the spirit of things.

Ben took a quick sip of his champagne too and laughed nervously. 'This is going to sound stupid but when I got that call from you to say you were unharmed, I made a list of all the things I should've done to save our marriage and I promised I would do every single one. And that's what I did over those few months you lived with your sister. Now look at us! When we kissed that night, and then it started to snow, it was just – well, perfect. I knew we were starting to heal ourselves then; heal our marriage.'

But Claire wasn't healed, was she? And she was going to be dragging Ben into a childless life with a wounded, barren her.

'Thank you, Claire,' Ben said, squeezing her hand. 'Thank you for giving us another chance.'

Was she really giving him a chance? He could be so much

happier with another woman: a *fertile* woman who could give him all he wanted. A woman who in turn would be happy too – because she herself wasn't happy, was she?

He raised his glass again. 'So another toast. The future!'

Claire lifted her glass, her hand shaking as she contemplated their future together. Champagne sloshed over the edge of the glass onto the sleeve of Ben's blue shirt.

'Sorry,' she gasped.

He quickly mopped it up with his napkin as he smiled at her. She looked into his eyes and realised with shock she desperately wanted to be looking into another pair of eyes: Milo's dark eyes.

'I can't do this to you,' she said. 'I can't pretend any more.'

His face drained of all its colour and Claire felt sick with guilt. But she couldn't carry on the charade, it wasn't fair on him.

'You deserve better than me,' she said, reaching for her bag, unable to see him looking at her like that. 'I'm sorry, Ben.'

Then she ran from the balcony, the roar of the regatta pounding in her ears.

Chapter Eight

'Can I ask why you didn't give a statement to the police after that night, Miss Shreve?' the barrister for the prosecution asked, a petite Indian woman with strange blue eyes that seemed to drill right into Claire's.

Claire felt her heart thump like a boxer's fist, the gravity of what she was doing really hitting her. She looked up at Milo but his head was still bowed, his black suit loose on his now-thin frame.

It had been an impulsive decision to call his barrister when she arrived back in the UK a couple of days before. On the flight home, she'd felt this overwhelming urge to help Milo by putting herself forward as a witness. If she could provide evidence about his state of mind before he shot his brother, perhaps it would add weight to the fact Dale's death wasn't premeditated as the press were trying to make out? His barrister had reassured her there was a low chance of her being prosecuted for lying to the police because she'd been one of the wedding guests the police had failed to question. But sitting there right now, with everyone's eyes on her, she was starting to regret her decision. Milo had

149

barely looked at her when she'd walked in, and now the prosecution's pit-bull of a barrister was laying into her.

She felt so desperately alone. She'd told Jodie about her decision to come here, but her friend had had to fly to Estonia that morning for a film festival she'd helped organise. She peered towards the public galleries. Among the sea of faces were the groom Matt Levine and his friend, Jay Hemingford. Jay had become a bit of a media star since that evening, giving interviews, even writing a few articles for the *Daily Telegraph* about what had happened. A few rows behind them was Nathan Styles, the journalist whose article she'd read in Venice.

Claire fiddled with one of the pearl earrings Jodie had suggested she wear and looked back at the barrister. 'I didn't want my husband to find out I'd been with another man. I was in shock too.'

'So to *hide* the fact you were being unfaithful to your husband, you decided to withhold vital information,' the barrister snapped.

'I—' Claire paused, her mouth going dry. She peered towards the public galleries again and Matt Levine stared back at her with red-rimmed eyes. Her own eyes started filling with tears. What the hell had she been thinking coming here? She looked up at Milo and was surprised to see his head was lifted now and he was staring at her with his intense brown gaze. Her stomach did a flip. He leaned forward, hands clutching at the rail in front of him, and mouthed two words: *It's okay.*

She took a deep breath and squared her shoulders. 'I apologise for that,' she said to the barrister, trying to keep the tremble from her voice. 'I was scared. But I'm here now and I'm telling the truth because it's the right thing to do.'

Milo leaned back, face unreadable again.

'You were scared? Do you mean scared of what Milo James would say if you went to the police?'

Milo frowned.

'No!' Claire said. 'I'm not scared of Milo, nobody should be, he's a kind—'

'Why are you coming forward now?' the barrister asked, her face hardening as she leaned towards Claire.

'People need to know I was with Milo before what happened and there was absolutely no suggestion he wanted to intentionally kill his brother. He loved his brother!'

'Have you been in contact with Milo James since that night, Miss Shreve?'

Claire looked up at him and noticed his shoulders tense.

'Miss Shreve?' the barrister pushed.

'No, I haven't seen Milo James since that night.'

'How would you describe your feelings towards him?'

'I barely know him. But what I do know of him, he's a good man and he was acting completely normal the moments before he saved all those people from his brother.'

Milo held Claire's gaze a few brief seconds, his face softening.

'But you clearly care for him,' the barrister said, 'so much so, you'd be willing to lie and say you spent time with him before the shooting?'

'I wouldn't do that.'

The barrister looked towards the jury. 'Most people wouldn't keep such a thing a secret for eight months. I think that's everything. Thank you.'

Claire stood up on shaky legs and walked away from the dock. As she passed under the area where Milo was sitting, he looked down at her, his brown eyes indecipherable. Had she made things worse for him? She thought she'd done a good job of explaining his state of mind when his defence barrister questioned her ten minutes ago. But it had all gone to pieces when the prosecution barrister had approached the witness stand.

She rushed down the walkway, desperate to get out as everyone's eyes focused on her. As soon as she got outside, she sank down onto a bench, putting her head in her hands. What if she *had* made things worse? If Milo was sent to prison, she'd never forgive herself.

Her phone buzzed. Her sister Sofia. Could she know already? She took a deep breath and put the phone to her ear.

'Claire, is that you?' Sofia's voice sounded panicked, out of breath.

She knew.

'Yes, Sofia.'

'My PA was just listening to the radio and told me you came forward as a witness for Milo James. Are you okay?'

'I guess.'

'What happened in Exmoor? Is it true you slept with him?'

'No! It was just a kiss. Is that what they said on the radio, that I slept with him?'

'They implied it. My God, Claire, the press are going to tear you apart.'

Claire's shoulders slumped. It was completely out of control, she'd been a fool to do this.

'I don't understand all this, why didn't you tell me?' Sofia asked.

'I – I don't know.'

'I thought you were still in Venice with Ben.'

Claire took in a deep breath. *Here goes.* 'Ben and I have split up.'

'When?'

'While in Venice.'

'And you didn't think to call me?'

'I didn't want to upset you.'

'Mum's going to have a hissy fit when she hears.'

Claire pressed her finger into a crack in the wall. 'Sofia, I—'

'Milo *James*, Claire? Milo bloody James?'

'I don't know what to say. It just happened.'

'With a murderer?'

'He saved people!'

'By killing his own brother.'

'Jesus, Sofia! He had no choice, Dale James was about to kill his niece.'

Sofia paused a few moments. 'Come stay with us, Claire,' she said after a while, her voice softer. 'We're all so worried about you. You need family at a time like this.'

Claire suddenly felt a need to be with her sister; to wrap herself up in her arms and cry like she used to when she was a kid, regardless of how judgemental she'd be when she arrived. She couldn't bear the thought of going back to Jodie's empty house. 'Okay, I'll drive back now.'

After they'd said their goodbyes, Claire leaned her head back against the cool wall, trying to pull herself together. At least she'd done it. Now she could put it behind her.

'Are you okay?' a familiar voice asked. She turned to see Matt Levine's friend Jay standing nearby wearing a navy suit and crisp white shirt. The last time she'd seen him, he'd been begging her not to go into the marquee. She wished she hadn't now: she'd made no difference to events and Milo wouldn't have had a chance to ask her to lie. She could have been open from the start.

'Not really,' Claire said.

Jay sat down on the bench next to her. 'It was very brave of you.'

'Stupid more like. I suppose Matt must hate me?'

He frowned. 'Why?'

'Fraternising with the brother of the man who killed his wife?'

'I think he's a bit shocked by the turn of events. But he doesn't *hate* you. You didn't pick up the gun and shoot Sarah, did you?'

Claire looked down at her hands. 'No.'

They both looked out into the large empty hallway, marble floors glistening under the sunlight streaming through the high windows above.

'I thought Sarah and Matt had got out,' Jay said after a while, raking his hands through his curly blond hair. 'I couldn't find them in all the madness, I had no idea they were under that table. I wouldn't have left the marquee if I'd known.'

Claire turned to him. 'I'm sorry, I know you were close to Sarah.'

'Yes, she was very special,' he said sadly. 'I was at the front of the marquee, you know, one of the first people to see Dale James when he marched in. Silly really,' he continued, smoothing a non-existent crease out of his trousers, 'but I thought at first that's what farmer types do, stroll into weddings with a gun in their hand. But then there was something in his eyes that made me change my mind. Then he lifted his gun and I managed to grab two little girls nearby and pull them away from sight. The gun shots . . .' He shuddered slightly. 'So loud. Then the screams, they were worse. I saw my friend Dean get a bullet to the arm. So I grabbed him and the girls then ran out with the other guests.' His eyes filled with tears. 'I really thought Sarah had got out already.'

Claire's heart went out to him and she put her hand on his arm.

154

'It must have been difficult for you too, seeing Dale James dead?' he said. 'Do you have nightmares about that night?'

She thought of the dreams she had most nights, cluttered with screams and blood and that hole in Dale James's head. 'Yes,' she said, sighing.

'Me too.'

They sat quietly for a few moments contemplating what they'd seen that night.

'So I presume your husband knows everything now?' Jay asked eventually.

Claire thought about that last night in Venice. After she'd walked from the restaurant, Ben had come to find her in their hotel room. She'd told him everything, the weight of it all finally breaking through the barriers she'd set up inside. He deserved the truth after all, no more secrets.

'You've never really left Exmoor, have you?' Ben said when Claire had finished telling him. 'You never really left *him*, did you?'

It had broken her heart to see Ben like that. On the plane journey back, she'd watched Ben as he'd slept, remembering all the times she'd done the same when they'd first married, coming home from a work trip and creeping upstairs to find him curled up with their dog Archie on the bed. She'd just stand in the doorway and watch them both, smiling. Now she was watching him with intense sadness.

As the plane had prepared to descend, she'd quickly got out her notepad, desperate to get all her feelings down. Words had always come easier to her when written down instead of spoken. So that's what she'd done – telling him how special he was, how wonderful and kind. And for this reason, he deserved someone who could give him a hundred per cent . . . a hundred per cent that included a family too. Then she'd slipped the letter into his bag.

Ben had insisted on going straight to his brother's after, so she'd returned home alone. She'd set her suitcase down in the hallway and stood quiet and still for a few moments as she'd taken in the mirrors they'd both sprayed together a year before, and the framed photos of their wedding they'd put up a week after they'd moved in. They'd been so excited and optimistic then, their terraced house with its huge garden the ideal family home. Claire had felt safe and secure in Ben's arms, excited about a future filled to the brim with babies and Sunday roasts and special memories.

How hopeful she'd been. How naïve.

Her heart ached as she thought of all that hope slowly and excruciatingly draining away; a house once filled with optimism and dreams becoming unbearable to live in, a daily reminder of the very thing she'd wished it to be but it had never become.

'Claire?' Jay said. 'I asked if your husband knows now?'

She was about to tell Jay things were over between her and Ben when something occurred to her. 'Are you trying to get a story out of me?'

He laughed. 'Claire, I'm a financial journalist, we write about stock markets and salaries. Trust me, I'm not. It's the creepy little hacks like Nathan Styles you want to watch out for.'

Claire thought of the article she'd read in Venice and the thin man sitting in the gallery. She sighed. 'Yes, my husband knows everything and it's over between us. And for the record, I didn't leave him for Milo, our marriage was over way before I met him.'

Jay tilted his head, examining her face. 'Why did you go to court for Milo James today then, bare your soul like that?'

'I don't want to see an innocent man go to prison. I thought it might help him if I told the truth.' She took in a deep breath. 'But now I think I've just made it worse.'

'Have you considered the possibility he might not be innocent? Maybe he purposefully killed his brother.'

Claire shook her head vehemently. 'No. He loved his brother.'

'They argued, according to Nathan Styles's report.'

'That's what siblings do, I argue with my sister all the time. That doesn't mean I want to kill her!'

Jay narrowed his blue eyes. 'There's something not right about Milo James. There are secrets there, I can tell. And it's not just me who thinks that. Other journalists do too. They're all digging, Claire, and one day, something will come out.'

'What do you mean?'

'I mean my antenna goes off when it comes to that family. Doesn't yours?'

She thought about seeing them all together in the pub all those months ago and how *off* it had all seemed.

'Dale James was a sick man,' she said. 'We'll never understand why he planned to do what he did, there are so many reasons – maybe it was like the psychiatrist the defence used said: post-traumatic stress from what he saw in the Falklands. Maybe it was the stress of running a farm during the BSE crisis, maybe it was because he had to bring up Holly on his own. But one thing I do know is Milo saved lives.'

'Well, all right, if you say so.' Jay adjusted his cufflinks. 'What now for you then?'

'What do you mean?'

'I mean now you and your husband have split up. People usually use it as a chance to change their lives, don't they? Yasmine, the editor I introduced you to at the wedding, thought you were great. Let me put you in touch with her again.'

'That's not exactly a drastic change, is it, working for another travel magazine? It's a superficial change, like dyeing my hair.'

157

'Then make a drastic change,' Jay said, his eyes running over Claire's newly highlighted hair. 'Run away abroad, maybe the States? That country's wonderful for journalists like you.'

She sighed. 'I don't—'

People started flooding out of the courtroom. Jay quickly reached into his pocket, pulling out a business card. 'If you ever need to talk . . .'

'I thought you weren't trying to get a story.'

'I'm not, I promise. I'm here for you, no strings attached, one Exmoor Shooting survivor to another.'

She looked into his eyes, seeing an honesty and compassion in them that made her realise he really was just trying to help. She took his business card and slipped it into her bag, then noticed Milo stride out of court with his barrister. Her heart-beat started thundering in her chest and she felt her face flush. He caught her eye then walked over as people turned to stare at them. Jay stepped away, peering down at his phone.

'Hello Claire,' Milo said quietly. He was so close, she could feel his breath on her cheek. He looked different: thinner, his hair longer, a haunting sadness in his eyes. But he was still the man she'd kissed that night in that field; who'd made her feel that old sense of adventure again.

'Hi Milo.'

He paused a moment then stepped even closer, lowering his voice. 'You shouldn't have done that, Claire.'

'I did it to protect you.'

'I appreciate that but now it's out, you'll understand why I didn't want you involved. The media won't leave you alone now. That's exactly what I was worried about.'

'I had to tell the truth,' she said. 'I couldn't let them think you planned to kill your brother. But I'm so worried I've made things worse for you. Have I?'

'I don't think they can get any worse, can they? I shot my own brother dead.' His voice cracked and he turned away. Claire put her hand on his arm, not caring if others saw, desperate to comfort him. He looked up, his face flooded with feeling and it was like it was just the two of them in that court foyer, everything around them dissolving.

Then Matt Levine walked past, throwing them a look of disgust. Reality returned and the whispers of people nearby throbbed in Claire's ears.

Milo moved away from her. 'I shouldn't have come to talk to you, it'll only make things worse for you.'

'I don't care what other people think!'

'You don't care that people know I grabbed your tits in a dark field while my brother was planning to shoot all those people?'

Her whole body turned to ice. She stepped away from him, face flushed. 'Well, if you put it like that . . .'

'Claire,' he said, his voice cracking. 'I didn't . . .'

His barrister walked over. 'We should go now, Milo.'

Claire turned away, still humiliated by what he'd said. Grabbed her tits? He made it sound like a teenage fumble. Maybe that's exactly what it was? A grubby little fumble in the dark.

She refused to turn around until she heard the click of his shoes as he walked away. The whispering grew louder, the stares even harder. She wrapped her arms around herself and bit her lip to stop the tears coming.

'Claire Shreve?' She turned to see Nathan Styles, the journalist Jay had mentioned, standing beside her. He watched her through his squinting eye, making her skin crawl. 'That was an interesting little exchange between you and Milo James.'

God, he'd heard that?

'Please, I don't need this right now,' she said, going to walk past him.

He blocked her way, slipping his business card into her bag. 'If you need to unload on anyone, I'm right here.'

'I've seen the articles you've written about Milo. There's no chance I'd talk to you.'

He raised an eyebrow, his beady eyes hardening. 'Now that's not the way to talk to someone like me.'

'That's enough, Nathan,' Jay said, stepping between them both.

'Ah, Daddy's boy comes to the rescue,' Nathan hissed, looking Jay up and down.

'Oh shut up, Styles, at least I don't ruin people's lives for a living.' He put his hand out to Claire. 'Come on. Let's get you out of here.'

She hesitated a moment then took his hand, letting him lead her from the court.

Chapter Nine

San Francisco, USA
1999

'So, what do you think?' Yasmine asked Claire as people danced behind her, working themselves into a frenzy as the countdown to the millennium approached. 'Can I tell everyone you'll be a permanent member of staff when we get back in the New Year?'

Claire hesitated a moment, peering out of the vast windows that overlooked Golden Gate Bridge. It shone bright red against the stark black sky, making everything else seem tiny and insignificant: the moon a tiny pinprick of silver in the distance, the headlights of the cars that crossed the bridge just tiny drops of white. Even the ocean seemed insignificant, its inky blackness merging into the dark sky above.

She turned back to Yasmine. 'I think I need some time to mull it over.'

A small frown appeared on Yasmine's face. She'd clearly expected Claire to say yes straight away. Hell, Claire had expected to as well! As soon as her divorce had come through, she'd decided to do what Jay had recommended and taken Yasmine up on a job offer, moving to the States to work in *Travel* magazine's West Coast office. Staying in her old job would have been a daily reminder of what she'd once hoped to be: a secure, happy mother. She needed a clean slate without remnants of her dreams staring back at her each day, and this had seemed like the ideal solution.

And it had been ideal for a while as she made new friends and travelled the world for the magazine. She'd even rented a room in one of San Francisco's 'painted ladies', the multi-coloured Edwardian houses that lined the city's Haight-Ashbury district. When its owners told her the houses had survived the 1906 earthquake despite many of the mansions in the affluent Nob Hill district crumbling to the ground, it felt like fate, staying somewhere that had survived something tragic. Maybe she'd have a chance too?

But if it was all so perfect, why was she hesitating now?

Maybe it was because it was New Year's Eve and old memories were resurfacing. When she and Ben had been trying for a baby, this had always been the hardest time of year. It all started with the Christmas cards featuring photos of new babies and happy families that landed with a thud on her doormat. Each year, those children would get older and older, another reminder of how long they'd been trying to conceive. When New Year arrived, Claire would promise herself things would be different, that by the time next Christmas arrived, she'd either be pregnant or nursing a newborn. She'd even cram pâté and brie into her mouth, joking with Ben that she wouldn't get the chance next Christmas. But as each year went by with no baby to show off, she became less and less hopeful, the reminder of the fact she hadn't fulfilled last year's resolution even more brutal.

What was her resolution this year?

'Looks like you both need a top-up,' Jay said, wandering over in his lilac designer suit and black shirt, his blond hair gelled back. They'd grown close since the court case, the occasional email turning into regular visits from Jay, both of them opening up to each other as they explored the city together, eating clam chowder on Pier 39 and shopping in the atmospheric hippy neighbourhood of Haight Street.

They were in one of his father's many houses at that very moment, a plush mansion in the middle of Nob Hill or 'Snob Hill' as Claire liked to call it. There were traces of Jay's stockbroker dad everywhere in the cold marble floors and impersonal pieces of art – except for one painting, a beautiful portrait of his mum, her curly blonde hair spilling over the shoulders of the electric-blue material of a dress she'd designed.

'I've just asked Claire if she'd like to join us as a permanent member of staff,' Yasmine said as Jay poured more champagne in both their glasses.

His face lit up. 'That's fantastic news!'

Yasmine raised a perfect eyebrow. 'She hasn't said yes yet.'

Jay shot Claire a quizzical look.

'Don't worry,' Yasmine said, putting her hand on Claire's arm. 'You can give me an answer when we're back in the New Year.' She peered around the room. 'Now, I really must find my drunk husband before he makes us both social outcasts.'

As she walked away, Jay turned to Claire. 'I thought you wanted to be made permanent?'

'I thought I did too. Now I'm wondering if it's really what I want to do with my life.'

'Why do you need to figure that out now? Nobody knows what they want to do with their life, I certainly don't.'

'You're wrong.' Claire looked around them. 'Look at all these people. No matter how much stumbling happens now, ultimately, they see security, companionship, *children* at the end of the line. What about me?'

'Oh come on. You'll meet someone new and have a zillion little brats.'

'Unlikely.' She paused. 'I'm infertile.'

Jay's blue eyes widened. 'Christ, I'm so sorry, Claire. You should have said.' He put his hand on her arm. She took a gulp of champagne, forcing the pain away. 'When did you find out?' he asked.

'About five years ago now. I have dodgy eggs.'

'You shouldn't lose hope,' Jay said. 'I know someone who had problems conceiving. They saw this wonderful doctor in Los Angeles and—'

'Let me guess, they fell pregnant, a miracle? I've heard it all before.'

'That must have been very hard for you,' he said softly.

'It was but I'm starting to accept it isn't going to happen now. I just need to figure out what my life holds without children in it. I thought this was it,' she added, gesturing around her.

'Not everyone sees children in their future, sweetheart. I'm not even sure I do.'

'Liar.' She looked towards his date, a tall black woman with the highest cheekbones Claire had ever seen. 'What was it you said about Petra earlier? "Imagine what our children will look like, Claire."'

'It's just an expression.'

'Is it? Are you really saying you'll never have kids?'

'I don't know, maybe not,' he replied in an unconvincing voice.

'You will. It's how we're programmed to think. Think of all the books you've read, the films you've seen. There's one lesson that usually runs through them: children are the greatest gift of all. Work means nothing. Ambition means nothing. As long as you have children, that's all that matters.'

'Who cares what society thinks? I think you can make a life here, you know.'

'Really? It all feels like Polyfilla.'

'Polly who?'

'Polyfilla, the gooey stuff that fills in cracks. Look at me, Jay,' she said, gesturing to her designer dress and shoes. 'Is this the Claire you met two years ago, the colour-clashing mess who placed more importance on the memories her clothes held than how they looked? We've both said how right it is that we're here in San Francisco considering it was ravished by an earthquake but was able to rise from the flames. But you do know there are still scars in the earth from the earthquake, don't you? They do a bloody Earthquake Trail so people can see them. It's like us. The scars will never go away, no matter how much we try to paper them over. We have to accept them, dig down to our true selves, not try to cover the pain with gloss.'

'We?'

'Yeah. You deal with your mum's death by dating one gorgeous stick-thin model after another. And me? I work harder, party harder. And now here we are, waiting for the century to tick over at a party to end all parties, packed with the great and good of San Francisco's media set. It's just—'

A man walked past. A dash of brown hair, pale skin, dark stubble. He slowly turned and Claire held her breath, heart like thunder.

Blue eyes.

It wasn't Milo.

'Just what?' Jay asked.

'Oh, I don't know.'

She turned to stare at her face in the reflection of the window. It blended into the ocean below. A gust of winter wind swept over the water, the ripples creating scars on her skin.

Where was Milo right now? He wasn't behind bars, she knew that. He'd been found not guilty and now his family farm had been sold, there were rumours he was working at a friend's farm in Norfolk. But that was all Claire had heard over those months. That and the occasional blurry photo of Holly, who was sixteen now and living with her aunt, Milo's sister Jen.

Maybe he was travelling? She hoped so. She'd like to think her encouragement during their talks in Exmoor would make him follow his heart. Despite how awkward things had been between them outside court that day, she wished the best for him.

Then it occurred to her. Was *she* following her heart? Meeting Milo and sharing their desire to travel had set something off in her. Maybe the hesitation she felt at Yasmine's job offer meant that old wanderlust was stirring again. Short trips for the magazine didn't feel like enough; she needed more, no strings attached.

'Okay, so you say there's no place in society for a woman like you,' Jay said. 'But maybe you can carve out a role for yourself in another way, use your writing skills to shine the spotlight on something important? God knows there's more to life than what's the latest hip city to visit and which hotels have the best spas. Only earlier, I was chatting to an old friend about what's going on in Serbia. You know they actually think ethnic cleansing is going on out there? Maybe you can look into becoming a reporter and writing about issues like that?'

Something inside Claire fluttered. 'What charity did Sarah work for, the one that helps animals during war situations?' she asked Jay.

'The Audrey Monroe Foundation. Why?'

'Sarah told me she was due to fly out to Serbia this year.'

'And?'

'And maybe you're right, maybe I need to do something with a bit more substance.'

Jay frowned. 'Like work for a charity?'

'Like go to Serbia.'

'Jesus Christ, Claire, haven't you seen the news?'

'Yes. Maybe I can be of some use?'

Jay laughed. 'Helping bloody *dogs*?'

'Why not?'

'You know how this sounds,' Jay said softly. 'You can't nurture your own children but maybe you can make a difference to the lives of vulnerable animals?'

Claire took a quick sip of her champagne, a sense of anticipation beginning to build in her stomach. 'I don't care how it sounds. It *feels* right.'

The music was suddenly turned down and someone shouted out, 'Two minutes to go!'

'You're crazy,' Jay said to Claire, smiling slightly. He peered towards a waiter standing at the corner of the large room who nodded and started handing out glasses of champagne. Jay then jumped onto a nearby chair, his shiny shoes sinking into the silky cushion. 'Everyone,' he said, banging his fist onto the wall. A small painting fell to the floor, the frame splintering. 'Ah well, it's only a Hockney,' he added with a wink.

'Oh, just a few hundred thousand dollars then,' Yasmine said, rolling her eyes.

Jay waved his hand in the air. 'Bah. Anyway, listen, I have important things to say, my wonderful wonderful friends.' His face grew sombre. 'Under a century ago, this wonderful city was ravaged by an earthquake. As I walk around these now-pristine streets, I also think of the fact Claire and I could so easily have been killed that fateful night. But like

167

San Francisco,' Jay continued as he peered out at the Golden Gate Bridge, 'we've come back stronger and fitter than ever just in time to cheer in the millennium – even if the scars are still visible,' he added, looking meaningfully at Claire. 'I want to thank you all for joining me on this special evening to celebrate life.' He lifted his glass. 'To life!'

Everyone cheered. 'To life!'

The lights in the room dimmed and Claire stood in the semi-darkness, her heart pounding. Could she really go to Serbia? She'd never been before but it had only been bombed a few months ago. That hadn't stopped her dad, had it? Would it stop her?

Everyone around her started counting down the seconds to the millennium, the room flooded with a different dazzling colour for each of those seconds. Jay jumped off his chair and pulled Claire close to him.

'I suppose dogs aren't so bad,' he said. 'Just don't go getting yourself blown up, all right?'

She smiled. 'I won't.'

As they turned to watch fireworks light up the sky over Golden Gate Bridge, Claire felt the wanderlust inside her batting its wings. She imagined it soaring up into the sky, circling a bright red Catherine Wheel before swooping towards the gleaming silver moon.

Chapter Ten

Ko Phi Phi Don, Thailand
2004

The rickety old boat bobs up and down on the turquoise seas and I press my hand against my flyaway hair, trying not to get sick. The girls had been so excited when I told them I was going to Ko Phi Phi Don by boat, especially when they heard the boat's name meant 'sea monkey' in Thai. I wish I could share their excitement but instead, my tummy's full of nausea and dread as I look out to sea, every shadow I see beneath the surface making my heart shudder because there's a chance it could be a body.

I've only been on a boat once before, nearly fifteen years ago. It had been with Mum just a couple of years after she'd left us. It was my fourteenth birthday and I was staying at the tiny beach house she'd rented in Brighton. She wanted to treat me to a boat trip around the coast, which included lunch too. But the combination of sea-sickness and food wasn't good. Plus I hadn't heard from her for four months so had been particularly resentful.

'Oh Lou,' she'd laughed as she'd held my hair back for the fifth time while I puked my guts up in the onboard toilets. 'We're so very different, aren't we? You're so fragile when it comes to things like this.'

I'd felt a stab of hurt and anger then. 'I'm fine now,' I'd said, swallowing down the bile and slamming from the cubicle, splashing water over my face and avoiding her gaze in the mirror's reflection.

'You're not upset, are you?' she'd asked, putting her hand on my shoulder. 'I meant it as a compliment. Why on earth would you want to be like me?'

I'd forced myself to laugh, turning around to look her up and down. 'I'm not upset. I just feel better, that's all. And you're right, why on earth would I want to be like *you*?'

Her face had gone ashen and she'd turned away.

I flinch at the memory now. I was just angry that she'd only got in touch every now and again. The truth was, I was desperate to be like her, this bohemian beautiful wisp of a woman who had men flocking around her. She was so confident and full of life. But every time I looked in the mirror or messed up in art class, I was reminded of the fact I was nothing like her . . . and never would be. I still feel like that in less confident moments, especially when at one of Will's work dos surrounded by all his snobby work colleagues. But I always remind myself: at least I have my girls.

At least I have my girls.

Is that just an excuse for not getting off my butt and doing something with my life? Being a mother is something but is it enough all on its own? Aren't plenty of people perfectly good parents? Maybe it's *not* a good enough excuse to justify the way I've sat back most of my life and watched the world go by instead of living life to the full like Mum does . . . and like Claire Shreve did.

'We're here,' Sam says, bringing me back to the here and now.

I follow his gaze to see we're close to Ko Phi Phi Don's shore now. There are dozens of palm trees in the distance, debris scattered around them, making it look like they've shed their clothes. Except a small voice inside me tells me those items were the flattened walls and roofs of the bungalows and villas that once sat there.

'It doesn't seem possible my mum could've survived this,' I whisper, all my inner torment just now seeming so insignificant.

Sam puts his hand on my shoulder as his friend anchors up next to the remains of a small rickety pier, shattered wood and upturned boats floating around us.

'This place is usually packed with tourists arriving and leaving,' Sam says sadly as his friend jumps off the boat and approaches a Thai official. They exchange a few words then the official peers over at us. I hold my breath. What if he doesn't let us onto the island? What chance have I got of finding Mum then?

But then the official nods and Sam's friend gestures for us to disembark. I let out a breath of relief. Sam helps me step off the boat and we pick our way through the wrecked labyrinth that was once Ko Phi Phi Don, feeling like we're searching the remains of an earthquake. It's so much worse here than in the parts of Krabi I've seen. I stop anyone I see to show them Mum's photo, which isn't many considering the place was evacuated straight after the tsunami and is only just starting to open up again.

'Hey, you!' says an American voice.

I look up to see a couple I'd just handed Mum's photo to walking back towards us.

My heartbeat turns up a notch. 'Do you recognise my mum?'

'Just a painting of her,' the man says.

'Where'd you see the painting?' Sam asks.

'Just down there,' the woman replies, pointing down the beach. 'It's where some bungalows used to be. You won't miss it.'

Used to be. If Mum had painted something, did that suggest she'd been staying in the bungalows?

After saying our thanks, we make our way down the beach. Smashed bottles lie everywhere, the sand stained by the liquid spilling from them. People are walking back and forth between a pile of debris and a makeshift skip, throwing stuff in it, faces exhausted, skin grimy with sand and dirt. In the distance, people in blue scrubs, like those I saw at the temple, scour the beach. I know what they're trying to find: bodies buried beneath the sand, many still being washed up ashore each day. I try not to think about Mum being one of them.

Then I notice something else a few metres away, a large blue elephant ornament with small mirrors dotted over it. It's lying on its side, and is surrounded by the remains of a restaurant, a sign snagged into a half-broken palm tree with the words 'Blue Elephant Restaurant' etched into it, the tables and chairs that were once there no doubt swept away in the tide. There's a Thai man of about sixty sitting on a chair in the middle of it all, looking down at a large framed photo of a woman, its wooden frame splintered, the glass broken.

'What's wrong?' Sam asks.

'I've seen that elephant before.' I reach into my bag and take out Claire's atlas to find the photo next to the map of Thailand. Sam looks over my shoulder as I hold it up and compare it to the blue elephant.

'It's the same restaurant,' he says.

'Yep. Holly James and Claire Shreve were here. Maybe Mum was too if she was looking for Erin.'

I walk over to the man and he peers up. He looks exhausted, his black hair dishevelled. 'Sorry to disturb you,' I say, showing him the photo. 'But is this the same restaurant?'

He takes it warily like he's been used to looking at family photos the past few days. 'Yes,' he says, pointing to Holly. 'I know that girl, very pretty.'

I show him a photo of my mum. 'Did you see this woman too?'

He sighs. 'Yes. She upset girl with red hair.'

'*Upset* her. What do you mean?'

'She try to talk to her but girl get upset, tell me to take lady away.'

'Anything else you remember?' I ask, trying not to dwell on the image of my mum being forcibly removed from the restaurant.

'I see lady arguing with man in that bar day before tsunami,' he says, pointing towards where the Thai couple were clearing up.

'Do you know who the man was?' Sam asks.

The restaurant owner shakes his head.

'What did he look like?' I ask.

'Thin, big nose, squint in eye. That's all I know. Good luck to you, Miss.'

'Thank you.' I look around me. 'Was this your restaurant?' He nods sadly. 'I'm sorry.'

'I'm alive, my son's alive. I very lucky. My wife die years ago, she looking down on us,' he says, peering down at the framed photo.

I stare at it, wondering who's looking down on Mum.

'We better find your mum's painting,' Sam says softly.

'My mum wasn't the type to get into arguments,' I say as we continue walking down the beach. Sam doesn't say anything and I realise why. 'Okay, I know Mum and I had that big argument two years ago but that was half my fault too.'

'I hope you don't mind me asking, but what happened the last time you saw each other?'

I sigh. 'It was Will's thirtieth birthday so his parents arranged a garden lunch party at theirs and invited my mum. I was surprised; they didn't seem to like her when they'd met her at our wedding. It was only later that I discovered the mayor's wife was a fan of Mum's art and Will's mother is a fan of climbing the social ladder,' I added, raising an eyebrow. 'Anyway, Mum turned up and, at first, it was great, she looked lovely and was charming everyone. But then it all went downhill. Mum drank too much, argued with Will's boss about politics, danced erratically, her hair falling from her grips, making her look wild, unkempt.'

Sam sighs. 'Awkward.'

'Yes. Will was mortified and pulled me aside, telling me to "Deal with your bloody mother before she ruins any chance of me getting a promotion." So that's what I did.' I flinch at the memory. 'We argued, Mum said I was a stick in the mud like Dad, and I told her I'd rather be like Dad than some drunk, failed artist who insisted on ruining my life.' I shake my head. It's awful remembering it now. 'Mum ran out. I knew I'd gone too far then and tried to apologise but she refused to talk to me. Will gave her a lift home; she was silent the entire car journey apparently. And then nothing. No more phone calls, no more emails, no more dinners.'

'You mustn't dwell on that, Louise.'

'But wouldn't you? It was awful, the things I said to her, the way she looked at me.'

I choke on a sob and go to turn away, but Sam puts his

hands on my shoulders, making me look at him. 'Tell me about a time you saw her smile,' he says. 'Any time. Just close your eyes and think.'

'That's silly.'

'Do it! Trust me.'

I peer back up at him. He looks so hopeful, so desperate to help. I take in a deep breath, close my eyes and suddenly I'm seeing Mum's smile, that big wide all-encompassing smile of hers. She's sitting in front of a window in her seaside beach house in Brighton, the sun shrouding her in a soft white glow. Strands of her hair float up in static, making her seem ethereal, like an angel. I'm sixteen and in front of me is an easel. I feel nervous, excited.

'Just follow your instincts,' Mum had said. 'Don't think too hard about it.'

'I don't want to get it wrong. You might hate it.'

She'd laughed. 'By whose definition of wrong? Remember what I always say, beauty is truth, truth—'

'Beauty,' I'd finished, doing an eye roll, having heard the phrase so many times from her.

'Exactly! Truth is what you feel here,' she'd said, ignoring my eye roll and placing her fist against her heart. 'Regardless of what others say. So just do what you think is good and beautiful and it will be wonderful, I swear!'

So I'd done just that, painting a picture of me and Mum eating ice creams. Mum had stared at it in wonder afterwards, her eyes filling with tears, her hand going to her mouth, a huge smile on her face.

'It's beautiful,' she'd said.

As I'd looked at the strange mish-mash of colours I'd used, the awful blunt lines, I couldn't fathom what she saw in it. But now I'm a mother, I understand. Her daughter had done it and that was enough.

I open my eyes, smiling at the memory.

'See?' Sam says. 'Hold onto that, okay?'

'I will.' I squeeze his hand. 'Thank you, Sam. You don't know what a godsend you've been.'

He shrugs, embarrassed. 'That's what I'm here for.'

We fall into silence. As we walk on, the beach around us gets steadily worse. It looks like it's littered with driftwood cast ashore, the only sign bungalows were ever there the concrete slabs that were used for their foundations. I can't even bear to think about the fact Mum might've been here when the tsunami hit.

We step over the debris just as we've been doing all day, scouring the rubbish for Mum's painting. And then it's right there: Mum's face, eight foot tall, painted in swirls of red and orange on a wall.

Sam places his hand on my back, doesn't say anything, just encourages me with that gesture. I feel uncharacteristically brave, something I rarely experience when I'm at home. Maybe that's why Will was so surprised when I'd told him I was coming out here to find Mum? He was so used to me being meek and mild.

Not any more.

'You okay?' Sam says.

I close my eyes briefly and imagine seeing Mum in the distance, hair stirring in the wind, long skirt swishing around her legs. She waves, smiling that same smile she wore when she looked at the painting I'd done of her . . . like she's proud of my work, moved by it even. She shields her eyes with the sun and shouts out, 'You're getting close, Lou!'

I open my eyes and look towards Mum's painting, taking a deep breath. 'I'm fine. Let's go look at the painting.'

Chapter Eleven

Fruška Gora, Serbia
2000

Claire tried to conceal her shock as she took in her first views of Belgrade. The buildings outside her taxi window were scorched and windowless, like charred paper decorations hanging from the sky, ready to crumble at one puff of breath. She'd been aware of what she might see when she'd agreed to a three-month volunteering stint at the animal sanctuary Sarah Levine's boss was setting up here. NATO had only just bombed the city the year before in an attempt to end President Slobodan Milošević's oppression of Albanians. But she'd never dreamed it would be this bad.

Her sister Sofia had been incredulous when Claire had told her she'd be coming here. It amazed Claire how quickly Sofia had forgotten the way things had been when they'd travelled as kids, the war-torn countries they'd trekked through. Sofia had also pointed out how damaging it could be for Claire to be in such a fragile country so close to the three-year anniversary of the shooting. Claire needed peace and security, she reasoned. But Claire thought it was just right. There was no gloss here like in San Francisco, just the truth. That meant no more burying her head in the sand. Claire wanted to get

177

on with discovering her place in the world and, to do that, she needed to be somewhere real and true.

As the taxi left ravaged buildings and cratered roads behind, the views were soon replaced by lush green plains and beautiful little villages. Rusty tractors passed by on country roads, the faces of the young men riding them dusty and red from the heat. In the distance, gleaming white monasteries overlooked the hills, the black metal crosses rising from their grey domes puncturing bright blue skies.

She wound the window down to relieve the stifling heat inside the taxi, the strong scent of roses from a roadside flower cart drifting into the car. The woman behind it waved at her, the large bells on the red bracelet wrapped around her wrist tinkling, the skirt of her long black dress lifting in the breeze. Claire smiled, breathing it all in, such a contrast to San Francisco.

That all changed when the farm she was staying at came into view. It was like a stray NATO bomb had rolled onto it. Fences slid into sludgy ditches, old stone walls crumbled onto the muddy road, weeds strangled abandoned troughs. In the middle of the farm's yard was a large skip surrounded by three buildings – a tall white stone house that might have been grand once except half its ceiling was now missing, and two collapsed wooden barns, one with a rusty old tractor peeking out of its innards. Even the view was savage. The farm squatted at the top of the hill and looked out over the worst-hit parts of Belgrade through a tangle of hedges snagged with rubbish.

'I'm told the view will improve, once the hedges are cut down,' an accented voice said from behind Claire as she stepped from her taxi.

She turned to see a tall man with short blond hair and black-rimmed glasses standing nearby. He was wearing a black polo neck and jeans, which struck Claire as quite insane in the heat.

'Filipe,' he said, putting his hand out.

'Claire,' she said, shaking it. 'You're not Serbian, are you? Your accent is different.'

He smiled. 'I'm from Finland. Audrey tells me you will be documenting our work here. I'm the resident vet.'

'Very impressive. My PR role seems wholly inadequate now.'

'Oh, don't worry, you'll be roped in too. Shall I show you to your room, madam?' he joked.

She looked up at the crumbling house. 'Will there be a fruit basket?'

'No, just a chocolate mint on your freshly washed pillow.'

They both laughed and Claire knew right then they were going to be great friends.

The farmhouse wasn't much better inside. Most of the rooms didn't have walls or windows, the floors grimy with rancid hay and chicken muck. As they walked past the kitchen, Claire took in the torn-out cupboards and ancient-looking oven. In the corner was a pile of books – stained, dusty classics like *Paradise Lost* and *The Odyssey*.

'How many people are staying here?' she asked.

'It depends what day it is,' Filipe said, shrugging. 'We have builders and different volunteers turning up every now again. But there are three permanent residents for now: you, me and . . .' He sighed. 'Nikola.'

'Why the sigh?'

'You might find him a little hostile. He lost a friend during the NATO bombings and what with British forces being so heavily involved . . .'

'But I was so annoyed when our government got involved!'

Filipe put his hands up. 'Don't shoot the messenger.'

'Sorry, it's been a while since I've got het up about a

political situation.' She smiled to herself. 'It feels quite refreshing actually. When are the animals arriving?'

'They'll arrive in two weeks when the main barn is finished.'

Claire peered out of a window towards the collapsed wooden barn. 'Just two weeks?'

'Yes, it will happen, you'll see.' Filipe led her to the back of the farmhouse and opened a door. 'Your five-star room,' he said with a sarcastic flourish.

It was tiny with a single bed and a see-through plastic sheet for a ceiling. In the corner was a box draped with a pink shawl, which acted as a makeshift table. It even came with its own pets: three gigantic spiders hanging from a dusty web in the far corner.

Four hours later, the light beige vest top she'd changed into was soaking with sweat and smeared with mud. She leaned against the good side of the wrecked wooden barn and gulped down the water Filipe had brought out for her.

'You've done a good job,' he said, looking towards the skip, which was now full of old chairs, troughs, glasses, dead birds and more. He'd been boarding up parts of the more intact barn all afternoon, which they were planning to use as kennels.

Claire smiled. She *had* done well. Just a few hours in and she finally felt she was doing something right instead of simply papering over the gaping hole left by her infertility.

'Nikola, how many times do I have to tell you? I'm not going to stick that bloody thing up, Audrey won't have it,' Filipe said, sucking in a mouthful of smoke and blowing it out. They were sitting in the ramshackle kitchen after an awkward dinner during which Nikola, a young Serbian man with caramel-coloured hair, glared at Claire with open hostility just as Filipe had predicted.

Claire watched the smoke from Filipe's cigarette circle his head then drift towards the black and white poster Nikola was proudly holding up. On it was an illustration of a clenched fist next to a photo of Milošević's back. Beneath it in large white font against a black background were two words: '*Gotov je!*'

'But this isn't just *politics*,' Nikola said in good English. 'It's what we must do.'

'What does the poster say, Nikola?' Claire asked, trying to show him that, just because she was British, it didn't mean she wasn't interested in his views. He'd barely said a word to her since arriving, just glaring at her over his glass every now and again. But she was determined to win him over.

He contemplated her for a few moments then laid the black and white poster on the table, pointing at the clenched fist at its middle. 'This is our – how do you say?' He looked towards Filipe.

'Logo, symbol,' he said.

'Yes,' Nikola said, face full of energy, 'this fist is a symbol of the courage of people who want change. Not just *want* it,' he said, leaning towards Claire. '*Demand* it.'

Claire felt a small burst of triumph. This was exactly what *she* was doing by coming to Serbia, demanding a change in her life. Even Nikola's open hostility wouldn't ruin the sense of liberation she was feeling at that moment.

'Except we don't demand with violence like your country did,' Nikola added, leaning back and assuming his standard glare.

Claire nodded. 'Good. I don't agree with what NATO did. You can't fight violence with violence.'

He tilted his head, examining her face. 'Yes, exactly. And this,' he said, running his slim fingers over the black Serbian words beneath the clenched fist, 'this means "He's finished" because there's no hope for Milošević now, do you understand?'

'I fear you're going to be disappointed when the elections come next month,' Filipe said.

Nikola muttered something to him in Serbian, and Filipe turned to Claire. 'He says I'm old and cynical.' He looked back at Nikola. 'No, I'm just realistic. I respect what you Otpor boys are doing but—'

'Otpor?' Claire asked.

'It's the youth movement Nikola's a member of,' Filipe explained to her. 'It was formed by a group of university students to resist Milošević's rule. They've been very effective in getting people behind Milošević's opposition candidate Vojislav Koštunica in the lead up to the elections.'

Nikola puffed his chest out. 'Yes, Otpor is very strong here. Everyone's talking about us.'

'They're also talking about how naïve you all are,' Filipe said, sighing.

'Why naïve?' Nikola asked, glaring at him.

'Because I heard all this talk when I was here before. But look, Milošević is still in power! Things don't change so quickly. Once something bad happens, it takes time to heal, sometimes a lifetime.'

Would it take Claire a lifetime to heal too?

'This time is different,' Nikola said. 'Can't you feel it in the air?' He slugged back some beer, peering out into the darkness, his hazel eyes blazing. 'Next month, Serbia will change. Milošević will be gone and you will be too embarrassed to sit at the table with me because it will remind you of how wrong you were.'

'It sounds like Nikola might be right,' Claire said. 'I saw a news item in the UK the other day saying support for Milošević is dwindling.'

Nikola looked at her again with that inquisitive stare, like he was trying to figure her out. Then he smiled slightly.

'Right, enough of this,' Filipe said, placing a bottle of gold liquid on the table and looking at Claire. 'A new member of the team means *slivovica*.'

An hour later, that *slivovica* seemed to be pulsing right in Claire's temples, its plummy flavours making her lips tingle. Other Serbians had turned up, including a girl with cat-like eyes who entwined herself around Nikola. As the night wore on, Claire heard less and less English and more Serbian.

Feeling left out, she and Filipe scraped their chairs back into the corner and bent their heads together as they talked about travelling and their pets, especially how much Claire missed Archie, who was staying with Ben. After five glasses of *slivovica*, Filipe leaned back in his chair and fixed Claire with his steel-like stare. 'So why are you *fractured*?'

'What do you mean?'

'Audrey only invites certain people to work here. A certain damaged kind of people.'

Claire thought of the conversation she'd had with Audrey when she'd called her the morning after the New Year's Eve party a few months ago to ask about volunteering. She had seemed inordinately interested in Claire's reasons for going out there. When she'd impulsively mentioned her infertility and a need for a fresh start, Audrey had instantly said yes.

'Then I presume that means you're fractured too?' Claire asked, avoiding answering the question.

Filipe smiled sadly, swilling what remained of his *slivovica* around the bottom of his glass. 'I found my ex-boyfriend Kaarle kissing another man.'

'I'm so sorry.'

'Don't be. The Kaarle I thought I knew wouldn't do that, I'd clearly just loved someone who never existed, a ghost.

So how can my heart be broken when the love hadn't been true in the first place?'

Claire thought of Milo then, of the contrast between the man she'd known in the short time they'd spent together and the man who'd hung his head low and barked those bitter words that day in court.

Was the Milo she thought she'd known just a ghost?

She sighed. It had been a while since she'd thought about him properly, the papers hardly mentioning him nowadays.

'Now you must tell me about your fractured heart,' Filipe said.

And so she did, every little bit, from the time she found out she was infertile to that night in Exmoor and the months that followed. It felt good to talk about it so openly to a near stranger. In fact, it reminded her of how she'd unburdened herself on Milo in that beachside café nearly three years ago.

'Do you miss Milo?' Filipe asked when she finished.

'What is there to miss? I only knew him a couple of days. It's like you said, he's a ghost.'

He frowned. 'I don't think he's a ghost. He's more like an iceberg. A part of him broke away when his brother did what he did, the same part that made you fall for him. Without that part, he doesn't know how to love anyone.'

'Maybe I don't know how to love anyone either.'

He tilted his head. 'Why do you say that?'

'The day I found out I was infertile, it felt like something broke away from me too. That's why Milo and I never had a chance in hell, neither of us capable of loving. It's like you said earlier, wounds can take a lifetime to heal.'

Filipe pushed his glasses up his nose. 'You know, in Finnish mythology, there's a place called Tuonela, the sphere of the dead. It's not usually possible for a living person to go there but if a shaman is brave enough, Death's Maid will let them pass through.'

'Lucky shaman,' Claire said sarcastically.

'What I'm trying to say is, maybe you can find that piece of you that was lost and bring it back? Maybe Milo can find his too. Maybe you can help each other find your missing pieces.'

Was Filipe right: had she been too hasty in giving up on her and Milo and the pieces they'd lost? She closed her eyes, saw his scarred face looking so real she could almost reach out and touch it.

No, Milo was part of her past, not her future.

She slugged her glass back, felt the warm liquid pinching at her throat, her head growing woozy again. 'I'd rather stay in the land of the living, thanks,' she said, holding her glass out for more.

That night, all she could hear was the sounds of Nikola's feline girlfriend moaning, the thud of the headboard against the thin walls, his Serbian whispers husky, urgent. When Claire finally slept, the sounds seeped into her dreams, and it wasn't long before she saw Milo in her dreams, Nikola and his girlfriend's moans becoming theirs as she returned to the river that fateful night and what might have happened if Dale hadn't done what he did. She woke angry with herself. Why was she still thinking of Milo? She needed to leave him behind.

But still she dreamt the same dream every night over those next two weeks, the feel of Milo's touch, the sound of his moans growing more and more intense, so intense she woke frequently in the night, hot and frustrated.

When Filipe noticed how tired Claire was looking, she said it was just work, which was easy to believe as it was non-stop at the sanctuary. The whole point of her being there was to bring attention to the charity's work in the UK as a way to get donations from the animal-loving British public. This didn't just mean writing press releases and web copy but also pitching articles to the UK media about the sanctuary, just like she had when she was seventeen and trying to fund her travels to find her dad. Then, when she wasn't in the makeshift office Nikola had set up for her, she was tidying more rubbish away in the yard.

In fact, it was so busy that, before Claire knew it, they were ready to receive their canine guests. The kennels were housed in the less debilitated barn, twenty kennels running down its length with a walkway down the middle and a small veterinary surgery for Filipe at the back. Nikola and his friends had laid the floor with concrete and each kennel had access to an outdoor run that wrapped around the barn. Now they just needed to restore the second barn and they'd have even more space for the animals.

'They're here,' Filipe said as Claire heard the rumble of tyres on stone.

The truck came into sight and behind it, a modern-looking van with a pristine blue exterior.

'Our new air-conditioned van thanks to Claire's efforts,' Filipe said, referring to the coverage Claire had already managed to drum up in national newspapers.

Claire smiled to herself. It felt good to see the results of all her hard work. She really was making a difference here.

The sound of barks echoed out of it, and Filipe and Claire exchanged excited looks. This is what it was all about, after all: saving the animals that had slipped between the lines of war.

'Time to enter the world of the living, yes?' Filipe asked Claire.

'Definitely,' she replied, laughing.

The truck and van both rolled to the stop. Doors slammed, people jumped out. Then one person came into view. Sad brown eyes, dark hair. Claire choked on her laughter.

There Milo was, right there in the land of the living.

Chapter Twelve

Fruška Gora, Serbia
2000

Milo's dark hair had been shaved into a buzz cut, his beautiful fringe gone. The scar on his right cheek looked raw and ragged under the midday sun and he was even thinner, the grubby jeans he was wearing hanging from his hips, the sleeves of his blue T-shirt loose around his arms. There was a look in his eyes too: a feral despairing look, like a starving dog.

Claire froze, mind whirring as his gaze burned into hers.

Filipe frowned as he looked between them. 'You know each other?' he asked.

Milo's brow puckered, his scar stretching. 'We—'

'It was a long time ago,' Claire said, sweeping her trembling fingers through her tangled hair. She hated herself for being aware that she was wearing ripped denim shorts that did nothing to hide her cellulite and that her brown roots were showing under the faded black of her hair dye.

'How are you doing?' she asked Milo in as casual a voice as she could muster given the confused emotions whirring inside.

'Okay,' he said, his brow furrowing.

'Shall we get the dogs out?' she said to Filipe. 'That's why we're here, right?'

Everyone stood still, eyes darting between Claire and Milo, and all Claire could think was: *I need to be strong.*

'Claire's right,' Nikola said, clapping his hands together. 'Let's get those dogs out and into their new homes.'

'Iceberg?' Filipe whispered to Claire.

She nodded curtly, her neck aching from keeping it upright. Filipe squeezed her hand then strode over to the van. Over the next few hours, Claire was grateful that she didn't have a chance to see Milo as she helped Filipe with the dogs. She needed time to process her thoughts. This wasn't part of the plan, Milo being here. A positive life-affirming experience was now getting all scratched up with negativity.

And why *was* he here? Surely it couldn't just be a coincidence?

She channelled her nervous energy into shampooing the fleas and ticks out of over twenty dogs that were all different sizes, colours and breeds. There was one that reminded Claire of Archie because of its black and white colouring, a terrier that peered up at her with sad brown eyes as it huddled in the corner of its kennel.

Finally, as darkness fell, their work was finished and she stepped out into the yard. As she crossed it to get to the house, Milo stepped out of the shadows and stood in front of her, fingers twisting at a bit of oily cloth. His jeans were now caked with sawdust and cobwebs, his face smeared with dirt.

When he looked at Claire, she thought of her dreams and her body stirred.

'Can we talk?' he asked in a stilted voice.

She gave herself a few seconds until she was able to muster a casual, 'Sure.'

'I wasn't aware you'd be here. I can leave if you don't feel comfortable.'

'Comfortable? Why wouldn't I feel comfortable?'

He sighed. 'I don't know, I just—'

'Honestly, I don't care, stay for as long or as short as you want.' She inwardly flinched. Of *course* she cared.

Milo sighed. 'I know I was out of order saying what I said that day in court. It's just . . . complicated.'

'Then uncomplicate it. It's nothing, honestly. Nothing.'

She quickly turned and strode towards the farmhouse, the word 'nothing' echoing between them. When she got to her room, she slammed the door so hard one of the spiders fell from its cobweb and onto the floor. She thought it had ended, the pain she felt when she thought of Milo and that terrible night. But now here he was and the pain was filling her again, pressing into all the dusty corners of her and squeezing out the light.

After a while, there was a soft knock on the door and Filipe walked in.

'I called Audrey,' he said, sighing. 'She told me she was desperate for a farmhand who worked with animals and, after reading your story, thought Milo would be ideal. So she tracked him down to his friend's farm in Norfolk. She meant to tell you but never got around to it. I don't think she told Milo you were here either.'

Claire shook her head. 'She must've known what she was doing.'

'Yes, Audrey has a tendency to try to force people together.' Filipe leaned against the wall, folding his arms. 'Maybe this is good though, maybe you need time together to heal?'

'This isn't the Priory Clinic, Filipe. To make matters worse, the anniversary of the shooting is next week. You know what, I'm quite tempted to fly back to the UK.'

Filipe pushed away from the wall and grabbed Claire's hand. 'No, you can't let your past ruin your future. This place has been good for you. I've seen it with other volunteers too. When people come here, they begin to heal, just like the dogs. That black and white terrier that came in? You just see, in a week, that wound will be half the size and she'll be wagging her tail. A lot can happen in seven days.'

Dinner was painful. Milo was seated at the other end of the table from Claire, and Nikola took the other seat next to her so she was hemmed in by him and Filipe as though they were making a buffer for her. She forced dinner down and contributed to the conversation in a fake bright voice. Sometimes, she dared to peer over at Milo. But he just kept his eyes on his bowl and barely ate as he jogged his leg up and down. Claire wanted to slam her hand onto his knee and stop it. She also, inexplicably, wanted to wrap her arms around him, trace the contours of his scar with her fingers.

She hated herself for wanting all that.

When he finished eating, he left the dinner table abruptly, inviting raised eyebrows from the others.

Later, as Claire came back from the bathroom after getting ready for bed, she glimpsed Milo playing cards outside with two Serbian builders, a battered old copy of *Paradise Lost* by his hand. There were several empty shot glasses by his side, and the tops of his cheeks were red from the drink. When he noticed Claire watching him, his eyes travelled down the length of her. She pulled her towel closer around herself and strode to her room, feeling his eyes burning into her back.

She didn't sleep that night. All she could hear was the slap of playing cards on the tinny table outside, so loud she had to smash her pillow over her ears to drive away the sound. Not just the sound but also the image of Milo's calloused hands; the feel of them against her skin.

She barely saw him over the next couple of days, Filipe sending him out for supplies. Claire was relieved as she sat at the dinner table those nights, staring at his empty seat. It was too painful having him around.

She focused on working as hard as she could, taking photos of the dogs and writing short pieces about them for the website while helping Filipe where she could. A couple of nights after Milo arrived, Claire woke to the sound of a horrific howling coming from the kennels. She didn't even stop to grab her dressing gown, instead running out into the yard in just shorts and a vest top, her feet bare as she called out to Filipe. Lights went on in the farmhouse and there was the sound of running behind her. She turned, thinking it was Filipe, but it was Milo in just a pair of tracksuits bottoms. He looked like a soldier with his jagged scar, his buzz cut, the contour of his chest under the moonlight.

Except there was a shot glass in his hand and his eyes looked dazed.

He followed her into the darkness of the kennels. She could sense him behind her as she followed the source of the sound, feel his breath on her neck, smell the plummy *slivovica* in it. When they got to the kennel of the black and white terrier – Luna as they now called her – the dog peered up at Claire, eyes soft with pain. Claire slowly approached her, and was surprised when she let her bend down and stroke her.

'What's wrong with you, girl?' Filipe asked, appearing in the entrance, his tired eyes drifting to the glass Milo was holding. He exchanged a look with Claire then crouched down in front of Luna. She recoiled away from him, eyes wide with fear. But Claire leaned down, whispering into her ear as Milo watched, his eyes growing soft. Luna relaxed slightly, letting Filipe examine her.

After a while, he leaned back on his haunches, shaking his head. 'I can't believe I didn't notice this before. This one's full of pups.'

Claire stared at Luna's belly. It was round and taut but she'd presumed that was from lack of food the past few months.

'Is she in labour?' she asked.

'Not yet. A month, maybe two?'

'But why was she howling?'

'I think she has an infection, maybe strep. That could be bad for the puppies.'

'One of our bitches at the farm had strep,' Milo said matter-of-factly. 'Grapefruit seed extract helps.'

'Yes, I've heard that,' Filipe said, frowning at the slur in his voice. 'Do you think you can get some when you're next in Belgrade, Milo?'

He didn't answer, his eyes fixed on Claire, face intense.

'Milo?' Filipe repeated.

Milo blinked then dragged his eyes away from Claire. 'Yes, yes, that's fine.'

Then he turned on his heel and disappeared down the walkway.

'He was drunk at lunch too,' Filipe said. 'He shouldn't drink while working, especially around animals.'

Claire looked down at Luna, trying to keep her face steady. 'No, he shouldn't.'

She sought Milo out the next day, finding him sheltering under the patio from the light rain with Nikola and a couple of other Serbs, smoking.

They all went quiet when she approached.

'Can we talk?' she asked Milo.

He shrugged, stubbing out his cigarette on the wall. 'Sure.' He followed her inside to the empty kitchen as the others whistled.

'Everything okay?' he asked, leaning against one of the debilitated kitchen units and examining a cut in his hand.

'I noticed you were a bit wasted last night.' He looked up at her, brow creased. 'You're driving, operating machinery. It's dangerous.'

His face hardened. 'Was I driving and operating machinery last night?'

'No. But you do during the day and I know you *drink* during the day, people have told me.' Her voice softened. 'I know the anniversary of your brother's death is coming up.'

'It's got nothing to do with that!' He pushed away from the unit, eyes fierce. Claire stepped back, bumping into the wall as he leaned very close to her, his face just a millimetre away. She stared into his brown eyes, saw the pores in his skin, the dark stubble and shape of his lips. 'Am I drinking now?' he asked. 'Smell my breath? Am I drinking?'

She shoved him away from her, anger pulsing inside.

'Everything okay here?' Filipe was standing in the doorway, a mug in his hand.

Milo turned away with a wretched look on his face, the anger gone. He took one last look at Claire then stormed out.

'What was that all about?' Filipe asked, watching him stride down the hallway.

'He didn't take too kindly to me mentioning his drinking.' Claire shrugged, belying the emotions raging inside. 'At least I tried. If he wants to mess up his life, it's not my problem.'

Milo wasn't at dinner that night. Nor were Nikola and the men he'd been talking to earlier. Claire presumed he'd gone out drinking and part of her wanted to go out and find him, shake the stupidity out of him. The other part thought, what the hell? He didn't want her help so she wasn't going to give it.

In the night, she woke to the sound of raised voices. She jumped out of bed, wrapping her dressing gown around herself and stepping out of her room. The kitchen light was on and two Serbian workers who'd been staying the night were on their phones muttering in Serbian as Filipe stared out of the window.

'What's going on?' Claire asked.

'They think Nikola's been arrested,' Filipe said. 'There was a raid on the Otpor offices.'

'And you think Nikola was there?'

'He's not in his room, I just checked. He isn't answering his phone either. I've not seen him since this afternoon.' He raked his fingers through his blond hair. 'This isn't good. I promised Audrey I'd keep an eye on him.'

Claire hadn't seen Milo since that afternoon either. Panic started mounting inside. She strode down the hallway, knocking on Milo's door as her heart thumped a fearful beat against her chest. When there was no answer, she carefully pushed the door open. She took a moment to take everything in – the framed photo of Holly and Blue on the bedside table, a glass with brown liquid pooled at the bottom, that copy of *Paradise Lost*.

The room was empty.

As she rushed down the hallway to tell Filipe, Claire thought of the two British men who'd been arrested a few weeks before. Or, worse, the anti-Milošević official who'd gone missing, presumed executed. What if that happened to Milo and Nikola?

'Milo's not in his room,' she said when she got to the kitchen.

'Right, I'm going out to look for them.' Filipe grabbed his keys and went out, the two Serbian men following him.

As Claire waited for them, she paced the farmhouse, taking in the possibility Milo might be lost to her forever. Maybe Filipe had been right – maybe Milo had lost a part of himself too and they could help each other heal. She'd been stupid to turn her back on him.

As the sun rose, she heard the rumble of a van.

She ran outside, heart pounding painfully against her chest, the early morning sun glaring at her over the tangle of branches nearby.

She started trembling, the fear that had been mounting inside her the past few hours almost strangling her.

Then, as they drew closer, she saw Milo. He was sitting in the back, an ugly bruise around his eye, a cut lip.

'What happened?' Claire asked, striding towards them all, relief flooding through her.

'We fought like warriors,' Nikola said, voice slurred. 'And then we drank like warriors.' He went to walk away from the van but stumbled over a nearby bucket as Filipe rolled his eyes.

As Milo walked past Claire, she grabbed his wrist. He looked down at her hand then up at her face, his eyes bloodshot, the cut in his lip still bleeding.

'Why did you go?' she asked him. 'Didn't you realise it would be dangerous?'

He shrugged then strode into the farmhouse.

As she watched him, anger pulsed inside. He clearly didn't want to heal. She'd been a fool to think they could help each other.

Over the remainder of the week, she tried to avoid Milo as much as she could. When she did see him, the anniversary of the shooting hummed between the lines of everything that passed between them, reminding Claire of the progress she'd made the past three years and her absolute resolution not to return to that time. He hadn't healed, but she would.

One day, when she was sitting on her own with Luna, she looked up to see him watching them from the entrance of the kennel. His white T-shirt was wet from the rain outside, his blue jeans grubby as always.

'Everything okay?' Claire asked.

'I brought Luna some rice pudding.' He held up a can. 'One of the British guys I know in Belgrade brought some over from his trip back to the UK last week.'

Claire frowned. 'Why rice pudding?'

'One of the pregnant bitches on the farm loved it. I thought you might want to try it with Luna.'

He held out the can to Claire and she took it. 'Thanks.'

He leaned down, tickling the fur behind Luna's ear. 'I found her, you know. She was in Freedom Square in Novi Sad crunched up behind a rubbish bin. She was in a real state, her wound badly infected. Filipe thinks she got hurt in the NATO bombings last year.' He sighed. 'War wounds. I guess we all have them.'

She peered at his scar and his eye caught hers. There was an awkward silence.

'I'm not drinking during the day now,' Milo said after a while.

'Good.' Claire kept her eyes on Luna, her nerves right at the surface. It was clear he was trying to be normal, to make amends somehow.

'Have you written about the lead up to the elections?' he asked.

'No, just the sanctuary.'

'You should. It's a unique situation we're in, living twenty miles from the city in the same house as an Otpor member. It'd make a good article.'

She looked up at him. 'Maybe you can be an undercover reporter yourself considering you've infiltrated Nikola's group?'

'I'm an old fogey compared to those lot.'

They both smiled at each other and Claire felt her tummy whir with emotion.

When she got back to her room a couple of hours later, there was a package outside her room containing a small notepad with pretty patterns on the front, a note scrawled on the first page.

Something to help with your writing. M.

Claire stared at it, eyes blinking, trying to calm her emotions.

That evening, Milo joined in with the conversation instead of shovelling his food into his mouth in silence or disappearing outside to get drunk with the Serbs. Filipe was talking about his childhood growing up on the reindeer farm his father ran in Finland.

'I spent my childhood there,' he said, 'schlepping up the shit and taking money from tourists.'

'Sounds familiar,' Milo said, peering up from his bowl. 'Well, the schlepping up the shit part anyway.'

'Whereabouts in Finland do your family come from?' Claire asked.

'Originally the far north. But my father bought a reindeer farm in the south to be near my mother's family.'

'I've always wanted to visit Lapland,' Claire said. 'It's one of the few places I haven't been. I spent my fourteenth birthday in North Carolina during the snowstorms there and loved every minute. While everyone was freaking out, me, my dad and my sister made snow angels outside our hotel. The snow was so soft!'

Milo rested his chin on his hand and stared at her. She felt her face flush.

'But Finland is hard beneath all that snow,' Filipe said. 'In the winter, the ice covers the land like a scab.'

'Scabs are good,' Milo said. 'They heal.'

'But they grow itchy too,' Filipe said. 'And when you scratch them off, they become infected.'

'You're making it sound like a hellhole!' Milo said as he laughed, the lines around his eyes crinkling. Claire hadn't seen him laugh since those days they'd spent together before the shooting.

'Fine,' Filipe said, flopping back into his chair and raising his arms in defeat. 'You can move to Lapland and I'll drive from my warm apartment in Helsinki just to hear you complain of the dark and the cold.'

'I might take you up on that offer,' Milo said. 'My niece Holly's always wanted to go to Lapland.'

'I've been thinking about Holly, she must be seventeen now,' Claire said. 'How is she?'

'She's okay. I've seen her a few times, not as much as I'd like. She wanted to come with me to Serbia actually, but Jen wasn't too hot on the idea.'

'Yes, I read your sister had taken her in. Any contact from her mum?'

His face stiffened. 'Nothing.'

'Okay, enough of this talk,' Nikola said, jumping onto his chair and clanging his fork against his glass. 'Tomorrow, we will make our case for freedom as we visit the polling booths. So I want to raise a glass. *Zivio Ziveli!*' he said, raising his glass high in the air. 'To democracy! To change!'

As everyone cheered and stamped their feet, Milo sought Claire's eyes across the dinner table and this time, she held his gaze too, her heartbeat matching the thump of those feet.

Chapter Thirteen

Luna was huge now, the skin of her belly stretched so tight, you could almost see the little pups inside. It was strange for Claire to watch over her and know she herself would never feel fat with baby. That fact was always inside her, like a lump of coal at the pit of her stomach. But she'd not dwelled on it as much since being at the sanctuary. Maybe it was because she was caring for wounded dogs, playing a part in their lives as a mother would in her child's life? Or maybe the grieving process at the loss of her fertility was truly entering the stage of acceptance? Just a few weeks here and she was starting to believe this really was the path for her, writing about things that slipped between the lines rather than reviews of glossy destinations.

When it was officially announced that Milošević had retained power because none of the candidates in the Serbian elections had won a majority vote, Nikola exploded with rage. He stomped around the house, calling his friends and throwing things about while Filipe looked on with an 'I told you so' look on his face. That evening, Claire picked up the notepad Milo had given her and started documenting all she'd seen in the lead up to the elections, what Milo had said in Luna's kennel striking a chord.

Soon the anniversary of the shooting arrived. Claire woke early and threw herself into her work, her mind spiked by the memory of blood, by the cries of the injured, by the sight of Milo holding his dead brother in his arms. She wondered briefly whether she should seek him out to check he was okay. But she reasoned that if he needed her, he'd come to her.

When evening came, Claire found Milo in the kitchen sharing a bottle of *slivovica* in silence with Filipe and Nikola. She sat down at the table and he looked at her with such sadness in his eyes, all she wanted to do was pull him into her arms, tell him everything was okay.

After a while, Filipe slid his chair across to her. 'Claire,' he whispered. 'I have something for you and your iceberg. Meet me outside in a couple of minutes, beyond the great spruce at the back.' He looked across at Milo. 'Both of you.'

Then he got up and left the room.

'Do you know what he's got planned?' she asked as she followed Milo outside.

'Nope.'

'How are you coping today? You okay?'

'Fine.' He looked at Claire sideways. 'You?'

'How I feel doesn't matter. Nothing really happened to me.'

'You were there. That was enough.'

She wrapped her arms around herself. She was just wearing a T-shirt and jeans and the nights were drawing in now, autumn digging her heels in.

Milo noticed her shivering and peered back at the farmhouse. 'Shall I get something to cover your arms?'

'I'm fine,' she said, smiling. 'Thanks for asking though.'

200

They entered a small meadow, the hedges around it frosted white by the moonlight and Claire could see Filipe had laid out a blanket on the ground and was holding something under the crook of his arm. He patted the blanket. 'Come, join me.'

They both hesitated a moment then sunk down across from Filipe. The ground felt cold and hard under the blanket and Claire was very aware of Milo's proximity to her.

'I know today is a very difficult day for you both,' Filipe said. 'For you especially, Milo.'

Milo kept his face expressionless and didn't say anything.

Filipe placed the item he'd been holding on the blanket in front of them. Beneath the moonlight, Claire could see it was a thick oval object with a white animal-skin top and wooden base. Milo caught her eye and she knew what he was thinking: it was like the drum she hauled around in her car.

'This is a Sami rune drum,' Filipe said. 'My father gave it to me.'

He pulled out a crooked birch stick from his pocket and lightly drummed it over the surface, the sound intimate, low, hypnotic. Milo peered into the distance, his eyes going some-where else – back to that night?

'Drums play an important role in Sami spiritual rituals,' Filipe said, increasing the pace of the drumstick. 'The Sami shamans use them to travel to the spiritual world. With every beat, their souls slowly inch out of the body and, when free, latch onto the wind and move onto another plane.'

At that moment, the wind seemed to grow more intense, the thud of the drum matching it as it whirled around them.

'The plane they enter is usually one of ecstasy and deep knowledge,' Filipe said, his voice barely discernable above the beat of the drum. 'But sometimes, the drum's used to cleanse the soul of harmful memories by easing them out and taking them away with the wind.'

As Filipe continued to play the drum, Claire closed her eyes, imagining each thump of his hand doing just as he said: easing the memories out, sending them away. She saw them all: her dad's sunken face as he took his last breaths; the flicker of the flames as she burned the photo she'd been given of her embryos after her last failed IVF round; then Milo, his face streaked with his brother's blood as he stared up at her.

She opened her eyes. Milo was watching her, his cheeks wet with tears. Those tears made her think of melting icebergs. She saw the river they'd lain down next to three years before. She saw Milo's brother lying dead in his arms. She thought of how quickly it had changed Milo. How the parts of the Milo she'd been kissing just a few moments before had, like Filipe said, cracked and broken away, drifting so far out to sea, she wasn't sure he could get them back again.

But then she focused on the tears sliding down his face and thought of the effort he'd made the past few days. What if the softer part of him, the iceberg that had broken away that night, was slowly coming back? And if so, what did that mean for him; for *her*?

She knew then she had a choice.

As the drumbeat continued to thud in time with the beat of her heart, all she knew was this: she needed Milo and he needed her, not as lovers, but as friends. She placed her arms around him. He tensed for a moment. Then he melted against her, his arms wrapping around hers.

Out of the corner of her eye, Claire noticed Filipe smiling.

They stayed like that for the next hour as Milo stared ahead of him, trying, as he told Claire later, to stop the memories he'd pushed away from seeping back into him again.

Then suddenly their peace was interrupted by someone running towards them in the darkness. Milo jumped up, placing his whole body in front of Claire's, making her think of that night three years before when his sister had stumbled towards them.

But as the figure drew closer, she realised it was Nikola.

'It's started,' he said, leaning down to catch his breath. 'Luna's giving birth.'

Milo looked at Claire, a small smile on his face. She knew what he was thinking: that Luna giving birth was a sign of new starts. He stood and put his hand out to her. She took it, smiling, and they both jogged to the kennels where they found Luna pacing up and down her kennel whining.

It took them several hours to deliver Luna's pups. When the first arrived, flopping onto the ground in front of her, black and covered with mucus, it didn't move.

'Is it okay?' Claire whispered, fear streaking through her. What if it couldn't breathe?

'Wait,' Milo said, putting his hand gently on her arm.

She followed his gaze to see Luna had started licking the pup, making it squirm and whimper. Then she chewed off the umbilical cord, whimpering with her new pup.

'You take it, there's a few more pups in there so I'd better get them out,' Filipe said, handing Claire a cloth. She gently picked the puppy up, wiping its face and nose just as Filipe had taught her to. It curled against her arm and her heart swelled. It was so tiny and innocent, eyes not even open yet, squirming with confusion and fear. Then she felt a trickle of sadness. She'd never hold her own newborn in her arms; never see its eyes open and latch onto hers for the first time.

Milo put his hand on her arm as though he could sense what she was thinking and the sadness ebbed away.

Over the next few days, Milo made excuses to be near Claire, offering to fix the trellis outside her office and bringing her post. And it wasn't long before she found herself hovering by the window to watch him work on the barn, even bringing him tea one day, ignoring the voice in her head that told her to keep her distance. She'd made a decision to be there for him, but as a friend, nothing more. The problem was, every time she was near him, all she thought about was *more*.

As September rolled into October, the feeling of revolution in the air intensified. Local radio stations stopped toeing Milošević's line, which Nikola assured them was a sign of real change; workers even went on strike in protest at Milošević's refusal to step down. Then one day, Nikola ran through the sanctuary, screaming 'revolution' at the top of his lungs. Even Luna left her precious pups behind and came out from her kennel, ears pricking at Nikola's excitable tones.

'What's going on?' Milo asked Nikola from the ladder he was standing on.

'Belgrade's on fire,' Nikola said, eyes sparking.

Claire thought of what her sister Sofia would say when she saw the news. She'd called a few times the past week, worried about what she'd been hearing. Jay had called too. The only person who thought it was exciting was her friend, Jodie. But then nothing scared her: she was currently in Colombia trying to get a book festival off the ground.

'It's the *Skupština*!' Nikola said. 'They're burning the parliament building.'

'I think Nikola's moment has finally come,' Filipe said, strolling outside as Milo made his way down the ladder. 'Maybe change is possible. Maybe a country can heal.'

Nikola's face exploded with happiness and he pulled Filipe into a hug, kissing his cheek as he rolled his eyes.

'You must come to Belgrade,' Nikola said to Claire and Milo. 'We'll take to the streets to celebrate Milošević's downfall.'

'I'm not sure,' Claire said, peering towards Luna's kennel.

'Don't worry,' Filipe said, looking between Claire and Milo with a small smile on his face. 'I'll keep an eye on Luna and her pups, I'm exhausted anyway. You go enjoy yourself. It's not often you get to witness a revolution. It'll be great for that article you're writing, Claire.'

'You're writing an article about all this?' Milo asked, a small smile on his face.

'Someone very wise suggested I do it,' Claire joked.

His smile deepened. 'Then I reckon Nikola and Filipe are right, I reckon we should go.'

'But it's not safe,' Claire said. 'Haven't you seen the scenes on TV?'

'Would the old Claire who made snow angels in a snow storm and travelled the world when she was seventeen say that?' Milo asked, his brown eyes shimmering with mischief. 'Taking the official path's overrated, remember?' He put his hand out to her and Claire felt her tummy whir, memories from their first few days in Exmoor spinning inside.

'Fine then,' she said. 'But if I get arrested, I'm blaming you.'

Nikola held the placard high above his head as he led them into the crowds a few hours later. The centre of Belgrade was jam-packed full of people, the atmosphere sparking with excitement. But there was an edge to it, like any minute something dark might erupt. Combined with the night skies above, Claire realised she ought to be scared. But instead she felt exhilarated, memories from the past and her old brave self floating back to her.

She peered around her, breathing it all in so she could write about it later. To the right of her was the Serbian parliament building with its distinctive green dome, smoke still weaving its way out from the back of it, scorching the air with its ashy stench. More buildings surrounded the crowds, pale cream walls a contrast to the colourful crowds. Buses and trucks were parked a few rows ahead of Claire with people jumping around on their roofs. Nikola told them that people had travelled from all over the country to join the protests, barging their way through police barricades in their trucks and coaches.

A cheer went up and Claire looked towards Belgrade City Hall, a square building with pillars adorning its entrance. On the balcony was the opposition leader, Vojislav Koštunica. Next to him, a man waved a huge blue, white and red flag, its colours catching in the light shining from the balcony's ceiling. A chant started, loud and fierce. Nikola joined in, the scarf covering his face billowing out with each word. People surged forward and Milo grabbed Claire's arm, pulling her close to him. She could feel the bare skin of his arms against her, the bristle of his hairs.

'You okay?' he asked.

A scream pierced the air and someone shouted out '*Crvene beretke!*'

It was like a war cry for the crowd. Everyone surged forward, and Nikola followed with his fist in the air, disappearing among a sea of people. Claire heard Milo shout her name.

Then suddenly, he was gone.

The crowd closed in around her, knocking the breath out of her chest. Her head swam, panic swelling inside. But then strong, cool hands were gripping her under her arms, pulling her through the crowds into the darkness of a nearby alleyway. She leaned down to take in huge gulps of air, the stink of rubbish and urine clogging her nostrils. Claire was starting to regret her choice of attire, a long patterned dress she'd bought in a Novi Sad flea market the week before.

When she looked up, Milo was standing in front of her, eyes frantic as they travelled all over her.

'Are you hurt?' he asked.

'No, I'm fine. Where'd you go?'

'I tried to hold onto you but you slipped away.' He took a step closer to her, his face intense. 'I don't like that, when you slip away.'

The sounds of the crowd dissipated slightly, the air between them wavering. Claire's eyes dropped to Milo's lips and she remembered how it had felt when they were pressed against hers.

But then she thought of all that came after.

No, she thought to herself, stepping away.

'Claire! Milo!'

They looked down the alleyway to see Nikola running towards them.

'Come!' Nikola said. 'We must celebrate.'

Nikola led them to one of the city's underground bars that had been set up for young people to escape to during the war, so underground a password was needed to get in. When they entered, it was as though they were in someone's shabby-chic front room with people draped across comfortable-looking chairs, others leaning against bookcases. The heady scent of perfume and sweat and beer and wine mingled with the smell of ashes from outside. The only thing that suggested this was more than a house party was the quaint little bar that sat in the corner of the room.

The rest of the night dissolved into a stream of *slivovica* as they all danced on the tables with Nikola's friends, screaming '*Zbogom Milošević*' at the top of their lungs. After a while, Milo pulled Claire against him, twirling her down the table and smashing glasses with his feet as people shouted expletives at him. Milo ignored them, pulling Claire even closer as the *slivovica* slithered into the restricted parts of her mind, memories from that autumn evening three years before trickling out: the feel of Milo's lips against hers; the way his fingers had trailed over her thighs.

'Let's get out of here,' he whispered to her, putting his hand out to her.

She hesitated a moment. She had to keep her wits about her. And yet the way he was standing there in his black cargo trousers and tight grey T-shirt, the way his cheeks were flushed . . . She felt her body respond, growing warm, almost feverish.

She took in a deep breath then grabbed his hand. He smiled, leading her out of the building and into the cold air which smelled of fire and revolution. They stumbled down a network of alleyways, his fingers wrapped around hers, a sense of urgency pulling them both along. Eventually, they reached a hidden patch of grass with a memorial at its centre, the sound of the Danube rippling nearby. Milo helped her climb over the black iron fence surrounding the memorial, then pulled her against him. They were still for a few moments, looking into each other's eyes, then Milo smashed his lips against hers. Her body reacted violently, her fingers digging into his hair as they stumbled across the garden and down towards the ground, the smell of mud and grass making memories from three years ago merge into now.

His fingers fumbled with the edge of her skirt as he pulled

it up and she undid his trousers, movements brisk. But as she did so, a thought shimmered into her mind. There was another time like this, wasn't there? Three years ago, Milo's eyes sweet, yearning, his fingers soft. Now they were hard and he could barely look into Claire's eyes. Something inside her *slivovica*-infested mind recognised the difference.

She placed her hand over his and he looked up, confused.

'Milo,' she said as softly as she could, suddenly feeling very sober. 'It's not the right time.'

For a fleeting second, she saw disappointment in his eyes. But it was quickly replaced by something softer. He removed his hand, and gently smoothed her skirt over her legs without saying a word.

He stood, put his hand out to her and helped her up.

When they got back to the sanctuary later that night, Milo took Claire's hand once more before she walked back into the farmhouse.

'Can you get the afternoon off tomorrow?' he asked.

'I think so, I haven't really had a day off since I arrived. Why?'

He smiled. 'You'll see.'

The next afternoon, as Koštunica was accepted as the country's new president, Milo and Claire disappeared into Serbia's countryside down the River Danube on a rickety old motorised boat he'd managed to get hold of, leaving the celebrations behind.

Trees bent over the river, their branches dipping into the water. All kinds of birds hopped from tree to tree, merrily chirping away as though they too understood what was happening to their country that day. It was warmer than it had been all week, giving Claire an excuse to wear the pretty eggshell-blue summer dress she'd bought.

As they drifted down the river, she peered over at Milo. He looked content, or as content as she'd seen him in a while anyway, his face relaxed, his eyes squinting as he looked up at the sun. She remembered the feel of his lips on hers the night before. She'd been drunk, both of them had, and now she felt that nervousness of the morning after, not quite believing the kiss had happened.

Milo moved the boat towards a small clearing at the side of the river surrounded by trees, the ground heavy with soft grass. The sun poured into the clearing, creating a soft yellow glow. As the boat bumped against the edge, Milo jumped out, tied the rope around a nearby tree and helped Claire onto land. Then he reached under a blanket and pulled out an old picnic basket.

'Hungry?' he asked.

Claire smiled.

He reached out for her and she took his hand, feeling the warmth of the sun on his skin. He spread the blanket on the floor and Claire sat, opening the basket to see huge chunks of bread, plump tomatoes still on their vine and jars of *kajmak*, a cheesy Serbian spread she'd grown to love. There was a bottle of *lozovača* too, a grape brandy she'd seen Nikola drinking, along with two plastic glasses.

'This is lovely,' Claire said.

'I wanted to do something special. I need you to know how much you mean to me.'

She didn't know what to say. It still felt so new, so fragile, and she wasn't sure where she wanted to take this.

There was a strange clicking noise from the river. They both turned to see two odd-looking birds with spiky black feathers on their heads floating across from each other, taking turns to shake their heads.

'What are they doing?' Claire asked.

'They're Great Crested Grebes,' Milo said. 'It's how they woo the ladies.'

Claire looked towards the food. 'But you do it with cheese spread and brandy.'

He shrugged. 'Hey, I'm a smooth operator.'

'Okay, you keep telling yourself that.'

Over the next hour, they ate and drank, laughing about things at the sanctuary, chatting about how much Holly was growing. After a while, Milo pulled out an old portable CD player with speakers attached to it, playing a Serbian folk CD he'd been given. As Claire listened to the low, sensuous voice of the woman singing against the background of a Serbian lute, she felt her head grow woozy from the sun and brandy.

'I think I'm going to end up in the Danube if I drink any more of this,' she said, gesturing to her glass.

'I'd like to see you in the Danube,' Milo said, his eyes running over the low neckline of Claire's dress. 'You know they call *lozovača* the juice of love?' he added, his face growing serious.

Claire smiled. 'You'll have to try better than that.'

He leaned over and grabbed two long leaves, jutting them out from the back of his head, shaking his head at her like one of the Great Crested Grebes.

She laughed.

'Did it work?' he asked, lowering the leaves, his face growing serious.

Her smile slipped from her face. She knew there'd be a moment like this, had agonised over it all night. Could this really work out between them, two people scarred by their own tragedies? Could it work out for *her*? She'd come here to leave the past behind, to make a go of a new future. But then hadn't meeting Milo paved the way for that new future?

It wasn't until she'd met him in Exmoor that she really understood what she wanted.

Without giving herself the chance to explore the answer to those questions, she impulsively leaned over and pressed her lips against his. It felt strange to kiss him without the blur of alcohol and cover of night. Strange and wonderful. He wound his arms around her and pulled her close to him. Their kiss deepened, making her feel like she was tumbling down a whirlpool.

He gently pulled her dress over her head and she leaned back onto the grass, feeling nervous as his eyes travelled all over her. She'd lost so much weight and the bra she was wearing was grey from being washed too much. But he didn't seem to notice, whispering she was beautiful as he pressed his lips against her collarbone and unhooked her bra. She stroked the bristles of his hair, felt the thud of his pulse as his chest pressed against hers. Then she pushed up his T-shirt, running her fingers over his chest, his arms. He was thinner than she remembered too, but she could feel the muscles, taut, wiry.

They carefully finished undressing each other, touching each other, kissing each other. Then he gently nudged her legs apart and it was like all that had happened since they'd first kissed no longer existed as he sunk into her.

Soon, they grew frantic, desperate to get past skin and flesh and feel as much of each other as they could, the trees stirring above, the river rippling nearby. When Milo came, he cried out, looking at Claire with raw desperation.

'Don't give up on me,' he said as he wrapped his arms around her, her head sinking against his chest. 'Promise me?'

'I promise,' she whispered.

When they got back to the sanctuary a few hours later, Nikola was passed out in the yard, his arms curled around a bottle of vodka, an Otpor flag in his outstretched hand. Claire and Milo smiled to each other as they stepped over him.

'He must've been drinking today too,' Claire said.

'He has a lot to celebrate. And so do we,' Milo said, leading her into the kitchen and pulling a chair out for her. 'That's why I'm going to make you the best supper this ramshackle kitchen can offer.'

She leaned her chin on her hand, unable to keep the smile off her face as she watched him potter about, remembering the feel of his fingers, his lips, everything still making her skin tingle. Yes, what they now had felt fragile, like those buildings she'd seen on the way into Belgrade, damaged, heavy with history, so brittle they might collapse at any moment. But they didn't collapse, did they? They remained standing, despite everything, and so would she and Milo.

And she knew Milo felt the same too, the look of disbelief on his face making him seem like a child contemplating something new and wonderful.

Then Filipe's deep voice filled the hallway, the sound of running echoing outside. Milo stepped away from Claire as Nikola walked in, face tense.

'What's going on?' Milo asked him.

'Luna ate one of the pups,' Nikola said in a slurred voice. 'She tried to eat the others too.'

Claire felt nausea rise inside. '*Ate?*'

'Same happened with one of our Jack Russell bitches back on the farm,' Milo said.

Claire gripped the edges of the table as uninvited images flooded her mind. 'But why?'

Nikola leaned against a chair, his eyes blinking like he was trying to get used to the idea himself. 'I've heard of it but never seen it until now. Four of them are fine, two not so much. Filipe said there's nothing that can be done for the two of them. They'll need to be put down, Filipe's doing it now.'

Claire put her head in her hands. It was all too much. 'Oh God.'

'It happens a lot, Claire,' Milo said softly as he placed his hand on her shoulder.

'It doesn't make it any less horrible! Will any survive?' she asked Nikola.

'Maybe a couple.'

Filipe appeared in the hallway, face livid with anger. 'The boxes were labelled wrong. It's the wrong fucking medication. The same happened with the eye drops last week. Audrey needs to bloody change suppliers.'

'Does that mean you can't put them down?' Claire asked.

Filipe shook his head.

'I have a shotgun,' Nikola said, ready to walk out.

Filipe blocked his way. 'No, you're too drunk.'

'I'll do it,' Milo said, striding towards the door.

'Wait!' Claire grabbed his wrist, thinking of the last time he'd held a gun. 'Are you sure that's a good idea?'

'You heard Filipe, they're in pain.'

'We should do it soon,' Filipe said.

Milo looked at Claire briefly then strode out of the farmhouse with Filipe. Nikola opened one of the cupboards, doing what he always did in a tense situation: reaching for a bottle of *slivovica*.

'I just don't get why Luna would do that,' Claire said, taking the glass Nikola had poured for her.

'Luna was there when NATO bombed Belgrade. It must've done something to her up here,' he said, tapping his temple with his finger.

'I wish the pups could be saved.'

'No, Claire. It's—'

A shot rang out and they both put their hands over their ears. When Claire lowered her hands, she heard shouting.

'Just the puppies,' Filipe shouted out, his voice ringing through the walls. 'Didn't you understand, Milo? Just the fucking puppies.'

Claire ran outside to see Milo standing in the middle of the yard, the shotgun hanging by his side. Filipe was striding up and down in front of him, shaking his head.

'What's going on?' Claire asked.

Filipe looked up at her. 'Milo shot Luna.'

'*Govno yedno*,' Nikola muttered, shaking his head in disgust.

Claire looked at Milo, not quite believing what Filipe had just told her.

'She was about to attack another one of the surviving pups. I had to stop her, Claire. It was the only way.'

'Not the only way, Milo,' Filipe said. 'You were – what do you Brits call it? – trigger-happy.'

Everything seemed to shift around Claire, the sky wobbling, the hills shimmering.

She ran to him, yanking the gun from his hand and throwing it across the yard. It clattered against a trough of water, knocking it over and spilling dirty water everywhere.

Milo stared at her blankly, his words from earlier ringing in her ears.

Don't give up on me, Claire.

215

Chapter Fourteen

Ko Phi Phi Don, Thailand
2004

Mum's painting is leaning against a large palm tree that must have withstood the force of the wave. There's a huge crack down the middle meaning half of it is hanging off, the paint smudged. It's of Mum, a turquoise sea spread out before her, and it doesn't look quite finished, one of the eyes missing, the one remaining eye seeming to stare right into my soul. She probably meant to paint her best friend Erin on it too. It's strange to see this new painting, Mum's once beautiful face hardened by age. The last time I saw one of Mum's paintings was a few months ago on a London events website when I was trying to find things to do with the girls over the summer holidays. I'd been scrolling through the pages then my eyes had snagged on her familiar brush strokes – yet another painting of her with Erin. This one showed them both underwater, faces blank. It terrifies me to think of that now. Next to the painting was a photo of Mum looking so different, older, more weary.

It made my heart hurt to see that she was exhibiting in London and yet hadn't been in touch to suggest meeting up. That's what we used to do when I reached my late teens and beyond: use her exhibitions as an excuse to meet up. I'd catch a train to her launches – London, Manchester, Liverpool, Brighton. I'd walk around, a glass of wine in hand, pretending I knew what I was looking at, all the time just wanting to watch my mum charming all the party-goers, swirling around some gallery or another in a long flowing dress, her dark hair loose and curly.

She'd always come to me at the end of the party, just when I was starting to get angry and frustrated that she wasn't paying me enough attention, and she'd sweep me around in her arms, shouting to the room, 'Look, it's my beautiful daughter!' making me feel like the most precious thing on earth.

And then we'd go out for dinner with her bohemian friends and they'd gush about my mum's talent, asking if I painted too. The special feeling would go then. Instead, I'd feel awkward, left out and humiliated, having done nothing but office work since leaving school. Mum would laugh, say, 'Of *course* not, Lou's too clever to splodge paint on canvas like me. She's wonderful at her job, her boss gave her a pay-rise last week, you know? Fastest typer in the West, she is.' And everyone would laugh and I'd feel even worse, sure my mum was ashamed of me, mocking me.

But looking back, I think she sensed my discomfort and was only trying to deflect attention away, make me feel better. I'd do the same for my girls.

Sam walks towards Mum's painting now and gently runs his fingers over the streaks of red and orange. 'Like fire,' he says. 'There's a question mark in her eye too, see?'

I see Sam's right, the pupil a circle in a question mark. 'She did the same in some other paintings,' I say. 'When I asked her why, she said it was a symbol of our desire to discover the truth about ourselves, the eternal question: who are we really? I think she often asked herself that, having not really known her parents.'

I used to think that was pretentious. But now I understand it, especially since that eternal question has burned into my mind during the past couple of days: who am I? What's my purpose? The only thing I'm sure of is my role as Chloe and Olivia's mother.

'She must've been staying here if she painted the walls,' Sam says. 'Or maybe the bungalow's owner paid her to do it?'

'She painted the walls at home sometimes. Drove Dad insane.' I can almost see Mum doing that now, standing on tiptoes, her arm moving in graceful arcs as she sweeps her paintbrush across the wall.

My mobile phone rings. We both look at it in surprise. Sam had warned me that though some networks had restored their connections, many hadn't. 'You must be one of the lucky ones,' he said, peering down at his phone. 'Still nothing for me. Though I managed to call my mum earlier from someone else's phone: she'd not heard of Claire, Milo or Holly. As far as she was concerned, your mum was out here for a change of scenery.'

I sigh. 'Worth a try.' I look down at my phone. 'It's my dad anyway. I better take it.'

'Of course,' he says. 'I'll go do some searching.'

He strolls off and I put the phone to my ear. 'Dad?'

'Louise? Is that you?' He's shouting the way he does whenever he talks on the phone. My heart goes out to him.

'Yes, Dad.'

'I called the girls earlier, Will said you were going to some island.'

'That's right, I'm here now.' I look around the shattered shore and try not to think about how Dad would feel if he saw all this.

'Any luck?' he asks.

'Nothing yet.'

'You know I would come if I could, Louise.'

'I know, Dad,' I say softly. He hates travelling on planes. In fact, he hates travelling on anything other than trains, his anxiety making it difficult for him.

'It'll be her birthday next month,' he says. There's a catch in his voice when he says that and I realise this must be hard for him too, Mum missing. He'd never stopped loving her, just hated the way she got when Erin disappeared.

I sink down onto the sand, and look at the photo of Mum and Erin. 'Mum's best friend, Erin,' I say. 'She came to stay a few times, didn't she?'

'Yes, why?'

I explain about finding Mum's bag and passport with Claire Shreve's atlas, and Claire's connection to Erin's daughter, Holly. 'I think Mum was trying to find Erin through her daughter, that's why she was out here. She could have seen photos of Holly in the papers and thought maybe Erin was out here with her. Maybe if I find Mum out here, I can help her try to track Erin down?'

There's silence from Dad at first then he sighs. 'I'm not sure finding Erin will be good for your mother.'

'Why?'

'She's very troubled,' Dad said after thinking about it for a few moments. 'I saw her at her worst when she stayed one Christmas. She was miserable, constantly crying and ranting.'

'Over what?'

'A man.'

'Her husband?'

Dad pauses. 'No.'

'She was having an affair then?'

'Yes. With her brother-in-law.'

219

I sit up straight, heart thumping. 'You mean Milo James?'

'Yes. I overheard her talking to your mother about it. What disgusted me was Milo was young at the time, just a teenager. Over sixteen but still. And, to make matters worse, it happened while Erin's husband was injured after serving in the Falklands. Your mother was very annoyed at her.'

'I'm not surprised. Is there anything else you can remember that might help me?'

'No, nothing else. Your mother didn't really tell me what Erin got up to and I didn't want to know after that.' He's quiet for a few moments. 'You'll find her, won't you? You'll find her and bring her home?'

My eyes fill with tears. 'I'll find her, Dad. I promise.'

'Good,' he says, his voice catching. 'That's good.'

When he's gone, I clutch my phone to my chest, tears starting to roll down my cheeks. 'Oh, Mum,' I whisper to myself. 'Please be alive.'

'Everything okay?' Sam says, jogging over and crouching down beside me.

'It's just difficult talking to Dad, that's all.'

He squeezes my hand. 'Of course it is.'

'He told me something interesting though. Apparently, Mum's best friend was having an affair with her brother-in-law, Milo James.'

Sam's eyebrows rise. 'Very interesting.'

'Did you find anything?' I ask, brushing my tears away.

'There's too much stuff here for me to make head or tail of it, and most of it will be from other parts of the island anyway, dumped here when the wave receded. Might be worth you having a look to see if you recognise anything though.'

I stand up, brushing the sand from my knees, and follow him down the beach, stepping over debris, a tangle of clothes, broken kettles, cupboard doors and so much more. There's half a boat turned on its side nearby and a whole bamboo roof that's somehow stayed intact but is now caught up in the branches of an upturned palm tree.

There are diggers on the side; the clear-up has already started, and people in blue scrubs scour the beach in the distance, no doubt looking for bodies.

I'm about to suggest heading back when a flash of yellow cloth catches my eye tangled in a palm tree nearby. I walk up to it. It looks just like the cardigan I got for Mum for her birthday with hearts on it.

Sam stands on tiptoes and carefully untangles it. He hands it to me and I hold it to my nose.

It's hers.

My legs seem to collapse beneath me and I sink down onto a spare patch of sand. I look up at Sam. 'Oh God, Sam, what if she was in these bungalows when the wave hit?'

Sam sits down next to me without saying a word, and we both stay like that for a while, taking in the ravished beach, the now-calm sea beyond it. Soon, it starts to grow dark, the debris around us like pieces of coal. So we head back to the stretch of beach where we were dropped off to wait for Sam's friend to return. As we wait, I look down at Mum's yellow cardigan, remembering when I'd given it to her. I'd treated her to lunch for her birthday and she'd put the cardigan straight on despite the fact it completely clashed with her tie-dye dress. I remember with a flinch how embarrassed I'd been as other diners had turned to look at her. Then I remember what happened next and laugh to myself: I was a few weeks pregnant with Chloe and was suffering from the worst kind of morning sickness, so I'd run to the toilet to puke. Mum joked that she really must've looked awful if *that* was my reaction.

'What are you laughing at?' Sam asks, a smile on his face.

'Oh, it's silly really, I was just . . .' I pause. There's something about that memory that's spinning just beyond my grasp.

I frown as it suddenly comes to me.

'What's wrong?' Sam asks.

'On the phone earlier, Dad mentioned one Christmas when Erin James came to stay. I just remembered I found her being sick in the toilet. Later, I overheard Mum asking her, "is it his?" Of course, I didn't understand what she meant at the time. But now I realise she must've been asking if the baby was Milo's.'

Sam's mouth drops open. 'Jesus. What a mess that family was.'

There's a noise nearby. We both look up to see the boat appear. Sam stands, putting his hand out to me. I take it, letting him pull me up.

'There's another passenger on there,' I say, noticing a man standing on the boat.

The moonlight shines down onto the boat and I squint my eyes, trying to get a better look. Then my breath catches in my mouth.

It's Will.

Chapter Fifteen

Iso-Syöte, Finland
2000

Claire looked out at the white landscape spread out before her – skies as pink as a child's blush; snow piled upon snow piled upon snow. It was like looking out at a scene from a Christmas card each morning, snow-clad fir trees as far as the eye could see with wooden huts like theirs dotted between them. It felt completely untouched, like she'd arrived at the beginning of the world.

Milo was in the distance, leaning against a tree, blowing out a circle of smoke as he stared into the forest. His hair had grown, his fringe now long enough to hang in his eyes the way Claire loved. He was dressed head to toe in black, stark and tall against the snowy backdrop, the opposite to Claire in her scuffed pink salopettes and the white moon boots she'd kept from her teenage winter travels.

She stepped outside and did what she'd been doing ever since they'd arrived a month ago: completely avoided the path he'd carefully dug out for them and jumped into the snow instead, sinking in up to her shins. Milo turned, face softening and opened his arms to her. Happiness tugged at her insides as she pumped her legs to get to him. By the time she was in his arms, she was out of breath, face tingling with cold, icicles already forming on her eyelashes and hair as she breathed in the pine-scented air.

'Do you know what time it is?' Milo murmured into her hair.

'I don't care. Time doesn't happen out here.'

'Easy for you to say, tucked away with your laptop.'

'But you make me so *tired*,' she whined, pressing herself against him, the sore parts of her throbbing so much, wanting him even more.

He pulled his gloves off and traced his cold thumb along her jaw line, his brown eyes flickering with emotion. She felt that magnetic pull of his making her lose focus.

'We can go back,' he said, his voice husky. 'We don't need to leave for another fifteen minutes.'

'It'll take us that long to get ourselves out of our snow gear.'

'But it's the only thing that works in these temperatures, this skin-on-skin thing.' He slid his hands under her coat and jumper, his cold fingertips making her flinch as he brushed them across the bare skin of her back.

The past two months had been a blur of his body against hers, lips pressed hard against every part of her, his fingers, his smell. They'd barely noticed the transition from one country to the next, both minds fuzzy from lack of sleep, every part of their bodies aching from what they did to each other and what they wanted to do again and again.

But beneath the surface was what Milo had done to Luna back in Serbia. Claire couldn't quite shake it off, despite Milo's explanation that it was a natural instinct drummed into him at the farm to protect the youngest, healthiest animals. He'd gone into autopilot, he told her, but had deeply regretted it after. She'd believed him, but it played on her mind, especially when she thought of what his brother had once said to her: 'If an animal needs to die – for food, to put it out of pain, to save a younger animal – you kill it.' She thought Milo was different from his brother, that the 'James Curse', as he called it, had bypassed him. But had killing his own brother brought something out in him?

She'd thought long and hard about how the impact of what he'd done to Luna would affect the fragile beginnings of their relationship. But she saw the vulnerability in him, and the damage that both his upbringing and his brother's death had wrought. If she had vowed to save animals that slipped between the lines, why not people? If she gave up on this damaged man, a man she was beginning to fall in love with, then what hope was there for her aspirations to be a woman who made a difference and didn't just observe?

It was hard after the incident though. Despite the wonder they shared at finally being together after all those years apart, the atmosphere at the sanctuary those last few weeks was horrid; Nikola cold, the other Serbians keeping their distance. Filipe was the only person who seemed to have forgiven Milo. When Filipe's father passed away and left the reindeer farm to him, he invited them to move out to Finland to help him run it – and so there they were, living on the earnings they made from Milo's work on the farm and Claire's freelancing, Milo's savings from his family's farm sale stowed away for future adventures.

Future adventures. That's exactly what Claire wanted right now. As she'd come to learn in San Francisco, her wanderlust was returning and it needed sating. Combined with her desire to make a stamp on the world with her writing, she felt like she was really getting into her stride as she marched down her chosen path. And Finland was ideal: she'd never been before so there were new vistas to explore, new foods to taste, new scents to smell . . . and something to get her writing teeth into: the land disputes between the indigenous Sami people and the Finnish government were ideal material for her.

Life was close to perfect those first few weeks in Finland. It wasn't just about the nights they spent exploring each other's bodies. There were snow fights, day-long expeditions on snow mobiles, just the two of them discovering Lapland's landscape. When they stayed in, they read each other passages from their books – Claire some travel memoir or another, Milo one of the classics he'd brought back from the sanctuary.

Living together had its quirks, of course, as it did for every couple. Claire was her usual messy self while Milo preferred no clutter. She slept in too, while Milo would rise with the sun. Then there were the nights Milo spent pacing the house with his copy of *Paradise Lost* as though something in those scuffed pages would give him the answer to all his internal troubles; the way, sometimes, his touch would grow too rough, his lips too forceful. The nightmares were bad too, Milo waking in the night and calling out his brother's name. When Claire tried to talk to him about it, he closed up, the usually happy air darkening. After all the darkness, Claire craved light. So that's what she tried to keep, her questions gradually dying away.

Excited families poured into the arrivals lounge at Kuusamo airport, reminding Claire of how it had felt two months ago, the reindeer and sled that greeted them in the baggage area making her giggle like a child. Three hours later, she'd been crying because her toes and fingers were so cold.

Among the sea of faces, a hint of red curls bounced towards them; a freckled face; a bright red coat and white woollen mittens. And then, two distinctive blond heads bopping above the crowds ahead.

Holly spotted Claire and Milo, her green eyes lighting up. Her face had thinned out, her high cheekbones exposed, and she had red tulip lips and eyes so big and slanted, they didn't look real. She was beautiful, breathtakingly so. Claire could hardly believe this was that fourteen-year-old girl who'd hidden under a table that night three years ago.

Holly ran towards them, throwing herself into Milo's arms as he laughed, twirling her around. People turned to stare at them both. Claire couldn't blame them. They looked stunning together, red hair against black, perfect skin, striking features.

In the distance, Claire's sister Sofia appeared, her son Alex checking his phone as he trailed after her. Ed, Sofia's husband, wasn't able to fly out due to business commitments, his usual excuse for missing get-togethers. Sofia looked as elegant as ever in smart blue jeans and a fluffy white jumper, her long blonde tresses twisted into a French plait, a contrast to Claire's messy brown hair. Despite how smartly she was dressed, she looked just like their dad with his light hair, but they couldn't be more different in personality.

'Look at you!' Sofia said when she reached Claire, holding her at arm's length. 'Your hair's the same colour it was when we were kids! You've put some weight on too,' her sister added, pinching the skin on Claire's arm.

Claire yelped. 'Sofia!'

'What? It suits you. You were too skinny after . . .' Her voice trailed off as she looked at Milo, her blue eyes narrowing as she did what she usually did, judging him before she'd even spoken to him. That had always struck Claire as strange – Sofia's penchant for jumping to conclusions, considering her job as a solicitor. Wasn't the idea 'innocent before proven guilty'?

'You been down the gym, Alex?' Claire asked her nephew as he joined them. He'd grown so much in the few months since she'd seen him last. He even had light gold stubble on his chin and cheeks, the thick jumper and baggy jeans he was wearing making him look like some famous football player.

She wrapped her arms around his broad shoulders, giving him a peck on the cheek.

'You all meet Holly at Gatwick okay?' she asked as they waited for Holly and Milo to finish hugging.

'Yeah,' Alex said. 'She's really cool.'

Sofia raised her eyebrow just long enough for Claire to notice. What could she possibly find wrong with Holly?

Holly pulled away from Milo and turned to Claire, a host of emotions running over her pretty face. Then she jogged over and wrapped her arms around Claire's shoulders. She was so tall now her curls muffled Claire's mouth.

Claire stood still at first, surprised. They barely knew each other and the last time they'd seen each other, Holly's father was lying dead in Milo's arms. But she was holding Claire so tight, with such enthusiasm, Claire couldn't help but relax against her, wrapping her arms around her too.

'You're a woman,' Claire whispered.

'I hope so,' Holly replied in a voice that had lost all its girlishness. She pulled away from Claire and searched her eyes. 'I'm so pleased you and Milo got together.'

Milo strolled over and shook Alex's hand before kissing Sofia on her powdered cheek.

'How was the journey?' he asked her, trying to hide his nerves with a bright smile. Claire had warned him what Sofia was like and it was obvious he was trying his best with her. Claire's heart went out to him.

'The food was dreadful,' Sofia replied as she looked him up and down, assessing him like a CT scanner. 'But the flight crew were nice enough.' Sofia pulled a letter from her designer bag. 'Right, we better get those bloody dogs.'

Claire and Milo smiled at each other. It had taken some persuading to convince Ben to let Archie stay with them for the next six months. They'd talked over email, curt, cold messages. When Claire told him she was with Milo, it made things even worse. But in the end, somehow, he relented, and they'd made arrangements for Archie *and* Blue to come over with her sister and nephew. Maybe it had something to do with the fact that, according to one of her old work colleagues, Ben had met someone, a perky blonde with a penchant for bright red lipstick and fifties-style dresses called Belle. Claire was pleased for him. Maybe Belle could give him everything she couldn't?

Holly slung her arms around Claire and Milo's shoulders, her face bright with happiness. 'It's so cool the dogs are coming too. Then we'll all be together again, just as it should be.'

Sofia raised an eyebrow again but Claire ignored her. She wouldn't let her sister's prejudgements about Milo and Holly ruin their first Christmas together.

Four hours later, they all arrived at Filipe's house – Claire and Milo's cabin was too small to host more than four people for dinner. Filipe may have had to leave his job and the conveniences of Helsinki behind when his father died, but he refused to give up the luxuries, his new house a modern building entrenched in a snowy mountain for insulation.

Everyone bundled out of their cars, including Archie who leapt out into the snow while Blue delicately sniffed it before cocking his leg and spraying it with his scent.

The door to the house opened and Filipe appeared at the entranceway in a thick grey jumper, his glasses perched on his nose. He gave Claire a kiss on the cheek then grabbed Milo into a hug. They'd grown close over the past couple of months, working day in and day out together on the reindeer farm.

'I don't think I've had so many Brits on my doorstep,' Filipe said, beaming at everyone. 'Come in, please!'

Everyone walked in, shaking the snow from their hair and handing their coats over to Filipe. Claire was surprised to see Holly was wearing a beautiful oriental-style dress with long sleeves and blue flowers all over it, a contrast to the jeans and wellies Claire had seen her wear three years ago.

'It's from Japan,' she said, noticing Claire's interest. 'I saw it on the internet, and it reminded me of the dress you wore to the wedding.'

Everyone went quiet at the mention of the wedding. Claire examined Holly's face. How could she mention it so nonchalantly? Milo must have thought the same as he regarded Holly with worried eyes.

Filipe smiled to ease the tension. 'Good choice, you look divine.'

'Lovely place,' Sofia said, smoothing her blonde hair down as she looked around. 'Worth a fortune too, I imagine?'

'Mum!' Alex said. 'You can't say things like that.'

'I can say what I want,' she said. 'Filipe's a successful man. He doesn't mind, do you, Filipe?'

'I don't mind at all,' he said, hooking his arm through Sofia's and winking at Claire. 'In fact, I'm going to invite you for Christmas every year to remind me of the fact.'

He led her down his wide hallway as Archie and Blue bounded off to explore the house, Filipe's two white cats darting out of their way. Filipe's house was exactly as you'd imagine a Scandinavian home ought to be: crisp white walls, heated pine floors and minimalist furniture in bright, primary colours. As they passed various rooms, Sofia peered in, raising an eyebrow. Clearly Filipe was going up and up in her estimation.

'Welcome,' Filipe said as he led them into his large kitchen-diner, inviting them to sit at his table. He poured wine into each of their glasses then lifted his glass. 'A very Finnish *tervetuloa* to you all.'

'*Kiitos paljon*,' Holly replied in near-perfect Finnish.

'Wonderful!' Filipe exclaimed as Milo smiled.

'Milo sent me a phrasebook,' Holly said. 'I haven't learned much, just a few bits and pieces.'

'Claire told me you're half-Sami, Filipe,' Sofia said, taking a sip of her wine and leaning back in her chair. 'She said she's writing an article about the land disputes here. I'm not sure if she mentioned that I'm a solicitor specialising in land disputes?'

Claire exchanged a look with Alex. Why did Sofia have to dive right in with the serious talk?

'Yes,' Filipe replied. 'My family come from the Inari region of Finland. The government's trying to log there, but I'm fighting them, of course.'

'You have legal representatives?' Sofia asked.

Alex rolled his eyes as Claire smiled to herself.

'I do. But let's not bore everyone with talk of land disputes,' Filipe said. 'I can tell you more when we visit.'

'We're going to the north?' Holly asked, face bright with excitement.

'I told Filipe you kept banging on about the Samis and their reindeer in your letters,' Milo said. 'So he invited us all to join him for their traditional Boxing Day activities. Plus Claire wants to interview them all for an article she's planning.'

Holly clapped her hands together. 'Awesome!'

Milo laughed. 'Thought you'd be happy.' He turned to Alex. 'I've arranged for a *Pesäpallo* match while we're there too. Claire told me you were into your sport.'

Alex smiled. 'Cheers, mate. But what's *Pesäpallo*?'

Everyone laughed.

'It's the Finnish national sport, you'll love it,' Milo explained.

'Tell Sofia what you've arranged for her,' Claire said, putting her hand over Milo's. He'd been working so hard the past few weeks arranging things for them. She wanted Sofia to see that and understand he wasn't just the farmer who shot his brother dead.

Milo turned to Sofia. 'Claire mentioned you've always been fascinated by the Northern Lights, so I've arranged for us to do a lantern procession up the hill where we'll have the best chance of seeing them.'

Sofia smiled tightly, her eyes lingering over Claire and Milo's joined hands. 'That's very kind of you, Milo.'

'This is going to be the best holiday *ever*,' Holly said.

'Definitely,' Alex said, smiling at her.

Milo squeezed Claire's hand, his face soft with contentment.

Filipe placed a bubbling Finnish meatball dish called *lihapullat* at the centre of the table alongside a basket of rye bread, the mouth-watering smell of paprika and garlic drifting towards Claire. After they'd finished eating, they all headed into the living room, a huge square room with a modern fireplace right at its centre dividing it in two. One side of the room was scattered with multi-coloured cushions, a large blue corner sofa stretching across its back. On the other side was a pool table and a wall of bookshelves, huge windows overlooking the snowy forest either side of the room.

Claire and Milo sat on the sofa as Holly placed herself neatly on one of the scatter cushions on the floor. Alex joined her on the cushion next to the fire and Holly shot him a big smile.

As Claire watched the flames flicker over their young faces, she felt old. The fact was, she was nearly twenty years older than Holly and Alex. And lately, she'd really begun to notice it, especially when looking in the mirror. Where once her full cheeks, bright eyes and pink lips were the focus, now all she saw were the bits in between: the circles under her eyes; the sunken dips under her cheeks; the fine lines around her lips.

She turned to look at Milo's profile as he smiled at Holly. But what did that matter? She might feel older, but she also felt happier. Like she was finally carving out a place for herself.

Milo turned to her as though sensing her thoughts and placed his lips against hers. She shivered, her whole body responding to him, and he pulled her even closer, wrapping his arms tight around her. Out of the corner of her eye, she saw Sofia watching them with that cynical look in her eyes.

'So, Milo tells me you want to be a journalist like Claire?' Filipe asked Holly.

'Yep,' Holly said. 'I want to travel the world and write about all the places I see.'

'So you'll study journalism at university?' Sofia asked.

She shrugged. 'Maybe, maybe not. Milo says qualifications aren't important.'

Sofia looked at Milo in surprise. 'You said that?'

'Of course.' He stretched his arm across the back of the chair. 'Nowadays, it's more important kids get out there and do the job, prove themselves.'

'Complete rubbish!' Sofia exclaimed, her cheeks red from all the wine she'd already drunk.

'Mum,' Alex said in a low voice.

Claire stared up at the ceiling, silently cursing Sofia and her blunt personality.

'Why's it rubbish?' Milo asked.

'Children need qualifications to get anywhere in the world nowadays,' Sofia replied.

'I didn't get any qualifications,' Milo said.

Sofia laughed. 'Well, that just proves my point then.'

'I think what Sofia means,' Filipe said, trying to ease the tension as always, 'is that *some* kind of qualification can give Holly a headstart. That's what Claire did in the end, go to university and get a degree.'

'You really think reading *Wuthering Heights* and postmodern poetry was the only thing that helped Claire's career?' Milo asked him.

Claire shot him a look. 'Look, let's change the—'

'Sentence structure. Words,' Sofia said, interrupting Claire. 'If Holly goes to university, she'll learn how to write essays to deadlines, how to write in a way that will be enjoyed and understood. She'll learn how to deal with the rigours of journalism.'

'I *am* here,' Holly murmured into her drink.

'Rigours?' Milo asked, ignoring Holly. 'Exactly how hard is it to place a Dictaphone in front of someone and ask a few questions?'

Claire looked at Milo. 'Excuse me?'

Milo's face softened. 'I just mean you either have it or you don't when it comes to writing, that's all. You have it, darling, and maybe Holly does too. So why would she need university?'

'The world's tougher now,' Sofia said, taking another sip of wine. 'Our children need foundations, qualifications, structure. They need the tools to follow the right path.'

'What's the right path?' Milo said, leaning forward, his whole body tense now. 'Holly's seventeen, for Christ's sake. She's better off spending some time figuring out if it's right for her before doing something *formal* like a degree to get there. Claire agrees, don't you, Claire?'

Everyone's eyes turned to Claire. She felt her face flush. Things had been going so well. Why had Sofia ruined it?

'I agree with both arguments actually,' she said, choosing the most diplomatic answer. 'Anyway, it's up to Holly, isn't it?'

'Are you joking?' Milo asked Claire. 'What about everything your dad used to say?'

Sofia tensed at the mention of their dad's name.

'Can we drop the subject please?' Claire said tightly, shooting Milo another warning look. 'This is all getting a bit serious.'

Milo stared back at her, his face taut with anger.

'One thing's for sure,' Filipe said, smiling at Holly. 'It's clear everyone cares about your future.'

Holly peered down at her hands, a sombre expression on her face.

'Fancy a game of pool?' Alex asked her, gesturing towards the pool table.

She smiled gratefully at him and let him help her up as Sofia watched the two of them with a grim expression on her face.

Milo stood abruptly. 'I better go find the dogs.' Then he marched from the room.

Claire watched him, confused. Surely he wasn't annoyed at *her*, she'd only been trying to keep the peace.

'First lovers' tiff?' Sofia asked.

'It wasn't a tiff,' Claire said in a voice that came out more strained than she'd intended. She caught Filipe's eye and he threw her a reassuring smile.

'You know I'm right though,' Sofia said in a low voice. She peered towards Holly and Alex to make sure they couldn't hear. 'I know Holly's not your daughter, but you have to accept you're a role model for her now. You need to—'

Claire sighed. 'Oh, just bloody leave it, Sofia.'

'I'm only thinking of you, Claire! Holly might be the only young woman you'll have an influence on.'

Claire shook her head. Her sister seemed to be obsessed with the fact Claire would never have children, somehow managing to bring it up in every phone conversation or email. But Claire had moved on, accepted her fate. How many times did she have to tell her sister that?

'I'm going to find Milo,' Claire said, standing up and taking the bottle of wine from the table next to Sofia. 'And I'm taking this to the kitchen, you've had enough.'

She left the room, searching the house for Milo without any luck. After a while, she caught sight of his tall figure standing among the trees outside, a plume of white smoke fanning out from his mouth. She pulled her boots and jacket on and let herself outside. It was bitterly cold, the freezing air biting at her cheeks. She scrunched her hands up in her pockets as the cold worked its way beneath her skin.

If Milo noticed her approaching, he didn't let on, just continued staring into the distance as the dogs bounced around in the snow together.

'I did warn you about Sofia,' she said when she got to him. 'She's a bit of a firecracker, always has been. You have to try to ignore her.'

He sighed, flicking his cigarette into the snow. It fizzled and melted the ice around it into a sludgy mess. 'It's not her.'

'Then what's wrong?'

'I felt ganged up on.'

'And I didn't? That was quite insulting what you said in there, you know – the Dictaphone thing.'

'I didn't mean it like that.'

'Well, it came out just like *that*. Look,' she said, taking his hand, 'I actually agreed with a lot of what you said. But maybe you *should* be encouraging Holly to go to uni? I don't mean in terms of qualifications. I mean so she can meet kids her own age, have fun.'

'She's doing that now.'

'Is she? We did ask her to bring a friend with her, remember? What was it she said? "Oh, I don't have close friends, they're too immature." Is that right for a girl her age?'

'Maybe she's different from other kids her age. Maybe that's a good thing?'

Claire thought of how Holly had mentioned the wedding earlier without a hint of emotion. 'Friendship's really important at that age, especially for someone who's been through what Holly has.'

Milo took in a sharp breath, staring out into the distance, his hand cold and stiff in Claire's.

'What I'm trying to say is,' Claire continued, 'she's partly your responsibility now, so you have a duty to—'

He pulled his hand away from her. 'Have a duty to do what, Claire? A duty to do what my parents did to Dale and force him down a path he should never have taken?'

Claire looked into his eyes, which were alive with anger and pain. He'd not once uttered Dale's name in the months they'd been together.

'Is that what this is all about?' she said softly.

He looked down at the snowy ground, jaw clenching. 'Yes. Jen's great but she can be a bit cold sometimes. After everything that's happened to Holly, I feel this huge sense of responsibility. I know it must be difficult for you to understand, you're not often around children and don't plan to be around them so . . .'

Claire's insides froze as hard as the ice beneath their feet. 'You make me sound like a barren old hag.'

His face softened and he put his hand out to her. 'I'm sorry, I didn't mean—'

She shoved his hand away. 'Forget it.'

She turned on her heel and stormed off towards the house, kicking up puffs of powdery snow with her boots. Maybe she was over-reacting but to completely dismiss the chances of her even being around children – what if she decided to adopt? He didn't have a right to write off her chances like that. When she got to the front door, she paused: she couldn't go back in like this; Sofia would know they'd argued. So she went around the side of the house instead, ignoring Milo as he tried to look for her. After a while, she pulled her hands out of her pockets and stared at them, focusing on the pain as the freezing air circulated around them, watching as they turned red then white. When she couldn't take it any more, she walked back inside.

The journey home was oppressive, uncomfortable. When they got back to the cabin, Holly went straight to sleep and Claire, unable to face Milo, did the same as he stayed in the living room, pacing up and down then letting in cold air as he leaned out of the window to smoke.

Some time in the night, she woke to see his brown eyes blinking down at her. He pressed his lips softly against her forehead, the smell of the cigarettes he'd been smoking swirling around her. She pretended she was still sleeping.

'I know you're awake,' he said.

She didn't say anything, couldn't, the hurtful comment he'd made still scorching her insides.

'I didn't mean to upset you,' he said. 'You told me you'd resolved yourself to a life without children, I suppose I was referring to that.'

'I meant *conceiving* a child. What if I want to adopt? Or work around children? It was insensitive, Milo.'

He sighed. 'Sorry, I should have worded it better.'

She turned around to look at him. 'How would you have worded it better? The basic premise is "you're infertile so you'll never have any idea what's right for Holly or any child for that matter".'

He put his hands either side of her face and stared into her eyes. 'Claire, no! I didn't think, I was angry, I—'

'What's happening between us, Milo?' she asked him, moving away from him.

He frowned. 'What do you mean?'

'I mean, our relationship. Is this the real deal?'

'Of course, Claire.'

'Because you understand I can't give you a family, don't you?'

Milo took her hand in his. 'You're enough. Honestly. And what do you mean by "family" exactly? Family means more than just blood. Of course you have a family, your sister, your mum, aunts and uncles. And I do too. But then there are our friends, people we *choose* to see, not forced to see through blood.'

'Have you really thought about it though?' Claire said, tears filling her eyes. 'If we stay together, there's a chance you might never have a child of your own. I mentioned adoption but I don't even know if I'm ready for that.' She paused, looking into his eyes. 'Am I really enough?'

'Of course. I love you, Claire.'

She examined his face, heart thumping. Had he really just said that? 'You *love* me?'

'Yes. How could you not know that?'

She smiled. 'I love you too.' She'd never said those three words so soon, but he'd etched himself into her, right from the very start.

He wrapped his arms around her, tracing his lips along her neck. 'I love you, Claire Shreve,' he murmured. 'I love you, I love you, I love you.'

She felt him grow hard, heard his breath quicken as his hands moved towards her breasts. This time, when they made love, the urgency that had been there the past two months was gone and it was slower, softer, like finally they felt so secure in not losing each other, they could take their time.

After, Milo pulled the curtains aside so they could lie in each other's arms and look out of the cabin window. It was especially beautiful at night, the white of the snow making the sky shine midnight blue, any lights left on in the distance giving the impression the stars had fallen from the sky and were littering the snow.

Claire peered up at Milo, taking in the way the moonlight danced over his long dark eyelashes and high cheekbones.

'I have my own baggage too,' he said, lifting himself up onto his elbow and looking into her eyes. 'Are you sure you want me? I'm damaged goods, remember – the man who killed his own brother.'

'To save others,' Claire said softly. She placed her hand on his bare chest. 'Neither of us are perfect and, yes, we have our baggage. But we know all about that baggage because we know everything about each other, right?'

Milo hesitated, his eyes flickering with something indecipherable. Then he smiled. 'Right.'

Over the next few days, Milo ensured everyone experienced all the sights and activities Iso-Syöte and the surrounding area could offer. They whooshed through Finland's forests and over its frozen lakes on snowmobiles. They went ice-fishing, drilling holes and looping fishing lines in an attempt to get dinner for the evening. They visited the reindeer farm too, Milo leading the reindeer around on the figure-of-eight circuit as they followed behind on sledges.

Sofia missed out on a lot of the activities, using the law case she was working on as an excuse to constantly check her precious PalmPilot. Claire noticed Milo watching her disapprovingly sometimes, but he didn't say anything. Instead, he brought her hot chocolate every now and again and Sofia would look up at him, her eyes suspicious. But by the third day, Claire thought she saw a small smile appear on her sister's face. Milo was finally melting her icy heart.

Some nights Claire thought she could hear the sound of sobbing coming from Holly's room. But when Holly joined them for breakfast the next morning, she looked bright-eyed and happy, no sign of any night-time tears. So Claire wondered if she was imagining it.

One morning, Milo left early to check on the farm. After Claire got ready, she knocked on Holly's door.

'Come in,' Holly said.

She pushed the door open to find Holly standing in front of the mirror, tilting her head as she examined her reflection. She took ages getting ready each morning, checking and rechecking her hair and outfit, as though her appearance meant everything to her now, a contrast to the girl who'd run around the farm in jeans and wellies. And yet she wasn't vain or shallow. It was more like she saw her appearance as some kind of armour.

'Just wanted to see what you fancy for breakfast?' Claire asked her, hovering in the doorway.

'You can come in,' Holly said, smiling at her in the mirror.

Claire stepped in, looking around. She hadn't wanted to intrude so had barely come into the small room. It looked spotless, perfectly co-ordinated outfits lined up in the open wardrobe, matching shoes beneath each one. It was unsurprising considering how fastidiously tidy Holly was, even clearing up after Claire just as Milo did.

Claire sat on Holly's bed, smoothing down the silky material of the pink duvet cover Milo had got her. Holly turned to face her, gesturing at her blue dress. 'Do you think a black cardigan will look better with this, or a white one?'

'White,' Claire said. 'I like white on you.'

'Perfect,' Holly said, plucking a soft wool cardigan from her wardrobe and slipping it on.

Claire caught sight of a clip on Holly's bedside table – the clip she'd given her in Exmoor. She reached over, picking it up. 'You still have this?'

'Of course,' Holly said. 'It's the best present I ever got. It belonged to a freedom fighter, remember? Do you know how much street cred that gives me?' They both laughed. 'Plus there's the fact you gave it to me too, of course,' Holly added. 'That makes it extra special.'

Claire tried to keep her emotions in check as she smoothed her thumb over the blue jewels on the clip. Did she really mean that much to Holly?

'So, you enjoying yourself?' Claire asked her.

'I love it here,' Holly said, looking out of the window towards the snowy landscape. 'Not just because it's so beautiful. I love being here with you and Milo too. You make me happy. You make me feel . . .' She paused, her brow creasing slightly. 'You make me feel like I belong.'

'You don't feel that way at home?'

'Aunt Jen's sweet,' she said. 'But, I don't know, I always feel like a bit of an outsider.'

Claire thought of the fact Holly hadn't brought a friend with her. 'You mean at sixth form?'

Holly shrugged. 'I guess. All people talk about is doing the right thing, you know? Teachers, Jen, even other kids now we're doing our A levels and thinking about uni. But you and Milo, you don't talk like that. I don't feel cornered when I'm with you.'

'Cornered?'

'Like I have to make decisions about stuff *right now* or I'll – I'll ruin everything forever, you know?' She reached for a silver bracelet from the small table in front of the window, trying to fasten it to her wrist with trembling fingers.

'Here,' Claire said, walking over and taking the bracelet, circling it around Holly's wrist. 'You should never feel pressurised to make the right decisions,' she said, trying to connect the ends of the bracelet. 'We all make mistakes and take the wrong turns in the road sometimes. But that doesn't mean it's a disaster. Those wrong turns have to happen so we can recognise the right ones when they come along. And when I say right, I don't mean socially acceptable decisions or those decisions that lead to the most money or whatever. I mean the ones that are right for us as individuals.'

'See, this is what I mean!' Holly said. 'You and Milo are the only people I know who talk like that. I feel whatever I choose to do, you'll support me.'

'Of *course* we will because we know you're an intelligent girl who can make her own decisions.' Claire kept her eyes on Holly's bracelet, trying to keep her emotions in check. 'Okay, I'm going to say something really cheesy now so prepare yourself for it, all right?'

Holly matched Claire's mock-serious look. 'Okay, I think I'm ready.'

'You must never feel cornered knowing Milo and I are *in* your corner. See what I did there?'

Holly laughed. 'And you call yourself a writer?'

'The cheesiest there is, sweetie.' Claire clipped the bracelet together. 'There, all done.'

'You're the best, Claire,' Holly said, her green eyes glassy.

Claire squeezed her hand. 'And so are you.'

'What about me?' They both looked up to see Milo standing in the doorway, his face red from the cold, his brown eyes heavy with emotion. Claire wondered how long he'd been standing there.

'One thing I do know is you stink of reindeer,' Claire said, pushing him out of the room and pointing to the bathroom as Holly laughed.

On Christmas Eve a few days later, everyone turned up at Filipe's house, arms laden down with presents. In Finland, Christmas is celebrated on Christmas Eve so Filipe had slung a colourful banner across the hallway with '*Hyvää Joulua!*' scrawled across it and golden stars were draped along the walls. Sitting on every surface were jolly Santas, reindeers of course and also more traditional straw ornaments wrapped in red ribbon.

After a dinner consisting of a huge plate of rutabaga casserole, a massive ham that exuded the most delicious scents, salmon and chunks of rye bread, Claire and Sofia washed up.

'Holly seems happy enough,' Sofia said.

Claire peered out of the window towards where Milo, Holly and Alex were walking the dogs in the snow. 'You sound surprised.'

'I said *seems*. We don't know what's going on beneath the surface. And what about that mother of hers?'

Claire smiled to herself. Typical of her sister to turn a compliment into a criticism.

'Even more reason why we ought to be impressed by how well-adjusted Holly is,' Claire said. 'What do you think of Milo?'

Sofia was too bloody judgemental sometimes but, despite this, her opinion mattered to Claire. With their mother tucked away in Hong Kong and other relatives spread around the UK, Sofia was the closest family she had.

'I *think* I like him,' Sofia said.

Claire smiled. That was good coming from Sofia.

'He clearly loves you,' Sofia continued, 'and Alex and I have noticed how much work he's put into making this holiday special. It's just . . .' She paused.

'Just what?'

'Something doesn't feel quite right.'

'Oh, Sofia! You just said you like him.'

'I can't explain it. Just . . . something's off. What's he like behind closed doors? I mean, he's great in front of all us but . . .'

Claire thought about their declaration of love for each other the night before. 'He's wonderful, Sofia! It's not just an act. Sure, he has his moments like any person does, we can't be perfect all the time. But he does these little things that make me feel special; things no other man I've been with has ever thought of doing.'

'Like what?'

Claire told Sofia about the time he left a notepad outside her room in Serbia, and the picnic he'd made for her. 'When I'm feeling crap about my writing, he reads his favourite passages out from articles I've written to make me feel better,' she continued. 'He does these silly little vouchers for me too, like "Private spa for two" or "Tea and scones". He makes me breakfast in bed and—'

'Okay, enough, you're making me sick. I get it. What about

security then, can he offer you that? Milo was telling Alex your visa only lasts a few months. What then?'

Claire shrugged. 'Who knows?'

Sofia paused, examining Claire's face. 'You don't mind living like this, on the edge all the time?'

'I *love* living like this. It's invigorating.'

Sofia frowned. 'But what about your career? It's kind of stalled, Claire.'

'No, it hasn't! You know I'm writing an article about the land disputes here. Plus I freelance, you'll be able to read the article I wrote about my time in Serbia in *The Sunday Times* magazine in a few months. And *Marie Claire*'s commissioned me to write an article about animal welfare during conflicts.' Claire smiled. 'Sofia, this is important stuff I'm finally writing about, not just articles commissioned by magazine advertisers.'

Her sister sighed. 'And I'm proud of you, really I am! But it's just the odd article here and there, not a guaranteed income. And I can't imagine Milo earns much money from the reindeer farm.'

'We have savings. Milo has money left over from the Exmoor farm sale and I have stuff left over from when I worked on the magazine. And anyway, who cares about money? We don't need new cars and big houses like most people do. We're fine as we are, really.'

'What about children?'

Claire sighed. Sofia was bringing her infertility up again, surprise surprise. 'You know that's not a possibility for me.'

'I know,' Sofia said, putting her hand on Claire's arm. 'I mean another round of IVF, even adoption? Isn't it something you and Milo might consider once you're married?'

'Milo and I aren't getting married.'

Sofia's smile froze. 'Why ever not?'

Claire hesitated a moment, remembering that dinner conversation about marriage all those years ago in Exmoor. They hadn't discussed marriage since – why would they after just a couple of months together? But Claire knew, even in a few years, it wouldn't happen. It was just the way it was between them. 'Milo and I don't need a marriage certificate to prove our love for each other,' she said to Sofia.

'Oh, Claire, really? You do realise you sound like a complete hippie! How does Milo feel about that?'

She thought of the conversation they'd had a couple of nights before. 'He's fine with it.'

'If it's money stopping you trying IVF, Ed and I—'

'Accept it, Sofia,' Claire snapped. 'I've resolved myself to never having children and you know what? I'm happier than I've been in a long time.'

Sofia's face softened. 'Isn't a girl allowed to worry about her sister?'

'Yes, you are allowed. But really, there's nothing—'

Claire suddenly felt a wet splat on her back. She turned around to see Milo, Holly and Alex standing in the kitchen's doorway, their faces red from the cold, mischievous looks on their faces.

'He did it,' Milo said, pointing to Alex.

Alex's eyes widened. 'Liar.'

Claire scooped up a handful of suds and marched towards the three of them as they darted away from her, Sofia watching with a sombre expression in the background. As she passed the hallway mirror, she caught sight of her reflection: eyes bright, cheeks pink, a wide smile on her face.

I am happy, she thought. *Really happy.*

'Okay, time for presents!' Filipe shouted out from the living room.

They went into the living room to find steaming mugs

of *glögi* – mulled wine – waiting for them. A beautiful fir tree sat in the corner draped with gold tinsel and stars that sparkled when the light caught them. They all sat down then handed each other gifts until there was a small pile in front of each of them.

'Ready?' Filipe said. 'One, two, three . . .'

Holly and Alex ripped the paper off their gifts as they giggled, the glass each of *glögi* they'd drunk turning their faces pink. Claire and Milo watched Holly open the presents they'd got her – piles of poetry books, a mobile phone and, finally, her favourite, a beautiful sheepskin coat and some bright red knitted gloves she'd seen in a nearby shop.

Then it was time for Milo and Claire to open their presents to each other. Claire had created a frame using knotty wood from a local fir tree then placed a photo Filipe had taken of them both in Serbia in it. When Milo opened it, his face filled with emotion.

Then he gave Claire a chunky, square-shaped present wrapped in plain gold paper with a green ribbon tied around it, a nervous smile playing on his lips. 'I hope you like it.'

She smiled at him then pulled the wrapping papers off to reveal a book made from fir wood. Etched onto its front and dyed in bright turquoise was a picture of the earth, the outlines of countries clear under the soft light in the room. Across the top in gold were four words. *The Atlas of Us*.

Claire peered up at Milo. 'It's beautiful.'

'Open it,' Milo said, his face eager.

She opened the heavy front cover, the smell of fir and ash bursting out at her. The pages were thick and colour-stained, as though they'd been thinly scraped straight from the bark of a tree. Carved into the first page were three lines:

To my darling, my life, my world. The atlas of my heart.

Your love, Milo

She looked up at Milo, her heart clenching. Then she turned the next page to see a beautiful drawing of the United Kingdom and Ireland on the right, its jagged outline dominating the whole page.

'I did the drawings before I came here,' Holly said.

'They're wonderful,' Claire said.

Milo hooked his fingers into the paper pocket opposite the map. 'I thought you could fill these with your notes, photos, anything you want from our travels, memories of when you and your family travelled too.'

'It has a lock,' Holly said. 'I told Milo to put it on so he can't peek. There's something in the first pocket.'

Claire pulled out a sheet of torn-out note paper with the line she'd written about Exmoor all those years ago on it. There was a drawing of a sheep beneath it now, teetering on a tightrope.

'Milo told me what you said about the sheep,' Holly said, 'so I drew you a picture.'

'It's lovely,' Claire said, stroking Holly's face. Then she turned to Milo, staring into his eyes. 'Thank you.'

'Please, stop, I'm sick with envy,' Sofia said, leaning back in her chair and taking another slug of *glögi*.

'Don't you like the breadmaker Dad got you?' Alex asked.

'Oh yes, it's a wonder.'

They all laughed as the dogs peered up from their bones, presents from Santa Paws as Holly called him.

Filipe bent down under the Christmas tree. 'There's another one,' he said, picking up a thin rectangular present wrapped in red paper with a UK stamp and the reindeer farm's address on it. He handed it over to Milo with a smile. 'For you. It came in the post a couple of days ago, I thought I'd save it for today.'

'Open it then!' Holly said.

Milo shrugged and unwrapped it to reveal a long flat box the colour of snow. He looked up at Claire, half-smiling.

'It's not from me!' she said. 'I swear.'

He narrowed his eyes at her like he didn't believe her then lifted off the lid.

It was an old Christmas card, the corners curled and dirty with age, a reindeer on the front with bulbous brown eyes staring out at them.

Milo frowned, recognition flickering in his eyes. Then he slowly opened it.

To Erin, it said inside in handwriting Claire recognised instantly as Milo's. *I'm sorry we argued. Please don't be sad. I don't regret what happened, you know I care for you. You just have to understand why it can't continue. Please come back for Christmas, we're all worried. Lots of love. M x*

Claire stared at the card, eyes blinking as she tried to wrap her head around it. Regret about *what*? Then she looked up and realised her sister was at the perfect vantage point to read it. Milo noticed too, his brow furrowing. Sofia shot Claire a look then turned to scrutinise Milo's face with cold eyes.

'What is it?' Holly asked, trying to look over Milo's shoulder. But he quickly snapped it shut, shoving it back into the box as he avoided Claire's gaze.

Claire tried to control her emotions, aware everyone was looking at her.

'Was it laced with poison?' Alex asked, clocking the look on their faces.

250

'It's a private joke,' Milo said, forcing a smile onto his face.

'Let us in on it,' Holly said, trying to grab it.

Milo shoved it into his pocket. 'It's silly, you wouldn't understand.'

The rest of the evening was tense, and they drove home in silence, the card and the words within it buzzing between them. As soon as Holly went to bed, Claire turned to Milo.

'Did something happen between you and Erin?' she asked quietly. He flexed his jaw, staring out of the window. Claire tucked her finger beneath his chin, making him look at her. 'Please, Milo. I wish you wouldn't keep things from me.'

He hung his head, his dark fringe in his eyes. 'We kissed. It was a long time ago.'

She tried to control the roar of emotion burning inside. 'When?'

'I was sixteen.'

'How old was she?'

'Twenty-something. It was stupid.'

'Did you love her?'

'No. I thought I did for a while, but I now know it for what it was: pure lust.' Claire felt her stomach crawl and Milo squeezed her hand. 'I was a teenager, remember? Hormones all over the place. My brother was in the Falklands, Erin and I grew close. She wanted to help on the farm so I showed her how to milk cows, how to shear the sheep. Then one day it just happened, we kissed. I felt disgusted with myself, especially when Dale came back after being in hospital with his injuries. So I told Erin just before Christmas it couldn't happen again. But she didn't want it to be over. So we argued and she ran off, going to stay with her best friend Nora for a few weeks.' He pulled the Christmas card out of his pocket, face flinching when he looked at it. 'That's

251

when I sent her this card. Dale was falling apart you see, he needed her.'

'Who posted it to you here then? Erin?'

Milo went quiet for a few moments, seeming to battle with something. Then he shrugged. 'I don't know.'

'Why did you lie to me about what happened between you?'

'I was ashamed.'

'If she sent you this card, what about Holly? Has Erin tried to contact her?'

'Holly hasn't mentioned anything. Anyway, Erin's banned from seeing her.'

'I've always wondered about that. It must have been pretty serious for the courts to ban her from seeing her own daughter. What happened? While you're in confession mode, you might as well tell me everything.'

Milo slumped down onto the sofa, running his fingers through his hair. 'Erin's always been mentally unstable. But when Dale had enough and asked for a divorce, she took Holly away in the night when she was just four and – and Holly nearly drowned.'

Claire sat down next to him, staring at the door to Holly's room. 'She tried to drown her own daughter?'

'I don't quite know what happened. Erin told the courts she'd decided it'd be a good idea to go night-swimming from the hotel they were staying at in Cornwall.'

'Jesus.'

'That, combined with some other things she did, made the courts decide she was an unfit mother. Not just unfit, dangerous.' His face hardened and he tore the card up, throwing it in the bin before pulling Claire into his arms. 'I won't let her spoil things for us.'

Chapter Sixteen

Inari, Finland
2000

The land Filipe's family lived on was a long drive from Iso-Syöte. They finally arrived just before lunch at a large flat plot surrounded by a pine fence, a huge forest of trees beyond it. In the middle of the plot were several pine houses, including tiny constructions Filipe explained were for storing food standing a few feet above ground on poles. In the centre were several teepee tents and then beyond, hundreds of grazing reindeer surrounding a hill.

Sofia stepped from the car she'd hired, patting down her dark jeans. When she looked up again, she caught Claire's eye. Things had been tense yesterday when they'd all spent the day together, Sofia watching Milo with narrowed eyes, Claire watching him too, hoping and praying that was it now, no more secrets.

'*Buorre idit,*' Filipe said as he approached them all. 'A Sami good morning.'

'*Buorre idit,*' Holly replied, pulling her red knitted gloves off.

Filipe smiled. 'Hungry?'

She nodded so he led them all towards a tepee made from a tan-coloured hide slung around several sturdy twigs.

'We call these *lavvus*,' Filipe said. 'They're temporary structures normally used for herding. We now use them for gathering and traditional days like this.'

Over the next hour, they gorged on a feast of traditional Sami food, including the *Bierggojubttsa* soup made by Filipe's aunt, as well as delicious cloudberries picked that very morning. They ate and drank from plates and cups made from reindeer antlers and wood, which Filipe explained were traditional 'Duodji' art.

When they'd finished lunch, they headed towards an area lined with several tree trunks, large antlers protruding from them.

'We practise lassoing our reindeer with those,' Filipe explained. 'I was going to suggest we all have a go.'

'Now this is more like it,' Sofia said, smiling. 'My Texan clients taught me how to lasso when I visited years ago.'

Alex rolled his eyes as Claire smiled to herself.

'Can I sit this bit out, it's freezing?' Holly asked, wrapping her arms around her slim frame as she watched Sofia with narrowed eyes.

Could she sense Sofia's distrust of her and Milo? Claire hoped not. She didn't want Holly to feel isolated. Claire had benefited from a tight family unit when she was a child. But when she was around Holly's age, her dad had smashed that all to pieces by leaving them. Claire had felt so disorientated and lost, she'd spent months trying to find him, desperate to bring him back and force that unit back together again. That destruction of the family unit had all happened to Holly when she was even younger, and to have the tragedy that followed . . . Claire looked into Holly's green eyes, thinking of the conversation they'd had in her room. She felt this overwhelming urge to recreate a family unit for Holly, to hold her close and make her feel safe and wanted.

'Of course you can,' Claire said. 'Why don't you take Archie back to the *lavvu*, he looks cold too?'

As Holly took Archie to the *lavvu* Claire strolled over to the fence, taking photos as the others played. It was clear Sofia *had* had a lot of practice, expertly snagging fake reindeer after fake reindeer along with the Sami men as Alex and Milo struggled to keep up. But despite this, Milo persevered, his face tense with concentration, brown eyes alert as Blue darted around with him. When they'd perfected their skills, Filipe gave them a chance to try lassoing the real thing. Alex grew bored after a while, wandering off in the direction Holly had gone. But Milo and Sofia stayed, competing with each other to catch a large reindeer. Beyond them, the sky was beginning to turn pink, a candyfloss of mist dipping into the azure hues of Lapland's twilight.

Just as Claire was beginning to feel too cold, Milo and Sofia both flung their lassos towards the reindeer. Milo's seemed to hang in the air for a few moments before floating down and entangling around the reindeer's antlers, Sofia's lasso falling short. Milo shot Claire a look of triumph but then the reindeer darted off, violently yanking his arm. Milo's feet lifted up underneath him and he landed with a hard thud on the ground, powdery snow puffing up around him as Sofia laughed.

Claire clambered over the fence and ran to him as Blue licked his face. Milo slowly opened his eyes, face softening when he saw Claire. Then he noticed Sofia smirking down at him and his face hardened again.

'Are you okay?' Claire asked.

'I'm fine,' he said, sitting up.

'Maybe we should go sit in the warmth and—'

'No way, I want to try again.' He jumped up, wincing slightly.

Claire frowned. 'Milo, I don't think—'

'What did I just say? I want to do this!'

She stood up, placing her camera in her bag. 'Fine. If you want to break your back, I'm not going to stick around and watch it happen.'

He sighed. 'Claire, I—'

She turned on her heel and strode towards the *lavvu*. She had a horrible feeling he was going to hurt himself and she couldn't bear to watch it happen.

When she got to the *lavvu*, she paused. She could hear Holly and Alex talking in hushed tones.

'You're not just saying that, are you?' Holly said. 'I can't do something like this unless you really mean it?'

'I swear,' Alex replied, his voice husky. 'I don't want to be a solicitor like Mum anyway and that's the only reason I'm in college. I'd rather travel with you. Plus I already told you I dumped Kirsty.'

There was the sound of clothes rustling then a soft moan. Claire coughed, waited a moment, then quickly strode in.

Alex was lying across one of the rugs, his trousers bunched around his knees. Holly was bent over him, her red hair spilling over his uncovered thighs, her top dragged up to reveal her small, bare breasts.

She lifted her head, exposing Alex, and Claire turned away, whispering 'Jesus' under her breath. Out of the corner of her eye, she saw him quickly scramble to cover himself as Holly pulled her top back down, her face pink. Archie peered up at them from the corner then leaned his chin back on the rug, closing his eyes again.

When Claire was sure they'd pulled themselves together, she turned back.

'Please don't tell my mum,' Alex said.

'Don't tell me what?' Sofia said. She was standing behind

Claire, her hands on her hips. Claire saw Holly and Alex through her eyes: faces pink, hair unruly, clothes dishevelled. Holly caught Claire's eye, silently pleading with her as Alex stood frozen with fear.

'Nothing,' Claire said.

They both visibly relaxed.

'I've always been able to tell when you're lying, Claire,' Sofia said. She marched over to her son, examining his face. Then her eyes moved down towards his trousers, which were still unzipped. She turned to Holly.

'I know your type,' she said, looking her up and down. 'You were probably rolling around in the hay with some farmhand when you were twelve.'

'Jesus, Sofia!' Claire cried.

Holly's face exploded with anger and she marched towards Sofia. Claire grabbed her arm and stood between them. She realised she was shielding Holly more than Sofia, despite Holly being the one who'd marched towards her sister. That yearning to look after her was there again, so strong. She wondered if this was how it felt to have a child, this fierce desire to protect someone.

'I was only stating the truth,' Sofia said.

'Shut up, you poisonous cow!' Holly shouted at Sofia over Claire's head, her face stretched with rage. 'You've been horrible to me and Milo all holiday and I haven't said anything 'cos you're Claire's sister but you're a—'

'What's going on?' Milo asked, limping into the *lavvu*.

'Your niece just had her grubby paws all over my son,' Sofia hissed.

Milo looked at Holly then at Alex, his eyes lingering on Alex's unzipped trousers.

'What did you do to Holly?' he asked Alex as Blue circled him, sensing his master's displeasure.

Alex's face went pale.

'I'm serious,' Milo said. 'It's much better you tell me the truth than lie to me.'

'Calm down, Milo,' Claire said. 'He's just a kid.'

'He's seventeen, virtually a man.'

'You were a teenager once, remember?'

'Yes and that's why I want to know what the hell you were both doing.' He turned to Holly. 'Holly?'

'N-nothing,' she stammered.

'Nothing?' Sofia said. 'I have a feeling you're the one who instigated it all.'

'Somebody tell me what they were bloody doing!' Milo shouted.

Claire stepped towards him. 'They were just making out. They're seventeen, remember? Not children any more.'

'No, this one certainly isn't a child any more,' Sofia said, looking Holly up and down.

'Oh, just fuck off and die, will you, Sofia?' Holly hissed.

'Holly!' Claire said. 'Calm down.'

'The apple doesn't fall far from the tree, does it?' Sofia said under her breath. 'You might want to rein her in a bit.'

Milo's face exploded with anger. 'How dare you give me a lecture on how to influence Holly when you've spent half this holiday working on a law case, not paying any attention to your son. If I were him, I'd fucking smash that PalmPilot of yours apart and scatter it all over the snow.'

Sofia stepped away from him, her cheeks flushed as Holly smiled to herself.

'I'll deal with this,' Claire said to Milo. 'Take Holly and Alex, and go outside, all right?'

He held Claire's gaze a few moments, his jaw flexing and unflexing. Then he grabbed Holly's hand and slammed out of the *lavvu* as Alex followed, his head down.

When they were out of earshot, Claire turned to face Sofia. 'You disgust me, Sofia. Do you understand what that girl's been through, what she's seen?'

Sofia said nothing, just looked down at the ground.

'Despite all that,' Claire continued, 'she's one of the loveliest girls I've ever met and Alex would be a very lucky man if they ended up together. So don't you ever *ever* talk about her like that again, understand?'

Sofia eyes widened at the tone of Claire's voice. 'Can't you see why I'm acting like this? Alex is *everything* to me. Why do you think I'm on my PalmPilot all bloody day, for the joy of it? No, it's all for Alex. So when I see him with a girl who's had the kind of past Holly has, I worry. I just want the best for him, that's all.'

'What if Holly *is* the best? And anyway, it doesn't look like he's getting the best of things right now, does it?' They peered towards Alex who was leaning against a tree, his blond hair in his eyes as he kicked miserably at the snow. 'Maybe Alex needs to see his mother show some compassion once in a while?'

Claire looked her sister up and down then walked out of the *lavvu* towards Milo and Holly. She'd put up with Sofia's obnoxious ways all her life but she was beginning to come to the end of her tether now.

'You okay?' she asked Holly.

Holly kept her eyes on the ground. 'I guess.'

Milo took Claire's hand. 'Sorry I lost my temper in there.'

'She deserved it.'

Blue padded over then and Holly leaned down, pressing her cheek against his furry face. Milo led Claire away a few metres and lowered his voice. 'What actually happened between Holly and Alex?' Claire told him and he shook his head. 'Christ. What the hell was he playing at?'

'It takes two to tango, Milo. And from what I heard, Holly was leading the tango.'

Milo shook his head. 'No, Holly's not like that.'

'*I* was like that at her age.' He frowned. 'Milo, she's not your little Snow White. She's an intelligent young woman who knows what she wants. This isn't a fairy tale you're living in where you can keep her locked away in a fairy castle.'

Milo leaned his forehead on Claire's shoulder. 'It scares me how much she's growing up.'

'I know.' She stroked his hair and they were quiet for a few moments. 'The thing is though, Milo, it's not just what they *did*, it's what they said too. I think they're making plans to give up sixth form and go travelling.'

Milo pulled away from Claire, looking her in the eye. 'Really?'

'Yep. You should probably talk to her.'

'Why don't you? She listens to you.'

'But you're her uncle.'

'We heard some of what you said to Sofia in there, Claire. I know you really care for Holly. You might as well accept she sees you as her aunt.' Claire felt a warm glow inside. 'Please talk to her? I think you'll be better at it than me.'

'All right.'

Claire went to walk towards Holly but Milo softly grasped her arm. 'Claire?'

'Yes?'

'You would've made a great mum.'

She swallowed, gently stepping away, his fingers dropping from her wrist.

Would've.

When she reached her, Holly had her head in her hands, spirals of red hair spilling over the shoulders of her coat as Blue leaned his chin on her knee.

'Oh sweetie,' Claire said, sitting on the bench and putting her arm around her shoulders. 'You know Sofia didn't mean what she said.'

'Of course she did,' Holly said without looking up, her voice muffled. 'She hates me and Milo.'

'She doesn't hate you. She just can't figure you both out and that scares her.'

Holly peered up at Claire. 'I can't ever imagine her scared.'

'Look, people have their reasons for being the way they are, so the best thing to do is feel sorry for them and ignore them, okay? And when I say ignore them, I don't mean telling them to fuck off and die.'

Holly sighed. 'Sorry about that. She just wound me up, that's all.'

'I understand. But like I said, sometimes the best thing to do is to walk away.' Claire took in a deep breath. She didn't think she'd ever be having a conversation like this with a girl. 'Another thing. I wanted to talk to you about what you and Alex did in there.'

Holly's face went red. 'I'm so sorry you had to see that, it must've been pretty gross for you.'

Claire laughed. 'Yeah, well, not what I hoped to be seeing on Boxing Day.' Her face grew serious. 'You've only known him a few days though, you shouldn't rush things.'

'I know.'

'It's not just that. I heard what you said to Alex about leaving sixth form and travelling.'

Holly's face dropped. 'Oh.'

'Are you really planning that?'

'Only so we can travel with you and Milo.'

'We'd love you to travel with us but now you've started your A levels, there's no point giving them up.'

'But Milo said they're not essential. And you said the other

261

day I shouldn't do what people expect of me unless it feels right for *me*.'

Claire sighed. 'And I still believe that. But it's not a good habit, giving up on things halfway through. You only have a year left.'

'Fine. Then I'll come live out here and carry on from Finland.'

'But you don't speak the language.'

'I'm a quick learner.'

'Oh, Holly. It just isn't going to happen.'

'But I hate living in the UK, it's so boring!'

Claire smiled. 'God, you sound like me at your age.'

'I *want* to sound like you.' She paused a moment, her green eyes flickering with emotion. 'Sometimes I imagine I'm like you, like I'm your daughter even. Does that sound weird?'

Claire had to fight hard to stop her eyes from welling up. It made her feel a mixture of sadness and joy: sadness for the child she'd never have, joy because maybe, just maybe, she *could* play a role in one girl's life.

But then she remembered Holly already had a mother.

'That doesn't sound weird, sweetie. But you do have a mother, remember?'

Holly turned away. 'She might as well be dead.'

'That's an awful thing to say!'

'You don't know what she's like, Claire. She's mental.'

Claire looked down at the snowy ground, trying to figure out what to say next. Then she caught sight of the silver globe her dad had got her hanging from her bag.

'My dad got me this,' she said, lifting it up to show to Holly. 'I used to think he was perfect. But eventually, I learned he wasn't, that nobody is.'

'Why wasn't your dad perfect? He sounds pretty perfect to me.'

'He based his whole life on the philosophy that all people need is themselves. No society and all its trappings, not even family. But in the end, he spent a year wasting away alone, too scared to ask for help from the very people he thought he didn't need.'

Claire thought of the sight that had greeted her when she'd found him in that flat. Dirty clothes sprawled all over the place; the smell of milk gone bad and rancid meat; the sound of rasping breath. Then him, lying in that sunken, single bed, face concave and pale, when she'd been so used to seeing it tanned and vibrant.

'If he'd got the help he needed,' she continued, 'he might be alive now. Everyone has their issues. No one's perfect, just like your mum's not perfect. She may have gone through more than you could ever know.'

'Like what?'

Like loving your uncle, she wanted to say. 'Milo said she lost her parents when she was very young,' Claire said instead. 'Maybe that's why she's the way she is.'

'Maybe.' Holly stood up, her face closing up, just as Milo's did whenever Erin was mentioned. 'I better do my hair before dinner, it looks a state.'

Claire grabbed her hand. 'Wait. You know I'm always here if you need to talk. I know you have Milo, and you must always talk to him, he's your uncle. But if you find you can't, I'm here too.'

'I know,' she said.

Before dinner that night, they all walked up the mountain holding lanterns. When they got close to the top, the white of the snow and the sparkle of the ice on the lake below shone bright, a strange snowy dreamscape. Claire looked at all the lanterns around her then caught her sister's eye, wondering if she too was thinking of the lanterns their dad used to set off, taking with them any negative thoughts.

They needed a few of those lanterns right now.

'Look!' Holly said, grabbing her arm and pointing up to the sky as giant multi-coloured ribbons of red, purple and green flexed up and down above them.

Milo wrapped his arms around Claire, pressing his cheek against hers. They'd seen the Northern Lights plenty of times since they'd got here but to see them through Holly's eyes made them extra special.

Holly peered over her shoulder at Alex, who was looking down at the ground, his face forlorn.

'Go talk to him,' Claire said to Holly. 'Clear the air.'

'No,' Holly said, shaking her head. 'I'd rather forget about everything.'

'But that's not fair on Alex, is it?' Milo said. 'Do you like him?'

Holly thought about it a moment then nodded. 'Yes, very much.'

'Then go talk to him!'

She smiled and walked over to Alex, taking his hand. He looked down at her, his face lighting up. Sofia watched them, her face darkening.

Claire thought of her conversation with Holly from earlier. 'There's something I wanted to talk about actually. When I spoke to Holly earlier, she said her mum might as well be dead.'

He went very still.

'It worries me,' Claire said. 'I feel she's keeping it all pent up. Maybe it'll be good for them to repair their relationship when Holly turns eighteen and is no longer a child in the eyes of the law?'

He shook his head. 'No. It wouldn't be healthy for Holly. I told you what Erin's like.'

'But Milo—'

He tipped her chin up, looking into her eyes. 'One of the reasons I love you so much – one of the *many* reasons – is that you help me forget the bad stuff, especially the look in Dale's eyes when he . . .' he looked towards Holly, his eyes watering, 'when he died. So can we focus on the positive tonight?'

She examined his face for a few moments. She'd said her piece. It wasn't her place to push it. So she pulled him close to her and he buried his face in her hair. A few moments later, Holly strolled back over.

'Where's your other glove?' Milo asked her.

She looked down at her bare hand and frowned. 'I must have dropped it on the way up.'

Milo took off his glove and gave it to her. She smiled, tugging it on. Then they all wrapped their arms around each other to keep warm, just the three of them on that little patch of snow, watching the Northern Lights stretch above them. In that moment, Claire felt the happiest she'd ever felt, standing there with the man she loved and a girl she'd grown to love too. It almost felt like they were family.

A few minutes later, they walked back down the hill and headed towards the main *lavvu* for dinner. As they drew closer, a small gasp rang out from the group in front of them and Claire heard her sister's voice, a hint of distress in it.

'What's wrong?' Claire asked, pushing her way through the small group with Milo and Holly.

'It's all my stuff,' Sofia said, her face pale under the moonlight. 'My PalmPilot, my folder, *everything*.' She let out a sob. 'It's all ruined, the whole case.'

Filipe shone his torch on the ground to reveal several pieces of paper tangled around a nearby fir tree, the red folders Sofia used to keep them in scattered all over the snow.

And there, in the middle of it all, was her precious PalmPilot, now smashed to pieces.

Sofia slowly turned towards Milo. 'You did this,' she shouted at him, spittle flying from her mouth. 'You fucking did this!'

'Milo wouldn't do that,' Claire said.

'Really?' Sofia asked. 'You heard what Milo said earlier.' She looked down at the remains of the PalmPilot then back up at Milo. 'Don't deny it, Milo.'

Milo's eyes found Claire's then he turned to Sofia, slowly nodding. 'You're right, I did it.'

Claire shook her head, not quite believing it. 'But why?'

He didn't say anything, just blinked at her.

As she tried to calm Sofia down, she looked over her sister's shoulder and watched as Milo discreetly reached for a red knitted glove and shoved it into his pocket.

Chapter Seventeen

Ko Phi Phi Don, Thailand
2004

As my husband Will jumps off the boat and strides towards us, I feel nothing but trepidation. No joy at him coming all this way, nor relief.

'Darling,' Will says, grabbing me into a hug, his dark eyes sliding over to Sam. He pulls away from me and holds me at arm's length. 'How are you?'

'I'm . . . I don't know. I've been too busy trying to find Mum to think about how I am.'

'Too busy to apply sun lotion too, it seems. Your nose is burned and look at your hair!'

I smooth my hand over my hair and Sam frowns. He's standing with his friend a few feet away. 'What are you doing here?' I ask Will.

'I booked a flight straight after our chat yesterday.'

I think of his harsh words about Mum and my grip tightens on her cardigan. This is so typical of Will, smoothing over an argument with some extravagant gesture.

'So you've left the girls with your parents?' I ask, voice stiff.

He frowns. 'I haven't left them to fend for themselves at home. You could at least look happy I'm here, Louise. And

267

anyway, they're with your father right now, my parents are picking them up tomorrow.'

I close my eyes. Of course he's right. He's my husband, for God's sake! Plus he came all this way, even if the gesture *is* a few days late.

'I'm sorry, I'm just – I'm surprised, that's all,' I say.

'Good, that was the whole point. I'm here to help you find your mother.'

'How did you know about the boat?' I say, gesturing towards Sam's friend's boat.

'The girls said the name of the boat you'd be travelling on means sea monkey in Thai. I asked around, found it, flashed the cash. Always works!' Will turns towards Sam and stretches out his hand. 'Will Kowalewski.'

Sam strolls over and shakes his hand, his eyes running over Will's immaculate dark jeans and white designer shirt. Will wipes his hand on his jeans, appraising Sam's scruffy gold hair, his stained shorts.

'Sam's a volunteer,' I say quickly. 'He helps people like me. Relatives, I mean. He's been wonderful.'

'Looks like we owe you,' he says, patting Sam on the back. 'You'll join us for dinner tonight?'

'We're not on holiday, Will,' I say, cheeks flushing with embarrassment at his lack of sensitivity. 'There are hardly any restaurants left standing, you know.'

'Don't worry, I have it all arranged,' Will says. 'A contact of my father owns a hotel on the north-east coast of the island, turns out it was hardly touched by the tsunami.'

I look at Sam. 'I thought the whole island was affected?'

He shrugs. 'Maybe not. The north-east is pretty sheltered.'

Hope blossoms. 'Maybe Mum stayed there?'

'There's a chance.' He quickly glances at the cardigan in

268

my hand then away again. I can see what he's thinking. There's too much evidence Mum was staying in those ravished bungalows.

'It's a thirty-minute boat ride away,' Will says, looking Sam up and down again. 'Your friend said he'd take us.'

'I better leave you to it then,' Sam says. He turns to me, and the look on his face reminds me of how Mum had looked the first time she'd met Will. It was after he'd proposed to me. I'd set up a lunch, just the three of us. She'd walked into the restaurant, late of course, dressed in one of her trademark long skirts, rushing towards the table with a smile on her face. But when she'd caught sight of Will, she'd slowed down, her smile disappearing. I'd wondered if it was because he screamed of money in his expensive suit, slicked-back hair, uptight smile, her socialist tendencies making her take an instant dislike to him. But then she'd married Dad, hadn't she?

Maybe that was exactly why she'd looked so disappointed: she was worried our marriage would end like just like theirs had.

'Good luck, Louise,' Sam says now, forcing a smile onto his face. 'I'd like to know how you get on so call me once you find your mum, all right?'

I suddenly feel lost and realise I don't want him to go, not like this.

Will frowns when he notices the look on my face. 'I won't hear of it,' he says, turning to Sam. 'We owe you dinner and, anyway, how will you get back without your friend's boat?'

Sam's brow furrows. 'But I—'

'We better hurry, I'm starving.' Will takes my arm and marches me down the beach towards the boat without waiting to hear Sam's response. I twist around to see Sam standing there, watching us for a few moments. Then he sighs and follows us.

During the boat ride to the other side of the island, I just stare out into the darkness as Will regales Sam with stories about his job, his black hair blowing in the breeze. He barely notices the destruction around him. Even though it's dark, it's still possible to see the wrecked shoreline in the moonlight, outlines once smooth and curved now jagged and ruined. Every now and again, the boat bumps into something, despite Sam's friend trying his best to avoid whatever's being brought in by the tide. I can't bear to think what that something might be. I can't bear to see how indifferent Will is to it too. Instead, I focus on my theory that Milo James is Holly James's father. Did Mum suspect? Did she know? It wasn't widely known considering Dale James was referred to as her father in the article I read.

The boat soon begins to slow and I look up, surprised to see lights dotted over a shoreline that looks completely normal and intact palm trees swaying in the breeze. We're approaching what looks like a cove, a mountain shrouded with trees curving around it to its right. I can smell barbeque food, I can even hear music, a Thai woman's voice lifting in the warm night air. It's a complete contrast to the other side of the island.

We have to step through the sea to get to the hotel, a strangely warm and soft sea. I think about the destruction it wrought a few days ago and can't quite believe it. As we approach the complex, it's clear it's five star, with a huge rectangular pool and straw-roofed villas dotted here and there.

Despite the smell of food and laughter, when we walk through the resort there's a sombre feeling in the air, people watching BBC News 24 in the bar, others on their phones. It feels quiet and I wonder if people have checked out early, not willing to take the risk in case another wave hits.

A fat Thai man is waiting for us when we walk through a reception area housed in a larger version of the surrounding villas, the floors a shiny white marble. I think of the scene that greeted us when we arrived earlier in the day. For such a tiny island, it's amazing to think this part of it was barely touched.

The manager shakes Will's hand vigorously. 'Welcome, Mr Kowalewski. I'm very pleased to see you here.'

'And I'm very pleased to see your hotel still standing, Niran. My father sends his regards. This is my wife, Louise,' Will says. 'And this good man is Sam, he's a volunteer who's been helping Louise to find her mother.'

'Very good,' Niran says, bowing low to us. 'I got that information for you, Mr Kowalewski.'

He looks at me quickly then hands an envelope over to Will.

'What's that?' I ask Will.

'Oh, nothing, darling, just business stuff for my dad.' He turns back to Niran. 'So, what's on the menu for dinner? I'm starving.'

I muffle a sigh. Will seems more concerned about the food than whether Niran lost any family in the tsunami. I can see Sam notices it too, his brow creasing. I look between them both. It's funny, how someone's faults can suddenly come to light when you see them through another person's eyes.

Niran bows down. 'You are welcome to eat at any of our restaurants, just give your name to one of the staff,' he says, gesturing towards a board featuring menus from three on-site restaurants.

Will smiles. 'Wonderful.'

'I've also arranged a room for you, Mr Kowalewski. I can arrange one for your friend too?' He peers at Sam.

Sam shakes his head. 'No, really, I'm—'

'You have to freshen up before dinner,' Will says, looking him up and down. 'And it's unlikely we'll be going back tonight. Might as well make the most of the luxury here. I expect you don't get much of it usually?'

Sam's face flushes and I close my eyes, pinching the bridge of my nose. This is unbearable.

When we get to our rooms – two villas next to each other with their own private pools – Sam looks at me with a bemused expression on his face before he walks into his room. It's obvious he'd rather not be here but Will's known for bulldozing people into doing what he wants them to, it's the reason he's risen so quickly in the recruitment firm he works at. Maybe the reason I've stayed with him too, despite the way he treats me, the things he does.

'Funny chap, that Sam,' Will says as we walk into our room.

'What do you mean?'

'I don't know, just . . . different, I suppose.'

He closes the door and I fling my bag on the bed, Claire's atlas tumbling out.

He walks over and picks it up. 'What on earth is this?'

'I found it in Mum's bag. It belongs to a journalist called Claire Shreve, she was connected to Mum's best friend's daughter, Holly James. We think that's why she was out here.'

'Ah, yes, your father mentioned something about all that when I checked in on the girls earlier.' He flicks through it. 'There's stuff in these pockets.'

'I know, I think Claire kept mementoes of her travels. She was a travel journalist.'

'Journalist, huh? Maybe I can recognise something. I read a lot of newspapers.' He digs around the folder next to the map of the UK, tearing a bit of the pocket. I flinch. 'Ah-hah,' he says, waving the awards invite about. '*This* I know about.'

I take it from him, staring at it. 'The Flora Matthews Foundation Prize,' I say. 'How do you know about this?'

'Your mother.'

'Mum went to this?'

'She tried to. She called me on the evening of the awards and asked if I could pull some strings to get her in.'

'Why didn't you tell me?'

He shrugged. 'No need. Plus I was working on a big account then, I didn't have time to tell you every detail of my life.'

I sigh. 'Why did she want an invite?'

'She didn't say.'

'Did you get her one?'

He laughs. 'Of course not! She gave me two hours' notice! I don't know why she thought I could. I know my job's very important, but even *I* can't perform miracles.' He takes my hand. 'Enough about all that though. It's so wonderful to see you, darling.'

I look down at his hand. This is just like the time when he whisked me off to a plush hotel in Edinburgh after I'd found a saucy text on his phone from one of the firm's secretaries.

I pull my hand away from him. 'Why did you come? I asked you as soon as I found out Mum was missing and you refused.'

'I didn't realise how serious it was then.' His face softens. 'I love you, Louise. I want to be here for you.'

'Are you really sure about that?'

'How could you say that? You're my wife, the mother of my children.'

I think of that photo of Claire and Milo, their eyes so full of love. 'That's not enough of a reason to love someone. There needs to be more to it than that.'

He wraps his arms around my waist. 'Then let me show you.'

I step away from him. 'No, Will. That's not enough to show me either. And you can't just pretend you didn't say all that stuff about my mum yesterday. Just because you came all this way doesn't erase the things you said from my mind.'

His nostrils flare. 'Fine. Looks like I'll be needing a cold shower then.'

He marches to the bathroom, slamming the door behind him, and I lean my forehead against the wall in frustration, trying to suppress the tears. It's all too much, having Will here. And yet shouldn't I be delighted? What does that say about our marriage if all his presence does is make me feel anxious?

For the first time in a long time, I'm desperate for Mum's advice. I imagine her right here with me, twirling around in the swivel chair, her dark hair flying about. She stops suddenly, grabbing the table to steady herself, her face growing serious as she looks at me.

'If your first feeling is one of apprehension instead of happiness when you see your husband, my darling,' I imagine her saying, 'something isn't right, is it?'

'But he's the father of my children,' I say, lowering my voice so Will doesn't think me mad.

I see her getting up, a sad smile on her face as she walks over to me, taking my hand. I can almost smell her perfume, the soft smell of lavender. 'If that's the only value you can place on him, that he's the father of your children . . . oh darling, don't waste your life with him.'

I feel angry then. What does she know? She never put family first, put *me* first. So how can she understand how important keeping my family together is?

I look towards Claire's atlas and the awards ticket lying on top of it. It can't be a coincidence Mum wanted to attend an event Claire Shreve had a ticket for. If Mum wanted to find Erin – hence why she came out here after seeing photos of Holly in the papers – what made her go to the awards ceremony? Was she hoping to find Milo there so she could ask him about her best friend's whereabouts?

So many questions and not enough bloody answers!

'I need answers, Mum!' I say to her imaginary figure. 'Why did you come here? And why did you attend Claire's awards ceremony? Why the hell did Claire have your bag? Is it all about Erin? And for God's sake, where are you *now*?'

I reach out to her, tears falling down my cheeks, but she just fades away.

Chapter Eighteen

The Red Centre. Australia
2001

The Red Centre of Australia is a land on fire, burned up with fever, hot and agitated. A few weeks into the New Year, Milo drove Claire down the Red Centre's dusty roads flanked either side by the sparsest, driest land they'd ever seen, trees just spindly stubs in the distance. The further away they got from the sight of people, the more Milo's shoulders relaxed, the smile returning to his face.

This hadn't been the plan initially. In fact, there'd been a brief period when Claire thought they might go their separate ways.

When she'd confronted him as they'd lain in their *lavvu* that night about hiding Holly's red glove, he'd denied it and that had infuriated her. She knew what she'd seen.

'Think twice before you lie to me like you did about you and Erin. I won't take it again,' she'd said.

He'd hesitated a moment then he'd sighed. 'When I saw the glove, it crossed my mind Holly might have ruined your sister's stuff, she'd been so angry with her after all. So I took the blame, I just did it without thinking properly.'

'You "just do" a lot of things without thinking properly,'

Claire had said, thinking of poor Luna. 'Sometimes it's better to just leave things as they are, let the chips fall as they may. Holly's a big girl now, she needs to take responsibility for her actions.'

'I need some air.' He'd tugged the zip of their sleeping bag down and jumped out of it, pulling on his boots and coat.

'So you're pretending this discussion didn't happen then?' Claire had said, kneeling up in bed now. 'Just keeping quiet and walking away like you always do?'

He'd looked down at her, his dark eyes blazing in the light from the lantern they'd lit. Then he stormed from the *lavvu*, the freezing cold air rushing in at Claire.

The next morning, she woke to find she was still alone. When she went outside there was no sign of Milo . . . nor Holly. And their car was gone. By the time lunch arrived and there was still no sign of Milo, she was furious. How dare he just leave her like that with no word? Filipe gave her a lift back to Iso-Syöte in the end and when she'd found Milo sitting in their living room, Claire had turned on her heel and stormed right back out again, jumping into Filipe's car and asking him to take her to his. See how Milo liked being abandoned for an evening. An hour later, the doorbell went and Filipe walked in with her atlas in his hands, Milo having dropped it off. When she'd flicked through it, she'd noticed more items had been placed in the pockets: her dad's postcards, a copy of that photo Filipe had taken in Serbia, then a leaflet from Nunney Castle, bringing back memories from how it had felt that day to feel Milo so close as they'd watched the sun set above the broken structure.

Then, next to the map of Australia was a postcard showing rows and rows of trees with pale green fruits hanging from their branches – mangoes. Scrawled across it was a note in Milo's writing:

Claire,

I understand how upset you must be, it must seem like I just left with no word.

But the plan had been for me to be back by the time the sun rose. After thinking about what you'd said, I went to Holly and she confessed what had happened. Then she got very upset, talking about Dale. She begged me to take her back to the cabin so I did, planning to be back to get you. But then the car broke down and I couldn't call you. I'm so sorry, Claire.

But as we waited for help, I had time to think. There's an Aboriginal saying, 'Those who lose dreaming are lost'. Remember that conversation we had about our dreams of just being free and travelling? And remember what you said about the Outback making you feel like you're the only person on the planet because it's so vast and so wonderful? I think that's what we need, just for a few months. Just us, masters of our own universe, no distractions so we can see if we can make something of our dream, of US.

I'm sorry. I love you, the atlas of my heart.

Milo x

Claire had read that note over and over, then she'd grabbed her coat and ran from Filipe's. As she'd neared the long road leading towards their cabin, she'd seen Milo sitting on a bench, his head in his hands. When he'd looked up, she'd run to him and pressed her lips against his cold ones, promising herself things would be better. But in the back of her mind, Claire couldn't help but worry about Holly. Sofia had been a bitch but had her harsh words been enough to justify what Holly had done?

A month later, with Archie back at Ben's and Blue with Jen and Holly, they arrived in the Red Centre and the mango farm Milo had bought fifty per cent ownership of from his friend Joe. The deal was done the first night they arrived in the tin house that came with the farm as the sun set in the background, a wad of cash from Milo's savings and a handshake sealing the deal. As far as the Australian government were concerned, they were there on an extended holiday visiting Joe, meaning they could wrangle a visa allowing them to stay for twelve months. Claire knew this made their situation precarious – what would happen after twelve months? And surely the government would find out they were actually working there, despite the fact it was all done under the table?

But she tried not to dwell on that too much. Instead, she did what the Aborigines do with plants that get infested: burned the negative thoughts away so new ones could grow in their place.

And it worked for a while. In those first few months in Australia, they felt they were masters of their own world living alone among the rows of green trees motionless in a windless terrain. It reminded Claire of when she used to stay in isolated caravan parks in the States as a kid, all wrapped up in her tight family unit. Except now her family were barely talking to her, apart from the occasional letter from Alex, though Claire suspected half the reason he kept in touch was for news of Holly, who he said hadn't replied to any of his letters or text messages.

The farm kept them busy as they prepared for the high season in September, the sun beating down on them, making their skin so scorched they'd have to stop and dunk themselves in a metal bath of cold water. When their work was over, they ate whatever meat they could afford, grilled over a barbeque as they watched the sun set over Uluru.

It was good to work with Milo, no distractions from other people. They got back into that comfortable routine they'd shared in those first couple of months in Finland, Claire regaling him with the stories her dad had told her of Aboriginal Dreamtime and the rainbow serpent that created all humans then swallowed them whole. And later, in the bed Milo had created for them with narrow crates and sacks stuffed with old clothes, he'd whisper the stories back to her as he explored every inch of her dusty skin.

Her hair grew long and light, bleached gold by the sun just as it had been when she'd travelled as a teenager. Milo's hair grew long too, so long he had to tie it back with an old cord he'd found. Their skin was constantly sunburned and dusty, the red earth seeming to sink right into it, making them merge with the land around them. Sometimes, Claire imagined their feet rooted into the sand, entwining them together like one of the parched trees dotted here and there. At the same time, she knew she could pull those roots from the sand any time she wanted. That gave her a special sense of satisfaction. Many people needed to set down long-term roots to feel content, the idea of travelling from one place to the next every few months disorientating. Not her.

Claire was starting to understand herself more and more: she was like her dad, able to feel secure and comfortable anywhere she chose to travel, settling in just fine as long as she knew she could extract herself when the need for flight overwhelmed her. Milo was the same, and knowing that gave her a sense of contentment she'd not felt in a long time, that bubbling restless energy she'd struggled with while living with Ben finally quiet. Her writing helped too, the change in direction from generic travel articles to issue-driven global features making her feel like she was carving a place for herself. Who needed a fixed long-term dwelling when you had the consistency of one man's love and a calling like her writing?

Holly came to visit near the end of her summer holidays just in time to watch the mangoes begin to appear. She was taller, thinner, even more grown up, her red hair curling down to her waist now. Claire had been surprised to hear she'd signed up to study English Literature at a university in London after all her talk of travelling. And now there she was, on the other side of the world, her long legs stretched over Claire's as she lay across the red soil like a lizard, Claire's head on Milo's lap, the evening sun twinkling through the branches as though it were spying on them. She was aware Claire had guessed it was her who'd destroyed Sofia's belongings so Claire had been hoping for some sort of apology when she'd met her at the airport with Milo. But instead, she got a big smile and a huge hug, with no mention of their time in Finland, just like she'd never been there.

'We should make wine from the mangoes next season,' Holly said.

Milo laughed. '*Wine?*'

'What?' Holly exclaimed. 'They sell mango wine in that farm we passed, didn't you see? Maybe we should go talk to them about it?'

'Oh, I'm sure they'd be thrilled to give all their secrets away to the competition,' Milo said.

'We'll go in disguise,' Claire said, winking at Holly.

They both burst out laughing and Milo smiled, his face

soft with contentment. He seemed at his happiest when it was just the three of them together, like those evenings in the log cabin in Lapland. Claire thought she might be happiest in those moments too. Despite what Holly had done, Holly had this knack of making Claire feel special and wanted.

'Fine, then let's make mango soap instead,' Holly said. 'I think people would like that.'

'Good idea,' Claire said. 'We can go into town to get some ingredients.'

'Do you even *know* how to make soap?' Milo asked her.

'My dad showed me once, he . . .' Claire paused as something occurred to her.

'You okay?' Milo asked her.

'I just remembered it would've been my dad's birthday tomorrow, that's all. He would've been sixty.' Milo squeezed her hand and she smiled to herself. 'The last birthday we spent with him, my sister and I hung piñatas from trees, like we'd learned in Mexico one summer.'

'Piñatas?' Holly asked.

'You know, those paper donkey things,' Milo explained. 'Kids smash them apart and sweets fall out.'

Claire nodded. 'They're used there to honour the gods who then give their thanks by helping the crops grow. I still remember the way Dad smiled when he saw all the colourful shapes hanging from the trees outside the hut we were renting. I miss him,' she added, her voice trembling.

Holly took her hand as Milo leaned down and kissed Claire's forehead, his eyes deep in hers. 'He'd be very proud of you.'

She smiled at him. This is what he did to her, make her feel special, important, just like Holly did.

'Look,' Holly said, pointing into the distance. 'The sun's starting to set.'

They all turned towards the horizon and watched as the huge orange sun began to dip beneath a hazy Uluru in the distance. Claire watched Milo and Holly, smiling to herself as she thought of the quote in Milo's note. *Those who lose dreaming are lost.*

She wasn't lost, she was home.

The next morning, Claire woke to find Milo and Holly gone, the house very quiet. So she took the chance to lie in bed a few extra moments, thinking of her dad and wondering what he'd think of Milo. He'd like him, probably call him the 'salt of the earth', a phrase he used for men who worked with their hands, who liked the outdoors. He'd understand his fiery personality too, maybe even respect him for it. He'd especially respect what Milo had done to save all those people in Exmoor all those years ago – maybe he'd understand his secrets too.

'A man needs to keep some of himself to himself,' he used to say.

She thought of the secret Milo had kept from her about Erin and the way he'd tried to cover for Holly. They didn't talk about any of that now. But there was always something niggling at the back of her mind.

'Oh, just leave it,' she snapped at herself as she jumped out of bed, pulling the curtains apart to let some sun in. She let out a gasp. Dozens of piñatas of all different shapes and sizes – nine-pointed stars, pink, yellow and turquoise; thick-legged donkeys, green, brown and red – were hanging from the trees. They swayed in the breeze, their colours twinkling in the sunlight. Sitting at a table laid out with food and wine in the middle of it all were Holly and Milo. Milo jumped up, beckoning her outside with a huge smile on his face.

'This is amazing,' Claire exclaimed as she walked outside.

'It was Milo's idea,' Holly said. 'We thought we'd celebrate your dad's birthday. We went into town this morning while you were asleep and got everything.'

'You made the piñatas while I was *sleeping*?' Claire asked.

Milo looked at his watch. 'It *is* eleven thirty, Claire.'

She laughed. 'God, I'm terrible.' She took his hand, staring into his eyes. 'But you're wonderful. Thank you *so* much for this.'

'You won't be saying that when I get all the sweets.' He handed her a stick he'd fashioned out of an old branch. 'Ready?'

She laughed. 'I've been ready all my life.'

They all raced each other to the trees and started bashing the piñatas, sweets falling to the floor.

Later, they sat in the shade finishing their second bottle of wine, sweet wrappings littered on the ground around them. It was strange to see Holly drinking but then she was eighteen now. As Claire sipped wine and watched as Milo and Holly chattered away, she felt her heart contract.

This is what it's like to have a family, she thought to herself.

'Oh, I forgot to tell you!' Holly said, her cheeks flushed from the wine. 'We got ingredients for soap too so we can start doing that later.'

'Excellent. In fact, I know who can be our first tester,' Claire said, lifting Milo's sleeve up and kissing the grimy skin there. Then she paused. 'What's this?' she asked, noticing an angry red circle just above his bicep.

He peered down it and shrugged. 'I don't know, a bite?'

'A bite? What if it's a Black Widow bite? Or a snake bite?'

He laughed. 'I wouldn't be here if that was the case. I'd be six feet under with red dust in my mouth.'

'That's a horrible image!' Claire exclaimed.

'I'd rather be six feet under than paralysed with pain from a toxic snake bite.'

'Milo, stop being so bloody morbid!'

His fingers danced up and down her bare arm. 'Don't get upset, Claire.'

'He's right though,' Holly said, covering her eyes with her hand and blinking up at the sun as she took another sip of wine. 'Sometimes, death's a better option. Like what happened with Dad.'

Milo's fingers paused on Claire's arm and they both looked at Holly in surprise.

'I miss him loads, of course,' Holly continued, still blinking at the sun, taking yet another sip of wine. 'But now I've had time to think about it, I'm pleased he died.'

'Holly, honestly!' Claire said, Milo's face dropping.

'But he would have shot us,' Holly said, shrugging.

Milo leaned forward, clasping Holly's hand. 'Holly, please . . .'

'But I don't understand why Claire's looking so upset?'

'I just – I'm not sure how comfortable I feel about what you just said.' Holly frowned and Claire quickly took her other hand. 'What I mean is, he was still your father so—'

'Oh, Claire,' she said, her hand slipping away from Claire's. 'I love you but you're so naïve sometimes.'

'Holly,' Milo said in a low voice.

'What do you mean, I'm naïve?' Claire asked her.

Holly shrugged. 'It's little things, like when you got upset about Milo having to shoot Luna, the bitch that ate her pups.'

Claire turned to Milo. 'You told her about that?'

He looked confused. 'Of course.'

Holly tangled one of her curls around her finger and examined its ends. 'I guess it sounds cold to you, but when you're brought up on a farm, you're taught to make snap decisions for the greater good. Kill one animal to save two, like Milo did to save those pups.'

'But life isn't a farm,' Claire said, unable to help herself, the patronising tone Holly was using making her angry, upset. 'It's no excuse to be trigger-happy.'

Milo looked down at his clenched fist.

'Trigger-happy?' Holly said, her voice heavy with hurt. 'Is that what you think happened with my dad?'

'Jesus, no.' Claire put her face in her hands and moaned. This was all going so badly. 'I completely understand what happened with your father, Holly.'

'But not Luna?' Milo said. 'I thought you said you understood about that?'

'It doesn't matter,' Claire said, not quite believing the conversation they'd all just had. 'I think we've all had too much to drink, me especially.' She stood up, unsteady on her feet. 'I'm going to lie down.'

She stumbled inside. How could Holly discuss her dad's death so nonchalantly? And how could Milo get upset when she brought up what happened with Luna? He'd been the one in the wrong, after all.

When she got to her room, she lay back on her bed and turned to look out of the window. Milo was examining a tree as Holly read a book of poetry. It was like the conversation had never happened. What was *wrong* with them both?

Henry's words echoed in her ears then. *I told you that family is nuts, something runs through those veins of theirs, a connection gone wrong in their set up.*

She sighed and fell into a confused, wine-drenched sleep where she dreamt of the rainbow serpent slinking across the desert towards her, its head huge, its forked tongue flickering out at her. She woke muffling a scream, her heartbeat pounding so hard she thought she might have a heart attack.

She turned on the light then noticed Milo sitting in the chair in the corner of the room.

'How long have you been there?' she asked, clutching her head as she sat up.

'Just a few minutes. I was waiting for you to wake so we could talk. You shouldn't have said all that in front of Holly.'

She felt a tremor of anger. 'But doesn't it concern you how nonchalantly she talked about Dale's death?'

'She deals with it in her own way.'

'By keeping it all buried deep inside?'

'If she wants.'

'Is that healthy?'

'Is it healthy you thinking I shouldn't have shot my brother?'

'I've never thought that. You probably saved my life, for Christ's sake!'

He sighed, turning to look out of the window. Claire examined his profile, his tanned skin, his full lips, the way his fringe fell into his brown eyes. She thought of what he'd done for her that morning, all that effort to celebrate her dad's birthday. Then she thought about what he and Holly had been through, witnessing Dale try to do what he did, then seeing him dead.

'I just worry for Holly, that's all,' she said softly.

'So do I, Claire,' he said, his voice low. 'It's all I think about sometimes.'

'Oh darling.' She shuffled over the bed and wrapped her arms around him. At first, he didn't move, just stayed stiff in her arms. But eventually, he turned and wrapped his arms around her too. They stayed like that for a while, just holding each other and looking into each other's eyes. But soon, his hand started travelling down the back of Claire's shorts, his breath quickening.

Later, they held each other, Milo tracing the shape of the Milky Way in the sky outside with his fingertips. Then he peered over at Claire's dad's postcards that she'd stuck to the wall above her desk.

'Happy birthday, Bo,' he whispered.

Claire closed her eyes, seeing her dad as he'd looked those last few moments she'd spent with him. 'Happy birthday, Dad.'

In the night, Claire woke to the sound of sobbing. She peered out of the window to see Holly sitting in the dark, staring out at Uluru as she rocked back and forth, tears streaming down her face. Claire ran outside, bare feet sinking into the dust, and wrapped her arms around Holly, feeling like her heart was breaking into a million pieces seeing her like that.

'What's wrong, Holly?'

Holly didn't say anything, just stared into the distance. Claire followed her gaze, thought for a moment she could see the rainbow serpent from her dream slithering towards them. But when she blinked, it was gone.

Eventually, she managed to get Holly up and inside, brushing the dust off her feet as she sat on her bed with that same expressionless stare.

'You know you can talk to me,' Claire said.

Still nothing. So Claire got up and gave Holly a kiss on the forehead then went to walk out but Holly grabbed her hand. 'Stay,' she whispered, staring up at Claire through her tear-drenched eyelashes.

So Claire did, curling up next to her and watching as she fell asleep. When she woke in the morning, she found Milo standing in the doorway, a confused look on his face. So she gently disentangled herself from Holly and led Milo to the kitchen where she explained what had happened.

'I'm worried about her,' Claire said. 'I think she holds everything in too much and when it comes out . . .' She sighed, letting her voice trail off. 'Will you talk to her?'

Milo nodded, brow creased.

Ten minutes later, Holly strolled in, spreading her new university books over the table and smiling at Claire as though the night before hadn't even happened.

Milo watched her for a while, brow puckered. Then he strolled over, picking up one of her books and casually reading the back. 'I was thinking we could go into town to get some supplies for the farm, Holly,' he said without looking up. 'Just the two of us?'

'Why not Claire too?' Holly asked.

'I need to start work on an article,' Claire said. 'You two go, it'll be fun.'

She shrugged. 'Okay.'

During the day, Claire tried to focus on her article about Finland's land ownership battle then wrote a letter to Jay. He wrote the most wonderful letters, pages and pages long, regaling Claire with stories about all the wonderful parties and beautiful women he'd met since starting his new PR contract in Paris. Even though the job was still in the financial area, at least it hadn't been his dad who'd got it for him. In his spare time, he was running an art and fashion e-zine too. He seemed happier in his letters, more comfortable in his own skin, and she'd often get an email or phone call from an editor friend of his, asking her to write an article, something she relished not just because of the money it brought in but also the opportunity it gave her to escape the mango trees and write.

But she couldn't concentrate this time, her mind returning to how Holly had looked the night before. She sighed, reaching for her mobile phone to find Jodie's number. Maybe she'd give her a call, they hadn't spoken for a few weeks. Then she paused: there was a text message from Ben. The reception was rubbish out here but the occasional message slipped through. She quickly opened it: what if Archie was ill?

Hi Claire. I just wanted to tell you before you heard it from anyone else that Belle is pregnant. Archie's doing well, he loves our garden. He can stay as long as he wants, even when our daughter's born in February. He's always been good with kids. I hope you're enjoying it out there. Ben.

Claire was surprised to feel tears flood to her eyes. She felt like she'd been hit with a sledgehammer. She'd known this might happen: Ben had bought a house with Belle very quickly and a proposal of marriage followed soon after. She'd been happy for him when she'd heard. She sunk into her chair and stared at the message. So why was she feeling like this now? She thought she'd come to terms with her inability to have children.

She heard the door open and quickly closed her phone, forcing a smile onto her face as Milo and Holly walked in. They both seemed relaxed.

'Did you talk to her?' Claire asked in a low voice as Holly changed clothes in her room a few minutes later.

'Yep.'

'And?'

'And she said she's just feeling tired and emotional from the jetlag.'

Claire shook her head. 'It was more than that.'

Milo stroked her cheek, his face softening. 'I love it that you worry so much but she's fine, really.' He held up one of the shopping bags. 'We got some pork so I thought I could do pulled pork?'

Claire hesitated a moment. When it came to Holly, it felt like she was walking a tightrope between helping out and poking her nose in where it wasn't wanted. She scrutinised Milo's face for a few moments then sighed. 'Sure.'

The next day, the three of them woke at the crack of dawn to watch the sun rise over Uluru. Claire had done the same with her dad when she was a kid, leaving her mum and sister in bed and going out, just the two of them. He'd told some tourists off for climbing the rock and she remembered thinking he was the most special person on the earth, to be sticking up so passionately for such sacred beliefs. When she'd found him in that flat a few years later, she recalled that moment and wondered if society had climbed all over him, ruining him as a result.

Claire squeezed the memory away, turned her attention back to the red rock, watching how the sun crept up from its hiding place and changed its colour, just as it had the time she'd watched it with her dad. It seemed as though it changed shape too, a living thing that stretched and yawned right before them. Around it, green shrubs sat like solemn parishioners in the red sand, paying homage to Uluru. Groups of tourists took photos, others gathered around an Aboriginal man playing a didgeridoo decorated with bright blue eyes, white dots and rainbow serpents, always rainbow serpents. Its hypnotic thrumming sound filled Claire's ears, taking her back to her visits here as a child.

There was a couple sitting next to her. They looked young, happy – honeymooners maybe. The man peered at the painting Holly had brought of the rainbow serpent coiled around itself, bright red like fire.

291

'Symbolises fertility apparently,' he whispered to his wife.

Claire thought of Ben's text message and felt that sting again. Milo squeezed her hand and she looked up into his brown eyes. Maybe she needed to accept the pain would never go away. But she had Milo and he loved her, dodgy eggs and all.

But later, as they drove back, she found her eyes seeking out the painting again.

The fertile rainbow serpent.

She peered at Holly who was staring gloomily out of the window. She remembered reading once about snakes who ate their own eggs, just as Luna had eaten her own puppies. Is that what Erin was doing to Holly, slowly eating away at her with her abandonment and the dark memories she'd left behind?

But over the next couple of weeks, as the mangoes began to mature into fat, green plumps of fruit, Holly seemed to return to her normal self.

Then an editor who'd commissioned Claire's Finland article got in touch requesting an up-to-date photo, so she asked Holly to give her a haircut. Holly sat her on a stool in the kitchen and carefully cut her hair.

'Will you cut my hair too?' Holly asked Claire after she'd finished.

'God, are you kidding? I'm terrible at stuff like that.'

'Please! It's too long, it's annoying me. All you need to do is chop a few inches off then I can tidy it up if you hold the mirror up for me.'

'Fine. But don't have a go at me if you end up looking like Worzel Gummidge.' She sat Holly down and placed a tea towel around her shoulders. 'You seem happier,' she said as she began snipping at Holly's hair, trying to keep her voice casual.

'Yeah, I *finally* finished that book on post-modern poetry.' She sighed. 'I really hate all that stuff, I much prefer old school poets like Edmund Spenser. Have you read *The Faerie Queene*, the iambic pentameter in it is—'

'I meant happier after that night I found you outside,' Claire said softly.

Holly flicked some hair off her hands. 'I'm fine. I just get stroppy in this heat, that's all.'

'Are you sure? After what happened—'

'Really! I'm still officially a teenager. I wouldn't be normal if I didn't get a strop on every now and again.'

'But you've been through a lot more than most teenagers.'

'And so did you with your dad leaving. Didn't you have a few tantrums as a result?'

Claire thought of the hell she'd given her mum the weeks after her dad had left. 'Yeah, I did. That's why I know how important it is to talk about it.'

'Fine. So we've talked about it now and it's cool.' Holly held the mirror up and tilted her head as she examined her reflection. 'I think shoulder-length would be best. What do you think?'

Claire paused a few moments, considering whether to push the subject further. She wanted to bring up what had happened in Finland but she couldn't force Holly to confide in her, just as she couldn't force Milo to.

So instead she focused on cutting Holly's hair. When it reached her collarbone, Holly asked for more to be cut, then more, then more until eventually, it fell to her jaw, so much shorter than Claire had intended.

Claire held the mirror up so Holly could see it from all angles.

'Can I have the scissors?' Holly asked as she stared at herself, tilting her head.

Claire handed them to her and watched as she started snipping at her fringe until it framed her pretty face. When Claire stepped back to look at her, her blood turned to ice.

She looked just like her mum.

'What do you think?' Holly asked.

'It's just like . . .' Claire paused. Maybe she had no idea? 'It's lovely,' she said instead. 'Very different.'

'I'll go show Milo,' Holly said.

Claire frowned. Would Milo notice it too?

She watched Holly run outside to him. He peered up, half a smile on his face. Then he frowned.

'What's wrong?' Holly asked, her footsteps slowing. 'Don't you like it?'

'Why did you cut it?' he asked her, his voice tight.

'I fancied a change. Don't you like it?'

'I preferred it long.' He turned back to the tree he'd been examining and Holly kicked at the dust then ran inside, shoving past Claire and slamming her bedroom door. But over dinner later, Holly did her usual and pretended like nothing had happened. Milo, however, still seemed tense, his eyes running over Holly's hair every now and again, his brow creased.

'Must've been strange seeing Holly's hair like that?' Claire said as they got into bed later. 'I've seen photos of Erin, I know they look very similar now.'

He pulled his T-shirt off and carefully folded it, placing it in their tiny wardrobe. 'You're reading into things. I just don't think it suits her, that's all.'

'But Milo, I—'

'—need to get ready for bed.' He pulled her close to him, pulling up her T-shirt as his brown eyes sparkled with mischief.

But it felt odd, like Erin was sitting there watching them somehow.

She pulled away from him. 'Don't.' He scrutinised her face for a few moments then sighed, getting into bed and staring up at the ceiling. She got in next to him and placed her head against his heaving chest. 'What I mean is, maybe we should just hold each other and talk?'

His eyes shifted to hers, scarily intense. 'I love you, Claire, more than you know.'

'I *do* know.'

'I don't think you do, not really. I feel like I can never do enough to show you. That's why when we . . .' His eyes slipped down her body, his voice growing husky. 'When we make love, I feel like that's the only time I can really show you.'

She looked at his bare chest, his taut stomach and felt her body start to pulse. Why was she letting a spectre from his past get in the way of things? Wasn't coming here supposed to be about getting away from all that?

So she pushed the sheet down, exposing him, running her fingers over him as he moaned. 'I don't think I do actually. I think you need to show me.'

He pulled her towards him and Claire thought she saw fear in his eyes, a desperate, haunting fear.

Chapter Nineteen

The Red Centre. Australia
2001

Over the next week, Holly's last week in Australia, Milo continued to watch her with his brow furrowed, as if he couldn't quite figure out if it was Holly or her mum. One afternoon, when Claire was working on her article, she heard shouting in the distance. She looked out to see Holly and Milo arguing. She shoved her hand into his chest and stormed away, her hair wild against the red landscape.

Claire walked outside. 'What's up?'

Milo raked his fingers through his hair. 'Nothing, she's just being a grumpy teenager.'

'It didn't look like nothing to me.'

He paused a moment, looking in the direction Holly had run. 'I'll go find her.' He gave Claire a quick peck on the cheek then disappeared after Holly.

That night, Claire dreamt of the rainbow serpent again. This time its jaws were opening to consume her. When she woke, there was the sound of footsteps outside. She looked out of the window to see Milo pacing around in the darkness. She went outside and slipped her hand into his hot one.

'What's wrong?' she asked him.

He looked up, a fleeting look of misery crossing his face. But then he quickly recomposed his features. 'Just needed some fresh air. Let's get you back inside before all those spiders and snakes you're scared of come and bite your bare feet.'

He went to take her hand but she stepped back, crossing her arms. 'You're lying, I can tell. We promised no more secrets.'

He sighed. 'Fine. Come see.' He led her towards the closest mango tree and pulled down one of the branches. Then he reached into his pocket for his torch, shining its light onto the mango there. At first, Claire didn't see anything. But when she peered closer, it jumped out at her: faded blotchy spots near the base of the mango.

'I noticed it last week,' he said. 'I think it's phomopsis mangiferae disease.'

'What on earth does that mean?'

'It means if I don't stop it spreading, every mango out here will rot before it even has a chance to finish ripening.'

Claire took the mango in her hand, feeling its smooth surface. 'Are you sure?'

He shoved the branch away and raked his fingers through his dark hair. 'Yes, I'm very sure. It's ruined, everything always ruins.'

'Don't think that, surely we can do something? Let's visit Joe on the way back from the airport tomorrow. He used to run the farm, he'll know what to do.'

'I've talked to him. Once the infection sets in, we're fucked. It's my fault, I should have noticed weeks ago.' He kicked at the dust then slid down the tree, putting his head in his hands. Claire sat next to him and held his hand as they looked out at the swaying trees, the mangos like clots of blood in the darkness. 'I'm being punished,' he said after a while. 'Bad stuff always happens in September. This, what Dale did and then . . .'

'Then what?' Claire asked, her heart slamming against her chest.

'Nothing,' he said, jabbing his fingers into the red dust. 'I'm bad, rotten, just like Dale, my dad, granddad and God knows who else in the James family.'

'Oh Milo, you're being silly, you're wonderful.' She wrapped her arms around him and he sunk his head onto her shoulder. After a while, he pulled away from Claire. 'It's getting cold, you better head in. I think I'd like to stay out here alone for a bit, is that okay? I'll be in soon.'

'Of course.'

But when the sun started to rise, he still hadn't come to bed, so Claire peered out of the window to find him sitting in the same position. But this time, there was a photo in his hands – a photo of Erin, her red hair a fiery cloud around her head.

Claire's eyes filled up with tears as she said goodbye to Holly that day. She'd miss her and still felt there was more she could do for her. When Milo held Holly, his face was heavy with worry.

With Holly back in the UK, Claire and Milo set about trying to save the mangoes. Joe – a tall wiry man with bleached white hair and wrinkled skin – came out to look at them and Milo used some of his savings trying everything Joe suggested, including injections of a ridiculously expensive copper sulphate. But the infection continued to spread from tree to tree, from branch to branch, the mangoes they'd so carefully cultivated becoming discoloured and polluted. As he worked, Claire watched him, unable to stop wondering if he really was still fixated with – maybe even in love with – Erin. She was a beautiful woman, no denying it. And he always seemed to clam up whenever Erin was mentioned.

She thought of Ben's text. Maybe Milo was starting to feel broody and Claire wasn't enough any more.

She shook her head. She was being silly. She *knew* Milo loved her.

But he started to turn in on himself, worrying her even more. As his hard work failed to pay off, Milo stopped eating and sleeping, growing thin beneath his T-shirt, often staring out at the dying trees with a forlorn look on his face. He didn't reach for Claire at night like he usually did, instead pacing up and down the rows of trees as the sun set, face feverish with concern.

So Claire sat in the house alone, trying to write, watching as Milo did what he could to save the trees. They were slipping into Australia's spring, the sun beating down on them even harder than before, turning their small house into a sauna by midday. Milo's body dripped with sweat, his arms bright red with sunburn. When he eventually came in to eat, he muttered to himself as he stared out at the trees as if he too had become riddled with disease.

After a week like that, Claire started to feel she was losing her mind too. The red sand clogged her lungs, the sun stifled her and her head swam with the madness of it all as she dreamt of the rainbow serpent each night, its face merging into Erin's. She started to yearn for concrete pavements and glass windows, for people, sane people. She even wrote four letters to Jay in that week. Four long, desperate letters telling him about their problems, none of which she sent because she didn't want to appear to be betraying Milo. And knowing Jay, he'd turn up to 'rescue her'. She started dreaming about his smile, the curls in his blond hair, his clean crisp shirts. And one night, she dreamt of him lying next to her, reaching for her, moving inside her.

She woke burning with shame.

In the middle of one of those dreams, Claire woke to the

sound of the phone ringing. She pulled herself from her bed and walked into the kitchen to see Milo leaning against the wall with the phone tucked under his chin, his forehead creased.

'Who is it?' she asked.

He handed the phone over to her, his face unreadable as he went to sit at the table. 'Jay.'

Claire's chest exploded with happiness and she grabbed the phone.

'Hello, my princess,' Jay said in a slurred voice.

'Jay!'

'I know it's the middle of the night there, darling, but I just went for a boozy lunch and needed to hear your voice.'

'It's so good to hear from you. I've missed you.'

Milo shifted uncomfortably in his chair. She turned away from him, leaning her forehead against the wall and closing her eyes.

Jay laughed. God, she missed that laugh. 'I'm not surprised you miss me! Must be driving you crazy out there, just you and Milo. Have any of your family been to visit?'

Things were still tense between her and her sister. She'd received an email from Alex with a photo of him picking up a football medal and a brief 'Hope things are good, xx' message, which also included a request to pass on his hellos to Holly. But that was it, certainly nothing from Sofia.

'Not yet,' Claire said.

'I had a – how shall I put this? *Pleasant* conversation with your beloved just now.'

'What do you mean?'

'He refused to get you out of bed, said you were sleeping.'

'That's unfair,' she said. 'I'll have a word.'

'Yes, you do that. How are things out there in the sweaty Outback?'

'Sweaty. Hard work too.'

'Do I need to come rescue you?'

She laughed. It sounded shrill. 'Don't be silly. Unless you're serious, you want to visit?' She felt a shimmer of excitement. To see a familiar face again, a face that wasn't twisted with anxiety and silent rage.

'I'd love to visit, darling, but I've been to Oz before and I have to say, the twenty-four-hour long flight just isn't for me. I'll be seeing you in London next spring though, surely?' he said.

'No, why would I?'

'Darling, don't tell me you don't know.'

'Know what?'

'You've won the Flora Matthews Foundation Prize for your piece on Otpor's role in the Serbian elections.'

The room span. She put her hand against the wall, steadying herself.

Milo strode towards her, face heavy with anxiety. 'Claire?'

She took his hand. 'I won the award my dad won for my Serbian piece.'

A huge smile spread over his face.

'You really didn't know?' Jay asked. 'They sent an email.'

'No, I had no idea. I haven't checked my email in ages. When was it decided?'

'Last week.'

'God, I'm – I can't believe it.'

She looked up at the ceiling, trying to grapple with how she felt about it. It was wonderful, of course, but all the memories it held made it difficult to digest. Her dad had left just after the awards ceremony, after all.

'Believe it, sweetie,' Jay said. 'It's a fantastic article, the way you captured those young men's passion for their cause, your descriptions of the rally the night of the protests, just fantastic. And believe it when I tell you you *are* coming to the presentation ceremony. You're guaranteed to make wonderful contacts. It'll be perfect for your career.'

Milo leaned down and kissed Claire's neck. She pulled away from him slightly, trying to focus on Jay's voice. He frowned then walked to the window and stared outside. Claire twisted the cord around her fingers, watching him. His chest was bare, the moonlight tickling his skin, picking out the hair on his chest, the shape of his biceps. His hair fell like a shadow over his eye, his lips slightly open.

'I don't know,' she said to Jay. 'Money's a bit tight right now.'

'I'll get you tickets.'

'Don't be silly.'

Jay paused. 'I think you need it, Claire. I think you need *home*, I can hear it in your voice.'

She noticed Milo stiffen a little. Could he hear Jay from there?

'Maybe,' she said. 'It's a lot to digest. Look, I better go. It's late. But thank you for calling.'

'I'll call you every week until you agree to book your trip to London. If I'm making a special trip back for the ceremony, you damn well are.' His voice grew serious. 'And whenever you need to talk – *whenever*, Claire – call me? You don't quite sound like your old self.'

'I'm fine, really. Take care.'

He was quiet for a few moments. 'You too, my darling. Speak very soon?'

She placed the phone in its cradle and smiled to herself. She'd won an award!

Milo strolled back over. 'I'm so proud of you, darling,' he said. 'I don't think I tell you enough what a wonderful writer I think you are.'

'Yes, you do. You're the one who encouraged me to write the article in Serbia!'

He took her hand. 'I know the awards must hold difficult memories for you but you mustn't think of that. You should think about how proud your dad would be.'

She smiled. 'I know.' Then she remembered what Jay had said about Milo not waking her up. 'Why did you tell Jay I was asleep?'

He shrugged as he walked over to the fridge. 'Because you were.' He pulled a bottle of wine out of the fridge and placed it on the table. 'I think we should celebrate.'

'But it's four in the morning!'

'So what? You're an award-winner. We're going to share this bottle of wine then we're going to watch the sun rise.' He walked over and took her face between his hands, staring into her eyes. 'A new start, all right? I know I've been a bit rubbish lately.'

She looked into his eyes, feeling hope flourish inside. 'New start.'

It felt like a new start that week. Milo's obsession with the mango trees seemed to ease and they even took a break from the farm, hiking across Kata Tjuta National Park, eating lunch – what Milo called his 'bush tucker', fistfuls of gooseberries, round yams and bush tomatoes, all eaten under the shade of the huge orange boulders. At night, Milo was tender, his eyes deep in Claire's as they made love, whispering her name over and over and kissing every inch of her 'award-winning skin' as he called it.

Yet all the time, Claire couldn't help but think about the awards presentation taking place in a few months, especially after Jay called again to tell her a features editor he knew at *Time* magazine wanted to meet her at the ceremony. It felt as though all the opportunities she'd once coveted were slipping through her fingers.

And while Milo seemed excited about the award too, he never asked Claire if there was any kind of presentation and she thought she knew why: money. Though Milo still had money left over from the farm sale years ago, he was reluctant to use more than was necessary, wanting to save as much of it as he could for the life he hoped they could build together. They barely had enough to feed themselves with any other money they made either, let alone pay hundreds of dollars to fly to London. But oh, for the chance! Claire had begun to grow tired of the red sand and the endless land with no people, no purpose, no links to the outside world. She was getting itchy feet again, that urge of hers to move on. Plus she'd dreamed of winning an award like this all her life. Why did it feel like she was pushing it aside?

Milo sensed her growing unease and soon his mood began to darken again in response. He began spending more and more of his time outside, staring up at the mango trees as if they held the answer to everything.

One afternoon, Claire marched out there. 'Milo, can you please stop fixating on those bloody trees? Surely you're sick of the sight of them? I know I am! Not just them but this place,' she said, sweeping her hand out. 'It's so isolated. I feel like I'm going mad sometimes.'

'I don't understand. I thought you wanted this? No people, no crowds. We both did.'

'But that's just the problem, it's too isolated. I feel like we're running away from everything here.' She swallowed, finally admitting to herself what she'd been thinking the past few weeks. 'We said we'd carve out a new path for ourselves and at first I loved it here. But now it's like we're on the same path we were on before we met, except we're running in the opposite direction; running *away* from what happened in Exmoor and everyone who reminds us of it. Not just Exmoor but everything that happened before . . .' She let her voice trail off as she thought of her dad's sunken face and her defunct ovaries. 'I think it's time to move on, Milo. I'm sick of bloody mangoes and Uluru and kangaroo meat and—'

Milo went very still. 'And me?'

'Don't be silly. I love you, you know that.'

He looked away and Claire felt a sudden thump of panic. So she stood on her tiptoes, wrapping her arms around him. 'Everyone gets homesick,' she whispered into his ear. 'It's not you.'

'I know.' He relaxed against her and they stayed like that for a while. After a few minutes, he pulled away from her and walked to the fridge. 'I forgot to tell you,' he said as he pulled a bottle of beer out. 'I've agreed to help Joe out with his house over the next few weeks.'

'But he's miles away.'

'Yeah, I'll be back pretty late.'

'Then why are you doing it?'

'It's money, Claire. Money we desperately need.' He sighed. 'Look, maybe it'll be good for us? We've been in each other's pockets the past few months. Maybe this is what we need?'

Her stomach dropped. 'What we *need*?'

He stared down at his beer, his hair in his eyes. 'I didn't mean it like that. I understand how you feel, hemmed in. I was used to it at the farm, working with my family, living with them. But you've always been so independent. You can write more articles, read more while I'm away. And then I'll be back in the evenings.' He walked over to her and stroked her cheek, his fingers cold from the bottle of beer. 'You'll see, it'll be good for us.'

But it wasn't good for them. It took Milo three hours to drive to Joe's, meaning he had to wake at five each morning, not returning until ten, sometimes eleven in the evening.

305

When they slipped into the New Year, the heat intensified, the acrid air suffocating them. The date of the awards presentation was fast approaching and Claire felt sick to her stomach. It didn't help that she had a tense phone call with her friend Jodie the week before who told her she was crazy not to come back to the UK for something so important.

So Claire read the faded copy of the article that had won her the award over and over, and stared out of the window at the terracotta landscape on those long lonely days without Milo. She felt as though she was being buried alive beneath those sands, the red dust seeping into her throat as she desperately tried to claw her way back up and find the life she'd left behind. When she considered her reflection in the mirror each morning, she even began to see her dad and the way he'd looked at her in that flat: face weary with lost chances and bitter disappointments.

A week before the award ceremony, it got too much. Claire woke to find Milo staring up at the trees again and the air in the bedroom felt congested, became unbearable. So without changing, without even putting any shoes on, Claire ran outside. Milo didn't even notice as she sprinted past him in her nightie, the searing air and red dust swirling around her thighs. She just wanted to run, alone. And that's what she did. She ran and ran until there was nothing but red and dust.

Then there was a hissing sound.

She paused, eyes gliding towards the noise, whole body going rigid with fear as she saw a long brown snake curled around itself a few metres away, scales gleaming red under the morning sun.

The rainbow serpent of her dreams.

Except this snake was real, very real.

It slowly lifted its head, the rest of its body uncoiling, its green eyes settling on Claire's. She saw something in those eyes, like it thought she'd overstayed her welcome. She could feel that inside too. She'd been so content to begin with, but now she felt trapped, old negative thoughts resurfacing: her infertility rearing its ugly head again, Erin intruding on her and Milo's happiness. She was pushing her luck. If she stayed, something bad would happen, she could feel it.

The snake hissed and Claire stumbled, feet scrambling against the dust as she ran back towards the farm. When she got there, Milo was gone, his truck tyres leaving tracks in the sand. She darted inside, slamming the door shut and sliding down the wall. What if she'd been bitten? She closed her eyes, saw herself lying in bed and dying alone like her dad, almost hearing the sound of rain beating against the window as though she was in his New York bedsit again.

She put her hand over her ears, the rain still pounding. Was she going mad?

No, a voice said inside her. *Get up, talk to someone, anyone. Don't be alone.*

She rose on shaky legs and stumbled to the phone, dialling Jay's number. On the fourth attempt, he finally picked up.

'Claire?' he asked.

'I – I'm going mad,' she said. 'This place, it's driving me insane.'

'Are you alone? Where's Milo?

'He's out. He's *always* out. And when he's here, he's tormented and it's not just about the rotting mangoes. There's more to it, I can tell.'

There was a sound behind her. Claire turned to see Milo standing in the doorway, a bottle of wine in one hand, a piece of paper in the other. He threw the paper across the room, then stormed out of the house.

Two plane tickets to London settled gently on the floor.

Chapter Twenty

London, UK
2002

'This place is amazing,' Claire said, looking around the hotel room Jay had booked for them as a surprise, just a five-minute walk from where the awards were taking place.

'Only the best room for my special guests,' Jay said, smiling a smile so wide Claire thought his face might break with the effort. He leaned back in his chair, carefully crossing his legs and smoothing his hand over the silky grey material of his trousers.

Milo, however, shifted awkwardly in his seat, pulling at the short-sleeved black shirt he was wearing, his tanned skin still blotchy from the shave he'd had before their flight, his first shave in weeks. 'The B&B I booked in Chiswick was nice enough,' he said, his eyes lingering on the necklace Jay had given Claire as congratulations for her award – an ornately designed typewriter made of gold with blue gems as keypads.

'Bit of a trek though,' Jay said.

Claire smiled at Milo. 'Chiswick's lovely, Milo. I've always liked it there. But we're here now, aren't we? We'll have a whole week in the hotel you booked from tomorrow.'

He smiled but Claire could sense the tension beneath it.

Jay checked his phone. 'Pinar's running late,' he said, referring to the *Time* features editor he'd mentioned to Claire. 'She'll meet us at our table. Shall we go?'

Claire's tummy bubbled with nerves. She finished the glass of champagne Jay had ordered for them. It fizzed down her throat then whirled in her chest, making her head sway. She hadn't had champagne in such a long time. She stood up and smiled to herself.

This is just what she needed – *they* needed.

Milo stood with her, placing his hand on her arm. 'Are you happy?' he asked her.

Was she happy? She could still see the rainbow serpent staring at her when she closed her eyes, still feel the heat of the Red Centre on her skin, still hear the sound of Milo's footsteps as he walked back and forth among the dying mango trees.

But they were here now thanks to the tickets Milo had worked so hard at Joe's to buy. Their visas would soon run out and they'd even discussed starting a new adventure on the journey over, maybe India or even Japan.

'Yes,' she said, smiling.

Milo matched her smile. 'Good.'

Jay frowned as he looked between them. He hadn't bought Claire's excuses for that frantic phone call she'd made to him a couple of days before. She knew he'd bring it up when he got her alone.

He went to the door and held it open. Claire looked down at the wispy black dress she was wearing, the only decent thing she could find at the airport, all her other outfits too old and faded. She'd set it off with an eye-catching Aboriginal necklace with red swirls and matching earrings, but it still felt dull compared to what she usually wore.

'You look gorgeous,' Milo said, as though sensing her thoughts.

'So do you,' she said, hooking her arm through his. 'So let's get our gorgeous selves there, shall we?'

'So I hear you both retreated from society?' one of the guests on their table, a writer for *The Times*, asked them an hour later.

Claire laughed. 'Not intentionally! Though we have been living in a virtual tin the past few months. It'll be nice to enjoy some luxury for a few days.' Milo's face clouded over. 'But it's been wonderful,' she quickly added. 'The Red Centre's an amazing place, isn't it, Milo?'

He nodded. 'Yes, wonderful. Have you been, Don?'

Claire's shoulders relaxed. She'd been worried when they'd first walked into the plush hotel where the awards ceremony was being held. Not just because it brought back memories from when she'd gone with her dad to pick up his award all those years back, but also because it was throbbing with people, with sounds, with smells they'd left behind when they went to Australia. But Milo was being so charming, almost like he'd been those first couple of days in Exmoor, that she needn't have worried.

'I've only been to Sydney,' Don replied. 'I come from your neck of the woods actually, Milo. Barnstaple area?'

Claire felt her smile trickle away. It was no surprise he recognised Milo, he *did* write for a major British newspaper after all.

But Milo just smiled. 'Good to have a fellow Westlander to chat to.'

'So this is a West Country reunion, is it?' a high-pitched voice asked from behind them.

Claire turned to see a man with a bald head, black eyes,

one of them squinting at her. Something about him rang a bell. Then it clicked: it was Nathan Styles, the journalist who'd written all those misleading articles about Milo and confronted her after her court appearance. He'd still sent her emails over the years, trying to get an interview with her, even calling her sister a couple of times. She'd ignored him, just like she ignored all those other nutters who had come out of the woodwork after she'd been in the papers.

'Good to see you again, Milo,' Nathan said sarcastically, taking the seat across from him.

Milo's jaw tensed and, for a moment, Claire thought he might punch Nathan. But instead, Milo frowned. 'Sorry, do we know each other?'

The smug look on Nathan's face faltered a little. Claire smiled to herself. Nathan was the type of person who'd rather be punched than not recognised.

Jay jumped up. 'Ah, there she is! Pinar!'

They all looked over to see a tall, impossibly beautiful woman walk in with wavy black hair to her waist and perfectly tanned skin, making Claire feel frumpy in her plain dress and peeling skin. Pinar caught sight of Jay and her face lit up. Claire wondered if she was more than just an acquaintance.

'I apologise for my tardiness,' she said in an accented voice when she arrived. She leaned towards Claire, clasping her hand. 'You must be Claire. I'm so pleased to finally meet you. And an award-winner, no less. You must tell me of your time in Serbia, especially all those details that didn't make that fascinating article.' She turned to Milo. 'And, Milo, I've heard much about you too. You're very brave and it's an honour to meet you too, truly.'

He frowned. 'Brave?'

'Yes. You saved many people. You're a real-life hero, no?'

His cheeks reddened and the table went quiet as Nathan raised an eyebrow.

'Don't be ashamed,' Pinar said. 'You did what you could to protect your family.'

'Interesting theory,' Nathan said.

Claire reached under the table, squeezing Milo's knee. He brushed his fingers over Claire's hand, a sign he was okay.

Nathan's phone buzzed and he stood up. 'Excuse me a moment.'

'Idiot,' Don said as he walked away. People around the table raised their eyebrows in surprise as Milo smiled to himself. 'Come on, we all think it,' Don said. 'We've all heard the rumours the only reason he managed to get that actress to talk to him about the abuse she endured as a child was because he stole her laptop and read her emails about it. She had no choice when he told her he'd found out through a "source",' he added, making quotation marks with his fingers.

'Oh come on, it's just a rumour,' one of the other journalists around the table said.

Don shook his head. 'He told a colleague when he was drunk and they told me! It'll be a travesty if he wins an award for that interview.'

The host for the evening walked to the stage then and the room went quiet. Claire felt her stomach fill with butterflies.

'You mustn't be nervous,' Pinar whispered, noticing the look on her face. 'You deserve this. In fact, I'd like to talk to you about a position that's opened at the magazine if you have time while you're here?'

Jay shot Claire an excited smile.

'Is it a freelance position?' Claire asked Pinar.

'Oh no, a proper salaried position based in Dubai.'

Claire imagined Milo walking around, staring up at all those new skyscrapers in Dubai.

She looked at Milo and he shrugged. 'Worth a chat,' he said.

She turned back to Pinar. 'Maybe we can meet for lunch later in the week?'

Pinar smiled. 'Of course. I think this could be a wonderful opportunity for someone with your talent, Claire.'

'Talent that shouldn't go to waste,' Jay said, his eyes drilling into Milo's. 'Picking mangoes all day a great journalist doth not make.'

'Claire still *writes* most days actually,' Milo said, his voice tense. 'I've always made sure she keeps her writing up.'

'How kind of you,' Jay replied.

'It looks like they're announcing the awards,' Pinar said, looking between Milo and Jay, her brow creased.

The next couple of hours passed in a wonderful blur despite the tension between Milo and Jay. The sound of Claire's name being called out, the sight of her article up on the screen, the words – her words – read out for all to hear. She imagined her dad there, watching with pride in his eyes. She'd even got another text message from Ben the day before, congratulating her on her award. She thought of his pretty fiancé growing fat with child. The sting that news had brought was dissipating. Maybe she'd just needed to get away from Australia to get back on track again and continue healing?

After she collected her award, Milo bought a bottle of champagne he couldn't afford and twirled her around the room, giddily introducing her to people as 'my award-winning girlfriend', making her feel even more like everything would be all right again.

When they got back to the table, Nathan was deep in

conversation with Don. They peered up when Claire and Milo approached, faces dark.

'Why so serious?' Milo asked Don, flopping down and pulling Claire onto his lap. She wrapped her arms around him, kissing his sweaty neck as he laughed.

'Quite a news story breaking in our part of the world, Milo,' Don said, his eyes passing over Claire.

Milo stiffened slightly.

'Skeletal remains of a body have been found in an old fishing hut,' Nathan said. 'It's just a mile from where your farm was, in fact. Been dead years, my sources are telling me. I'm going to head down there to do some poking around.'

A terrible wretchedness spread over Milo's face.

'You know the area,' Nathan said, his eyes drilling into Milo's. 'The police are currently making enquires into who owns the hut but maybe you—'

'It's been a long time since Milo's been back to Exmoor,' Claire said, her instincts to protect him overtaking her doubts. 'Shouldn't you be going now anyway? Exmoor's quite a drive.'

Nathan held her gaze for a few moments then he stood, flinging his jacket over his shoulder. 'Of course. I'm sure we'll be talking very soon anyway.' He shoved his business card into her bag then left the room.

Claire turned to Milo, seeing a look in his eyes that showed he wasn't surprised. She tried to open her mouth, to form some words, but nothing would come out. Then a journalist she knew came over to congratulate her. When he left them alone, Milo took her hand. 'We better go,' he said tightly, his breathing funny as he avoided her gaze. 'I've booked a table for dinner, remember?'

'But Milo—'

'Please, Claire,' he said, voice desperate. 'Let's not ruin today.'

'I don't want dinner, I want to know—'

'So, dinner next?' Jay said as he strolled over. He paused, finally noting the atmosphere. 'Everything okay?'

'I think we'll give dinner a miss,' Claire said. 'It was a long flight and—'

'No,' Milo said, shaking his head. 'Absolutely not. We can't stop the celebrations.'

Claire frowned. Why was he being like this? Hadn't he just looked like the world was falling apart?

'I agree,' Jay said, grabbing Claire's hand before she could protest any more and pulling her away. She twisted around to see Pinar tuck her arm into Milo's. There was a look in his eyes she'd only seen once, when she'd found him with his brother dead in his arms: a heart-rending vulnerability. That look made Claire's head spin, made her realise something was terribly, terribly wrong.

When they stepped outside, the sun was setting, spring making itself known with soft yellow skies and blossom-clogged pavements. It didn't seem right to watch a new season beginning when, right at that moment, it felt like they were on the precipice of the end.

Ten minutes later, they approached the restaurant but it looked dark inside.

'Are you sure it's open?' Claire asked, hoping Milo had got it wrong so they could go back to their hotel and talk alone.

'Sure I'm sure,' he replied, putting on what she could tell was a forced smile. 'Come on.'

He took her hand and pushed the door open, revealing a room shrouded in darkness.

'Milo, I really think—'

Suddenly, the lights flashed on and a sea of faces smiled out at them.

'Surprise!' they all shouted out.

Her family and friends! She could even see Sofia in the crowds, her face tense. Claire stumbled back and Milo took her arm, a flicker of his old natural smile appearing. It felt like a dream. A wonderfully shocking dream.

'You arranged this?' she asked Milo.

He nodded. Now she understood why he'd been so keen not to go back to the hotel. But still, that didn't change what had happened earlier. What could she do though – insist on leaving? She looked into Milo's brown eyes. It had to all just be a coincidence. She needed to put it to the back of her mind.

Over the next couple of hours, they worked their way around the room, Claire introducing Milo to everyone. He put on a fine act, laughing at the right moments, but Claire could tell beneath it all he was tense.

Then they got to Sofia, Alex and Ed, the latter a handsome blond man with a kind smile. Milo and Ed shook hands, and Sofia nervously smoothed down the red material of her dress. She looked thin, her face lined. She'd managed to get a promotion in the end and the extra hours were showing.

Claire pulled her sister into a hug. 'Lovely to see you,' she whispered into her ear, desperate for something not to be broken tonight. 'Can we be friends?'

Her sister pulled away, examining Claire's face. Then she smiled. 'Of course. I've missed you.' Claire felt relief rush through her.

'Mum couldn't come then?' she asked.

Sofia rolled her eyes. 'You know what she's like about flying with her bad back.'

'Oh yes, her bad back,' Claire said sarcastically.

Milo shot Sofia an awkward smile. 'Hello, Sofia.'

She didn't say anything, turning away instead as Alex and

Ed looked on, embarrassed. Claire wanted to grab her sister by the shoulders and tell her it was Holly who'd destroyed all her work. But she knew Milo wouldn't want that. She resolved to tell her one day though; she couldn't have Sofia hating the man she loved for all the wrong reasons.

'You look well tanned,' Alex said, giving Claire a peck on the cheek before awkwardly shaking Milo's hand.

'Alex helped me organise this,' Milo explained to Claire.

'Ah, bless you,' Claire said to Alex, giving him a hug, pleased things were better between him and Milo.

Jodie bounded over then with her husband Paul. They both looked so young and blond and happy with their boho-chic clothes and trendy haircuts. Sofia smiled tightly at Jodie, no love lost between the two women, then led Alex and Ed away, shouting 'Catch you later, Claire,' over her shoulder.

After Claire introduced them, Paul dragged Milo to the bar, shouting above the music that he wanted to hear all about his 'peach farm'.

'So,' Jodie said, turning to Claire. 'I finally get to meet the elusive Milo.'

'Yes, finally,' Claire said, squeezing Jodie's hand. 'And I finally get to see you again. You look great.'

'You look fab too, hon, though what's with the black?'

'Only thing I could find at the airport.'

'Yeah, I heard it was all a bit last minute. I was hoping to come visit you in Lapland before you suddenly upped sticks. What happened there? You fobbed me off last time I asked. I thought you were planning to stay a year or so.'

'Long story,' Claire said, nervously fiddling with her type-writer necklace as she looked over at Milo. He was leaning against a pillar, nursing a bottle of beer as Paul talked to him. He'd taken off his tie and his face was red from the heat in the room, his hair dishevelled.

'He's definitely the dark, brooding type, isn't he?' Jodie said, following Claire's gaze. 'You always went for boys like that when we were kids, that's why I was surprised when you fell for Ben. He was more Labrador puppy than wolf.'

'Milo's not a wolf!'

'I was joking, babe!' Jodie frowned. 'Are you okay?'

Claire sighed. 'Sorry, I guess I'm just jetlagged.'

Jodie put her hand on Claire's arm. 'You've heard from Ben, haven't you?'

'About his girlfriend being pregnant?'

'Yeah. Paul heard about it. Must be difficult.'

'It was at first,' Claire admitted. 'I felt like I'd been hit by a bulldozer when Ben told me. My reaction surprised me, you know? I think I was a bit naïve to think I could completely get over being infertile. I guess it goes to show the pain never goes away.'

'That's a healthy attitude,' Jodie said. 'I'd be more worried if you were in denial, it's a big part of your life and will be forever. But look at you! I'm so proud of you, hon. This award is amazing and the article you wrote is the kind of thing you always dreamed of writing.' She took the award from Claire's hand and examined it. 'Daddy Bo would be so proud.'

Claire squeezed her friend's hand. 'You're a sentimental old bag, you know.'

'I can't help it, it's just so wonderful seeing you like you are, travelling the world with a hot farmer, writing the stories you always dreamed of writing. You were so unhappy with Ben, Claire. I didn't think it was my place to intrude but it worried me, how separately you seemed to live your lives and the mechanical way you approached those IVF rounds.' Jodie looked into Claire's eyes, her own filling with tears. 'You know, you always pretended it was like water off a duck's back. What you just said now, about the pain never going away, it's the first time you've admitted to me how hard it was for you. It's great to see you open and honest and grabbing life with both hands.'

Jodie was right, Claire really did feel she was finally finding her way. But she couldn't feel happy right at that moment after what Nathan Styles had just revealed. Stormy waters were coming her way, she could feel it.

'Thanks,' Claire said to Jodie. 'We've both found our way, haven't we?' She peered towards Milo. 'I better go check on my hot farmer.' She gave Jodie a quick hug then walked over to Milo. His face lit up when he saw her, making her heart leap. Maybe everything would be okay?

But then someone was walking towards her. She thought it was a mirage at first, the woman's red hair lifting as she walked towards Milo, her skirt swishing around her legs, the setting sun shimmering into the window above like a spinning top. Milo froze, his eyes wide, his face pale.

The woman stopped before him, her head tilting. 'Milo?'

Irish accent.

Erin?

'I heard the news,' the woman said. 'It's Erin's body, isn't it?'

Claire's head swam with confusion. 'I don't understand. Who are you?'

The woman stepped towards Claire, the bells around the hem of her long pink skirt jingling, the sun moving from behind her head, taking the red glow with it. Now Claire could see that the woman's hair was brown, like her own.

'Nora,' the woman said. 'Nora McKenzie. I'm Erin's best friend. I've been looking for her for years.'

'Erin's in Ireland,' Claire said, not believing the words as they came out of her mouth.

'I haven't heard from Erin in over fifteen years.'

Claire looked at Milo.

'It was just after Dale got sole custody of Holly. We argued about you, Milo,' Nora continued. 'Her daughter had been taken away from her and yet all Erin could talk about was *you*. That's the last time I heard from her. I refused to believe she'd block me out like that, I even filed a missing person's report. But no one took me seriously. And now they've found a body.' Her voice broke. 'It's her, isn't it?'

Milo didn't say anything, just blinked at her.

Claire put her hand up to her head, massaging her throbbing temple as though she could massage the dawning terror away. Erin had been missing for years. A body had been found in Exmoor. Could it really be her?

People were turning to look at them now, noticing the look on Claire's face, the tears running down Nora's face.

'Claire,' Jay asked, striding over. 'Are you okay?'

But she ignored him, looking into Milo's eyes. She saw something there, a horrible dread.

As she looked at Nora, something occurred to her. 'Did *you* send Milo that Christmas card when we were in Finland?'

'Yes,' Nora said, her voice trembling slightly. 'I got the address after seeing one of your articles online saying you were both staying at the reindeer farm. I had the card from the time Erin stayed with us when she'd just found out she was pregnant with Holly. I got a little drunk and sent it impulsively as a little reminder to Milo that she wasn't forgotten, and that I knew what happened between you both,' she added, eyes drilling into Milo's.

'What happened between you both?' Jay asked Milo. 'What's going on?'

Nora turned to Jay. 'Milo and Erin had an affair. Erin James is my best friend and she's dead.' Her voice broke as she said that and Claire could see in Nora's brown eyes the gradual dawning that the best friend she'd been searching for all these years might be dead.

'It's her body they've found in Exmoor,' Nora said, her jaw tight as she tried to contain her emotions. 'I know it is.'

'What body?' Sofia asked. 'What's going on, Claire?'

Claire looked at Milo. 'Tell me, Milo. I know something's wrong. I think I've always known.'

'She loved you, you know,' Nora said, her voice filled with sadness. 'More than she ever loved that unstable brother of yours. Did he kill her, Milo?' Nora stepped towards him. 'Or did you?'

Milo's face crumpled.

'No,' Claire said, shaking her head. 'No.'

Jay took Claire by the shoulders and shook her. 'Look at his face, Claire! He doesn't even have to say it out loud, that's confession enough.'

The room went quiet, everyone looking at them now. But all Claire could see was Milo and the wretched look in his eyes.

'Okay, I think the party's over,' Jay said, nodding at the bar's manager who opened the doors. People hesitated a moment then started walking out, leaving just Claire, Milo and Nora.

'Is it true?' Claire asked Milo, suddenly feeling very calm as Nora stood close to her. 'Is Erin dead?'

He slumped against the pillar, covering his face with his hands.

That was all Claire needed for an answer.

Nora looked up at the ceiling, tears streaming down her face. 'What happened to Erin?' she asked.

'Holly went missing a few weeks after the court order, and when we searched for her, we found her at Hope's Mouth with Erin,' Milo said in a wretched voice. 'I thought she was going to jump with Holly in her arms. I tried to stop her but – but she slipped.'

Nora let out a sob, putting her hand to her mouth.

'So Holly saw everything,' Claire said.

Milo nodded. 'Yes.'

'That poor poor girl,' Nora whispered.

'I'm so sorry for everything, Claire,' Milo said. 'For the lies, for what happened.'

Milo put his hand out to Claire but she stepped away from him. 'No more lies.'

Chapter Twenty-One

Ko Phi Phi Don, Thailand
2004

I sit at the table, smoothing my hair down. I must look a
right state compared to my usual neat self. But I haven't got
the time or the heart to make myself look good for Will.
Anyway, he's still in a mood with me, I can tell, despite how
relaxed he's pretending to be.

Sam approaches the table looking uncomfortable, his
usually relaxed pose replaced by a straight back, rigid arms.

As we order our food, we make small talk. Or Will does,
telling Sam all about his father's job as a finance director of
a top haulage company, emphasising how important he is
by association. When our food arrives, I look at the salad
Will ordered for me then at Sam's curry and suddenly have
a craving for it.

'Want to swap?' Sam asks, noticing me looking at it.

'You don't mind?'

Will laughs. 'You hate spicy curry, Louise. That stuff'll
take your head off.'

'Maybe that's what I need right now,' I say, swapping my
plate with Sam's as he smiles to himself.

Will looks between us, his lips getting that pinched look

they get when he's annoyed. 'It doesn't sound like you've made much progress searching for your mother. Just as well I'm here, isn't it?'

I'm about to tell him this isn't some kind of competition but then he places a large envelope onto the table and leans back, folding his arms.

'What's this?' I ask, picking it up.

'As I mentioned, I called your father when I landed to check on the girls, and he told me your mother was looking for her best friend out here. You do realise Erin James is dead, don't you?'

I look at him in shock. 'Dead?'

Will nods. 'Yes, her body was found over two years ago. Your father did some digging after he spoke to you. He asked me to let you know.'

Two years. Chloe would've just been five, Olivia two, so my TV had been full of kids' stuff, my newspaper rack crammed with parenting magazines, the real world not getting a look-in. Plus Mum and I hadn't been talking during that time, so if she'd known about Erin, I'd not have heard it from her. She must've been devastated. Why didn't she tell me? It breaks my heart to think she couldn't share something like this with me. When she lost contact with Erin, she struggled to cope. How would she have coped to know she was dead? Has she had anyone to turn to for comfort?

Oh Mum.

I take a deep breath, blinking the tears away. I can't fall apart now, not when she needs me the most.

'How did Erin die?' I ask Will.

'An accident, apparently. She was arguing with Milo James,' he says, making quotation marks with his fingers, 'and she stumbled off a cliff. Her daughter witnessed it all.'

324

'My God, that poor girl,' I say. 'First she sees her mother die then had to witness what her father did a few years later.'

I think of what that boy in the café had said about Mum asking about Holly James. 'If Mum hadn't been searching for Erin, why was she searching for Holly?'

'Maybe she saw the photos,' Sam says, 'and was worried about her? She may have felt a responsibility for her now Holly's mother was gone?'

I can't help but wonder why Mum didn't feel that same responsibility to me.

'That's exactly the conclusion I came to,' Will says. 'So I called Niran from the airport and got him to do some digging.' He taps the envelope in front of me and raises an eyebrow.

I go to open it then pause. 'Is this what Niran gave you when we arrived?'

'Yes, he had it all ready for me. He'd be a brilliant detective, that one.'

I feel anger well up inside. 'Why didn't you show it to me then, for Christ's sake? This isn't a game, Will! Time is of the essence, what if Mum's injured somewhere?'

The smug smile drops off his face. 'Well, if you're going to be like that.' He snatches the envelope away from me.

'Give it to her,' Sam says in a low voice. 'Louise is right, this isn't a game. Her mother's missing.'

Will slowly turns to Sam. 'Your mother was friends with Nora, wasn't she? Oh, that's right. I remember Louise saying something about her mother's sad old divorcée friend Jane who drank too much.'

I almost choke on my drink as Sam's whole face goes bright red. What the hell is Will playing at?

'I certainly did not say that,' I say.

Sam stands, throwing his napkin on the table. 'I'll leave you both to it.'

'Please don't go,' I say, half standing.

Will places his hand firmly over mine. 'Let him go, Louise.'

Sam goes to walk away then pauses, turning to me. 'You might want to ask your husband what he said to your mum when he dropped her off after his birthday party. I might be wrong, it's just a hunch.' He strides away.

I watch him leave, my stomach twisting inside. Then I look at Will.

'I have *no* idea what he's talking about,' he says before I have a chance to say anything.

'You're lying. I always know when you're lying. If our marriage matters to you at all, you can't lie to me. Do you understand?'

I imagine Mum sitting at the chair Sam's left behind, smiling to herself. *That's right, Lou. Beauty is truth and truth beauty.*

Will searches my eyes then blinks a few times. 'Fine,' he says eventually. 'I only did it because I love you.'

My heart ricochets against my chest. 'Did what?'

'It's nothing really, your mother took it too literally and—'

'Took what too literally?'

Will rakes his fingers through his short dark hair, avoiding my gaze. 'All I said was she was holding you back.'

'Holding me back?'

'Yes. I said you fixated too much on your relationship, that you couldn't really grow into the real Louise, that she was ruining your life.'

'What the hell, Will? Did you also say I'd be better off without her, like you said on the phone the other day?'

He doesn't say anything and I know in that moment he *did* say that. And Mum, being the way she was, took it right to her heart, thinking it would just be better for me and the girls if she stepped quietly out of our lives.

326

I feel a horrible buzzing in my head. Will's trying to say my name, trying to make me look at him and it's suffocating me. I jump up and run out of the restaurant, shouting 'Don't follow me' over my shoulder, nearly bumping into Niran whose smile freezes when he sees the look on my face.

When I get down to the beach, the heat presses into me, the sound of crickets, the ripple of the ocean wrapping itself around me.

'Oh, Mum,' I whisper, sinking down onto the sand.

'Louise?' I look up to see Sam standing nearby. He must have noticed the tears on my cheeks because he quickly strolls towards me, crouching down in front of me. 'Are you okay?'

'I didn't say that about your mum, Sam. I swear.'

He sighs and sits down next to me. 'I know. It's not the sort of thing you'd say.'

'You were right, you know. Will told Mum I'd be better off without her in my life.'

He shakes his head. 'I'm sorry. I had a feeling he had something to do with it after you told me he'd given her a lift back from the party. It couldn't be a coincidence you haven't heard from her since that night.'

'I realise now she never thought she was good enough for me,' I say. 'To have Will confirm that to her . . .' I shake my head. 'I think she was just exhausted with it all. It was easier to simply walk away, just as she had when she and Dad argued that last time. Nothing in her life ever made her feel wanted or deserving of love. *I* never made her feel wanted. Why hang around?'

I feel the weight of everything pressing down upon me and put my face in my hands, starting to sob. Sam puts his arm around me and I lean against his shoulder.

'Well, I can't say I'm surprised.' We pull apart to see Will standing a few metres away, watching us with crossed arms. 'Let me guess, you knew each other before you came out here?'

I stand. 'Of course we didn't. I was upset, Sam was just comforting me.'

Will raises an eyebrow. 'Comforting. Is that what they call it now? Come on, Louise, admit it. You saw him at some gig or other, started emailing him and came out here to meet him. That's the way it happens, isn't it?'

'We didn't know each other until two days ago,' Sam says, his voice weary.

'Rubbish,' Will snaps. 'Why else would you be so keen to run away from the father of your children, Louise?'

'Father?' I find myself saying. 'What kind of father have you been the past few years, not spending one moment alone with the girls until this week? You go on about my mum not being in touch but what about you? You'd rather spend weekends away with some tart at work than take the girls away.'

Sam's eyes widen and Will does what he always does: opens his mouth in mock-indignation.

'Don't try to deny it,' I say before he has a chance to speak, feeling the burden lifting from my shoulders as I finally admit what I know in my heart. 'God knows I've denied it the past few years but not any more. And as for why I came here, why do you think? For my mum, for Christ's sake!' I shout that bit out, making people in the distance turn to stare, all the resentment over the years about the way Will's dismissed Mum, the way *everyone* does, bubbling to the surface. 'You really don't get it, do you? Despite everything you've seen today, the way this island's been torn apart, you still don't get it. My mum's missing and the chances are, she's dead. And yet still, a few hours after we heard about the tsunami on the news, *still* you pretended like nothing happened.'

My voice breaks and Sam steps close to me.

'I don't get it?' Will says, waving the envelope in front of me. 'Then why have I gone to all these lengths to get this information for you?'

'Don't you mean the lengths *Niran* went to?' Sam asks softly.

Will turns to him. 'Oh fuck off, you New-Age loser.'

I feel a burst of anger. 'How dare you speak to Sam like that? He does more for people's lives than you bloody do!' I put my hand out. 'Hand that envelope over.'

'Why should I give it to you? You're clearly not grateful for the work I've done here.'

'This is my missing mum we're talking about,' I say, trying to keep my voice calm. 'You've already ruined things between us, don't ruin my chance of finding my mum.'

'Ruined things between us? If you mean those text messages you found—'

'Not just that! I can't believe what you said to my mum, Will! You know how vulnerable she was.'

'I did it because I love you.'

'Did you really?' I ask. 'Or did you do it for you? I saw how annoyed you were when Mum argued with your director in front of your parents. It was neater if she was out of the picture, right?'

Will doesn't say anything and I know I'm right.

'You know what?' he says, looking me up and down. 'I don't care. You've changed and I don't like it, not one little bit. I should never have come here.' He shoves the envelope into my hand. 'Here, don't say I didn't try to help you.' Then he strides away.

As I watch him, I understand it's now over between us.

I feel a heady mixture of nausea and relief, nausea at how upset the girls will be but relief I've finally admitted to myself: there's something deeply wrong with our relationship. As for the girls, I've learned from bitter experience, if a relationship is flawed, no good can come of it for the children involved.

I look down at the envelope then tear it open. It's a leaflet from an accommodation complex called The Lotus in Tonsai Bay, the area we first arrived in when we got here. Attached to it is a note in Thai.

Sam takes it. 'I know a bit of Thai.' He scans the note then peers up at me. 'Looks like Niran has a contact in the Thai police who's been compiling names of people who stayed in resorts on the south of the island. Turns out Holly James was staying at The Lotus. So was Claire Shreve.'

'Then we have to go there,' I say. 'If Mum was looking for Holly, maybe she went to this hotel too?'

I take in a deep breath and brace myself for what I'm soon to see.

Chapter Twenty-Two

Dubai, UAE
2004

Dubai astounded Claire when she first arrived: a mirage of a city erupting from the sand with its glistening skyscrapers and robotic cranes. It felt like the beginning of something hopeful and ambitious. And though Claire soon learned of the sacrifices made to bring it that far and the tragedies that had brought it to life, she couldn't help but still regard it in awe.

As for the gaping hole left by Milo's absence, she stared it in the face and it stared right back at her. She'd refused to see him after his confession about Erin. He'd written to her, begging her not to give up on him. But she couldn't handle the lies any more, despite how much she desperately loved him. She'd worked so hard to face the truth of her own tragedy, her infertility, that she craved honesty. Milo was too entangled in lies, not just small lies but the worst kind of lies. For her own well-being, she needed to be away from all that. So that's what she told him in her reply to his letter. What she didn't tell him was that each morning when she woke, her mind hiccupped and floundered like an old computer as it tried to grapple with the concept of him not being there beside her.

Claire stayed with her sister in the grim year following the award ceremony, freelancing from their spare room, trying to figure out what was next for her. It felt like without Milo, she'd lost her compass. When it was confirmed that the body that had been found was Erin's, and the fisherman's hut she'd been found in belonged to Dale, there had been an inquest into her death. Claire accompanied Holly to the inquest after she begged her to and it had been heart-wrenching to see the way Milo had looked at her with such desperate sadness in his eyes as he gave his evidence. After a while, she couldn't take it any more and had to look away, just as he had looked away all those years ago in that court-room in Exeter. When it came to him providing evidence, he recounted exactly what he'd told Claire, adding that he'd presumed Erin's body had simply disappeared into the sea. But as the inquest went on, it became clear Dale must have found Erin's body then hidden it in his hut after a local coastguard logged his boat circling the coastline in the weeks following her accident. In the end, the coroner returned a verdict of misadventure.

She left the inquest before Milo could talk to her, knowing her resolve would falter being in such close proximity to him. The inquest seemed to create a new resolve in Claire too. It had felt as though she'd been living in limbo at her sister's in the year since the awards ceremony. But after the inquest, she decided to rent a small flat in London and got a tempo-rary contract working for a travel magazine for a few months. Then a few months later, Jay's editor friend Pinar offered her a contract with *Time* magazine based in Dubai. She took it up without hesitation, seeing in 2004 on the plane ride out there. It was the accumulation of everything she'd been working towards these past few years: writing articles of substance. She even wrote about her experiences with infertility, and it allowed her to map out her journey of grief, a journey she was still on. First the horror she felt at never holding a child in her arms, then her anger at a society that refused to acknowledge the validity of a woman who couldn't be a mother. And then her struggle to prove her validity through her writing before, finally, a calm acceptance of the path that was weaving its way before her.

She made new friends in Dubai, had old friends come to stay. And they all commented at how together she seemed. Only one friend, Jodie, seemed to notice the sadness Claire saw in her own eyes each morning when she woke to find Milo not there. But Jodie didn't say anything, nor did Claire. What use was it? Everyone has their ghosts, as Filipe had once said. They haunt us but we grow so used to them, it isn't long before they're another shadow, another cloud.

Jay visited her in November. She hadn't seen him in a while and when he approached her as she waited in the rusty old car she'd won in a bet with another journalist – same plush suit, same curly blond hair – it hit her just how much she'd missed him. She pushed open the passenger door. 'Come on, you old snob. I know it's not an Aston Martin but you have no choice.'

He slung his Louis Vuitton bag into the back and slipped into the passenger seat, throwing her his trademark smile. 'As long as I get to choose where we go for lunch.'

'Don't you always?'

His eyes softened. 'God, I've missed you.'

'Me too.'

He pulled her into a hug and she smiled as she breathed in the familiar scent of his aftershave.

Two hours later, they were looking out over the turquoise Persian Gulf in one of Dubai's most luxurious restaurants.

Nearby, the windows of steel buildings laddered up into a hazy blue sky, the sea shimmering below. Combined with the shiny cars that glided past and pavements so pristine they glistened, it felt as though they were surrounded by mirrors. It was such a contrast to Australia with its curves and soft reds.

'Jesus, Jay, I thought you said we were getting a bite to eat?' Claire said.

'Have you learned nothing about me?'

She laughed and three businessmen turned to look at them. Claire wondered what they thought: Jay with his ridiculously expensive suit and glossy blond curls, Claire with her messy dark hair and frayed T-shirt. Maybe they looked just as they should, a rich flamboyant man talking to a busy journalist.

'I can't believe you haven't been here already,' Jay said, nodding at the waiter hovering over them to pour more champagne in their glasses.

'If you knew what construction workers had to go through to build this place, you might think twice.'

'Ah, I sense the award-winning journalist has her teeth sunk into a story.'

'I've just finished the first draft actually,' she said, popping a shawarma into her mouth, the delicious mixture of soft lamb, zingy spices and nutty tahini dip bursting in her mouth.

He peered towards Claire's bag. 'Do you have a copy?'

'It's not exactly what Pinar had in mind.'

'So you're going off the grid, are you? Be careful, my dear. Pinar doesn't like it when people disobey her orders.' He put his hand out. 'Do share.'

'I don't know. It needs a lot of work.'

'Oh come now, don't be coy with me.'

334

She sighed, reaching into her bag. Whenever she wrote something new and fresh, it felt so delicate, like someone else's touch might make it crumble away. She handed the print-out over and Jay took it, leaning back in his chair.

As he read it, Claire drank her champagne, nervously watching his face for signs of response. She'd been working on the article for weeks now. Only that morning, she'd been interviewing a construction worker willing to go on record about the appalling conditions he lived in as the city he helped build grew bigger and richer. Maybe she was becoming a little obsessed with that, finding the reality beneath the veil of happiness, having denied the truth coiled up beneath her and Milo's veil of happiness for too long.

She studied Jay's face as he read her article, his white eyelashes, his plump lips. She was so used to seeing Milo's dusky skin and dark eyes, he looked almost alien to Claire.

He peered up at her. 'Your writing's changed.'

'How do you mean?'

'There's a fierce, frantic *rawness* to this.'

'Is that a good thing?'

'I think so. Though it scares me a little.'

'Why?'

'What was it your father said in the note he wrote before he left? Marching off the map, darling, that's why.'

'I'm not marching off the map!' Claire said, annoyed Jay had brought that note up. 'I'm firmly on the map, thanks.'

'Hmmm,' he said, looking unconvinced. 'Speaking of which, I've seen the stories about Holly.'

Claire sighed. Holly was taking a gap year, using the money she'd been given from the farm sale travelling around Thailand with some friends she'd made at university. Occasionally, the tabloids ran photos of her, stumbling out of clubs, eyes glazed. Claire often wondered if Milo had seen those photos, wherever he was. Holly had told her he was travelling around various farms in Europe, getting work where he could.

'I've spoken to Holly a few times,' Claire said to Jay. 'She assures me she's just doing what most twenty-one-year-olds do: having fun. I can't say I led a sober life myself at that age so it's difficult to judge.'

'But you didn't see your uncle shoot your father,' Jay said quietly. 'Nor your mother fall over the edge of a cliff.'

Claire sighed. 'I suppose.'

'Enough of this morbid talk,' Jay said, making his voice bright again, sensing her discomfort. 'Over the next three days, you're going to take a break from your scribbling and we're going to have the time of our lives, how does that sound?'

'That sounds wonderful.'

And it was as he dragged her on lots of adventures, from camel rides and a desert safari in a four-by-four where they smashed over sandy dunes, to evening river cruises and an oasis experience in the desert with belly dancers and henna tattoos where they both got horribly drunk on yet more champagne.

On the third night, they stumbled back to the house Jay had hired for his stay, a sprawling one-storey condo overlooking a stretch of beach, Dubai's stunning skyline glimmering in the distance. Claire sunk down onto one of the massive plump cushions as Jay poured her some wine, the exotic smell of spices and perfumes drifting from the market below and making her feel even more heady.

'You could get put away for that,' she said, peering at the bottle. 'You're not supposed to keep alcohol.'

'Who's going to tell?'

'Maybe me.'

'You'll be too drunk, they won't believe you.'

She laughed as he handed over her glass of wine. 'You really are changing, my dear. It's not just your writing.'

'God, Jay, you're making me paranoid.'

'Really! Your face is changing. The way you hold yourself too.' He put his glass on the ground and took Claire's glass, placing it next to his. Then he took her hand. 'Come see,' he said, pulling her up.

She let him lead her towards a huge gilded mirror inside, her head spinning slightly from the wine she'd been drinking all night.

'Stand here,' he said, placing his hands on her shoulders and making her stand right in front of the mirror. 'Look at yourself.'

She let her eyes travel up and down the reflection in front of her. She'd put on the weight she'd lost in Australia thanks to her love of Middle Eastern food. Beneath the eggshell-coloured dress she'd bought in the Gold Souk the week before, her legs looked bronzed, her arms too. Her hair was very long and dark now, curling down to her elbows.

Apart from the lines around her eyes, she looked like the old Claire, the carefree traveller she was as a teenager before she'd discovered her dad in that bedsit.

'Step closer,' Jay said, making her shuffle forward. 'Look into your eyes.'

'You sound like an actor in a cheesy film.'

'I'm serious, Claire.'

She looked at Jay in the reflection. His face *was* very serious, his eyes searching out hers in the reflection. She sighed, and did as he asked, looking right into her own eyes. They blinked back at her, brown, tired, eyelids drooping slightly from the wine.

'I said it scared me but the fact is, you've carved a place for yourself,' Jay said. 'You're strong, you're independent, you have a wonderful career. It's everything you ever dreamed of.'

Except for Milo, she wanted to whisper, *the love of my life.*

For a second, she thought she could see him reflected in her eyes. She closed them, heart pounding. Jay was right. She was finally finding her way in life and that way had to be without Milo. But she hadn't changed *there*, in Dubai. She'd started changing the moment she met Milo. And that's why it had all been so painful. Weren't all metamorphoses? Bones crunching into place, skin stretching. Now it was complete, no wonder she was starting to feel healed.

Was it the same for Milo, wherever he was? Was he feeling healed?

Jay suddenly leaned down, pressing his lips softly against her neck.

She stepped away from him in surprise.

His face dropped.

'I adore you, Jay, and think you're bloody gorgeous—'

'But?'

'But I value our friendship *so* much, I don't want to ruin it. Not just that, what I had with Milo was so overwhelming, I know it would be a mistake to jump into another relationship, because I know that's what this would become if we let it go further. Do you understand?'

Claire's phone started buzzing. She went to press the ignore button then hesitated. It was an international number, one she didn't recognise.

'Get it,' Jay said, sighing.

She went to tuck her phone away. 'No, Jay.'

'Please.' He turned away, taking in the cityscape with a sad look on his face.

She hesitated a moment then answered the phone. 'Hello?'

'Claire?'

She recognised the voice instantly. 'Alex! Is everything okay?'

'It's Holly,' her nephew replied.

'What's wrong? Is she okay?'

'I think she wants to kill herself.'

Panic mounted inside. 'My God. What happened?'

'I found her in the sea. She nearly drowned, Claire.'

'Is she in hospital?'

Jay turned back to her, frowning.

'No,' Alex said. 'She's with me, she's safe for now.'

'Is she still in Thailand?'

'Yes, we're in Ko Phi Phi Don. She's asking for you, Claire. Will you come?'

Claire took a deep breath. 'Of course. I'll book a flight out as soon as I can. I'll call you once I know. Keep Holly close, Alex. Don't let her out of your sight.'

'I won't. Thanks, Claire.'

She put the phone down then looked up at Jay. 'That was my nephew. Holly's in trouble. I need to book a flight out to Thailand.' Jay didn't say anything. 'Jay?'

'I've tried to keep up with you, Claire, I really have,' he said. 'I knew as soon as I got here a few days ago you've got itchy feet again. Dubai can't keep hold of you, just like Australia couldn't, nor Serbia or Finland. You're more like your father than you know.'

'I'm doing this for Holly, Jay.'

'Yes, but what's the betting you'll stay there a few weeks, maybe months? That wanderlust inside you is batting its wings, I can almost hear it from here. You yearn to march off the map.'

Claire frowned.

'I know you don't like me using that quote,' Jay said, 'but your father's problem wasn't marching off the map, darling, it was the fact he was alone when he did it. If you're with Milo, you won't be alone.'

'Milo isn't there, I swear. This is for Holly, you know how much she means to me.'

He sighed. 'Holly. Milo. Either of them. They've both engrained themselves into you. If you're with one of them, you'll be fine. Let me make some calls, see if I can get you on the next flight.'

'Are you sure?'

He shrugged. 'I suppose we do these things for the people we love.'

'Love?'

His blue eyes sunk into hers. 'You've never understood, have you? You're my Milo.'

'Oh Jay . . .'

Claire reached out for him but he turned away, picking up his phone. 'I'll get your flight sorted,' he said with a resigned sigh.

Chapter Twenty-Three

Ko Phi Phi Don, Thailand
2004

When Claire arrived in Ao Nang two days later, she felt swallowed up by the place. The rush of colourful tuk-tuks along the dusty roads and the screech of the monkeys hanging from the shoulders of passing men disorientated her, so much so she had to sit down to regain her composure. And yet she'd been to far busier places. Perhaps her heart was longing for some time away from the heat after the stretches of time she'd spent travelling hot lands lately. She almost found herself yearning for the cold of Finland.

Just as she was thinking that, she noticed Alex walking towards her, even taller and broader than he'd been before. She called out his name and ran towards him, shoving in between shoulders and shopping bags.

He smiled when he saw her. 'Aunt Claire!'

'How are you?' she asked, standing on tiptoes to kiss his cheek.

'All right. You?'

'Not bad.'

'You didn't tell Mum, did you? She thinks I'm still at uni.'

'Of course not. Have you actually dropped out?'

Alex shrugged. 'They'll probably take me back but I don't want to be a solicitor, never have really.'

'No, I thought not. Shall we walk to the pier?'

'Cool.'

'So you've been with Holly the past few weeks?' she asked as they fell into step with one another.

He nodded, brow creasing. 'I hadn't heard from her since what happened. I tried, as you know, but she wouldn't take my calls. Then I get this random phone call from her a few weeks ago. She told me she missed me and loved me.' His face flushed. 'Her voice was slurred.'

Claire's stomach sank. 'Did she call from Ko Phi Phi Don?'

'No, here in Ao Nang, she'd been staying here with some uni friends. She called again and she sounded . . .' He paused. 'She didn't sound right, you know? Up here,' he said, tapping his head. 'So I said I'd fly out.'

'Just like that?'

'Of course! Wouldn't you do the same for Milo?'

Claire didn't say anything. This wasn't about Milo.

'It was good to begin with,' Alex continued. 'Holly seemed okay, so I thought I'd got it wrong about her being messed up. When I mentioned her strange phone call, she told me it was jetlag.'

Same excuse she used in Australia that time, Claire thought.

'She told everyone I was her boyfriend,' he said, his face softening, 'and the first week here was like paradise with new friends and a beautiful girl, a girl I love. That sounds cheesy, doesn't it?'

His face flushed again and Claire's heart went out to him. He was so enraptured by Holly. 'No, it's lovely, Alex,' she said.

'Anyway, one night, I woke to find Holly gone. I looked outside and saw someone just standing in the sea with water up to their waist . . . it was her.' He shook his head. 'I thought

I wouldn't get to her in time, the tide was so bad, but I did in the end. When I brought her back to shore, she wasn't breathing. So I used the first aid stuff I'd learned at school and gave her mouth-to-mouth. I think I must have been screaming at her to wake up as her friends came out too.'

'Jesus, Alex. You saved her life.'

He nodded, blue eyes haunted with the memory. 'When I asked her why she did it, she told me she wanted to die like her mum.'

Claire's eyes filled with tears. Someone pedalled towards them on a bike. The bike blurred in front of her, seeming to disappear. Alex grabbed her arm, pulling her out of the way.

'You okay?' Alex asked her.

'Yes. So when did this happen with Holly?'

'Just before I called you. I tried to get her to go home to Jen but she begged me not to make her. So I took her to Ko Phi Phi Don just to get her away from her so-called druggie friends. Then I called you.'

The small wood-slatted pier appeared in the distance then. People were milling around on it, tanned and happy. Next to it, a wooden boat with Thai writing in bright yellow on its front bobbed up and down, a Thai man with long hair standing on its roof, smiling and beckoning people on. In the distance, the calm azure waves of the Andaman Sea lapped against white sands. Claire thought of Holly disappearing beneath those waves, just as Erin had disappeared beneath the Bristol channel, and she promised herself she wouldn't let that happen.

When they arrived on Ko Phi Phi Don, Holly was sitting on a large, turquoise cushion at the Lotus Resort's poolside, her legs crossed, her head bent to hear what the woman next to her was saying. Claire stopped at the veranda leading to the pool area and watched her. Her hair was longer again, tumbling halfway down her back and she looked very thin, too thin.

Claire stepped out of the shadows of the veranda and Holly turned. Her face looked different, more grown up than ever. But worst of all, her eyes were empty, like something inside her had given up. It made Claire think of her own reflection in the mirror in the weeks after she'd seen her dad die.

Claire opened her arms to her and Holly ran into them, leaning her cheek on her shoulder. Claire could feel her tears sinking through the thin material of her cardigan and she started crying too, for herself, for Holly . . . and for Milo.

Claire tilted her chin up, examining Holly's tear-drenched face. 'How are you?'

'Perfect now you're here. Did Alex get you to come?'

'Yes. He's been very worried.'

She wiped her tears away with her thin fingers. 'God, he's such a worrier! I just got a bit carried away with the partying. How long are you staying?'

'I don't know. I wanted to make sure you were okay.'

'I will be when Milo joins us.'

Claire's heart skipped a beat. 'He's coming too?'

Holly sighed. 'I wrote him a letter, he never checks the email I set up for him. I hope he comes.'

'Where is he now?'

'France, at some little farm. But I'm worried he's moved on from there without telling me. He didn't reply to my last letter and he moves from one place to the next so quickly.'

Claire linked her arm through Holly's. 'This place is lovely,' she said, desperate to change the subject. She wasn't here to talk about Milo. She looked around at the laidback complex of villas and bungalows, young people walking around in flip-flops, the sea glistening in the background. She'd heard a lot about Ko Phi Phi Don, especially the relaxed backpacker's vibe

344

of Tonsai Bay. It was just as she'd imagined, with its swaying palm trees, white sands and stunning views of hilly rocks and shining waves. 'Do you think I can book a room here?'

Holly shot Claire a beautiful smile. 'You're staying?'

'Of course!'

That evening, the three of them had dinner at a nearby restaurant with a blue elephant statue at its centre. Holly and Alex had been a few times before and raved about how good it was. Holly sat in the chair next to Claire and held her hand as Alex watched, a slight crease in his tanned forehead. He could see it too, what was brimming beneath the surface. Add to that the fact Holly had absent-mindedly doodled an image of a woman standing on a rock overlooking the sea on her napkin, they were both worried.

'So what are you planning to do with your English degree?' Claire asked Holly, her eyes still on the drawing.

Holly noticed her looking and crunched the napkin up. 'I'm not sure really. We've been talking about travelling, haven't we, Alex?'

Alex nodded, his eyes still heavy with worry.

'Sounds fun,' Claire said.

'Maybe the four of us can travel together?'

'Four?'

Holly nodded. 'You, me, Alex and Milo.'

Claire sighed. 'Holly, Milo and I—'

'You want a photo?' They all looked up to see a man standing over them with a Polaroid camera.

'Oh, yes please!' Holly said, putting her arms around Claire and Alex's shoulders. Just at the moment that the camera flashed, Holly's smile slipped from her face as she stared into the distance. Claire followed her gaze to see a woman striding towards their table wearing a long flowery dress stained with dry mud at the bottom.

Nora McKenzie.

The last time Claire had seen Nora was at the inquest. She'd watched her cry as the verdict was returned and her heart had gone out to her as she imagined how it must have felt to be estranged from her best friend all these years only to discover she'd been dead the whole time. Afterwards, Claire had been so desperate to get away to avoid Milo, she hadn't had a chance to talk to Nora.

But what on earth was she doing here now?

Holly's eyes darted to Claire's face then to Nora's. 'Go away,' she said, scraping her chair back.

'Why are you doing this, Holly?' Nora said, face pained. 'You must tell Claire what you told me a few days ago, it'll destroy you if you don't.'

'Tell me what?' Claire asked, looking between them both.

Nora looked at Holly, her eyes pleading. 'Holly, please. If you don't say anything, I'll have no choice but to—'

Holly put her hands to her ears. 'No, no, no, no!'

The manager jogged over with a waiter. 'Is everything okay?'

'Take her away,' Holly said. 'She's harassing me, take her away!'

The manager clasped Nora's arm and dragged her away as Holly buried her face in Alex's chest. Before she got to the exit, Nora turned. 'I'm staying at the bungalows down the beach,' she said to Holly. 'Number eight. Please, Holly, please come see me.' There was something in her eyes, a desperate pleading that made Claire's heart almost stop.

Surely no more secrets?

After the manager steered her out, Claire turned to Holly. 'What was she talking about? Why's she here?'

'She's mad.'

'Holly . . .'

'Really, Claire. I have no idea. I think she's not right in the head.'

'She got it right about your mum though.'

Holly took a deep breath then reached for the menu. 'Now, what shall we eat?'

Alex and Claire exchanged worried looks. But what could they do? Claire sensed the tightrope Holly was walking and was terrified of pushing her over the edge. So, promising herself she'd talk to her in the morning, Claire picked up her menu too, Nora's outburst still lacing the atmosphere.

That night, Claire fell asleep to the ripple of waves, the sound seeping into her dreams. She found herself at Hope's Mouth where Erin had died. A figure approached from the sea and Claire presumed it was Erin. But as she drew closer, she realised it was Holly.

Claire woke with a start, heart pounding. She looked towards her window and, at first, she didn't notice Holly in the darkness, just saw the rocks in the distance heaped like bones in the hazy moonlight. But then she saw a figure standing on a rock like a ghost in a white nightdress, hair turned silver by the moonlight. Her arms were spread out against the black sky as in her drawing and there was something about the way she held herself that made Claire realise straight away it was Holly.

She didn't bother grabbing her dressing gown or shoes. She just ran outside towards the rock, calling Holly's name as the waves lapped at her bare feet. As she approached the rock, she heard movement behind her. She turned, thought she saw a shadow disappear behind a nearby palm tree.

Holly sobbed and Claire turned her attention back to her, scrambling up the rock. When she reached the top, she

347

stepped forward, the oppressive night air pressing against her, urging her to the edge, taking her back to Hope's Mouth and that first day she'd spent with Milo as he'd looked out to sea with tears in his eyes.

'Can I stand with you?' Claire asked Holly.

She nodded, her face very still. So Claire stood next to her, taking her hand. They both looked down into the moonlit waves below.

'It's the look in my mum's eyes when she fell that haunts me,' Holly said very quietly. 'She turned up on my birthday and grabbed me while I was alone, taking me to Hope's Mouth and pulling me beyond the barriers. We were right at the edge and I remember being so scared. She – she was going on about not wanting to live if I wasn't in her life.'

Claire squeezed her hand. Hearing this story for the second time as she had at the inquest didn't make it any less painful.

'Then she started going on about loving my dad,' Holly continued, 'but he didn't love her back and that's why things had to be the way they were.' She peered behind her. 'There was a sound behind us and we turned: it was Milo. And Mum whispered to me, "There he is, there's your dad."'

'Your *dad*?'

Holly nodded, making Claire's very core shift. She closed her eyes, saw Holly's face transplanted over Milo's, high cheekbones and perfect skin blurring into one. She saw the way he looked at Holly, with such pure love, and the way she looked at him too.

'I didn't know until that moment,' Holly said. 'And then my other dad turned up and, even at that age, I could see it in his eyes: that he knew I wasn't his, but he loved me anyway.'

Holly let out a sob, putting her hands to her face, and Claire hugged her close.

'Mum just said it out loud then, right in front of Dad,' Holly said. 'She said, "I love you, Milo. I really do." Then she took a step towards the edge and Milo ran to us and . . .'

Her face crumpled and she put her fist to her mouth, sobbing into it. Claire took the chance to shuffle her further away from the edge.

'All he wanted to do was make sure I wasn't hurt, that's all,' Holly mumbled into her fist. 'But when he ran towards us, Mum was surprised, she stumbled and – oh God, Claire.' Claire pressed her cheek against Holly's, feeling her tears slide over her face. 'She fell backwards and she screamed at us to help her. But it was too late, she'd gone and . . . and the last thing I saw was her . . . her head smashing on the rocks before Milo made me look away.'

'Oh Holly,' Claire said.

'When we got back, they made me go to my room but I overheard them tell Jen what happened. They called me down and convinced me to keep it a secret, that if we told the truth, Milo might get sent to prison. We never talked about it after and Milo never knew Mum told me he was my dad.'

But Claire knew right then Milo had always known. She could see it in the way he looked at Holly, spoke of her, took the blame for her actions the way he had in Finland. And yet he thought Holly didn't know she was his. It was a strange stalemate.

Claire pulled Holly into the middle of the rock, away from the sea, and Holly contemplated the waves with wide eyes as if shocked she'd been so close to the edge.

The next evening, Claire took Holly down to the beach after dinner. It was very warm when they got there, the stars above vivid, the leaves of the palm trees above rustling in the breeze.

The smell of Thai spices drifted over to them, laughter rising and falling in the wind. In the distance, over the sea, a light grey cloud hovered, lightning occasionally darting through it.

'Close your eyes,' Claire said to Holly, 'and only open them when I say.'

Holly did as she asked, excited like a child.

When Claire was ready, she told Holly to open her eyes again and Holly let out a small gasp when she saw the Chinese lantern Claire was holding. It was bright orange and decorated in flower symbols, just like one of the lanterns Claire's dad had let off their last New Year's Eve together as a family.

Claire handed Holly a small notepad and pen. 'We need to write down anything we want to leave behind,' she said. 'Then I'll attach our notes to the lantern and when it floats up into the sky and disappears, so will whatever you've written on your note. We used to do it when we were kids.'

Holly's face went very serious. 'A family tradition.'

'That's right.'

'We're family, aren't we, Claire?'

Claire smiled, her heart aching. She was right. Holly was her family, whatever had happened between her and Milo. She would always be there for her. 'Yes, Holly.' She reached into her pocket, pulling out a folded piece of paper. 'I did the same, see? Now your turn.'

Holly turned away and quickly scribbled something on the notepad. When she was finished, she folded it and handed it to Claire. Claire attached it to the thin material of the lantern with a tiny safety pin without looking, just like her dad used to do, then lit the lantern before flinging it into the sky. It caught onto a whisper of a breeze and drifted upwards. Holly leaned her cheek against Claire's shoulder, peering up at her under her long eyelashes. 'Thank you,' she whispered.

Out of the corner of her eye, Claire noticed the lantern

get whipped about by the sea breeze before snagging onto a nearby palm tree, the light flickering out.

'Let's head back,' Claire said, not wanting Holly to see what had happened. She was so vulnerable right now, she'd just presume it was an omen. Claire would retrieve it the next morning, make sure she didn't see it.

As they walked back to the resort, Claire sensed someone watching them.

She turned, peering into the trees nearby.

Nothing.

But still, the hairs on the back of her neck stood on end.

That night, as she fell asleep, Claire thought of the note she'd written. It was just one word.

Nothing.

The reason? She had no regrets, every moment, good or bad, the threads of the fabric that formed the path beneath her feet.

The next day, Claire woke to the sound of a child laughing outside. She got up and looked out of her window to see a boy with dark hair plucking shells from the sand. It had been so long since she'd done something so simple. So she got dressed and ran outside, collecting shells in her skirt as she walked towards the palm tree where the lantern had got tangled up. Children played in the sands, the sea lapping at their toes as they giggled. Couples lounged on the verandas of their bungalows and villas, sipping tea or orange juice as they looked out at the stunning scenery. Long-tail boats bobbed up and down, colourful ribbons hanging off their wooden shafts.

When Claire got to the palm tree, she pulled over a deckchair and balanced on it to free what remained of the lantern. As she yanked it down, Holly's note fell to the sand below. Before she knew what she was doing, she was reading the charred scrap of paper.

> *The bad things I want to leave behind are the memories and guilt from the day I shot my other dad. H x*

Claire stared at those words, hardly able to breathe.

Holly had shot Dale?

She sank into the sand, putting her head in her hands. Holly was just a child, how could this be possible?

But then life was a little different on a farm, Holly had once told Claire. A girl learns to hold a gun, to shoot accurately when she must. Puppies born wrong? You shoot them. A dog loses its mind and eats its pups? You shoot it. A woman is cruel to you and your dad? You tear apart her work. And then: the man you thought was your father loses control and tries to shoot the man who *is* your father? You shoot him.

And now Claire understood why Milo changed so after what happened that fateful night. To watch a child pick up a gun and shoot the man everyone thought was her father would break even the strongest of men, wouldn't it? Make him fiercely protective too. Milo loved his daughter so very much, he'd been willing to sacrifice everything for her, to take the blame for everything she did . . . to lie. Those lies suddenly made sense in some way now. People did anything for their children, didn't they, including lying to protect them. But surely he knew Claire cared deeply for Holly and would never have betrayed her secret. Why couldn't he tell her? Why so many lies?

Claire walked back to her hotel room in a trance, Holly's confession still in her hand. When she got to her room, she reached for her atlas and slipped the note into the paper pocket next to the map of Thailand before locking it and hiding the key in her pocket.

She then turned to watch Holly dance on the beach, her red hair a flame on the horizon. Though she didn't agree with how he'd kept it all buried away, all Milo had ever wanted was to protect and fix his daughter, just as Claire once wanted to protect and fix him. And as she sat watching Holly, she realised that's all she wanted to do now. Protect Holly, fix her, make sure she became the woman she was meant to be.

She didn't want to be like a bull in a china shop, confronting Holly with no thoughts of knowing how to get her help. So she took the next day – Christmas Day – to digest it all and give Holly a chance to enjoy the special day without bringing up her dreadful secret.

The resort put on a traditional Christmas dinner over lunch, setting up a long table on the beach full of turkey, potatoes and even Brussels sprouts. As Holly ate, Claire watched her, thinking of how cruel life can be, to bring such tragedy into such a young girl's life.

With their bellies full of food and wine, they headed back to their rooms for a siesta, promising to meet again in an hour to watch the Christmas entertainment the hotel had planned. Claire was pleased for the chance to be alone. The night before, she'd stayed up, staring at the confession, trying to wrap her head around it. Now all she wanted to do was make sure all traces of it were gone; to go back to her room and burn it.

But as Claire headed towards her room, she noticed her door was ajar.

She hadn't left it open, had she?

She walked towards it, heart thumping, then felt relief flood through her when she realised her mobile phone was still on the side, her purse where she'd left it on the bed.

But then she looked towards the desk where she'd left her atlas and froze.

It was gone.

Maybe she was wrong, maybe she'd put it somewhere else? She strode around the room, flinging items about, searching everywhere she could think of, but not finding any trace of it. Had it really been stolen? But why not steal her purse and phone too? Had someone broken in just for the atlas?

She felt her phone buzzing and saw Jay's name flash up. She felt a shimmer of guilt. To hear his confession of love to her after she'd rejected his advances had been so difficult. But it wouldn't have been right to let things develop between them both; she'd done the right thing.

She took a deep breath then answered her phone. 'Hello, Jay. Merry Christmas.'

He sighed. 'Not so merry, I'm afraid. I'm hearing on the grapevine Nathan Styles has a story on Holly.' He hesitated a moment. 'It's rather shocking, Claire.'

He knew. But Claire didn't say anything. What if he didn't know the specifics?

'You know too, don't you?' Jay asked her.

'How did you find out?'

'I have a friend who's a sub on the paper Nathan writes for. I managed to bury a story about her father who's a banker, she owes me. As soon as she heard Nathan Styles had called the editor to hold some space, she called me. She knows you and I are good friends. How did Nathan find out, Claire? How did you?'

That's when it hit her. 'Oh God, the atlas.'

She explained about the atlas and Holly's crumpled confession. 'But would Nathan Styles really break into my room? He's a journalist, for Christ's sake, not a criminal.'

'There have always been rumours he arranged for that

actress's laptop to be stolen, remember? And didn't he rifle through your bins? He's scum, Claire. He'd do anything for a good story because something of this magnitude means a spectacular bonus from his editor.'

'But why did he come out to Thailand? He didn't have a story before the atlas.'

'My friend said he'd heard Holly tried to kill herself out here,' Jay said softly. 'Is that true?'

'She's in a vulnerable place,' Claire said, thinking of what Alex had told her. Had one of her friends called the papers after she'd waded into the sea? Claire peered into the shadow of the palm trees nearby. 'I had a feeling someone was following us the past couple of days. When's the article being published?'

'The day after Boxing Day. It'll be their big post-Christmas splash according to my friend.'

Claire felt her legs go weak and sunk into a nearby chair. 'God.'

'Good news is, Styles won't have had time to file it yet. He'll still be working on it, probably there in Thailand. Styles has always had a thing for lady boys. No point flying back to dreary old England when he can email it to his editor from paradise.' He paused. 'But once he gets back, he'll have a duty to hand any evidence to the police. I presume he has other sources too, otherwise he wouldn't be able to get the article published based on just a scrap of paper. But it's evidence for the police all the same.'

Claire watched Holly put a paper hat on her head and pull a funny face at Alex. 'Could they arrest Holly?' she asked.

'I don't know, she was a child when she did it. She clearly needs help though, Claire.'

Claire anxiously bit her nails. 'I know. But having her story splashed all over the papers isn't going to help the situation. What can I do, Jay?'

'I've tried to do what I can, pulled in some favours, no luck. Next step is to speak to Styles himself, that despicable piece of crap.' He paused a moment. 'I can fly over if you want, help you find him? There are ways a greedy man like him can be persuaded to get a story dropped, even if he files it before I get there.'

Claire's shoulders slumped with relief. She wasn't sure she could deal with this alone. 'Thank you, Jay. That would be great.'

'Fine, I'll try to get a flight as soon as I can.'

'But it's Christmas Day, are you sure?'

'Any excuse to get out of my father's traditional Boxing Day party.'

'You're wonderful, you know, helping Holly like this.'

'I'm not doing this for Holly, Claire. I'm doing this for you. I know how much you care for her.'

When Claire put the phone down, she leaned over and put her head in her hands, the horror of what Jay had just told her engulfing her. Why hadn't she just bloody burned Holly's confession as soon as she found it?

'Claire?' She looked up to see Holly standing in front of her, the sun winking over her shoulder. 'What's wrong?'

Claire took Holly's warm hand in hers. She had to be prepared for the worst. 'I know what really happened at the wedding in Exmoor, Holly.'

Holly snatched her hand away from Claire's, as if she'd set her fingers alight. She started shaking, eyes wide, face suddenly very pale under her tan.

'I saw the note you pinned to the sky lantern,' Claire said quickly. 'I didn't mean to, it got tangled up in a palm tree.'

Holly put her hand to her mouth. 'Oh God. Y-you must hate me now.'

'I don't hate you, I *love* you, Holly,' she said, realising then she really did. 'I locked the note in my atlas but someone stole it, a journalist. I'm so sorry.'

Holly crumpled to her knees and Claire pulled her into her arms, whispering sorry over and over. People sunbathing nearby peered up, frowning at the two grown women crying in paradise.

'I had to do it, Claire,' Holly said, voice trembling. 'He was going to shoot me, he said I was better off dead than in this horrible world. When Milo tackled him and he dropped the gun, I – I didn't think, I just panicked and picked it up and before I knew it, the gun went off.'

They were silent for a moment, Claire simply holding Holly's hand.

'I never wanted him dead,' Holly whispered after a while. She closed her eyes, her long eyelashes wet with tears. 'When Milo told me to say it was him who'd shot Dad, I just went along with it. I was so terrified, barely aware of what I'd done. And I've lived with the guilt ever since. Milo's always been there for me, but he can't help me now.' Her face hardened. 'Maybe that's good. Maybe he can finally think about himself for once.'

After a while, Alex appeared in the distance. Holly ran towards him, throwing herself into his arms. Then something changed in the air; a shift in Claire's skin; the soft hair on the back of her neck rising.

There was someone watching her from a path of palm trees nearby.

She turned, saw dark hair, tanned arms, a white scar that ran ragged over brown skin.

Milo.

Chapter Twenty-Four

Ko Phi Phi Don, Thailand
2004

Milo was standing under a nearby palm tree dressed in grey shorts and a black vest top, a rucksack slung over his shoulders. As Claire looked at him, it was like the sun had dropped from the sky and was scorching her insides, sending her mind and heart and soul into overdrive.

Milo stayed where he was for a few moments, eyes running all over Claire as though he couldn't quite believe she was real.

'Why are you here?' Claire asked, trying to keep her voice steady.

'I saw the photos of Holly in the press. I needed to make sure she was okay.'

'Just like you've been doing all these years,' she said, unable to help herself. 'Making sure she's okay, protecting her, taking the blame for her actions . . . I know what she did.'

Milo's eyes widened with shock.

'I know everything, Milo. I know you're Holly's dad too; so does she.'

His whole body slumped against the tree as he put his face in his hands. Claire's heart went out to him and she reached towards him then let her hand drop to her side again. He peered up at her, his dark eyelashes drenched with tears.

'You know,' he whispered. 'You finally know.' There was relief in his voice, years of pent-up secrets finally being unburdened.

'You should've told me,' Claire said. 'We could have shared the burden together.'

He turned to look at Holly. She was sitting on the sand with Alex and hadn't yet noticed Milo. 'How could I?' he said. 'I couldn't even resolve myself to it, seeing my daughter lift that gun and shoot my brother. I couldn't comprehend how it could've got to that stage, for her to do it so coldly.'

'What happened in those moments, Milo?'

He took in a deep shuddering breath and it occurred to Claire this might be the first time he had said it out loud. 'When I got into the marquee, Dale had his gun pointed at Holly. He said she was better off dead than living in this messed-up world. I ran at him, we fought and Dale dropped the gun. Holly grabbed it. Then . . .'

He closed his eyes.

'Oh, Milo.'

'I took the gun straight off Holly after. She was paralysed with shock,' he continued, eyes still closed, like he was replaying it in his mind. 'I wiped it clean of her fingerprints and I told her it was me who'd shot him and that's all there was to it. I made her hide under the table, and I pulled my brother into my arms.' He opened his eyes. 'Then you walked in. When I was given bail and could return home, I tried to talk to Holly but she refused to acknowledge what had happened, she was in complete denial.'

'It's such a terrible secret to hold inside.'

Milo nodded. 'Over the years, I've tried everything I can to help her. I couldn't tell the police what she'd done, she'd just end up in the system. But I thought I could help by keeping an eye on her, trying to talk to her about it. I arranged for her to see a therapist. But she just clammed up every time. Remember that argument you saw us having in the desert in Australia?'

Claire nodded.

'I was trying to get Holly to admit she was struggling more than ever with what had happened. It's difficult enough for a child to deal with something so terrible but add teenage hormones . . .' He sighed. 'But she wasn't having any of it, she just insisted on not talking about it.'

'What about the fact Holly was your daughter? Why didn't you talk about that?'

'I hoped she didn't know. Best she didn't think she was mine, best no one did. She'd had enough to deal with already.'

'You're a good man, Milo – look at what you've done for Holly all these years, taking the blame, trying to help her.'

'So you *do* think I'm a good man then, despite the lies?'

'I understand some of the lies, you had to for your daughter,' Claire said softly. 'But the other lies – what happened between you and Erin, Erin's death – are difficult to forgive.'

He stepped forward, his eyes deep in hers. 'I was terrified you'd leave me if I told you.'

'Jesus, Milo, I told you everything about me, including the fact I'd never be able to give you children. Don't you think I was frightened of the same thing?'

'But that was your own personal secret,' Milo said. 'My secrets were tangled up in my family's messed-up lives. But that's over now, I swear, every secret is out, every lie in the open. I promise on Holly's life.' He took her hand and the feel of his skin against hers set every nerve on fire. 'I love you, Claire. I've never stopped loving you. Please forgive me.'

Claire avoided his gaze, trying to keep her wits about her. She couldn't fall into his arms like she always used to. Yes, she still loved him but feelings weren't enough. She was on her own path now, she was making something of herself, something she'd been so desperate for all those years ago when she first arrived in Exmoor.

'Claire?' Milo asked.

'We have more important things to talk about,' she said, letting her hand slip from his. She couldn't make such a huge decision at that moment.

He was quiet for a few seconds then nodded, jaw clenching. 'What else do you want to talk about?'

She told him about what had unfolded over the past twenty-four hours and his face went white. 'Jay doesn't need to come over,' he said. 'I'll find Nathan Styles, it's a small island.'

He started backing away but Claire grabbed his wrist. 'What about Holly? She'll want to see you.'

'I'll come back.'

'Will you?' She realised then she wasn't just asking for Holly, but for her too. Despite her resolve not to fall into his arms, she needed just a few more moments with him, a chance for some proper closure.

His face softened. 'Of course.' Then he turned on his heel and jogged away.

She leaned against the tree behind her and stared up at the blue sky through its leaves, Milo's face still scorched onto her mind, his touch still making her skin glow. She stayed like that for a very long time until she started seeing someone else's face in her mind.

Nora.

What was it she'd said the other night? *You must tell Claire what you told me, it'll destroy you if you don't.* Had Holly told Nora she'd shot Dale or was Milo lying again – were there yet more secrets? She needed to find out.

When Claire got to the sweet little bungalow where Nora

had said she was staying, Nora's door was wide open and she was standing on tiptoes on a chair, sweeping her paintbrush over the wall. She was painting a large face – her own – and it was mind-blowing, a vibrant, torrid mix of red and orange, like flames.

Nora sensed Claire standing behind her and turned, red paint dripping from her brush onto the floor below. She was wearing a long red skirt over gold sandals and a beaded vest top, her dark hair twisted in a coil.

'You'll get fined for that,' Claire said. 'Though they ought to *pay* you. It's wonderful.'

Nora smiled and stepped off the chair, placing her paintbrush in a jar of water nearby and cleaning her hands on an old rag. 'So you came.'

'Yes.'

'I hoped you might when I told Holly where I was staying. I would have come to find you if you hadn't. Would you like a drink?' she asked, gesturing towards the small fridge nearby.

'No thanks. Why did you come out here, Nora?'

She looked out at the sea for a few moments. 'I saw photos of Holly splashed all over the papers. Drunk, on drugs, whatever it was, she didn't look right. I could see she was on a downward spiral. Most of all, I could see Erin's fragility in her. I realised I couldn't help Erin in the end, but I had a chance to help Erin's daughter. So I flew out a few days ago and found Holly in a bar, drunk. Maybe that's what loosened her tongue?'

'What did she tell you?'

She stepped towards Claire, taking her hands. 'It's not my place to say. But you must ask Holly what really happened the night of that wedding in Exmoor. What she did.'

'I know what happened.'

Her hands dropped from Claire's. 'You know?'

'Yes. Was there anything else?'

Nora shook her head. 'Just that.'

Claire felt a shimmer of relief. Did that really mean there were no more secrets; that Milo had really meant it when he said all the lies were out in the open now?

'So you'll get Holly help?' Nora asked Claire.

'Yes, I'll make sure of it.'

'It'll destroy her, you know, keeping it bottled up.' She looked towards a photo of a blonde woman and two young girls. 'Something I know a little bit about.'

'Who are they?'

'My daughter Louise and my two beautiful granddaughters.'

'I didn't realise you had a daughter.'

'No, neither did I.'

'Excuse me?'

Her eyes lifted to meet Claire's and Claire could see they were full of pain. 'I took her for granted, never really realised she means everything. I haven't spoken to her for two years.' She paused. 'Do you have children?'

Claire took a deep breath. 'I can't.'

'Oh sweetheart, I'm so sorry.'

'It's fine. I've learned to accept it.' She realised then she really had. It didn't hurt to say it out loud like it used to do. The pain was there but it was distant, like an echo.

'You have Milo and Holly though, don't you, they're your little family?' Nora said. 'Holly adores you and I can see you adore her. And as for Milo, he's your core, and you his.' She paused a moment. 'I was wrong about Milo, you know. I realised that after seeing him give evidence at the inquest into Erin's death.'

'I think a lot of people get him wrong.'

'But not you, you see him for the good person he is. That's what Holly said. You help each other know who you are, even when you're going off-song.'

'Marching off the map,' Claire said. Hadn't Jay said something similar? And yet, if Milo was her core, why did things keep going wrong with them?

Nora smiled to herself. 'I like that, marching off the map. I suppose I've been doing that for a long time now.'

'Who's your core?'

'My daughter, Louise. It's always been my beautiful darling Louise. What a fool I was not to see that. I've been too obsessed chasing a ghost all these years.'

'What was Erin like?' Claire asked.

She hadn't realised she wanted to know that until then. But Erin had been there all the time, from the moment she and Milo had met, the secret that burned bright. And Erin had loved Milo too, as Claire did, desperately.

'She was beautiful and fragile,' Nora said, her eyes filling with tears. 'Like a child, really, fascinated by everything from tiny insects to the shape of a cloud. She used to be so carefree, dancing and singing and telling me not to worry so much about things when all the time she was the one who worried too much.'

Claire hardly knew Nora but looking at her now, seeing how calm and composed she was, she couldn't imagine her being a worrier.

Nora stepped towards Claire, smiling slightly as she lifted the gold typewriter necklace Jay had given her. 'This necklace makes me think of the old typewriter Erin used to practise on in the room we shared. She always said she'd get a job as a secretary to a rich managing director and he'd sweep her off her feet.' She sighed as she dropped the pendant back against Claire's skin. 'But instead she met a poor farmer's son with a penchant for guns.'

'How did Erin and Dale meet?'

'He was posted out in Dublin and we met him on a night

364

out. We were just sixteen and had pretended we were staying at a friend's house. Instead, we used the birthday money I'd got from my nan and got a coach to Dublin, dressed up to the nines, nowhere to stay. Dale was at the bar of the first nightclub we visited, holding court with all his soldier friends. As soon as he saw Erin, he stopped talking and that was it. I could see it in his eyes. She was going to be his and that was that.' Her face hardened. 'She was swept away by his bravado, his boasts about inheriting his parents' land. Erin fell for every word. They were married a month later.' Nora laughed bitterly. 'Boy, was Erin disappointed when she discovered the land Dale was talking about was a crappy little farm in the middle of nowhere and she'd be stuck there on her own while he toured overseas.'

Claire thought about how it must have been for Erin, alone and disillusioned at such a young age. No wonder she turned to Milo.

Nora's eyes filled with tears. 'Now she's gone forever. Yet seeing Holly, it's like Erin is still alive, they're so alike. And that terrifies me because I'm so worried Holly will go the same way. I feel this awful guilt about Erin, like I should've tried harder to make amends after our argument, marched to that bloody farm and forced her to speak to me. Maybe I'd have seen how desperate she was, maybe I could've brought her back to mine, looked after her.' Her voice cracked. 'But you can't turn back time, can you? Instead, all I can do is make sure her daughter doesn't meet the same fate.'

Claire thought of the story brewing back home about Holly. 'I'm worried things aren't going to go very well for Holly over the coming days.'

Nora frowned. 'What do you mean?'

Claire explained about her atlas being stolen by Nathan Styles and the story he was writing as a result. Nora shook her head, her dark eyes sparking with anger. 'Nathan Styles left a message on my phone the other day,' she said. 'Not the first time, either. Ever since Erin's body was found, he's been hounding me for her story. He's a nasty piece of work. What are you going to do?'

'I don't know. Milo's looking for him.'

'So Nathan Styles is still on the island?'

'I think so. I better leave you to it,' Claire said, gesturing towards Nora's painting.

Nora followed her gaze. 'I think I rather like it without an eye, don't you?'

Claire smiled. 'It's different. Are you going to stay here?'

'I've booked a flight back to the UK for the morning after Boxing Day.'

'Have a safe flight. It was good to finally talk properly.'

Nora smiled. 'Yes, it was, wasn't it?'

Claire went to walk away then paused, turning back to her. 'Happy Christmas.'

Nora lifted her eyebrows in surprise. 'Of course, it's Christmas Day, isn't it? Funny the rituals you forget when you're travelling the road less travelled.'

'What are your plans after this?'

'I think it's time I found my core again,' Nora said, smiling. 'I think I'll return home to my daughter.'

'You do that,' Claire said.

*

When Claire got back to the hotel, Holly was waiting for her.

'Milo's here,' Claire said as soon as she saw her. 'He's going to try to help us.'

Holly looked around her, her eyes frantic. 'Where is he?'

'He's gone to find the journalist.'

'Is he coming back?'

'That's what he said.'

But by the time darkness fell, there was no sign of Milo. Holly was bitterly disappointed, and Claire realised she was too. But then, in the early hours, a sound outside woke Claire. She sat up in bed, heart hammering against her chest. She'd dreamt Milo was there, right there with her in bed. She reached over, swept her hand over the sheets but it was just her, alone. Then she noticed a streak of shadow outside the window. She got out of bed and opened the door.

He was standing outside her room, staring out to sea, his rucksack over his arm like he might leave any minute. His dark eyes travelled the length of Claire's body, the look in his eyes making it difficult for her to breathe.

'I think I made things worse,' he said.

'You found Nathan?'

'Yes, in a bar, drunk. I punched him.'

'Oh, Milo.'

'He wouldn't listen to me.'

'So what next?' she asked.

'Holly and I disappear off the face of the map.'

'Sorry?'

'I can't let Holly get prosecuted for this. We can just disappear, she can dye her hair, I can—'

'Run away again?' Claire shook her head. 'No more running away, Milo. Holly needs help. Bottling things up, pretending they never happened . . . we know now that's the wrong path to choose. It's time for you two to stop running from the truth and try to live some kind of life together.'

He thought about it for a few moments. 'Okay, maybe you're right. But it shouldn't just be me and Holly. We need you too, the three of us together.' Milo gently took her hand. She tried to resist him by stepping away. But it had been so long and her whole body craved him, every fibre and every pore. 'I know how you feel about me, I can see it in your eyes,' he said.

'You're right, I love you. Always have, always will. And I believe you when you say the lies are over.' Milo smiled, moving closer to her, putting his hand on her face. But she gently pulled his hand away. 'But I love myself too. I didn't go to Exmoor all those years ago just to figure things out with Ben and me, I did it to find myself, find my path. And now I finally feel like I'm finding my feet, I'm terrified they'll be pulled out from beneath me.'

'I helped you find that path,' Milo said softly. 'We've been travelling it together the past few years.'

'But when you were on it, it was cracked and full of lies. I suppose I've got used to a simple clean path.'

'I *told* you there are no more lies,' Milo said, his face intense. 'You know all of me now and I've learned so much about myself through your eyes.'

And she through his, she realised then. She'd gone to Exmoor so confused about her future as a divorced infertile woman. But within just a few hours of being with Milo, she'd begun to see a new path stretching out before her. And with each new experience they had shared over the years, that path had grown stronger and stronger, despite all the cracks. She wondered what it would be like without those cracks.

As Claire looked into Milo's eyes, she realised she wanted to find out. She loved him so much, could feel it in every part of her. It was like Nora said earlier, he was her core.

And so, as the sea roared in the distance and the moon sat watching from above, she stood on her tiptoes and pressed her lips against his. The kiss they shared felt different, somehow, because it wasn't burdened with secrets, nor weighed down by lies. And wherever their new path led them, it didn't matter because they'd be together as they marched off the edge of the map.

Chapter Twenty-Five

Ko Phi Phi Don, Thailand
2004

In the short walk from the pier on the south of the island to the area where Holly and Claire's resort is, the scenery gets harder and harder to look at. Palm trees lie strewn across the sand, clothes tangled in their branches, and whole shards of concrete point up into the night sky, the force of the wave so strong on this stretch of beach, it even took whole walls with it. In the distance, there's a large group of Thai people holding a vigil as they stand around a bonfire with candles in their hands, chanting some kind of Buddhist prayer.

'The map on the leaflet suggests the resort was here,' Sam says.

Except it isn't a resort any more. The black and white marble floor of what may have once been the reception hut is still there, but parts of it are smashed, making it look like a wrecked chessboard beneath the moonlight. In the distance are semblances of what may have once been bungalows, bed frames jagged in the dark, large TVs on their sides, the moon and stars warped in their shattered glass.

I take a deep breath, looking towards the carnage and

trying to figure out where we go from here. Then I notice a curved rock standing nearby, a little offshore, surrounded by a clutch of more rocks. I pull Claire's atlas out, finding the drawing of the rock I'd found next to the map of Thailand with a girl standing on it.

'It's the same shape,' I say, holding the drawing up to it. 'Do you think it could be the view from Claire or Holly's bungalow?'

'Maybe.'

I stare at what remains of the bungalow that once stood there. It's not as devastated as the others, sheltered by the rock. But the wave still got to it, meaning Claire might well have met her fate right there before she was found and taken to that makeshift morgue in Krabi.

What about Holly?

I stride towards the rock as Sam follows. Three crumbling walls remain, a bed frame on its back at the centre, a green fishing net tangled around its upturned legs. A palm tree is lying across its front and a suitcase is bent over one of the taller walls, clothes spilling everywhere. Sam pulls his phone out and sweeps the light over the room as we step over the palm tree to get in. There's a jumble of clothes, more debris, smashed glass. I imagine Claire here, watching aghast as the wave came for her, my mum's bag and the atlas inside clutched tight to her chest.

I go to put the atlas back in my bag, but something falls out then, swirling down and landing on the ground. I crouch down, see it's a torn note smudged by water and dotted with sand. Sam shines his phone on it and I can just about make out what's written on it:

. . . I want to leave behind are the memories and guilt from . . .

370

'Wait, there's someone there,' Sam says, shining the light away from the note towards what remains of the bungalow.

I gasp.

In the corner is a figure sitting cross-legged on the floor.

'Mum?' I whisper, my heartbeat a cascade of hope-filled beats.

The figure slowly turns and I step forward, the sound of the waves nearby seeming to stutter and stop.

Chapter Twenty-Six

Ko Phi Phi Don, Thailand
2004

'This is officially the *best* scrambled egg on toast I've ever had,' Holly said.

Milo smiled. 'Told you this place did the best English breakfast in Thailand.'

They were sitting outside a tiny café in Tonsai Village, the bustling heart of Ko Phi Phi Don. The sea was just out of sight beyond a patch of palm trees and the area around them throbbed with over-enthusiastic shopkeepers trying to sell their wares to tourists fresh from the ferry. The café they were sitting in had just seven wooden tables scattered beneath a low bamboo roof, a turned-over boat acting as a till. People chattered and laughed around them while others sat quietly eating, no doubt nursing hangovers from the night before.

As Claire watched Milo and Holly eat while Alex took photos nearby, she felt a sense of relief. She knew they had a lot to deal with considering the article was due to be published tomorrow, their efforts to track down Nathan Styles and her atlas fruitless. But finally everything was out in the open and they were dealing with this together, no more secrets or lies. That was enough for Claire. Milo caught her watching him and he smiled, taking her hand.

Yes, this felt right. No more running away, no more hiding. Time to face reality, whatever that may turn out to be.

'We could stay here, you know,' Holly said, looking around her. 'Buy a house, maybe even a café like this to make money?'

Claire and Milo exchanged a look. They knew what Holly was trying to do.

'We spoke about this earlier, Holly,' Milo said gently. 'We need to go home.'

Holly looked down at the table, her brow creased.

They were all quiet for a while then she peered up at them. 'Do you think Nora's still here? I'd like to see her before we go. I feel bad for the way I was with her. She was Mum's best friend after all and she's only been trying to help.'

Claire looked through the trees. 'She told me she was flying out tomorrow. Her bungalow's just a few minutes' walk away, we can both go if you want?'

Holly nodded, her face sombre. Not long after, they were both standing outside Nora's bungalow. Claire peered in the window, saw the blinds were up, the room empty – and that huge painted face staring out at her, its one strange eye seeming to look right into her soul.

'Maybe she's at breakfast?' Holly said.

'Maybe. Why don't you write her a note, give her your number or something?'

Claire handed her notepad and pen to Holly. Holly paused a moment, nibbling on the end of the pen as she thought about what to write. Then she quickly scrawled a message before giving it to Claire.

'Is this all right?' she asked her.

Nora,

Thank you for looking over me the past few months, and for how much you cared for my mum. You were the closest thing she had to family really - apart from me, of course. I hope we can keep in touch. My number and email address are below.

Take care, Holly x

Claire gave her a quick hug. 'It's very sweet.'

'She seemed sad when I spoke to her in that bar the other week. I hope whatever was on her mind sorts itself out.'

Claire thought back to the conversation she and Nora had had the day before. 'Me too.'

Something else from her and Nora's chat came back to her then. She impulsively reached into her bag, finding her necklace and wrapping it around the door handle, the turquoise jewels of the typewriter glinting in the rising sun: a small token of thanks for looking out for Holly. Jay wouldn't mind, he'd bought her so much jewellery in the past.

They walked back to the café and, just as Holly went to sit down, her phone started ringing. She rummaged around in her bag and pulled it out, frowning. 'Five missed calls, bugger.' She put it to her ear then her face lit up. 'It's Nora!'

Milo and Claire exchanged a smile.

As Holly talked to Nora, a huge smile spread across her face. 'Oh my God, that's amazing! Thank you, thank you so much . . . yes, of course. Just five minutes. Yes, yes, we'll see you there. Oh Nora, I don't know what to say.' She smiled, tears filling her pretty eyes. 'Yes, Mum would be very grateful.'

She put her phone down and grabbed Milo's hand in

excitement as Alex jogged back over. 'Nora got the atlas back from Nathan Styles!' she said. 'She just took it off him and ran. My note's in there too,' she added, her face flushing.

Relief flooded through Claire as Milo looked up at the sky, a big smile on his face.

'Thank God,' Claire said. 'I know Nathan Styles still has his story but it's something, isn't it, getting my atlas back?'

Milo nodded. 'It's something. Without your note, Holly, the police won't have much to go on. Good old Nora. I wonder what she did to get it off Nathan Styles?'

'Not punch him,' Claire said, raising an eyebrow.

'She got my note a few minutes ago and has been trying to call,' Holly said. 'She's headed straight for your bungalow, Claire, and she'll meet us there.'

'I'll get the bill.' Claire stood up to get the waiter's attention then paused, peering out to the sea. It looked like it was miles away, shimmering under the morning sun, a huge expanse of beach dividing it from the café. 'Wow, the tide's gone really far out – look.'

Milo followed her gaze. 'That's strange.'

A couple standing at the sea's edge knelt down to look at something. They waved some friends over who jogged over and did the same.

'Shall we go look?' Holly asked Alex.

'Don't be long, Nora's waiting,' Milo said.

Holly smiled. 'All right, *Dad*,' she said.

A small smile appeared on Milo's face as Holly grabbed Alex and led him towards the sea.

'Dad, hey?' Claire said, jogging her shoulder into his.

His smile deepened. 'It feels pretty damn good to hear her say that. Not just that, it feels good to have it all out in the open.'

'No more lies,' Claire said, lifting his hand and kissing it.

'No more lies,' he said, pressing his lips against hers. 'I know the threat of the article being published hasn't gone, but Nora getting the atlas off Nathan makes me think things will work themselves out. She must really care for Holly to do that.'

'I guess she's like Holly's aunt in a way, considering Erin was like a sister to her.' Claire sighed, thinking of their conversation from the day before. 'She's estranged from her own daughter, you know, they've not spoken for two years. I hope she patches things up with her.'

Holly and Alex jogged back over.

'The water's really frothy and bubbling,' Holly said, slightly out of breath, eyes bright. 'It's really cool.'

Claire and Milo exchanged a smile. She was so much like a child sometimes, innocent and easily excited. She'd been through so much and had such a journey ahead of her, but, like Milo, Claire too felt like things might just work out.

'Let's not keep Nora waiting,' Milo said, standing up. 'We ought to—' He paused as a flock of colourful-looking birds flew over their heads, wings flapping frantically, squawks shrill.

Someone nearby shouted something in Thai. A plate crashed to the ground, chairs scraping back.

'What's going on?' Claire said, slowly rising from her chair.

People around them peered up from their meals, eyes widening as they looked out towards the sea. Claire followed their gaze and let out a gasp as she saw a line of white foam rapidly approaching in the distance.

'What is that?' Holly asked.

'A wave,' Claire whispered, heart pounding with fear in her chest.

The Thai people working behind the counter started talking in urgent voices, one grabbing the phone.

A couple came running through the trees, their movements

frantic, faces white. One of them was dressed in just their underwear as though they'd got straight out of bed.

Claire grabbed the arm of the passing girl. 'What's going on?' she asked her.

The girl said something in German and peered behind her, a look of horror on her face. A roar like a jet engine echoed around them and for a moment Claire wondered if a plane was crashing.

'Tsunami!' an American man shouted out from behind them, jumping up from his table, knocking over a glass of water. 'She said it's a tsunami.'

People screamed, jumping up, tables overturning.

'Oh God,' Claire said, not quite believing what she was seeing as she watched the frothing wave work its way towards shore, eating up a small boat in its path.

She'd written about the Papua New Guinea tsunami that had killed over two thousand people a few years ago. Could this really be happening here?

Milo grabbed Holly's arm, pulling her from the table as he put his hand out to Claire. 'We need to get to safety.' Claire took his hand, stumbling out from behind the table, looking around for Alex. He was standing nearby, his camera to his face as he took photos of the emerging wave.

'Alex, for God's sake, come on!' Milo said, reaching across the table to grab him.

The wave reached the beach, gushing over abandoned sun loungers, knocking over a small cart selling souvenirs. People screamed, running from the water as it seemed to surge higher and higher, swirling around the base of palm trees, gobbling up beach bags and tables. People darted between the five of them, knocking Claire off her feet. She managed to stop herself from falling and frantically looked for Milo among the stampede.

'Claire!' Holly screamed. Claire shoved her way through the crowd of people and grabbed hold of Holly's hand, somehow keeping her balance as a huge man thundered into her.

Claire twisted around, standing on her tiptoes to try to see Milo and Alex above everyone's heads. But they seemed to have disappeared from sight. Holly tried to run back to their table to find them but Claire yanked her back. 'We have to get to safety.'

'No!' Holly screamed. But Claire pulled her back again. It would be stupid to run towards the water. They had to get away.

She pulled Holly away from the beach, aware of the thunderous noise in her ears, the hysterical panic in the air, the elbows digging into her sides as people shoved past her. She focused on Holly's hand in hers, praying Milo and Alex were running too.

Up ahead was one of the island's only hotels. Claire peered up to see people on its main balcony, looking out at the approaching sea in horror. Others rushed into the hotel's reception, some slipping on the concrete stairs, crying out in pain.

'Come on,' Claire said, hauling Holly towards the hotel. They ran inside, their flip-flops slapping onto the marble floors, and headed towards a small crowd of people trying to scramble up the narrow flight of stairs and away from the oncoming water, which was splashing into the reception area now.

'There won't be space for us,' Holly said as she peered up the crowded stairwell.

'We'll make space,' Claire said, squeezing onto the first step and pulling Holly with her.

Claire quickly turned again and saw people succumbing

to the wave, simply disappearing under its depths as it flooded the reception area, speeding towards them. She tried to spot Milo and Alex but couldn't see any sign of them.

She turned back to the stairs, using all her strength to drag Holly up them before running with everyone else towards the balcony she'd seen earlier. There were dozens of people on there, huddling close, eyes wide with panic. Holly and Claire pushed their way on then both fell silent as they took in the view over everyone's heads. It was like they'd been dropped into the middle of the ocean, water as far as the eye could see, the tide continuing on past the hotel into the mainland. Below them, a terrible process line of broken palm trees, boats and debris swept past . . . and people too, so many of them.

A terrible sound of creaking rang out in the air. Claire turned and saw the roof of a small shop nearby collapsing, the man who'd been standing on it disappearing into the building's belly.

'What if this doesn't hold? What if the water keeps coming?' Holly said, clutching onto Claire's arm as she looked around her.

'It will hold.' But she wasn't sure. She stood on tiptoes, scouring the water below. 'Milo!' She screamed. 'Alex!'

Her cries triggered a chorus of other cries, the people around them calling the names of their loved ones over and over. It felt unbearably hopeless.

She wrapped her arms around Holly, squeezing her eyes shut.

Milo would be fine, Alex too. They had to be.

Someone screamed, pointing out to the ocean.

'Another wave!' Holly gasped.

'Oh God,' Claire whispered, watching as it swept towards them, crashing into trees, sending the people hanging onto them flying off in its whirlpool of horror. Claire watched, helpless, as the wave approached the small balcony of a nearby building, its fragile structure crumbling, sending the people standing on it toppling into the waves. The hotel they were in seemed to shudder as the wave smashed against it and she imagined the same happening to their balcony. She braced herself, pulling Holly even closer to her.

'I'm scared,' Holly said, pressing her face into Claire's neck.

'We'll be fine,' Claire said to her even though she didn't believe it herself.

Somehow the building held and Claire and Holly stayed on that balcony for some time, clinging onto each other, eyes scouring the water for Milo and Alex. Time seemed to pass in a blur and Claire wasn't sure whether it was a few minutes or an hour before the water started to recede, bringing with it more debris, more bodies. People appeared, wading through the water, many helping badly injured people. This prompted some people on the balcony to make their way down too, the waters calm now.

'I'm not sure it's safe up here any more,' Claire said through chattering teeth as she looked towards a new crack that had appeared in the balcony wall. 'We have to try to find Milo and Alex. And then we have to get away from here.'

They carefully made their way down the stairs, pausing before they got to the bottom. This close, the view was even more harrowing. Though the water was only shin-deep now, sinks lay on their sides, clothes tangled around fallen palm trees, suitcases swollen alongside mattresses and old kettles. And then the bodies – people lying face down, others slumped against what remained of some of the structures nursing terrible injuries.

'I'll go first,' Claire said, carefully lowering herself until her feet found ground, crunching through the dirty water and debris.

Water rushed in between her toes, gritty and warm. She looked down, saw it was a filthy brown colour.

'It's fine,' she said, putting her hand out to Holly.

A man floated by them then, his arm clutched around a bag of beach balls, his leg at an awkward angle, face bloody. He reached his hand towards Claire, eyes desperate. Claire tried to grab him but his fingers slipped through hers. A woman a few metres away managed to get hold of him, stopping him from floating further as he looked up at her with grateful eyes.

Claire hoped someone would be there for Milo or Alex if they were injured too.

Over the next few minutes, they trod through the shallow water, pushing debris aside and calling Alex and Milo's names out, Claire's heart stuttering each time she considered the possibility that they might be dead. It was eerily quiet compared to when the wave had hit, just the occasional sob and crunching sound, the air stinking of brine and gasoline.

Other people limped past, many having lost their footwear, yelping as they trod on jagged debris.

After a while, Holly shouted out, 'There! Look!'

Claire followed the direction she was pointing in to see a man floating face down nearby: dark hair, long limbs, tanned arms . . . and a purple T-shirt just like the one Milo had been wearing that day.

No.

Could it be him?

Claire stifled a sob and limped through the water towards him. 'Please, please, please,' she whispered to herself, tears running down her cheeks, leg aching from the searing pain of her cut. When they got to him, Holly let out a sob and turned away as she took in the blue tinge of his skin.

Claire closed her eyes, seeing all those moments she'd spent with Milo flash through her mind: those quiet few moments in Nunney Castle as the sun set; the feel of his skin against hers as they sank into the grass the next day; the way his eyes turned bronze in the sunlight as he rowed them down the Danube; the feel of his cold lips against hers as snow fell around them in Finland . . .

She reached her hand out, whole body trembling and—

'Holly! Claire!'

She looked up at a tree nearby and caught sight of a thatch of blond hair through the leaves. 'Alex!' He was sitting astride one of the branches, his arms around the trunk. Holly started crashing through the debris to get to him as Claire looked back at the body.

If that was Alex, was this . . .?

There was the sound of splashing and she turned to see Milo wading through the water towards her. He was limping, a bloody T-shirt tied around his thigh.

Relief flooded through her.

'Oh God,' Claire sobbed, grabbing hold of him. 'You're alive.'

Milo looked down at her, brown eyes filled with tears. 'Told you I'd never leave you.'

Claire surveyed the scene before her, unable to believe her eyes. They'd eventually made their way to higher ground, finding themselves at a large hotel full of survivors, a handful of medical staff trying their best to help. People were sobbing, rocking back and forth. Others cried out people's names in forlorn voices. Children wandered about, asking for their mummies and daddies. Families hugged each other like they'd never let each other go again.

The scene laid out below was one of complete devastation, once smooth white perfect beaches a tangle of debris, corpses and filthy water. It was how Claire imagined a bombed beach might look. Every now and again, rumours spread of another wave so the four of them huddled together, eyes on a now-calm sea as they braced themselves for what might come next.

After an hour there, a gruesome convoy started to flow in – bodies on rickety old trucks, people with missing loved ones looking on in horror. Claire thought of Nora then. If she'd been waiting for them at Claire's bungalow, she wouldn't have had a chance.

'What do we do now?' Holly asked, leaning against a wall and wiping her grimy face. 'We left all our phones at the café so we can't call anyone. Do we just wait?'

Claire looked at Alex, thinking about how frantic her sister would be. And what about Jay, arriving in Bangkok to discover the island Claire had been staying at had been devastated by a tidal wave?

Claire looked towards the children and the injured. There'd be people worrying about them too. At least the four of them were together and mobile.

'We help,' she said simply.

So that's what they did over the next couple of days, hardly aware when day turned into night then day again. They spent the hours searching for the injured, using plastic pool beds that floated upstream as temporary stretchers. Some of the injuries were horrific, and at first, Claire struggled to cope – they all did. But as time went by, she grew stronger, even arranging for water and supplies to be handed out to the injured as they waited for transport to either the makeshift hospital on the island or the mainland. She saw Holly grow in strength too, distracting children desperate to find their parents by playing games with them. And Milo and Alex were pulled in to help carry the injured, working well into the early hours despite both of them looking exhausted, especially Milo whose limp was getting worse. Claire had tried to get him to have his leg seen to, but he refused, saying it was clear the doctors were overwhelmed with injuries so much worse than his.

All the time, Claire looked out for Nora, scared every time she saw a woman brought in with dark hair and a long, sea-drenched skirt. She looked for Jay too, wondering if he was searching for her and thinking the worst. She wished she could call him and Sofia and tell them she was fine. But the times when someone was kind enough to offer them their phones to call home, there was no connection, the networks struggling to serve the devastated area.

But after Claire borrowed a nurse's phone to call Sofia, she managed to connect. 'Alex is fine,' she said as soon as her sister answered.

'My God,' Sofia said. 'I've been frantic. And you? Are you OK?'

'I'm fine. Bit shaken up, but fine.'

'Can I talk to Alex?'

Claire gestured to Alex who was helping lift a man onto a truck. 'He'll be over in a minute. I'm so sorry, Sof. It's been impossible to call until now.'

'Is Alex really okay, no injuries?'

'He's fine, just a scratch to the head.'

'A scratch? Could it become infected, could—'

'Sofia, really, he's fine. They got caught up in the wave, but Milo saw Alex as he was being swept inshore and grabbed him. They clambered onto the roof of a building. Milo got hurt in the process but he'll be fine.'

Sofia let out a sob. 'Oh, thank God. Please thank Milo for me.'

Alex started jogging over. 'Alex is here now so I'll hand him over. We'll get him home soon, Sof.'

'Thank you, Claire. And – and remember to thank Milo, won't you?'

Claire looked towards Milo who was helping a Thai man carry two young boys to the concrete building. 'I will.'

'Wait, before you go!' Sofia said. 'Your friend Jay called yesterday to see if you'd called me. When I told him you hadn't, he said he was in Bangkok but he'd try to get over to the island to find you all. I took his number but when I tried to call this morning, it said the number didn't exist. I must've taken down one of the digits wrong, I was so frantic, Claire, I couldn't do anything right really. Do you remember his number?'

Claire sighed. 'No, I don't. Poor Jay, he must be so worried. Look, if he calls again, tell him I'm fine, won't you?' Claire looked towards Holly who was hugging a little girl. 'There's not been anything in the papers about me or Milo, has there? Or Holly?'

'No, the tsunami's the only thing people are talking about. It's affected a huge area, the images are just horrible.'

'I'd heard it wasn't just here. How awful. Look, as soon as flights are available, we'll get Alex to you.'

'What about you?'

She thought of Nora. 'There's a friend we haven't found yet so I might be back a little later than Alex. I'd like to find her before I leave.'

'A friend?'

'I'll explain when I get back.'

Claire could hear her sister's breathing on the other end of the phone.

'Something else, Claire.'

'Yes?'

Sofia let out a sob. 'I love you.'

Claire leaned against the concrete wall, trying to hold back her own tears. 'Love you too, sis.'

That evening, just before the sun set, the four of them made their way back to the shore. As they drew closer to the sea, there were more bodies, more debris, more smashed boats and flattened roofs. People walked down the dusty road, faces bloody and dazed, eyes wide. Claire tried to find Nora's face among them, Jay's too. But nothing.

As they headed towards Claire's bungalow, they passed Nora's resort. There was almost nothing left, though Nora's distinctive painting was just discernible, lying against a palm tree in the distance, wrecked and broken.

A man was walking through the debris with a little boy, calling out a woman's name. In the distance, volunteers loaded bodies onto the back of a truck.

Claire could hardly believe she'd been there on Christmas Day, the sea so calm and beautiful nearby, no clue of what was to come.

'Your bungalow might not be so bad,' Milo said, squeezing Claire's hand as he noticed the look on her face.

But when they drew closer to the complex of bungalows where Claire had been staying, it was even worse. The huts were mostly flattened, victims laid out nearby covered in plastic sheets , volunteers looking over them with clipboards in their hands.

'Jesus,' Alex said. 'Nora wouldn't have survived this if she was here when the wave hit.'

'If she ran she might have,' Holly said, her voice trembling. 'We did.'

'Wait here a minute,' Milo said to Holly and Alex. He took Claire's hand and they walked over to the volunteers, trying not to look at the bodies, their hands over their noses, still not quite used to the smell.

The volunteers looked up as they approached. Their eyes looked exhausted over the top of their masks, red-rimmed and glassy.

'We're looking for our friend,' Claire said. 'A woman called Nora McKenzie? She's British, dark curly hair, in her late forties or early fifties, I think.'

One of the volunteers, a woman with a shock of red hair, shook her head. 'We haven't come across her,' she said in a German accent. 'She doesn't fit the description of any of these people either,' she added, looking down at the bodies laid out before her, her eyes sad.

Claire sighed and looked towards where her bungalow had been. It seemed more intact than the others. Maybe Nora had a chance? She quickened her step, clambering over a broken suitcase and a mangled bed frame, the remains of the bed she'd slept in during her time there. There were just three walls remaining, the roof completely gone. Lying in the middle of it all was a palm tree. Milo walked around, manoeuvring items to look under them. They didn't say it, but the truth was, they were searching for Nora's body . . . or some trace of her anyway.

'Claire!'

They both turned to see a man running towards them in a tan suit, blond curly hair lifting with each step.

'Jay!' Claire ran towards him and he picked her up, twirling her around.

'You're alive!' he said, blue eyes filled with tears. He sounded frantic, his voice full of emotion. He set her down, eyes exploring her face. 'I thought you were dead. I – I saw your body, I—'

'My body?'

Jay nodded. 'I managed to get to Ko Pho Phi Don a couple of days after I arrived. I couldn't believe what a state this place was in. I searched the island, trying to find a trace of you. Nothing. Then someone told me they were taking bodies over to a temple in Krabi. So I went straight to the temple yesterday. That's when I thought I saw your body.'

Claire put her hand on his arm.

'She was wearing the typewriter necklace I got you. It was custom-made, I knew straight away it was yours, she had your atlas in her bag.'

'Oh God,' Claire said, putting her face in her hands as the realisation dawned on her.

'What's wrong?' Jay asked.

'Nora McKenzie, Erin's best friend,' she said, looking up at him. 'I gave her the necklace to say thanks.'

Jay raked his fingers through his curly blond hair. 'Christ, poor woman. I told her daughter I recognised the name but—'

'Daughter?' Claire asked.

'Yes, Louise. She was at the temple trying to find her mother yesterday. She has your atlas.'

Claire nodded sadly. 'Nora retrieved it from Nathan Styles.'

'Then the body's definitely hers, isn't it?' Milo said.

Jay nodded. 'Must be.'

'Where's Louise now?' Claire asked Jay.

'I feel terrible. I was supposed to be meeting her this morning.'

Claire sank down onto the bed frame. 'So Louise has no idea her mum's dead?'

'I presume not. Look, I can get my man to take us back to Krabi, but he won't be available for another few hours. I haven't eaten all day. There's volunteers serving food at a café down the road, shall we wait there?'

'Good idea.' Milo stood and put his hand out to Claire but she stayed where she was. 'We can go to the temple, make sure Nora's body is looked after then try to get hold of her daughter when we get back to the UK. Let's get something to eat first.'

'I want to stay here,' Claire said. 'Just for a bit.'

'It's getting dark,' Milo said, peering towards the setting sun. 'I'll stay with you.'

'I'd like to be alone if that's all right. Come get me after you've eaten, I'm not hungry anyway.'

He scrutinised her face then nodded. 'Okay.' He turned to Jay. It was strange seeing them together, Milo's yin to Jay's yang. 'Thanks for coming out here, Jay,' he said, putting his hand out to him.

Jay hesitated a moment then shook it. 'You'd have done the same.'

'I would.'

They went to walk away then Jay paused, turning back to Claire. 'I forgot to say, Nathan Styles is missing. His article was never filed, not that it would have made it anyway with this all over the news,' he said, looking around him with sad eyes.

When they were gone, Claire walked around what remained of her bungalow. Was it possible Nora had been here when the wave hit? She peered towards the toppled palm tree blocking the door to the bathroom. Maybe she got trapped?

Claire sunk to the ground, watching as the sun cast a fiery glow over the sea.

'Oh Nora,' she whispered, a tear sliding down her cheek.

Chapter Twenty-Seven

Ko Phi Phi Don, Thailand
2004

I hold my breath as the woman kneeling in the sand turns.

Is it Mum?

But as she comes into view, I realise this woman is younger than my mum, her brown eyes larger, her cheeks fuller. She stands and, in that moment, I realise who she is, her face instantly recognisable from the photos in her atlas.

'Claire Shreve,' I say, even though I know that can't be possible.

She frowns and I can tell from the way she's looking at me, I'm right. It feels strange to see her standing before me, the very woman whose atlas I've been travelling with the past two days; whose life I've been dipping in and out of. She seems different from how I imagined: a little older, even more petite than in her photos.

And she's alive.

'Do I know you?' Claire asks us.

'I'm Louise. Nora's daughter?'

She puts her hand to her mouth, and there's a horrible feeling in the pit of my stomach as I take in the expression on her face.

'You must be wondering what we're talking about,' Sam says as I find it difficult to talk, my mouth opening and closing, head spinning. 'I volunteer at a temple in Krabi and a man named Jay Hemingford identified you – well, I guess it wasn't *you*. There was a necklace . . .?'

'My necklace,' Claire says. She turns to me. 'I'm sorry, Louise. I gave your mum my necklace as a gift.'

I think of the typewriter necklace tangled around that body's swollen neck and start trembling.

'Do you think we could go somewhere to talk?' Claire asks. 'There's a café that's open up—'

'No!' I say, trying to muffle the rising panic inside. 'If you have something to say, say it now.'

She pauses, her eyes flittering to Sam then back to me. Then she steps towards me, putting her hand on my arm. 'I'm so sorry, Louise, but – but your mother didn't make it. We think it's her at the temple.'

I feel my legs go weak and slowly sink down to the sand, looking up at the star-speckled sky. Every clue, every step of this journey has been taking me to Claire, not Mum. All this time, it *was* Mum's body lying in that morgue. My God, how could I have left her alone there?

'I'm so sorry,' Sam says, sinking down beside me and taking my hand.

I look up at Claire, the tears in my eyes distorting her face, making her look like a ghost. 'Do you know what happened?'

'No,' Claire said. 'But I think she might have been here when the wave hit.'

'Why do you think that?' I ask, needing to be sure.

'A journalist stole my atlas, the one you found in your mother's bag. It had something sensitive in there, something that meant he could run a horrible story back home about the daughter of your mother's best friend. Your mother got the atlas back for me.'

'But why was Mum here at your bungalow when the wave hit?'

Claire puts her hand on my arm, her dark eyes in mine. 'She called just before the tsunami hit to say she'd be waiting here to give me my atlas back.' She peers at the palm tree blocking the door. 'I think she got trapped.'

I follow her gaze and feel sick at the thought of Mum being trapped here, helpless as the wave headed for her.

'Just because Mum got the atlas doesn't mean the story's not going to be published,' I say.

'The journalist is missing,' says Claire.

Anger surges through me. 'That just makes it seem even more bloody pointless, Mum retrieved the atlas for nothing, she *died* for nothing.'

'No, Louise,' Claire says. 'Don't you see? What your mum did by getting the atlas off the journalist was amazing, brave, utterly selfless.'

'Claire's right,' Sam says softly. 'It was her final, selfless act.'

'Yeah, well she thought she was doing that by not talking to me for two years too, but she got that wrong. She just made it worse by keeping away.'

'We *all* get it wrong,' Claire says. 'We're just human. My dad did the same, he didn't want to bother us with his illness. But in the end, he needed me, just like your mum needed you to come back to find her. Your mum loved you very much, Louise, she made that clear to me when I saw her last on Christmas Day.'

I pause, so wishing I'd seen my mum on Christmas Day too. 'What was she like the last time you saw her?'

Claire smiles sadly. 'Good, actually. She talked about you.'

Her eyes sink into mine. 'I think it finally dawned on her she needed to make amends with you.'

I look down at the atlas and imagine Mum protecting it as the wave rushed towards her. I trace my finger over the bumpy cover then hand it to Claire.

'I suppose this is me completing my mum's mission then,' I say, trying not to get choked up. 'Make sure you don't have her dying for nothing, all right? Make sure you get her best friend's daughter the help she needs.'

Claire smiles, a tear crawling down her cheek as she looks at the atlas. 'I will. Thank you, Louise.'

'Thank my mum,' I say.

In the distance, a red-haired young girl and two men appear.

'I'll leave you to it,' Claire says, placing her hand on my arm again. 'I'll be thinking of you.'

As I watch Claire approach her family, I wonder what's next for her. The man with brown hair leans down to kiss Claire's cheek and she says something to him. He turns, revealing a long dark fringe. He nods slightly then takes Claire and the girl's hands, and I watch them walk away together, their new path weaving a pattern beneath their feet.

I look up into Sam's eyes. I don't know what the future holds for me and my girls; all I know is that I need him by my side for what I must do next.

'Let's go find my mum,' I say.

Epilogue

Ko Phi Phi Don, Thailand
2014

When I close my eyes, the water still comes: the violent thud of waves, the tart smell of salty dampness seeping through the cracks of my dreams. But this time, I see Mum emerging from those waves, her face peaceful, a sad smile on her lips, Erin beside her.

'Does it look different?' Chloe asks.

I look out from the busy wooden dock we're standing on as backpackers and tourists jump off the ferry, many throwing off their flip-flops as they press their toes into the warm sand. Palm trees stand tall above us, their long leaves gracefully swaying in the breeze. The sun's rising in the distance, an arc of yellow across the horizon. No mangled beds or boats flung onto roofs; no suitcases lying in the sand, their innards exposed. Just tourists with red cheeks and food vendors with toothless smiles.

'It's like it never happened,' I tell Chloe, looking down at the soft white sand as it spills over my toes. I'd barely felt sand when I'd been to this part of the island last, just debris and grimy water.

'Must be weird seeing it all back to normal,' Chloe says.

She's so like me, her blonde hair a frizz around her shiny face, blue eyes sad. There's this look in her eyes too as she stares out at the sea, the same look I imagine I had on my face ten years ago: confusion and fear.

'Why's it so weird, it's been ten years,' Olivia says as we start walking across the beach, rolling her eyes in typical fourteen-year-old fashion. She's more like her dad, her dark hair still smooth despite the heat, cheeks rosy but not slick with perspiration. She's fearless too, sometimes oblivious. But there's a fierce compassion within her I never saw in Will that surprises me sometimes.

Chloe yawns, ignoring her sister as she places her book into her rucksack. She's due to start university next year and is planning to study geography. I think that comes from hearing my stories when I returned from Thailand ten years ago. I was only there for a couple of days and for such harrowing reasons too. But I squirrelled away good stuff to tell the girls – the monkey I saw weaving between the foreign embassy desks, the gold spikes of the temple gates, the beautiful traditional Thai dresses I'd seen. I wanted – no, *needed* – the girls to know the place their nanna spent her last hours was special.

Olivia opens her mouth to say something patronising to Chloe but Nora interrupts, already a diplomat at just seven years old. 'Were there really boats on roofs when you last came here, Mummy?'

I nod. 'That's right.'

Her dark eyes widen and I can see she's painting the picture in her head. She sees the things her sisters don't: a lone red flip-flop pressed into the sand; a young Thai girl sitting cross-legged on the ground outside a bamboo-roofed café, black hair dipping over one eye as she reads a magazine. She'll draw all this later and my heart will ache like it always does when I watch the way she paints, so much like her nanna.

'Don't worry, the memorial's not too far,' Sam says, putting his hand on my shoulder and shooting me a sympathetic smile. Once again, I'd be lost without his presence here. Visiting Thailand gave me a taste for travel and I've visited lots of interesting places, from Sri Lanka to Canada and even a cruise around Alaska. But coming here brings back so many memories, many of them very difficult, and I feel a little like I've gone back ten years and need Sam to guide me all over again.

'Look, Mum,' Olivia says, pointing towards a blue 'tsunami evacuation route' sign. Nora's eyes widen.

'Well, that's reassuring,' Sam says. 'It's good that the people here are safer now.'

I smile gratefully at him and for the next few minutes we all walk in silence, our flip-flops in our hands as we stare out at the sea.

'Here we are,' Sam says after a while. We all stop, taking in the simple memorial garden ahead of us. It's marked by a wooden sign standing on stilts over stone clad flowerbeds. A path made of light stone bricks curves beyond it, leading to a patch of green. Bright pink, red, blue and yellow flowers bloom among exotic-looking green plants, their perfume working its way towards us.

We walk towards the garden, and I see her straight away, head bent low as she examines a plaque. Her dark hair's shorter now, with streaks of grey in it, and she looks plumper, healthier. There's a small tan rucksack on her back, a bottle of water in her hand. She straightens up, wiping the sweat from her neck as she squints up at the blazing sun.

'Is that her?' Nora asks.

'Yes, that's Claire.'

Claire turns as though she can sense us talking about her. A wide smile spreads across her face and she beckons us over.

I stand where I am for a few moments, taking it all in. Last time I'd seen her had been on this very island just a few minutes' walk away as she told me the news I'd been dreading. It's a bittersweet feeling, a reminder of the sharp tang of grief I'd felt mixed with happiness at seeing her after all these years.

I take a deep breath, planting a smile on my face. 'Come on then,' I say to the girls. We all head over and Claire's smile deepens. We give each other a hug and it's silly, but I feel my eyes well up. I blink a few times, stopping any tears, not wanting to upset the girls. When Claire pulls away and looks into my face, she nods and I know she understands.

She turns to Sam, giving him a quick hug. 'Louise said you live on the island now?'

He nods. 'Yep, nearly ten years. After I stayed and helped clear up, I fell in love with the place.'

'And a certain beautiful Thai girl we met a few hours ago,' I say, smiling at Sam.

'Good for you,' Claire says. She looks towards my three girls and I feel that sense of pride I get whenever someone's meeting them all for the first time. I introduce her to each of them and, when we get to Nora, Claire's eyes light up. 'How lovely,' she says, shaking her little hand. 'You look just like your nanna too.'

'And I paint,' Nora says proudly.

'She's very good,' Chloe says.

'*I* write,' Olivia butts in, gesturing towards her travel journal. 'I plan to get this published when I return home.'

'Well, with determination like that, I'm sure you will,' Claire says, winking at me. I smile at her.

Chloe looks between us, then turns to her sisters. 'Shall we go look at the memorial?'

'Good idea,' Sam says, nodding at Claire as he leads the girls away.

'It's been too long,' Claire says when we're alone. 'We promised we'd keep in touch but—'

'Life gets in the way,' I finish for her, smiling. 'It was lovely to get your letter last year though. I'd been toying with the idea of bringing the girls here for the ten-year anniversary, but it wasn't until you got in touch again that it cemented my plans.'

'Must feel strange being back here,' Claire says, her voice soft.

'Yes, but at the same time . . .' I pause, watching Nora dip in and out from behind the trees. 'Happy. I feel like Mum's getting the chance to meet her namesake. Does that sound weird?'

'Not at all. She's just like your mum, you know.'

I smile. 'Very much so. Helps her dad's an artist too.'

'He is?'

I nod. 'Sounds like a cliché but I met Roger while doing an arts and crafts evening class. He was my tutor.'

'Worked out to be more than just a cliché though, didn't it?'

I nod as I look down at my wedding ring. 'Eight years next week, we've been married. He's wonderful. He'll be joining us later; he wanted me and the girls to do this alone.'

'Well, you deserve wonderful. I hope you don't mind me saying but I always wondered if you and Sam . . .' She lets her voice trail off.

'Me too for a while. We wrote, I even said I'd fly out. But, I don't know, I guess it's like you and your friend, Jay? He's brilliant but a friend, that's all. And anyway, the world's not big enough for another torrid love story. Speaking of which, how's Milo?'

Claire's eyes sparkle with happiness. 'He's great. He's in his element when he's at the farm.'

'Yes, I was surprised when I got your change of address card. I never thought you'd return to Exmoor.'

'Me neither. But we'd always talked about how running away from our tragedies do us no good. One day, he just woke up and said: "I need to go back home." So we just went for a week and you know what? Though there were bad memories, there were the good ones too. When we saw his parents' old farm for sale, we both knew we wanted to buy it and renovate it.'

'You can't be there much. I've read your articles, you seem to be everywhere all at once.'

Claire laughs. 'Oh, we'd never give the travelling up. Exmoor is just a base we return to every now and again. Milo took on an old friend who runs it while we're away and the profit goes towards funding our travels. Most of the time, we're travelling all over, me writing articles, Milo working on farms and bringing back what he's learned to make our Exmoor farm even better.'

I reach into my bag for my suntan lotion, the sun beating hard onto my neck, despite it starting to set. 'Like the water buffalo herd?' I say as I rub some lotion on my skin. 'Olivia saw Milo's vlog from last month.'

Claire nods. 'Yes, we went to India so I could write about how sand mining is encroaching on the Western Ghats, a mountain range there. While I did some research, Milo worked at a local farm. He learned so much. First thing he did when we got back was make enquiries about where he could get some water buffalo.'

I shake my head in admiration. 'What a life you two lead.'

Claire looks out to sea, her face soft with contentment. 'The life I've always wanted.'

I watch the girls as they chase each other around the garden. 'Chloe's reading your travel memoir, she says it's great.'

'Thanks, it was quite cathartic writing it. I'm working on another book actually, I'll—'

A scream of delight rings out from behind me, and Claire peers over my shoulder, her whole face lighting up. I turn and see a young girl about Nora's age running towards Claire, her arms open, dark hair like Claire and Milo's bouncing around her shoulders with every step. Claire swings her up in her arms and twirls her around, her nose pressed against the little girl's neck.

'*This* gorgeous little bundle is Scarlett,' Claire says, letting her down. Scarlett presses her cheek against Claire's arm, gazing up at her adoringly.

I think of the article Claire had written about her struggles with infertility and my heart swells. 'Oh Claire, she's beautiful! You must be so delighted after everything you went through.'

Claire smiles. 'Yes, I feel very lucky Holly had such a lovely little girl.'

I bite my lip. 'Oh, I'm sorry, I—'

'It's fine,' Claire says. She looks down at Scarlett. 'Why don't you go play with those children there, see?' she says, pointing towards my girls.

'Can I give them some sweets, Nanny?' Scarlett asks Claire in an Australian accent, pulling a packet of fruit gums from her pocket.

Claire nods. 'Of course, sweetheart.'

We watch her run off then I turn to Claire. 'Claire, I'm so sorry. I shouldn't have presumed she was yours.'

She shrugs. 'Easy mistake to make. I've never had children, never will. When I said I was infertile, I meant it.' She pauses a moment. 'You know, I really ought to stop using that word *infertile*. It suggests nothing has come of my life; that nothing has come from the love Milo and I share. But so much has

400

grown from what we have together. Holly. Scarlett. All the wonderful experiences we've shared, the people we've met.'

'That's a wonderful way of looking at it.' I watch Scarlett offering Nora a sweet. I can now see Erin and Holly in her wide cat-like eyes and high cheekbones.

'Do they live in Australia? I noticed Scarlett has an accent?' I ask.

Claire nods. 'Holly fell in love with the country when she stayed with me and Milo all those years ago. She's married my nephew, Alex. He runs a pro bono law firm out there while Holly writes articles.'

I smile. 'Are they here?'

'Just in the café,' she says, nodding towards the nearby café. 'They're feeding little Bo – he's six months old.'

'Wow. Holly and Alex must have their hands full.' I pause a few moments. 'How is Holly? She went through such a lot when she was young, didn't she?' I ask carefully. I never did discover the secret Mum protected by retrieving Claire's atlas but I could tell Holly was on a downward spiral when I saw those photos of her in the press ten years ago.

Claire smiles. 'She's good. After we returned to the UK, we headed out to the States for a few months where a therapist friend of Jay helped Holly sort through her demons. They're not gone, by any means. But she knows how to deal with them. Alex has helped too, as have the children. The memories will always be there, deep inside her, but she's good, really good.'

'Mummy, Mummy, look!' I hear Nora shout out at me. I look over to see her standing with Scarlett by a large stone memorial in the garden, black plaques dotted all over it.

'We better go see what they've found,' Claire says, smiling.

As we stroll over, something else comes into view: bright reds and oranges. A large eye. Dark hair.

Mum's painting.

It's the one Sam and I found flung onto the beach, her one eye blinking out at us, the vivid aqua sea beyond her. It's been re-touched very carefully, colours once faded by water and time bright and overwhelming. It's drilled into the marble wall to the left of the stone memorial, the sea beyond merging into the sea in the painting, creating a stunning effect. In a special plaque next to it are the words:

'Beauty is truth, truth beauty.'
In loving memory of Nora McKenzie, artist, mother
and grandmother, who joins her best friend Erin
James, finally found after many years of searching.

I purse my lips together, feel tears sting my eyes. 'It's wonderful,' I say. 'Who arranged this?'

'I did.' I turn to see Holly smiling at me. She looks the same, red hair even longer, beautiful green eyes slightly tired. There's a gorgeous red-haired baby with almond-brown eyes in her arms, a handsome blond man by her side.

Then Milo limps over, his dark hair long now, the skin around his eyes wrinkling as he smiles at me. Claire had told me his leg had been injured during the tsunami. I suppose we all still have our scars to bear from that terrible event.

'Hi Louise,' he says, putting his hand out and grasping mine. It's calloused and sandy, the farmer in him oozing out of his pores. I notice the scar on his face, white and faded with age, and I wonder if the pain of losing his brother has faded too. Probably not. It's like Claire says: the memories are always there, deep inside.

'Look,' Claire says, nodding towards Nora and Scarlett who are sitting cross-legged in the sand in front of the painting, both their heads tilted as they contemplate it.

'My nanna did that,' I hear Nora explain. 'I never met her, but Mummy says I'm like her. Your nanna Erin was her best friend.'

'I know,' Scarlett says matter-of-factly. 'Your nanna saved my mummy.'

'I hope Nora and Erin are looking down watching this all,' Claire says sadly.

'Do you think our paths continue after this life?' I ask her.

She smiles. 'I hope so.'

'Me too. I hope Mum knows I got this,' I say, reaching into my bag and getting the letter I'd found on my doormat when I returned home ten years ago. It was a short letter but meant so much, Mum finally telling me how deeply she regretted the two years of silence and how she planned to make amends when she returned home.

'Oh yes, I remember you mentioning it,' Claire says. 'She told me on Christmas Day that she was hoping to make amends.'

'She did. I just hope in her last moments she knew it would reach me.'

Milo puts his hand on Claire's shoulder. 'Ready?'

She nods so he reaches into the bag he's been holding and pulls out two flat square objects, one red, one orange. He hands one to Alex and they both pull the corners of each object out.

Sky lanterns.

'For Erin,' Milo says, passing his lighter to Holly. She lights one of the lanterns with Claire's help as Alex holds Bo.

Then Claire hands the lighter to me. 'For Nora,' she says.

'What is it, Nanny?' Scarlett asks Claire in awe as she watches me light the tiny tea light inside.

'Wait and see,' Claire says.

I hold my lantern up high above my head, Holly and Claire doing the same with their lantern. Then we throw them into the air.

They hover where they are for a few moments as though taking in the land below them one last time. Then they swoop up on the wings of a breeze, the lights inside trembling against the setting sun, before gliding up and up and away, two blinking lights above the calm aqua sea below.

Acknowledgements

This novel has been on quite a journey and there are many people who've helped along the way. My writing voyage started with my mum Dot Fountain who taught me to love words, setting a fabulous example by reading with a passion and teaching me how to form words from an early age. My journey then picked up speed when I met one of my closest friends, Elizabeth Richards. Always there to provide spot-on feedback and a swift kick up the arse, this book simply wouldn't be here without her. Alongside Liz and my mum, there are two brilliant 'readers' who I road test all my work on: Angela Cranfield and Emma Cash. Thank you, my love-lies! And I must thank the Hilary Johnson Authors' Advisory Service whose fabulous reader helped me too.

My journey to publication got serious when my agent Caroline Hardman plucked me from the slush pile. She believed in my writing right from the start and fought hard to get it out into the world. A brilliant editor, tough and funny too, I'll forever be grateful to her. It's thanks to her my novel arrived in the offices of my wonderful editor Eli Dryden who saw something special from the moment she read it and has worked tirelessly to get it to its final destination, the UK's bookshelves, teaching me so much about writing (and where to get the best vegetarian food in London!) along the way.

And finally, a heartfelt thanks to my husband who's been there every step of the way the past few years, looking after our beautiful daughter Scarlett and our Jack Russell Archie, cleaning and cooking when I was just too wrapped up in Louise and Claire's worlds to leave my laptop. Without Rob, there'd be no novel . . . and no gleaming kitchen surfaces.

AUTHOR Q&A

What was your inspiration for writing *The Atlas of Us*?
I knew I wanted to write about the countries I visited while working as a travel editor and my own experiences with infertility, but it wasn't until I went on holiday to Exmoor that the idea really came to life. During a walk, I saw a farmer standing outside a local pub, his wild-looking dog skulking next to him. The character of Milo instantly came to me then and I had to get back to our cabin to start writing. The rest just poured out!

Which of your characters do you identify with the most?
I started out identifying with Claire the most as I was struggling with infertility when I started writing *The Atlas of Us*. However, by the time I'd finished the final draft of the novel, I'd given birth to my 'miracle' daughter, Scarlett, so I really began to identify with Louise too, in particular her fierce love for her girls and the way motherhood can make you lose your identity a bit at the start.

Did you find infertility difficult to write about?
The first draft of *The Atlas of Us* was written just after a second failed round of IVF. So I have to confess to shedding a tear while writing the scene in the seaside café where Claire

unburdens herself on Milo. While I didn't experience the problems she did with her husband (though infertility certainly places a great deal of pressure on even the strongest of marriages), all the other stuff about her visits to clinics and the emotional toll of IVF were drawn from my own personal experiences. But I wouldn't call it *difficult*. It was more cathartic and helped me deal with feelings that were still very raw.

How did you own travel experiences help with writing about the settings in *The Atlas of Us*?
They were a wonderful help! I drew on my memories from all the press trips I'd enjoyed while working as a travel magazine editor, and also my own personal holidays over the years. It was lovely to revisit all those places.

Why did you choose to write about the 2004 tsunami?
I'd seen the scars left behind while visiting places like Thailand and the Maldives during my travels. It shocked me that an event could have such far-reaching reverberations, even years later. It was an event I'd wanted to write about for a while and it seemed to fit in perfectly with the overarching question at the heart of the novel: if someone's affected by a tragedy that changes them to the core, can you still love them?

The post-tsunami scenes are very vivid. How did you write about them without having been there yourself at the time?
I read harrowing first-hand accounts from families who'd gone out to Thailand to try to find their missing relatives. I also looked at photos taken at the time. It was a difficult thing to do, but it really helped me draw those vital scenes.

Which setting was your favourite to write about?

Definitely Finland! I went on holiday to Iso Syote a few years back and completely fell in love with the place. It's a true winter wonderland, so magical and it was lovely to bring those memories back to life again by writing about them. Funny thing is, I wrote those scenes on an unusually hot day in September while sitting in my warm conservatory. But I was so engrossed in my memories, and Claire and Milo's story, I barely noticed!

Dogs play a large role in your novel – Archie and Blue and then the dogs from the sanctuary in Serbia. Why did you choose to set the Serbian scenes in a dog sanctuary?

I adore all animals, but dogs hold a special place in my heart thanks to my one-eyed Jack Russell, Archie – yes, he makes a special guest appearance in the novel too! The reason I decided to set the Serbian scenes in a dog sanctuary was because of my memories of all the stray dogs when I visited Serbia. It broke my heart but at the same time, they all seemed quite robust and happy roaming about in their packs. But it did make me wonder what it must have been like for stray dogs during the Kosovo war. As an animal-lover, it was important for me to focus on this when I wrote about Serbia.

READING GROUP QUESTIONS

When Milo and Claire first meet, he kills an animal in front of her. What were your first impressions of Milo and did those impressions change the more you read it?

How do you think Claire and Milo's lives change after their initial meeting?

Claire is surprised when Jay makes a move on her. Were you? Jay ends up being one of Claire's closest friends. What impact does he have on her life? How important do you think his role is in the novel?

Claire and her sister Sofia are very different. How important do you think Sofia's opinion is to Claire?

Claire's infertility plays a big role in the novel. How do you feel about the fact that Claire doesn't end up having a child in the end? Would you have preferred it if she got pregnant?

Louise often wonders if she should be doing more with her life. By the time her search for her mother ends, do you think she's learnt to be satisfied with her role as a stay-at-home mum or do you think she yearns for more?

Louise has a difficult relationship with her mother. Do you think Nora is a bad mother, or do you think Louise never really gave her a chance?

Sam plays a significant role in helping Louise find her mother. Do you also think he helps her find herself? If so, how?

Louise doesn't end up with Sam. Do you think she should have?

Both Claire and Louise have life-changing events to deal with. How do you feel they both deal with those events?